The Green Dragon League

The Green Dragon League

Daniel Laskowski

Even the darkest magic has its logic.

Dr Miloš Jesenský – member of
the Czechoslovak Division
of the Hyborian Legion

LIST OF CONTENTS

1

⌒

IRIS FROM IANTHE

I

"Gods! If there is something more hopeless than the desert, it is only the taverns under the walls of Yezud[1]", I thought, when my little caravan left the sea of the Hyrkan sands, crossed the Kezankyan Mountains and finally began to tread on the firm ground of Zamora. "I can't believe I just went there!"

---

[1] The action of this novel takes place in the already literary existing world - in the world of the Hyborian Era invented by Robert E. Howard in his eighteen classic stories about the king-barbarian Conan the Cimmerian, as well as other heroes: Red Sonja and Prince Halidor. The world of Hyborian Age is a world after the Cataclysm that 20,000 years before the birth of Christ plunged the Platonic island of Atlantis into the ocean. Our hero lived eight thousand years after the events that changed permanently the face of the Earth and human civilization, which was the third human civilization on our planet. And the hero and narrator of the novel is Lestko from Vislania called Crossbowman, because of the masterful wielding of this weapon, which, however, he is not abused it in his adventures and not only. Most often he uses his knowledge and cleverness in the fight against opponents and adversity. He is not also indifferent to the charms of women who stand in his way. But he is not only a wandering hellraiser looking for fame, gold and adventures - he also fulfills a secret mission which details and meaning you will be getting to know, the Reader, as you read…

I hated Zamora from the very beginning, like anyone who had any decency. For shekel. Anyway, even worse in this respect was its capital - Shadizar, the city of thieves. And yet I had to go to Yezud to attend a meeting with the Brotherhood liaison. More like, he was supposed to come to collect what my horse carried on his back. I breathed a sigh of relief seeing that on the Yezud Route sandstorms did not cover a large pond; palms and flowering shrubs were sowing a pleasant scent of flowers - how different from the smell of the desert.

My horses speeded up and after a few moments they got to the water. I jumped from the saddle and also went to the pond. There was no one there, only traces of people, camels and horses could be seen on the bank. Apparently there was already a caravan before me, which now probably rode through the eastern gate of the city. I found traces of the camp, the smoke was still hovering over the fire. Someone did not extinguish the fire, leaving it to other wanderers. The unwritten law of the people of the steppe trails made it necessary to leave smoldering heat in order for it to be used by other wanderers who sometimes did not have enough strength to strike and kindle fire.

The sun was already well above the horizon and began to burn any exposed skin. I liked the sun, but in the deserts of Turan and Hyrkania I learned to hate it. It burned out the eyes and dried the brain. It struck a mirage, and when it finally went down, it was possible to breathe a sigh of relief just to chatter with teeth a quarter later because of cold. I was hoping that after the two years had passed away in the deserts of the East, the Brotherhood would take me somewhere into some more friendly and civilized country of the West. And for now, I had to wait two days for a meeting with a liaison, which should already approach the city from Nemedia. He was to take the artifact from me and take it to the headquarters of the Brotherhood in Belverus. His path was not easy, he had to overcome two Brythuan mountain chains with a route to Numalia along the border, and then across the plain to the capital of Nemedia - the largest city in this and neighboring countries.

I threw off my clothes and gladly immersed myself in the cool water. After a few moments, I rinsed off the dust and sweat of the desert trail. I filled the waterskins just in case - once I had to escape from the royal guards during the riots. I could defeat them without special difficulties, but on the other hand I did not have the slightest desire to attract the attention of the authorities. The Brotherhood worked outside all the structures of secular and spiritual power of all the Hyborian religions, and in the event of disclosure, it threatened with troublesome questions... - which we would have preferred to avoid. Torture and other such pleasures, too.

I left the water and let the sun and the wind dry myself and my horses, which unburden and unsaddled, also took a bath and cropped rare and hard grass. After the dry fodder and water from the snow on the mountain passes, they apparently thought they were in paradise... I sat in the shade of a palm tree and closed my eyes. The horses grazed and Arus, my dog, whom I took with me from Wislania when he was a puppy, lay down next to me. His wet fur quickly dried in the warm wind. It was noon and the sun was golden with the light of the towers and roofs of Yezud, a few yards away. I had time until evening. I did not have to hurry. I could stay here, but I had to stay in the inn "Under the Lion and Scorpio". That was the directive and the principle of the Brotherhood. Out of a dozen branches and dried palm leaves, I lit a fire and cooked myself a poor meal. Water, a few dates, a piece of dried meat... I did not need more. The dog demolished a piece of dry beef and rye cake. He stood with me staring lovingly at my eyes and waited for further morsels waving his short tail. Finally, seeing that he would not get any more he licked the crumbs from the ground and lay down by the fire.

I had to take a nap because Arus woke me with a short bark. I looked around and noticed the moving caravan that was approaching from the south. A dozen or so riders and several covered carriages. Sitting under the palm, I watched them from under half-closed eyelids. Who were they? Dark skin and dark hair seemed to speak for Shemites or even Stygians. Their accouterment and weapons also spoke about it. I was about to close my eyes and take a nap when something caught my attention. A large, heavy wagon passed us, and its chest was covered with a huge palanquin. I guessed that there were women in it who did not want the sun to burn them. I did not have to guess, because through the muslin curtains you could see their outlines and I could hear their voices and laughter.

At once the catara slid away for a moment and I saw her.

It lasted a moment, but I saw her face. She was very pretty, with regular features and a fair complexion. Dark straight hair ran down the bare neck, and the green eyes gleamed like two precious emeralds. She was dressed in an emerald dress with a deep cut at the front showing a light skin with a silk sheen. Smiley, she looked at me and for a moment our eyes met. I felt a sudden heartbeat. Then she covered the muslin curtain again and disappeared from my sight.

"Who was she?" I began to wonder. Judging from her beauty, she could have come from the south of Aquilonia, but she might be as well a resident of Shem or Ophir. She could have been the wife of a significant Stygian or his concubine. She did not look like a daughter, she could have been around thirty, so she could not be maidenhood. The people of the South quickly pushed their daughters to the husband, until the beauty of their daughters was destroyed by the sun and hard work...

The caravan slowly floated towards the city gates. Probably standing in a local tavern or inn before they returns to home. No reasonable person, having a women in the caravan will risk going west to Nemedia by two mountain chains, similarly with the opposite direction. The trails laid out there were difficult to overcome in the summer and intransitive in winter. Only troublemakers, witches, treasure hunters and Brotherhood couriers, just like me, ventured there. The passage to the deserts and steppes of Turan and Hyrkan located above the inland Vilayet Sea was especially dangerous. In the Kezankyan Mountains, apart from the frost and snow, besides the avalanches of stones and floodgates, Thaki was threatening the traveler - half monkeys and half-men, menacing and cruel. Only one man went out victoriously with the clash with them - Conan the Cimmerian in the house of the Red Priest Nabonidus in Corinthia, about which the bards sang later at the shepherds' fires and at the courts of rulers of the entire civilized world. Thakis, whose double-animal-human nature remained unknown to this day, tried to knock out the Hyrkanians and Zamorians - armed expeditions went to the mountains and returned with nothing, or did not return at all... and finally they gave them peace. Which was absolutely good for us, because the Brotherhood had its trail there and two camps. These mountains could not be jumped by one jump. It took three days and two nights to pass them. And the Brotherhood did not want anyone to disturb them. It was the surest and shortest way to the East. Another thing, it was very difficult and tiring. But it saved a lot of time. Time and trouble with the authorities of the not too stable kingdoms of Zamora and Corinthia.

Slowly, I got up and started packing. I still had four miles to the city gates and the tavern where I was supposed to stand. I was surprised to find that I can not stop thinking about the woman I saw for a short while. I was interested in where she came from and who she was. And what she did here. I forced myself to stop thinking about her and after two hours, when the sun was already hanging over the jagged saw of distant Zamorian Mountains, I finally stood in front of the "Under the Scorpion and the Lion" inn, which stood near the main eastern gate of the Yezud city.

The tavern looked like... like a tavern. Its walls with small windows were built of huge logs laden with tar. Over time, here and there, some additional annexes were added to it, and thanks to that the whole thing looked as if it crawled on the ground. On the square in front of it, a rabble milled around, multicolored and flickering. There was a fair there where you could sell and buy almost everything from the crabs of the overseas vanilla to the earrings of the Bamulas nose, from the Stygian gray lotus to the balls of the Khitayan opium. Perhaps here was the one I had to wait for. In the meantime, I was looking for a Stygian caravan. And though I looked out, I did not notice its wagons anywhere.

"Apparently they have already entered the city..." I thought, "and to the hell with them..."

I shrugged and slowly stepped out of the crowd and headed for my animals.

"Lestko Vislanin?" I heard behind me. "Is that who I think it is?"

I slowly turned away. Behind me stood a tall Nemedian clad in a gray-green, woolen coat with a hood. From behind his head stuck the hilt of a simple sword from distant Zipang, a standard weapon of Brotherhood members.

"Welcome to Zamor Tarkwinus Syxtus." I replied. "I don't need to say how much I enjoy your view."

We hugged. In fact, the sight of him made me very happy because it meant the end of my part of the mission. Now he has to bring what others have managed to get out of the Dead Marshes, which lay in the very south of Cambudia, transported through the countries of the South to the Vilayet Sea, where I took this shipment in the port of Shapur and drove to Yezud happily, where I passed this baton to the next participant this relay race. Now he was to take it to Belverus, where the members of the Brotherhood would take care of it content, who would decide on its future.

"Where do you have it?" Tarkwinus asked when we finished the greeting.

"In saddlebags," I replied, "follow me."

I moved towards my horses. I took off the saddlebag and opened it. The remains of sunlight fell on a small metal box covered with inscriptions containing a warning against attempts to open it.

"Beware Tarkwinus," I said in a very serious tone, "you can't open it under any circumstances. Death lurks in it. Invisible, imperceptible, but surely. If, however, it opens, you must immediately wash in the water, and its contents buried as deeply as possible into the ground. And that will be all you can do, because you'll have only two weeks of life ahead of you. It doesn't kill right away, but slowly. You die in horrible torment."

For a moment he chewed on the news he had heard.

"Sure, I'm not going with such packages for the first time," he said carelessly, but I knew he was worried about it. Just like me.

"Have you got something for me?" I asked.

"Yes, of course," he said hastily, "for now you got a month of rest, so you can go with me to Belverus and then to Vislania."

"Oh!" I was happy "I'll take this leave, but I'll stay here a day or two."

"Woman?" He asked with a smile on the face.

"As a matter of fact!" I replied.

"Well, I wish you good luck," he gave me a hand, "and see you in Belverus!"

"Are you going now?" I asked, "through the night?"

"I like to ride like this, and in the morning I will be at the foot of the mountains. I don't have to camp there. I camped there few times and twice fought with some lugs..."

He got on his horse and waved goodbye to me. He took my horse, leaving his. In his saddlebags, I found a purse and in it one hundred golden lunas. I slipped it into my pocket. I unsaddled and unburdened the horses. Arus stayed with me, launching raids with local dogs from time to time. I did not have to worry about him, because I knew he would come back for the night. The servants took the horses to the stables, and I entered the tavern, where the every-night bust was boiling.

II

Nothing has changed here. The interior was vibrant. People sat at long benches, and the tavern man stood by the counter, conducting a swarm of agile servants and maids. I approached him.

"Hello, Father Keen!" I shouted.

"Welcome Vislanian," he answered.

But there was no joy in his voice, and his eyes were searching.

"We'll have to talk," he said, "and it's a serious matter."

"About me or something else?" I asked, puzzled.

"Directly to you, and indirectly to the Brotherhood and myself," he said gravely, as we sat in his office, separated from the rest of the room and its noise.

"Will you tell me that the Royal Guard is interested in us?" I asked. The Zamorian Royal Guard, in addition to being an excellent, well-trained and equipped battle formation, additionally fulfilled the role of intelligence and counterintelligence service. Everyone knew that with their powers, it was not worth messing with them and everyone preferred to live with them in harmony. Father Keen knew it perfectly well, and he worked on two or maybe three fronts.

He certainly worked for us, for the Royal Guard and perhaps the Khauranians, who were a lot here.

"Ah, they," father Keen waved his hand, "no, guards aren't the worst here. I mean Stygians"

I put up my ears.

"What Stygian?" I asked cautiously. "I saw the caravan from Stygia today."

"This is already the third in this week." Father Keen looked around anxiously, "they're supposedly all right, they have goods and all the others things, but they're snooping too much."

"Were there women with them?" I asked with growing interest.

"Yes, there are several women in each of them, three to six. And about thirty men. You can see that they're familiarity guys," father Keen made a face that showed a deep disapproval.

"And those ladies?" I asked, winking.

"Not bad," he replied. "But be careful, they're not for you..."

"I know, you should rather to watch out," I said with a laugh, "I won't be here tomorrow. I'm going back to the Borderlands Kingdoms. Finally home.

I spent here three year, between Zamora and the Vilayet Sea, carrying people or various trumped goods in both directions. I've been lucky so far, but one day can come and my good luck will end and a good run will turn around."

"What can Stygians look for here?" I thought for a moment.

"You," said Father Keen. "And other liaisons: for example Syxtus, Gvalbert, Mahaviris. That's why I advise you, better run away. They learned from somewhere about the Brotherhood and what we do here."

"It would be even logical..." I said. "I heard a lot about the dark secrets of their gods... And one of them could have power over the world. Absolute power," I finished with a certain emphasis.

"For now, everyone except me and you are safe in the mountains," I said.

"And Syxtus?"

"He is on his way to Mountain pass," I replied. "What are you going to do?"

"I'm here for now, and in case of something, I will hide with my relatives." Father Keen shrugged. "And as if something happens, I'll always be able to hide our secrets in the arms of Dekerto..."

The prospect of committing suicide was always something unreal, I always wanted to die in battle, but the training in the Brotherhood's activity changed my attitude to death. We dealt with mysteries so gloomy, for which stories about Stygian gods sounded like fairy tales for children.

A sudden noise escaped through the dam of the solid door and turned our attention to what was happening in the room. Father Keen stood up, taking a solid club. He repeatedly called to order too-fiery revelers. From behind the door there were curses spoken in a heavy voice, the sounds of blows and a cry of a woman.

We left the back room. We saw a huge, bearded Kothiyan holding a woman on a chain, lying on the floor, whom he beat with a stick, shouting curses at the same time.

"You fucking bitch from Brythunia!!!" He shouted. "You're a stupid whore! I'll smash you, you Hyborian slut!!!"

Each punch was accompanied by a stick punch. As angry as a bull in heat, he beat his victim methodically, beating her to make her the biggest pain. The woman was lying motionless, I think she finally lost consciousness.

Nobody paid any attention to it. Most likely, no one wanted to deal with the ravaged and inserted giant. He just lifted the stick to hit her again when I shouted to him:

"Stop it, you carrion eater! Dekerto was asking about you..."

"Whaaaatttt???" He shouted and hit the lying one again.

"Stop beating her," I said calmly, "don't you see she's barely dead."

"It's my woman and my thing and you've nothing to do with it!" He replied, raising the stick again. "Maybe you want to forbid me, you borderland whoredog?" He asked mockingly.

There was silence. Everyone slowly moved to the wall feeling a fight.

"Surely, you Kothiyan punk!" I said brazenly looking into his eyes. "I forbid you."

He threw back the stick. He was a seven feet tall and could fit in him three such man as me. He straightened up to his entire height.

"You are already dead," he announced in a satisfied tone. "I'll gut you. Go to hell, you drowsy shit!"

A huge scimitar with a four-foot long blade flashed in his hand.

"And what now, you borderland dog?" He asked mockingly. "You've already made shit?"

He chortled and the rest of the room after him.

"So what?" I asked coldly, "Are you afraid? Come closer here, you Kothiyan bastard! Are you coward?"

"Go to the dung, where is your place!" He shouted.

I provoked him and he jumped in my direction taking a wide swing. Anger took away his senses, because he cut almost blindly. I dodged.

"You aren't so good?" I asked mockingly as he tried to snatch his weapon from the floor.

"You son of the bitch!!!" He yelled. "Look you rags, what will I do with you!"

He took a wide swing and cut the empty air again.

"Stop it!" I said, "because I will have to kill you and I don't want to."

I had to finish this spectacle, because I didn't want anyone to bring in a city guard or Royal Guard patrol. That was the last thing I could wish for. The Kothiyan chortled.

"You fool!!!" he roared. "I'll make marmalade from you!!!" And he swung for the third time.

I had enough of this fun. I reached out with my left hand behind my head and took out my sword with one smooth movement, and then I precisely punched him with a blow to the left temple. I had to take a step back, because the fat man fell like a beheaded oak. Scimitar fell out of his fainting hand and stuck to the floor. The fun was over.

I went slowly to the lying woman, crouched and touched her neck with my fingers. The pulse was weak but palpable. She was alive, but she was unconscious. Her back was covered with bleeding wounds and bruises. This fat sadist also beat her legs trying to hit her heels. She probably could not stand it, and then she cried out. I involuntarily admired her resistance to pain. I picked her up from the ground and took her in my arms.

"Help me, Father Keen," I said, "let's move her to some calm place."

"Upstairs," he replied, "to your room."

"Go ahead," I let him go ahead.

We went upstairs and after a while we found ourselves in a simple room. I put her on the bed and turned her on the stomach. She moaned regaining consciousness. She opened nicely cut gray eyes.

"Lie calmly," I said, "we will care for you."

Father Keen went for hot water and bandages. I reached for the pannier for ointments and painkillers and antipyretics. The woman lay calmly looking at me and what I was doing. And meanwhile, I took off the ruffled shirt and took it gently and looked at her naked body. She did not protest, she just lay quietly, pausing in pain. She was terribly beaten. Despite that, she closed her eyes with shame.

"I regret that I didn't kill him," I murmured.

"He lives?" She asked calmly. What did you do to him?"

"I hit him in head and I think he is still unconscious," I replied. "But at the first chance I'll kill him."

"It's a pig, it's not worth to burden your conscience with his death," she replied with remarkable calmness. "Don't do this, please"

"Would you like a replay?" I asked ironically. "If you want, then be my guest. He's down there. I don't know who you are, but there is a limit to forgiveness. One fight isn't enough to you?"

"I know but..."

"Are you a priestess?" I asked unkindly. "What can you know about it?"

"You're right," she said resignedly, "actually, nothing..."

III

Father Keen returned with a maid, a charming 18-year-old creature who brought the basin of steaming water and bandages. Then we set about dressing the wounds of an unknown woman. We finished after a hour. The stranger lay motionless on the bed, pale and breathing with difficulty. I gave her a concentrated bark extract and a swallow of willow to ease the pain. After two hours, she felt better and fell asleep. We left her with the maid, and left to the room.

The giant Kothiyan disappeared somewhere, and the whole company went to rest, sitting down and lying down where anyone could. I wondered what to do. I could stay here for a few days and find out about the situation and find out what the Stygian people are really up to, or take a holiday and go to Vislania. The road to Vislania would take me two weeks one way, then a month of rest and again two weeks back. Staying here threatened to uncover, and certainly sooner or later there would be a clash with this Kothiyan sadist. I would gladly have rip his guts out, but that could have threatened with unpredictable consequences on the part of the Zamora authorities, and that I wanted to avoid. So I decided to stay tuned for about two days with Father Keen and then leave Yesud for two months.

I escorted him to his back room, and I returned to my room. The woman slept quietly, apparently a concentrated mixture of painkillers and sleeping pills worked. I dismissed the girl who smiled at me with a sly smile, she winked at me and went to the door. I slapped her on the buttock. She squeaked and ran away. At other times, maybe I would like to have this girl, but not today. I blew out the lamp and the room darkened. Through the window one could see the bright stars shining over the steppe, in whose light one could see only the gloomy mountains closing the horizon in the field of view. I spread a blanket on the floor and put a saddle under my head, and after a while I fell asleep.

* * *

I woke up when the sun was already high above the mountains. I felt someone's eyes on me and looked back. The mysterious woman did not sleep anymore - she lay there staring at me. I went to her and sat on the bed.

"How are you?" I asked.

"Not bad, it was worse," she replied, trying to smile, which only flashed through her pale and drawn face. "To whom do I owe my salvation?"

"My name is Lestko son of Dzierżymir, and I come from Vislania," I introduced myself. "This is in the Borderlands Kingdoms, and you?"

"My name is Iris and I come from Ianthe in Ophir. I was born and brought up there. But my parents were Brythuans who emigrated after the palace revolution a dozen or so years ago.

"I see," I smiled at her, "gray eyes, a dark frame of eyes and brown hair, a light complexion... Ophirian women are much darker."

"Are you an artist or a doctor?" She asked. "Since you know so much about people."

"A bit of that and a little bit of that," I shrugged my shoulders, "I know a little bit about everything, as people are wandering around. And you? How did you get to this forbidden hole?"

She shrugged and waved her hand.

"It's a waste my breath," she sighed. "I'll tell you this, but not now."

"You don't have to hurry." I said. "We've some time."

"We'll have a lot of time for each other, because now you are mine." She said simply. "And I'm yours. You saved my life, you saw me naked and therefore you share the joss with me."

Yeah. I have heard about this habit and, in its defense, I should foresee the effects. Not that I would not associate with her, but because I was a member of the Brotherhood.

"You don't find me attractive?" She asked quietly. "Well, in such a condition only a blind man could take me... Of course, you can chase me off if you want. I won't hold you captive."

"No, that's not it," I said calmly, "the point is that you'd have to share the life of a wanderer with me, and that's probably not liked by any woman. Secondly, you are still weak and you've to lie here a little - about two or three days. Then I go to Vislania. You'll come with me, but I've to leave you to parents, because I'll go back on the trail alone. I have such... eh... a job."

"Are you a guide?"

"Well, you can call it in that way. I'm moving people and sometimes goods through the Kezankian Mountains."

She took my hand and put it to cheek. It was cool, so she did not get fever.

"Oh no, I'm yours and my place is with you," she said calmly and firmly, "and I can go with you to Vislania only as your fiancée, wife, concubine or slave girl - as you please. Nothing hold me here," she added enigmatically.

"And what are you useful for?" I asked maybe a little too rough. And she, to my amazement, smiled only.

"I can do a lot of things that can be useful to us on the trail," she said with a mysterious smile and insistence on the word 'us'. "Now look at how my back is healing."

I slid the duvet off her and looked at her body. I took off her bandages gently and lint. The wounds slowly closed and only the bruises ran nasty, almost black in color.

"Does it hurt a lot?" I asked. "We have a two-week drive to Vislania and it's through two mountain chains and the Nemedia's steppes."

"The labor pains are stronger, so I can stand it," she said.

"Did you give birth?" I asked, astonished. "Do you have children?"

She laughed and hissed in pain.

"No, I didn't give birth, but you know such things, if you'll give a new life to the world."

I quickly rubbed her wounds, changed the dressings and went to the main room to order a broth for her and something for us. Arus was waiting for me at the door of the tavern, so there was a morsel for him too. The guests sat eating and drinking, so I did not pay anyone's attention. Iris first slapped the broth and then with small nibbles she ate a roast beef, which I brought to us from downstairs.

"Actually, I don't eat meat, but I think I should get used to it," she said when she was satisfied with the first hunger.

"Are you a priestess or a nun?" I asked, because what she said seemed to indicate it.

"I was a Mitra priestess in Ianthe," she said simply, "I have lower orders behind me, but unfortunately, as you see, Mitra wanted differently. This... this... this breeding bull fell in love with me and kidnapped from the temple."

"Hmmm... so you can return to the priesthood?" I asked.

"Not anymore..." she said quietly. "He raped me because I didn't want to give myself to him.

Tears glowed in her eyes for a moment. It must have terribly humiliated her. I was not surprised by her. But now I understood her peace - it resulted from something transcendent, from her spiritual strength, not only physical.

"And you still defend him?" I asked in exorbitant astonishment, "you give him life?"

"Mitra is merciful and makes me forgive," she said seriously, looking into my eyes. "I forgave him and I don't want any harm to come to him..."

It was difficult for me to accept it. I did not understand her value system. This man did her terrible harm, he kidnapped her from the temple and desecrated her. Other woman would demand revenge and she would forgive him and even defend him...

"I won't kill him," I said, "because you ask for it, and not because Mitra wants it. Besides, I don't believe in any gods. But don't let this man stand in my way."

"Thank you," she said. And she breathed a sigh of relief.

"Iris," I called her by her first name, "you must understand that for him it won't be any lesson. Yesterday he beat you, tomorrow he'll do it with another woman who'll be less fortunate and no one will defend her. He'll kill her as he tried to kill you. Think about it."

She lowered her head.

"You're right, but I don't want to shed somebody's blood, even if it's a criminal's blood."

I waved my hand and left the room.

I went to father Keen and asked him to look after Iris, and I went to look around the city where there were more than one hundred and twenty Stygian people. In the morning another caravan entered the city. It was strange that they did not stop in taverns, inns, roadhouse and hostelry outside the city walls, and spent the night in a city where it was safer but also more expensive. In any case, not on my budget. Even with a hundred lunas, you could only spend a few nights in the city. The local innkeepers could make money from people with the skill of a professional milkmaid. You could spend all the money in one night. Like in every big city in the entire civilized world.

So I wandered around the city from the tavern to the tavern, from the saloon to the saloon in the hope that I would find a trace of Stygians and their vehicles, but I found nothing. It was really suspicious. I was extremely curious about the royal secret services, but I could not check it out. I did not have any fellows or friends here who could be a reliable source of information for me. So it seemed that the Stygian people disappeared among the streets and disappeared into the metropolis without leaving any trace...

IV

I returned to 'Scorpion and the Lion' concerned. I came to the conclusion that apparently one of the local magnates ordered a larger number of Stygian products or women or something else from that country, and therefore during two days in the city there were five caravans and more than hundred Stygian men and women. If they wanted to paralyze the Brotherhood's activities, they would first of all set a trap where quick meetings of his couriers took place. They could watch all the more important taverns and inns, pick out suspects and follow them. I did not saw anything like that, so their aim was not the Brotherhood. At least for now.

In the tavern, as always, the late afternoon noise and traffic prevailed. I looked around quickly and did not notice my yesterday opponent. I quickly went upstairs. Iris lay on the bed and slept. Her breath was even and calm. I did not have to worry too much about her, she was young and she recovered quickly. The element of uncertainty was the fact that she immediately got into my life and I did not know what to do with her. It would be nice to have a normal home and a family to come back to after a grueling walk through the mountains. Iris was pretty, even very pretty. Her beauty resulted more from excellent health and good physical condition, which was evident even from her lithe, shapely and harmoniously built body. She was damned unlucky that this brute fell in love with her... On the other hand, if not him...

"She would not even look at you," I replied in my mind.

I got up and at once heard the soft creak of the door. My right arm automatically stretched out to the sword, and the body turned one hundred and eighty degrees. The first thing I saw was a heavy scimitar in the hand, huge like a four-pound loaf of bread. I got the impression that the door had shrunk somewhat, because there was the same Kothiyan giant in it that so much hit Iris with the stick yesterday evening.

"And here you are a borderland bastard," he drawled with hatred. "You won't miss me now, and she too."

"I wouldn't do anything," I said, "I want you to know that she was asking for life for you."

"I've got it in..." he spat and then he carefully defined the place at the outfall of the anus, "and now I'm gonna kill you and that bitch, too."

His roar aroused Iris. For a moment I saw her terrified eyes staring at the scene taking place in front of them.

Meanwhile, the breeding bull moved in my direction. He led a treacherous thrust directed at my stomach. I made a quick dodge. The blade hit the wall and dug into it. He snatched it out with one jerk, led the cut, aiming again at the stomach. He came up with this idea because he was hoping that I would be able to get rid of him again, and he would immediately move on to my torso. In addition, such cuts and thrusts are difficult to repel.

He miscalculated. I blocked the blow. His right hand drew back slightly to the hit and this was his last mistake, because I cut him unexpectedly on the shoulder and chopped off his arm, and a second later I cut through the head until the scraps of what was his brain were splashing against the wall and ceiling. The massive bulk of his body fell to the floorboards that crackled under his weight. And then there was a deadly silence interrupted by the sound of convulsions and the lapping of blood flowing from the body of the enemy I had struck down.

"You killed him," Iris whispered.

"Yes, what else I had to wait to the time when he kill us." I growled. "And you pity him!"

"I'm sorry," she said in repentance, "you were right, he was a monster..."

She hid the face, pale like a paper, in her hands for a moment. Only now she had relieve fear. I nodded. I heard footsteps on the stairs and Father Keen and a few apprentices stood in the doorway.

"And how did he get here?" He asked in astonishment. "But how beautifully you got him," he said, looking at the corpse with his thumbs tucked in his belt. Master Trakketrai-san would be pleased with you..."

"Well, I think so." I said without boasting in my voice, because I sensed another problem.

"Take away the scum," Father Keen commanded his journeymen. "We have to clean up here for you."

"Who was it actually?" He asked, looking at Iris. She still hid her face in her hands. Finally she showed her face, which was completely calm. She finally pulled herself together.

"I'm afraid we are in serious trouble," she replied, "it was Count Savanarab, a friend and adviser to General Almaryk, commander-in-chief of the Kingdom of Koth."

"For Swarog's sake!" I moaned. "That's all I need."

"Oh, so you're professing faith in some gods?" Iris asked in a harsh voice. "Father Keen is right, you have to clean up run like hell. I have no reason to return to Ophir - as a kidnapped and disgraced priestess, I'm a bushwhacker. I don't have anyone, anyway. My parents are dead, and I don't have siblings..."

At last I understood her, she just burned all the bridges behind her and had to change everything in her life, she was alone like a finger. And she had to put everything on one card.

"So you go with me," I said, "to Vislania. We're not safe here. I'll stay in Belverus and contact the Council of the Brotherhood. Maybe they'll send somebody else for me here.

I started gathering quickly. Iris did not have any clothes, except for the dirty, torn and bloody dress I had thrown away. I gave her my old pants and a woolen hoodie and spare riding boots. It had to be enough for her, and she did not be fussy. She stuck her dark brown hair in ponytail and she stood next to me.

"I'm ready," she announced.

"Go away," said Father Keen, "he wasn't alone here, his adjutants would soon seek him, and then it could be very hot here. I'll take care of these Stygians myself. They're snooping about something, that's for sure. Let them send someone from Belverus here. I was told that the Stygians had installed themselves in the Sarharadon merchant's palace. Strange things people say about him, including the fact that he collects unusual items imported from distant lands. And this is already under the Brotherhood's interests. Now go quickly, because nobody give even a shackle for your heads..."

We quickly descended to the general room, where I caught a few research glances, maybe even from people accompanied to the count, so we immediately ran to the stable, we saddled the horses. To my amazement, Iris handled it perfectly. We jumped on horses and went towards the last fires of the evening aurora in the sky. We missed the city from the south making sure nobody was going after us, but no. There were no riders behind us, so for now we were safe. Nevertheless, we had to reckon with the pursuit and we could rest for the first time in the first camp on the pass. It was only there that we could feel safe. Kothiyans were well-trained fighters, but in the mountains the advantage was on my side. We drove into the woods at the foot of the mountains, but instead of west, we turned north.

"We won't take the trail to Corinthia?" Iris asked.

"No." I said. "Just in case we take a different route, less secure, but more dangerous for a possible pursuit. Besides, I hope that the pursuit will follow the Corinthian route, so we'll gain time before they realize that there is a different route and find it."

We rested on the snow Pass. After the murderous climb, we deserved that. Iris was already feel well enough to be able to overcome the hardships of travel. Everything was healed on her good, so we have hope for the best. Two more days and we will be relatively safe. And for now, we rested in the camp - one of two on the Brotherhood trail. Tomorrow we had a hard time crossing the second mountain chain, which cut from the north deep into Brythunia. Then four days drive up the foothills and jump over the border to Vislania.

"Have you had enough sleep?" I asked Iris, who stuck her nose out from under the huge, coarse hide of a cave bear.

"Wonderful," Iris stretched pleasantly, "and I hardly feel pain anymore."

She petted Arus lying with her, who licked her hand.

"Great." I said igniting the fire. "You have to prepare some food, and I'm going to look around. First of all, I will check if someone is following us. On the snow you can clearly see the traces of possible intruders, unfortunately ours too, so *they* could not be fooled..."

"Of course," she said, getting up and putting on a bit too bigger clothes, "go and I'll do something good for us."

I left the cottage. The sharp mountain air hit the nostrils. The sky was still dark, but the first bands of dawn appeared behind the mountain massifs, quickly brightened and the new day woke up. Above the mountains in the northwest, a large light appeared, which was rapidly and increasingly shining toward the zenith. The zenith passed and flashed with a strong white light in the almost navy blue sky, and then it began to quickly fade and disappeared in the south-east. It was the Little Guide. Once, still in Belverus, one of the astronomers working for the Brotherhood showed us what it really is. Through a long tube blinded on both sides with crystal lenses, we saw a white-light construction resembling a huge spider. Then he said strange words that I did not understand - *an orbital station...* Apparently, the other one was in the ether spaces, but it was visible only over the Black Kingdoms and was called the *Great Guide*. It shone apparently even brighter and was visible even during the day!

Something brushed against my leg. It was Arus who followed me. Now he looked around and aired. Suddenly he turned his ears and quietly growled. It was a warning. The dog has seen the foreign smell.

"Search." I directed.

Arus, still sniffing, slowly moved in the direction we came from.

"Oh!" I thought. "We have guests."

It could only be uninvited guests following us. It could only be Count Savanarab's companions and they followed us with only one purpose.

We saw them after half an hour. Four of the Kothiyans armed very well rode slowly on our tracks. I wondered what to do. I was absolutely sure of one - none of them should get away with life. This trail was the secret of the Brotherhood and it should remain so. Besides, as long as one of these Kothiyans was alive, we were both at risk. There was no turning back. I took off the crossbow and quickly jumped into the stone labyrinth rising below the Pass. The path our enemies traveled by was passing this maze, and on the right side there was an abyss. Here I was going to attack them.

The riders were already about three hundred paces away. I tugged on my bowstring and loaded a long bolt. I leaned in while taking aim at the last of them. I put myself into the shot by grabbing his character in the sight. In the bright circle of the sight, I saw his head.

V

I pressed the trigger. The bolt whistled flying towards him and hit Kothiyan in the neck. He grabbed his throat and silently slipped into the abyss with the horse, whose terrified snoring cut through the morning silence. I immediately loaded the crossbow and sent a long bolt to the other rider, who also collapsed from the horse. The confused animal stood as if unable to cross to two others. The Kothiyans were good soldiers. They did not panic, only drew weapons, looking around, trying to spot their opponents.

I loaded the crossbow and sent another bolt to the one who was on the left. And then thanks to the next shot, I took the last one from the horse. I did not have any remorse. It was them who wanted to kill us, if they did not, they would not be here. I approached three corpses. I took the arrows and slipped them into a quiver. I threw the bodies into the abyss. For a moment, I wondered what to do with their horses, finally I jumped on the first one and moved up. Arus chased the other two behind me.

I drove up to the hut. Hearing the horses' throbbing and snorting, Iris came out in front of me.

"You killed them." It was a statement, not a question.

I nodded.

"With a crossbow?" She asked.

"Yes, I couldn't do it myself," I said, "they were well-trained soldiers. However, now they are in the abyss."

I jumped from the horse and unsaddled the rest. I left the inspection of the saddlebags for later.

"Show it." Iris reached out for my crossbow. "I haven't seen anything like this yet!"

I smiled. Sure, she did not see it! It was a unique weapon with completely innovative solutions. Her arch was made not of wood but of elastic steel. Like the arrow slideway that is gun carriage. It was heavier than a standard crossbow equipped with many Hyborian armies, but it gave to it greater stability in shooting, minimal kickback and arrow throw. Instead of a chord from animal traps or a string, I used a steel cable with a tensioned lever, instead of a finger or a knob, which allowed it to be loaded within a few seconds and give the second shot. The downside was that the steel cable stretched after some time and it was necessary to replace it. The steel chord gave an extra "shot" to arrow, so that the initial speed of the missile was at least four times larger than a regular crossbow. For a thousand feet, a long arrow with a steel, hardened tip pierced through each armor or shield. A terrible weapon for a struggling war. Well, the gunpoint was made of a piece of straight pipe, so you could aim the crossbow at the target and hit it with incredible precision. Also innovative solutions, which I have not seen anywhere, and which use has multiplied the accuracy of this weapon.

"You won't tell me, that you know it?" I asked.

"A little," she answered with a wicked grin.

"Priestesses taught you how to use weapons?"

"Yes, a bit. And as you can see, it didn't help much..."

We sat down to breakfast, which consisted of thick pemmique soup and cakes. We ate it quickly and started to look through the contents of our persecutors' saddlebags and dorsels. There was nothing interesting there, a bit of dried meat and vegetables, not a very accurate map of those areas where no less-frequented routes were marked.

"I wonder what the Kothiyan military of this rank was looking for in Zamora?" I was thinking loudly. "I think it's not just a convenient hideout for you?"

"I was just an adventure on Savanarab's way," Iris throw the strands of dark-brown hair with a vigorous movement of her head, "I suspect they were just following the Stygians."

"What is happening in this Stygia, for Perkun sake, that everyone is interested in this?" I asked.

"You don't know?"

"No."

"Well, you must know that there has been a change of the ruling person. After the death of their king, his daughter, the young princess Ghe-drenh-ra, entered his throne. They say that she is too stupid to govern herself and, in fact, she is governed by the priesthood college of Amon Ra and its chairman, Mer-ankh-re-amer-ra, or somehow."

"Well, it often happens with young rulers," I said.

"Of course, but it's not good when the priests get to power," Iris said.

"And who is saying that?" I said with irony.

"*Former* priestess, after her lower ordination," she replied, "and you're right, it's hard to talk about gods. All priests have one god, whose name is power and money, now I see it..."

"It doesn't please me," I murmured.

"So what are we doing?" She asked.

I looked at the sky. It was enlisted in dark clouds from the north. It did not bode well for anything.

"For now, we're going to be here, like two hares under the mire," I said. "Do you see those clouds? In a few hours there will be a snowstorm."

She smiled and looked into my eyes.

"How long does it take?" She asked.

"Sometimes an hour, sometimes a few days..." I replied.

"That's great," she said quietly and took my hand, "at least it will be a chance to relax and... get to know each other better - isn't it? What do you think?"

"You want it very much?" I asked surreptitiously.

"Very much." She whispered.

Her lips touched my hand. I felt a wave of heat.

"All right," I said, "I'm going to take care the horses and prepare us for the dujawica."

"For what???" She asked, surprised.

"Dujawica," I said, "this is what we call a snowstorm and blizzard. And it looks like we'll wait here longer..."

Well, we waited. At first it got completely dark, and then a mass of snow fell on the mountains. And this wind. A huge gale of snow mass gave it completely horizontal, like a big broom. I thought that it would erase all traces of our escape. Syxtus, who drove a day earlier, should go to another shelter, or he was already on the Brythunia plain and he headed for Numalia. I could have been confident about him, he knew the trail as well as I did.

We had a fire in the fireplace and it got cozy. Outside, a blizzard broke out, and in the middle the fireplace sent out waves of heat. We sent out bears pelt near the fireplace. Iris threw off her clothes and lay down on her stomach, exposing her back curves.

"Take a look at my back, please," she said.

"With pleasure," I said and started my inspection.

It looked good. The wounds had already closed and began to heal. Bruises slowly began to descend and everything began to get faster and faster.

"It's good," I said, "there will not even be a mark in a week..."

At least that's what I hoped for.

Iris sat down and her hands slid under my sweatshirt. They were delicate and warm. Her lips were dangerously close to my lips at once. Then they touched them gently. The kiss was delicate and sweet.

"Take it off and come to me," she said pleadingly, "I'm not going to be alone here, and what else do you have to do?"

"You don't want to..." I said.

"Not yet," she smiled, "but..."

She lay on her back and covered with a misiura.

I took off my clothes and bare slipped under pelt. She hugged me quickly, embracing my neck. We lay silent. Each of us got used to each other, a warm presence of the other person.

"What we gonna do now?" Iris broke the silence.

"We're waiting," I said. "It's a pity I can't take you in."

"I can cuddle harder." And she hugged harder.

We fell silent again.

"I must confess to you," she said in a tone of confession, "I'm not a priestess of Mitra.

"So, who?" I asked, unable to stop my curiosity.

"I'm a priestess who belongs to the Inner Circle of the Shrine of Mother Earth in Eleusis..."

I felt a growing astonishment.

"Eleusis?" I asked, "but..."

"I know what you mean: Stygians attacked and murdered the priestesses of Mother Earth, but not all," she said calmly, "and I'm one of them. They think that they have introduced the cult of the Seth, the Old Viper in Eleusis, but this is a pretence. We still exist."

"So you can't be mine," it just came out from me.

"That's exactly what I can do," she replied, "but, of course, I won't be a priestess anymore, because all priestesses are virgins, but I can still be a member of the Inner Circle, with no voting rights and the right to sit in it. It is such an honorary title. And you?"

"As you know, I work for the Brotherhood of the Green Dragon. I'm his ordinary member."

"Women can be in the Brotherhood?"

"Of course, older brothers are married and have families. Our fellowship isn't religious. There are devotees of Mitra, Krom, Svetovid, Rama and others like me... Religion doesn't matter to us."

"So we can be together?" She asked hopefully.

"I think so."

"Then nothing prevents me from being yours?"

"If you're not connected to someone, there's nothing."

The answer was a hot kiss.

VI

The wind grew more and more, but it stopped snowing and the sky cleared. Stars appeared on it. It got cold. And it was heralding that you could go through the mountains, where the snow had already turned into rain, because after the night frosts, the next days were always warm. We fell asleep embraced and hugging each other. Iris from time to time moaned when I hugged her too tightly - hurting and scarring places still hurts her. But the night passed calmly. The fire on the chimney has go out, but we more tightly covered with pelt, which were in abundance and we clung firmly to each other. And so we lasted until morning.

The morning greeted us with a flaming sunrise. We stood in front of the shelter looking around. The bright light quickly extracted the mountain peaks from the shadows, the order prevailed around the cottage, because the snow had been swept away by the wind, while from Brythunia now blowing a warm zephyr. I was used to the fact that the mountain weather was as unpredictable as a capricious woman.

"And what now?" Iris asked, "are we going?"

"We'll wait another day," I said, "until the water from the melted snow flows."

"So we're slowly packing up the road?"

"We have one day back because of this snowstorm." I growled.

"Do you regret it?" She asked in a slightly pathetic tone.

I embraced her gently.

"No, I don't regret it. I think that all that's best is ahead of us..." I kissed her on the lips. "You have my word."

She brightened up. She was a priestess, but she liked such a tender word like any woman.

A thought suddenly dawned on my mind.

"Tell me, did you conduct any operation against the Stygians?"

She nodded her head.

"I can tell you now, because it does not matter. When Queen Ghe-drenh-ra ascended the throne, it will be Gedrena in Hyborian, we stated that she was behind this slaughter in Eleusis. What's more, she's interested in black magic... She ordered to murder us because someone told her that we have in our possession a jewel, a powerful magic item called the Heart of the Dragon."

"It's nonsense, there's no magic," I disapproved.

"As you wish," she waved her hand and continued, "as I was telling you, Gedrena got sniffed with the high priest of the temple of Set who changed his name to Mam-ehr-as-seth and with his support she established cult of Seth as a state religion in all Stygia. And now they are both looking for magical objects around the world for their sorcerous practices. That is why the Eleusisian Sanctuary undertook to observe its activities. Now you understand?"

"And you?" I asked.

"I kept an eye on the Stygians who came to Yezud. We managed to find out whom they came to and who they contacted with. Unfortunately, the Kothiyans are also interested in that, and the rest are familiar. This breeding-bull kidnapped, raped and almost killed me. If not you, then..."

She turned her thumb to the ground.

"Sure. It changes the form of things," I muttered, "and therefore the Brotherhood is in this game two points back."

"Why?"

"That before we can react, the Sarharadon merchant's artifacts will pass into Stygian hands."

"Arti... what?" Iris raised her eyebrows for a moment.

"Artifact, it's something artificially created," I explained, "and returning to the Stygians, they will either bribe him or murder him and take it out of the city quietly. After all, Yezud is an open city, so they'll do it without a problem... They will pay only for the route fee and leave without any obstacles."

"So?"

"So I'll have to contact the Brotherhood immediately," I decided, "and we're going to Belverus. Every hour counts. Does the Sanctuary have any branch in Nemedia?"

"From what I know, it's not. We didn't expect a threat from this side, so there was no point in creating it..."

* * *

We were already the fifth day on the way. The mountains remained behind us and we were moving towards the borders of

Nemedia, counting all the time with the possibility of encountering the Kothiyans who were hungry for our blood, but we were wrong. They were not on our way. We quickly crossed the Brythunia border but did not enter the Nemedia episode of the Way of Kings. There might be someone who was waiting for us - or for Iris or me. Or for both of us. Leaving the shelter she took some clothes and the same sword as mine, so she was not so defenceless. In addition, a heavy dagger closed the wide belt. A terrible weapon in hand-to-hand fighting. We once practiced a slashing and pushing at some stop - she was doing rather well. And she was very useful soon.

And it was like this. We traveled on the route from Numalia to Belverus. On the way, we decided to rest a bit and stretch our bones. We drove along the edge of the forest, so on one hand an ancient forest grew out of us, and on the other we had a steppe. The road led through not very deep gulch, where the stream flowed. A secluded and pleasant place, used by hikers to grazing. We also decided to go there for the grazing. Suddenly, I saw a faint ribbon of smoke and felt the smell of burning. They could be wanderers as we were. They could also be others with not very clean intentions. We slowly pulled up and we saw a small clearing over the stream where the campfire was still glowing. Arus growled warningly. Some people were nearby.

"Watch out." I said quietly to Iris.

Unnecessarily. She was uneasy too. If they did not have bad intentions, they would have come out from behind the trees...

I jumped from my horse and went to the fire. The heat was still smoldering, so someone was here lately. And then everything rolled out. I heard Arus barking and Iris shout. There were five of them. One jumped in the direction of Iris, who was standing motionless by her horse, and four rushed at me. The man came to her and saw only the flash of the sword. He was seduced by her girly figure and did not expect resistance, and now he lay on the ground with his head torn open. Four swordsmen caught up with me, their swords looked scary, but they wrestled them in the West fashion.

Iris jumped to me, holding her bloody *katana* in both hands. Two of the bullyboys fell on her and two on me. I drew my sword and cut the first one by the hand that fell from the body. The owner for a moment looked at it in disbelief, and after a while fell on the ground imbruing with blood. The sword of the second whistled near my ear. I did not come on strong with him – I took off his tip of the blade and cut through neck. His head slowly dropped to the ground in a rain of blood. I looked around and saw Iris throw a dagger in the throat of one of her opponents, a moment later her sword dug into the chest of the last man standing on his feet. The fight was over.

We looked around again, but there was no one among the trees anymore. I heard a moan and turned away. The man with the right hand cut off was sitting on the ground, his face contorted with terror. I approached him, he was pale even more. I searched him, but he did not have a hidden weapon. Muttered and defenseless, he made a pathetic impression. I reached for the belt at his pants, took it off, and made a tourniquet on his forearm. He lost a lot of blood.

"Will you talk, or I should leave you here to die?" I asked him not very kindly.

He nodded.

"Who told you to kill us?" I asked.

"I don't know," he replied.

"You don't know? It's your problem - but I advise you to remember. For your own good..."

"I really don't know!" He cried. "I swear! The order and money were sent to us by intentional..."

"How much did you get?" Iris asked.

"A thousand drachmas, two hundred for each of us..."

"Nice," I thought, "damn, someone really want to kill us..."

"Where are you from?"

"From Belverus."

"Mercenaries," I said to Iris, "they won't tell us anything."

We left him in the first inn and we drove on.

We soon got to Belverus and immediately went to the Brotherhood headquarters in the suburbs. We were took by the secretary of the Grand Master, to whom I gave in writing my report on the events we had lived through. He read it with an increasingly cloudy face.

"The Grand Master will have to read it, immediately," he declared, "the situation is very serious."

"I think so too," I said, "and the worst thing is that it's not very clear what's going on."

"So tomorrow, at noon, you have an audience with the Grand Master," he said, "and let us hope for all the gods that we will be able to penetrate it..."

Then we went to my accommodations. We were so tired that we fell on the bed and fell asleep in a dead sleep. We needed it after so many hardships...

VII

"...so it must be assumed that someone really cares about murdering members of the Brotherhood. The reason is most likely the artifacts that are in its possession." I finished my speech and sat down.

We sat with Iris in front of a semi-circle of armchairs on which sat the Grand Master and his two deputies and three advisers. The whole elders of the Brotherhood. The secretary who wrote the report sat on the right.

"Don't you think brother, that your application is premature and rash?" Asked Master Brontosphoros, one of the Grand Master's advisers. "After all, they tried to murder only you? The other couriers were not solicited or attacked."

"Therefore, it must be assumed that our branches in Zamora may be threatened."

"Branch in Zamora isn't in danger, but of course we'll take care of its security," said the Grand Master. "At the moment, several brothers are on their way to Zamora to investigate the situation."

The Master Brontosphoros moved in his chair.

"For now, you and your woman are in danger," he said slowly. "Most likely because you saw or heard something that wasn't meant for your eyes and ears."

He was thinking for a moment.

"And one more thing," he said, "tell us what a woman you saw in the oasis near Yezud?"

"This Stygian, Master?"

"Yes."

"I don't know. She looked like I described her. Who was she? Perhaps a wife or relative of a significant Stygian."

"Would you be able to recognize her in these images?" The secretary gave me a set of drawings, paintings and other graphics depicting the faces of different women. "Look at them closely."

The first four were unknown to me. Fifth also, the sixth was a bit similar, but her eyes were completely different. Sixth and seventh dissimilar again, as well as a few others, only eighteenth..."

"It she is, the Grand Master," I said in a tone of absolute certainty, which caused a stir. Only the Master Brontosphoros was not surprised, but rather pleased, like the man whose predictions worked. "Are you sure about that?" Asked the Grand Master.

"Completely." I confirmed. "Maybe she has a different hairstyle, but it's she."

"Do you know who she is?"

I shook my head.

"Then read on the back."

I turned the picture and read: Ghe-drenh-ra, the eldest daughter of Pharaoh Herkhrem-mer-amon-ra... Luxur and the date from the year before.

"Gedrena!" I exclaimed involuntarily. "Was it she???..."

"Yes," said the Grand Master, "and that means we have to change our plans. You can leave. Go to your quarters and wait for orders. It looks like we'll have to look for what the Stygians and other peoples of this region of the Earth are looking for. Perhaps it is the Heart of the Dragon, or something else, or this and something else."

I bowed to the Council and left, and Iris followed me. For a moment we wondered what the real picture of the situation was and how it could develop. But we had enough to discuss the political complexities, because we were once again called to the Grand Master. He was alone in the audience room and very concerned.

"Why did you call us the Great Master?" I asked.

"Where did you leave the mercenary who attacked you?" He asked without any introduction.

"In the tavern by the road, ten miles from the Belwerus craft settlement, it was the Golden Tiger tavern..."

"Did you tell someone about the circumstances in which this mercenary lost his hand?"

"No, and we have commanded him not to boast of it," I said.

"It didn't help much," said the Great Master grimly.

"???"

"I sent two brothers for him because I wanted him to be interrogated," he said in a grim voice, "but it was too late."

"He escaped?" Iris asked.

"In a way, yes," said the Great Master, "he was found dead. There're no wounds on the body except the one you gave him."

"Maybe he bled to death, it's a serious wound the Grand Master, and he lost a lot of blood."

The Grand Master shook his head.

"It would be too easy. In this case, the deceased is pale and has blue streaks of postmortem lividity. He was sandy blue and had foam on his lips.

"Poison?" I asked. "Or maybe it's just rabies?"

"The disease didn't kill him, but a rare mixture of poisons," explained the Grand Master, "the illness kills slowly, and he died by death, hmmm... very violent. According to the brothers who questioned the events, he drank before the death of wine with roots and died a few minutes later, throwing himself in an epileptic-like attack. It must have been very strong poisons that acted on the brain and blood vessels that were broken throughout the body."

"Stygians..."

"You're right," said the Grand Master, "so their tentacles reach up here.

"So we must be on our guard," I said.

"Yes," said the Grand Master calmly, "and you are their target. You and she," he pointed at Iris.

"What we do?" I asked.

"You've two options: either to hide here or..." he hung the voice for a moment.

"I prefer the second 'or', the Grand Master, whatever that means..."

"I knew that I would hear it," he smiled, "in that case you'll return to Zamora, but you won't go down the trail, but the Way of

Kings and not to Yezud, but to Shadizar. Well, not alone, but with Iris, because I'm sure that only you two you can handle there."

"And I can know why?" Iris asked this question abruptly.

"Of course. Your task will be to make the Zamoran Royal Guard become interested in Stygians and drive them out of Zamora. You have to be here tomorrow morning to discuss the details of this task. And for now, I wish you... have a nice evening."

The audience was over. We went back to the inner square flooded with the afternoon sun. Iris changed her clothes, and from mine, a bit not on her size, she jumped into a short cherry tunic and sandals. She looked like a flower, an exotic flower growing in the far south of the swamps. If it were not for the dressings on the back and the shins, she would look like Izis or another goddess of love. I embraced her and stood for a moment looking at the city bathed in the bright sun. I did not like Belverus, anyway, like every big city, its stink of districts of poverty and the glitter of the wealthy districts. It did not attract me. I preferred the fresh air of mountains and steppes. The smells of forest and sea salt were nicer to me. I hoped Iris thought and felt the same way.

"Do you like this place?" I asked.

"I don't know." She said skeptically. "A city like a city. I'm not happy. It's bigger than Ianthe, but much uglier. Ianthe is many times greener, and here ," she shook with disgust, "it reminds me of Shemu deserts stone."

I smiled.

"Do you prefer the village?"

"Yes, a smaller town, where everyone knows everyone, where everyone is helping each other. Where everyone is more sympathetic and kind to each other."

"Maybe someday we'll live in such a place," I said quietly, "you and me. And for now we have to face what tomorrow will bring us..."

2

⤳

STYGIAN'S ENIGMAS

I

We were traveling east again. Our horses treaded on the Way of Kings. We were silent from leaving the Belverus gates. To be safe, we left at night to get as far away from the city as possible, but we did not go to Numalia, but straight to the Way, so as not to waste time traveling through the city. Besides, someone could see us and send more assassins. As if everyone who had stumbled with us was dead, but one of them could have say something for his principal against a nasty death from poison.

Iris was silent, too. Now that she was in the knowledge, she knew for sure what was at stake in this game. On the morning audience with the Grand Master, her swear was sworn in and then we were instructed to report to Brother Hough. Brother Hough was waiting for us.

"Welcome," he said in greeting. "The Great Master has instructed me to familiarize you with what your task is about."

He showed us the entrance to his dungeon, but soon it turned out that there was a spacious and well-lit room.

"This show is for you Iris," he said, "because Lestek already saw it."

I nodded.

"So, not to waste time," he began his lecture. "You heard, of course, that there are combustible and flammable substances?"

Iris nodded.

"That's great. But among the flammable substances are those that burn violently with the access of air, such as flour or fine sawdust, which are sprayed in the air and set on fire, and sometimes cause terrible damage. Therefore, don't go in with an open fire to a mill or sawmill. Now find out that there are substances that burn even without air."

Hough removed a casket from a drawer and spilled a few teaspoons of black powder from it onto a metal table.

"Look," he pointed to a burning splinter.

The powder immediately burned with a bright flame, giving off a cloud of stinking smoke.

"It's a mixture of saltpetre with charcoal and sulfur, very finely ground and in appropriate proportions. If it's burning in the open air, we have this effect. But when we put it into even a paper tube, the result is different..."

He put a thick paper on the table and lit it with a long string. When the flame reached the tube, there was a loud explosion. Tube disappeared in the reddish flame, and her shreds fell to the floor after a while.

"With the help of this powder, you can smash stones, walls of fortresses or throw missiles at great distances. You can also construct missiles that are able to break away from the ground and not return to it anymore... But the phenomenon of an explosion can be achieved not only with the help of what you have seen. There are metals in the world that are thinned in water and rocks, diluted, so they aren't dangerous. But when it is extracted and collected in sufficient quantity, something strange begins to happen, namely, there is a terrible explosion several million times stronger than what I've shown you here. And this isn't the end of the possibility of matter, because the strongest explosive is one of the components of water, which after the appropriate preparation can give an explosion, accompanied by a flash stronger than a thousand Suns!"

"How is it known?" She asked in a calm voice, in which, however, she was amazed.

"This is the knowledge extracted from "Scrolls from Skelos" and other letters from Atlantis.

"But "Scrolls from Skelos" are..."

"You talk about the censored version and generally available in every temple or royal library, and even some private libraries," Hough said in a polite tone. "I'm talking about the full and uncensored version and secret protocols, which are annexes to them. This is secret knowledge, but I assure you, fully explainable based on the laws of Nature. And Nature has it to herself that it is honest and honestly answers every question.

"So what's the problem?" Iris asked.

We laughed.

"The problem is that we must learn to ask the right questions." I explained.

"And the Brotherhood...?"

"And the Brotherhood has the task of finding these questions and answers before we can harm ourselves. The Atlanteans left behind a whole lot of things that - like the dust you saw here - are potentially dangerous to humans. Eight thousand years ago, the island of Atlantis sank into the water of the Western Ocean, which happened due to a gigantic cataclysm. That's what official history says. Unofficially, it's known that this was the result of a failed experiment with a powerful weapon that could wipe out entire continents from the surface of the Earth."

"And this is the goal of the Brotherhood of the Green Dragon?"

Hough and I nodded.

"And this is the goal of our actions. We don't want the old mistakes to happen again and again lead to another terrible catastrophe," said Hough.

"But someday, it will be somehow invented by someone?" Iris raised her dark eyebrows.

"Of course," I nodded, "but let it happen when Humanity is prepared for it. Imagine what would happen if Gendera and the high priest who manipulated her got to something like that? Then Set's cult would not only prevail in Stygia, but all over the world.

Then he showed her other artifacts that could be and probably were weapons of a terrible power of destruction. They were most often longish metal constructions, up to ten to fifteen feet long and up to three in diameter. Of course, they were already disposed of and threatened nothing. People who found them and who manipulated them sometimes did not experience the month dying of horrible diseases. Some of them survived, but their offspring was born crippled and weak...

* * *

We left the kingdom of Hough in a grim mood and listened with pleasure to the sounds of the city and the chirping of birds. Then we went to the Grand Master, who commissioned us the task. We were to go to Shadizar and contact the commandant of the Royal Guard, and through him with the queen, to whom we had to influence the removal of the fugitives from Zamora and look for what they were so intruding on. The task was not particularly easy, but not difficult. The Stygians as a pair of black magic enjoyed a nasty opinion even in Zamora, famous for thievery, and it was enough to incite the people against them. But that's what we did not want, and it would be better if it dealt with this specialized military unit, not the dark mob. And then we started packing before the next mission. And now we were going along the Way of the Kings towards the border with Corinthia, to be in Zamora and its capital next week.

In fact, after a week of driving, we were not slandered by anyone outside the walls of Shadizar.

II

Shadizar rose above us on a high rock, and we were wondering how to do the task entrusted to us. We could enter the main gates of the city, or sneak into the royal palace unnoticed by sewers. After the death of Taramis, which took place in circumstances unknown to this day, her 17-year-old niece, Jenna, joined her throne. We had a letter of introduction from the Grand Master, but we did not know how much it would be useful for us. We did not know the commander of the Royal Guard, so it was hard to know what the chances of completing the task were. After a brief conference, we decided to enter the city normally, the main gate, which required at least a two-hour drive to it, because the city itself was surrounded on three sides by chasms and was accessible only from the east of the mountain range. We drove by admiring the giant statues standing on both sides of the avenue leading to the gate. Their magnitude indicated their origin from the time of Atlantis...

The city was reminiscent of every city in the region - great districts of the local establishment and districts of misery. The royal palace towered over all of its white towers, which shone in the light of the midday sun. We stood in a good tavern, where we had quite a short distance to the palace and what is more important urban buildings. We ate a meal, and went to sleep. But the dream did not come. Iris hugged me, and I embraced her and so we lay on the wide bed listening to the noises coming from the street.

"What are you going to do?" She asked.

"I'll write a letter to the commander of the guard asking for an audience and send it intentional to the palace," I said, "and then we'll introduce him to our case. And that would be everything."

Let it be that easy!

"I don't think it's that simple," Iris murmured.

We lay and finally dreamed.

The following day, after breakfast, I wrote a letter to the commander of the Royal Guard, in which I asked for an audience regarding the urgent and security-related person of the ruler, and attached our letter of recommendation. I sent the messenger to the palace and to my amazement around noon I received the answer that the commander intends to meet us today at six in the royal palace. We did not expect such a turn of events.

"Will it not be a trap?" Iris wondered.

"I don't think so," I said, "maybe it's just anxiety about the queen?"

"Maybe he's her lover?"

"I don't know. As far as I know, Queen Jenna didn't find a man worthy of her husband, and only one of them, Conan of Cymmeria, was worthy of this honor."

"But the Cimmerian is now the king of Aquilonia," Iris murmured.

"Well, we'll see what we can do, and for now we've to prepare for the audience."

* * *

We arrived at the royal palace at the appointed time. It was a huge building, which consisted of three gigantic column halls. White marble dominated everywhere. Some of the columns and walls bore traces of violent action of some forces that caused them to break or even ruin. However, now they were perfectly restored and only a trained eye could distinguish old walls and columns from new ones.

We gave the guard a letter from the commander. He saluted us kindly and showed us the way to the side rooms. We entered the side corridor, which most likely led to some barracks. It smelled of harness leather and accoutrement, olive oil for cleaning and preserving weapons, steel with sharpened swords and halberds. Indeed, there was the guardhouse of the Royal Guard, but we were directed towards a large courtyard, on the other side of which stood a stately home, an elegant villa adorned with small sculptures of animals and their larger heads. The sentry directed us to the main entrance. We entered a small foyer with reed seats. We were ordered to sit down. A cute girl served us a cool pomegranate juice in decorative gilt Shemit cups. We had to wait for the commander to arrive.

We looked around the room. It was decorated with taste, but in a feminine way. This person liked the strong colors and the soft fabrics at the same time, which were lined with floors and covered walls. Two colors predominated from the colors: rusty red and dark brown. In the corners stood strange sculptures of dark, almost black wood depicting naked, long-legged people with slender, agile figures.

"Our host has interesting taste," Iris said.

"Uhm..." I nodded, "some... feminine?"

"I've the same impression." Iris nodded.

"I think it's someone from the Black Kingdoms - look at these sculptures - I saw such people in the Southern caravans."

"That is from Kush, Darfaru or Keshan." Iris showed off her knowledge of geography.

"And from Punt. And this gives you some opportunities, because as far as I know, those people don't love Stygian people too much..." I murmured, "well, we'll see."

I stretched out in my chair. But after some time the door opened and two women stood in them.

We stood up from the armchairs. I looked at them closely. The first of them was a tall Kushytian, black as ebony. She was slim, but not skinny. There was an obvious similarity between her and the statues standing in the corners. Dark, curly hair cut almost to the skin. A slender face and dark eyes looking alert and boldly. A high forehead and small nose and full lips complemented the picture. She moved silently, graceful, catlike movements, like a black panther approaching her prey. She was about thirty years old. She was wearing a simple tunic in vivid red, yellow, green and black. Small footprints lay in costly slippers made of delicate leather embroidered with pearls and other precious stones - the only accent indicating its social status.

The second woman was a Hyborian girl with light long hair and blue eyes. Her complexion, by contrast with her black companion, was white, but not pale. She was younger than the first woman, she could be twenty-seven or eight, no more. The delicate face with expressive features was childishly beautiful, but it was a deceptive childishness, because her step was as resilient and sure but as silent as her black companion. She was dressed in a richly decorated, long robe in a straight cut, but it was very elegant. The black woman turned to her.

"It's they Your Highness," she said, "they came according to the command."

"Welcome to our doorstep," said the blonde, "I hope that you'll forgive us a bit longer waiting for our person?"

We bowed.

"Welcome, Your Highness," I answered with a nod, "of course, there is no question of any intrusiveness on the part of a woman so imperious and... beautiful."

Both women laughed.

"Your Highness," I continued, "I'd like to speak with your Royal Guard commander regarding the safety of your person and your kingdom."

"So we wait, say what you've to say," said the blonde. "This is Zela, my friend and Captain of the Royal Guard. Zela," she turned to black girl, "please do the house honors."

Zela opened the second door and gestured for us inside. We entered the cosily furnished room with a low table surrounded by soft pillows and a huge four-poster bed, but with a dense mosquito net.

"Please, sit down," she pointed to the pillows and took her place next to her queen. "First, satisfy our curiosity and tell who you are. And I hope that you'll not refuse to eat a simple soldier's supper with us?"

"We'll not deny Your Highness," I replied, knowing that the refusal would be tactless. Zela clapped her hands. And in fact, a few nice, very shapely and agile girls set the table with simple dishes, which, however, were very tasty, and when we ate them, wine and fruit appeared on the table.

"So we're waiting for a story about you," said the queen, "we are listening!"

"You must know Your Highness, that we've come here with a specific task," I said calmly, " to warn Your Highness about the possibility of a takeover or even a coup."

"But for now we're safe, and therefore we can afford for a moment of oblivion and pleasure of listening, and for a moment... of pleasure," said the queen, "and so we turn into hearing."

There was no advice, so I had to tell them a bit about myself and my adventures, bypassing some details of my work in the Brotherhood. At one point Zela interrupted me with the words:

"You don't drink wine? It's delicious!"

"Thank you, but I drink only water and milk."

"Me too," Iris answered.

"Are you monks or priests?" The queen asked with interest.

"You can call it that way, although it's not quite true," Iris said. "I've lower priesthood ordinations, but it so happened that unfortunately I couldn't become a priestess, Your Highness."

"Why is that?" Both women asked.

"Because I was kidnapped and desecrated, so you understand that I couldn't be a priestess, and therefore I got married and I'm the wife of this man..."

"Tell us about it, but first you finish your story," the queen has improved on the pillows.

Meanwhile, Zela lit an incense stick from the candle and put it in a decorative stand. The trance of Vendhian music came through the doorman.

"Well, that's all, Your Highness," I said, "I took Iris from the monster, I killed him in a duel and from now on we're together."

III

There was a moment of silence. Incense burned as the chamber covered with clouds of scented smoke. Its aroma was reminiscent of amber and sandalwood. I looked at Iris. Her gaze was glassy, her face still. In a fraction of a second, I realized that we were trying to get us into a trance and that now we are facing a test of truthfulness.

The queen's aunt, the evil queen Taramis was an adept of black magic, and really a fantastic hypnotist. She managed to hypnotize Conan, whom she persuaded him to be able to resurrect his late beloved Valeria from the Red Brotherhood. Actually, it was about Bêlit - the Queen of the Black Coast, which he lost during one of his crazy adventures. Some said this, others something else - the fact is that Conan undertook to do some work for her and then there was change on the throne of Zamora. And now she tried to give us a try. Iris did not undergo training in the Brotherhood and was therefore susceptible to hypnosis and suggestion. I smiled inwardly. A blend in wine did not work, because we did not drink either, it was decided to take us smoke from incense from dried Stygian plants and trance music from Vendhia.

I started to wonder what to do. I could, of course, say that they would give me peace and force them to take other steps, I could pretend to be stupid and simulate that this abomination works for me and tell them what I had to say to them. However, one thing puzzled me - why it did not work for them? But the most important thing was to make the right impression. I made the most dumb face and googly eyes. Jenna came up to us and very carefully checked if we were ready.

"Watch out. I count to ten," she said quietly, but clearly. "One, two, three," she began to count down, "you feel more and more tired and sleepy," she said it in an even, calm voice, in which there was something soothing, "four, five, six, hands and legs are getting heavier, your eyelids droop."

I looked at Iris from the corner of my eye. She lay completely relaxed, her eyelids drooping. Her breath barely lifted her breasts.

"Seven, eight," the queen continued, "you fall asleep, nine, ten, sleep. It's warm and good for you... And now you'll answer my questions."

We have not moved.

"We start," Zela said, and turned off the lights except one olive lamp. "First, this beautiful girl."

The queen sat opposite Iris.

"Who you are?" asked the first question.

"I'm Iris from the city of Ianthe," she replied in a monotonous voice.

The questions was asked one by one. These were the right questions that were meant to unmask the real purpose of our trip. I noticed with astonishment that Iris had missed the truth several times.

"But under hypnosis you can't lying!?" I thought in a certain panic, unless... Iris kept up what we told them in a real, and therefore she also pretended she was in a trance... After asking her dozens of questions, they gave her peace.

"So what, we are going to ask him now?" The queen changed place vis-à-vis me.

"I don't know." On Zela's black face showed a grimace of boredom, "he will tell us nothing more, and it's a waste of time."

"You think so?" The queen asked and a light smile and a delicate blush filled her face.

"What's going on here?" I thought. "Not about..."

"Wake them up?" She asked.

"No, they may not want to," said the black woman.

"Well, wait," she stared at me again, "Lestek, do you hear me? If so, then move your fingers with your right hand."

I obediently moved my fingers.

"Perfectly," she laughed, "and now stand up and come to me."

She got up and walked to the bed. I understood. Now I had to be very careful not to expose myself.

I stood up and slowly approached her. I stood unmoved.

"Okay, now undress me," she said, standing in front of me so that I could reach her within arms. I slowly reached to her shoulders, where she had the buckles of her robe. I pulled gently on the ribbons and the silk robe flowed from her revealing her naked, bright body.

I was curious about the further development of events. The queen came to Iris. She raised her hands.

"Come to me, my love," she said warmly and tenderly. "Take it off from yourself."

Iris rose and with a snakelike motion removed her tunic and softly slipped into her embrace. The queen began to kiss her face gently, her hands moved over her body, and Iris gave in to her caresses. After a moment, they fell onto the cushions. It was a wonderful sight of these two beautiful caressing women.

Meanwhile, Zela came to me and embraced me by the neck.

"Come with me," she said. "The queen doesn't want any man, but I do..."

...We lay panting heavily. Queen Jenna and Iris lay on the floor, on the unfolded hides and pillows. They no longer caressed as gently as at the beginning, but they did it - hard and nasty. Whistling breaths merged into one sound of the coming spasm of pleasure. I sat down looking at them and felt a growing wave of desire. And again, we plunged into the abyss of pleasure...

...Panting slowly, we calmed down. Finally, we returned to each other

"It was wonderful," Queen Jenna said, "how long are you going to stay with us?"

"Until we do our mission," Iris answered. "We want to find out what exactly Stygians are looking for in Zamora, or rather in Yezud. And there are over a hundred of them and their queen is there."

"Gedrena in Yezud?" They were amazed.

"Yes, incognito," I added.

"Well, this is something I should be interested in," Zela said, hugging my shoulder. "Don't be mad at me," she said to Iris. "I won't take him away from you, although I have an biiiiiiiiiiiiiiiiiiiig desire."

She went to Iris and embraced her.

"Don't be angry anymore," she kissed her heartily, "we have a local custom and you couldn't do anything. If your boyfriend wouldn't make love with me, he would lose his head. Literally, because the queen's insult is punished at the throat, and the refusal is offensive to us. This also applies to you. Here, you can't simply refuse! The host shares everything with the visitor - including yourself..." she smiled flirtatiously.

"An interesting habit," said Iris, "I've never made love with a woman by the way. This is a very interesting experience..."

"There you go," Queen Jenna smiled at her, "journeys educates!"

IV

When I woke up, Iris lay next to me on the floor, on the pelts, covered in the grip of my arms. The queen lay on the bed and was still asleep. Zela was not here. Apparently she returned to her duties.

Pale dawn filtered through the windows. Iris moved in my arms and opened her eyes. I kissed her, but she did not give me a kiss back.

"You bastard," she said in a low voice. "I'm mad. You made loved with this... this Negro, and not with me."

She turned her back to me. I embraced her and she clung to me. I knew he was just teasing.

"Don't be angry," I said, "I know what you think. I didn't enjoy it either, but sometimes we'll find ourselves in a similar situation. That's our fate. You've to get used to it..."

She sighed. After all, she was too difficult to accept it.

We were silent for some time. Iris sulked yet, but she was still hugged to me. We feel good and warm, we did not have to cover ourselves.

It brightened outside the window and Iris brightened up and then she turned with face to me and kissed me on the lips.

"You know what I'm thinking about?" She asked flirtatiously.

"Probably about breakfast?" I asked surreptitiously.

"No, about you for breakfast," her lips touched mine, and then began a hot walk around the neck and chest, and the hand slipped between the thighs and gently stroked their interiors...

...We were lying back to ourselves.

"It's completely different with you than with another woman," she whispered.

"You're crazy," I answered, kissing her in the ear.

"Bravo, bravo, bravo!" I heard over us.

I opened my eyes. Jenna sat cross-legged on the bed and clapped her hands.

"Excuse Your Highness, if we woke you," I mumbled.

"But no, indeed," she said with a laugh, "it was quite a pleasant awakening. I like to look at loving people. You were doing quite well!"

And she laughed.

"Do you want a bath?" She asked.

"Sure!" We shouted in unison.

"Come, then. First, a bath, then breakfast," Iris pulled her hand and we all crossed to the patio, where there was a small pool surrounded by dwarf palm trees. We immersed ourselves in cool and crystal clear water with pleasure. Both women thoroughly washed and splashed snorting from time to time, and all I could do was look at this beautiful and graceful spectacle that lasted for half an hour. We left when we got chilly. Covered with goose bumps we wiped with thick, fluffy towels.

"Okay," said Jenna, "and now come and eat. Breakfast on the table."

When we finished eating a belated breakfast, Zela came in. Her expression showed that she was very busy.

"And what did you do?" Jenna embraced her as she sat down next to her.

"I sent our trusted official to Yezud, Thera Amylles Capoor," she said.

"Who is this man?" I asked.

"Officially, it is a tax official who is to carry out the control of revenues and expenditures of companies in the entire Zamora kingdom. In fact, it is our gray eminence and the centaury of the Guard."

"As I understood, he is to carry out an inspection of companies belonging to this buyer who..."

"You're extremely astute," Jenna smiled patronizing. "Exactly."

"And he's going to conduct a reconnaissance in his business and contacts with Stygia," Iris finished. "Of all this, we're interested in what Stygian people are interested in and nothing more."

"Well, we've two weeks ahead of us for the first results of his investigation. So by that time you'll remain our guests. Oh, we brought your stuff, so you don't have to walk to the taverns..."

I thought that Zela is very predictable. Knowing that she has two spies from a foreign state on her territory, she preferred to keep them with her and keep an eye on them than to let them penetrate her country. Anyway, you do not become the commander of the Royal Guard for beautiful eyes. From what I heard about her, it showed that she was beautiful and wise, brave and cunning. Her enemies were at the same time the enemies of the Queen and the State - precisely in this order. They were tolerated until they became active. That is why Zamora was called the country of thieves because of the slack and the freedom of morals prevailing here. This state was maintained artificially, because in fact the Guard dressed in armor and plumes was only for show, and in fact she had her second face and in fact it was one of the most effective special services of our world...

"You live in a beautiful palace, queen," Iris said.

"You're right," the queen beamed, "it's really worthy of his destiny! It's very old and was created at least half a thousand years ago.

"But this isn't always the case," I said, "there are the traces of some... cataclysm or building disaster visible?"

"Oh, yes," the queen has overcast a bit, "these are the traces of my ascension. And Daggoth's actions."

"Daggoth?" We asked. "What is it?"

"You haven't heard this story?" The Queen's eyebrows went high above the line of light hair, "after all, all the bards from Vendhia to the Lightning River sing about it."

"But what else is to listen to it from them and listen to something different from the witness and participant of this drama!" Iris gracefully bowed to Jenna.

"If Your Highness has the time and willingness to tell us about it," I said with a low bow, "we are very pleasing..."

The queen smiled under the influence of flattery.

"Okay," she said after a moment's reflection, "for now I've to go, where state duties call me, but I promise that we meet in the evening."

"Thank you, Your Highness," Iris gracefully curtseyed the queen, "and we look forward to the evening with impatience!"

V

In the evening, the four of us met again for dinner. We waited for the queen to satisfy her hunger. After finishing eating, she washed her hands and rinsed her mouth with water, sat down in front of us and spoke these words:

"You said that there're signs of a powerful cataclysm on and in the palace. Well, you must know that all this happened when I celebrated my fifteenth birthday, or eleven years ago."

"So, something terrible happened here?" Iris asked.

"Yes, all because of the whim of my aunt, queen Taramis and her damned counselor, who baffled her with the idea of resurrecting our deity, the mighty Daggoth. Well, the priest decided to tell aunt Taramis that she would gain immortality and unlimited power by calling Daggoth alive. This man who was a magician and above all an interpretation of the 'Skelos Book' suggested to her that I should go with her Crown Guard to unlock the key with Daggoth's Horn who was supposed to be in the Tsoth-Amon sorcerer's castle somewhere on the Stygian-Shemits border in the Fire Mountains."

"A long way." I noticed.

"That's true," the queen said, "we've been going there for almost two months. Along the way, we released, or actually Conan did it, our Zela..."

"Why was Zela imprisoned?" Iris asked.

"Oh, I just belonged to the Brotherhood of the Desert, which Stygians didn't like very much, just like the Shemits. In other words, we were dealing in a charitable practice: we broke up the rich and supported the poor."

"And what happened next?" I asked.

"Well, if the poor people have become indulged and became rich, they said that we can plunder their turn..." Zela sighed, "and then they betrayed us. There were several regiments of regular Shemits troops, and our Brotherhood went into disarray. I was caught near Akbitan, and if not Conan, then..." she made a gesture with her hand cutting the throat.

I nodded.

"And what's next, Your Highness?" Iris asked in turn.

Then we finally arrived at the Tsoth-Amon Palace, located in the middle of a mountain lake. There I was kidnapped by him to the palace when he lulled my comrades. He sprayed some kind of intoxicant in the air, and the cloud that was created in this way rained at us... Fortunately, they managed to get under water to the Tsoth-Amon Palace and defeat its guards first - the weird apes of the Kezankih Mountains, and then Conan faced the sorcerer himself and having beaten him with his sword, he sent him to Hell... Gods! - what a fight it was!"

"And there really were so many of Thak's apelike people there?" I asked in disbelief.

"Yes ," both women nodded, "he had their entire kennel or if you prefer a colony. Anyway, Conan and Thak had a similar crossing at Nabonidus' house..."

"I know the Kenzankih Mountains a bit and I went there alone and with my companions many times, but I didn't meet any Thak," I said thoughtfully, "it's strange, but it was just that... Well, no matter. And what was next Your Higness?"

"Next? We continued searching for Key. It was the biggest diamond I've ever seen. I took the key and at that moment Tsoth-Amon's castle began to crumble. And it was from the mountain crystal and ice. The glass panes crumbled with a crack. At first we thought it was magic, but no, it was an ordinary earthquake, only very strong," the queen took a sip of wine from the cup and continued. "Then we went in search of Daggoth's Horn. From what we were told, it was supposed to be in the Sanctuary of the Haunted Pyramids, but in "Scrolls from Skelos" it was written that I had to find this horn. And I found - it wasn't at all in Stygia, but in the neighboring Khauran principality, where we fought a bloody battle with its guards. On the occasion of Bombaat, my guardian, he wanted to murder Conan, but he didn't give up and he reached Shadizar in our footsteps."

"How did he want to murder Conan? For what?" Iris asked.

"Taramis was afraid that Conan would steal the key jewel and the Horn of Daggoth," the queen replied. "After all, he had the opinion of a thief and an extra-ordinary bully who alone had a chance to lead me whole and healthy and get both jewels."

"I understand." I nodded.

"But on the other hand, I'm afraid she was afraid that Conan would want to wake Daggoth and use his power against her," Jenna said after a moment's thought. "You know what tyrants are."

"And what happened next, queen?" Iris asked.

"He managed to get to the castle through the sewer. Just in time, because Taramis gave me an intoxicating drink and was already running the helpless victim to Daggoth. I put a horn on his head - and you must know that Daggoth had the figure of a naked, handsome young man, and waited for the first sign of life. I didn't know that the first sign of his life was to be the last moment of my..."

She paused for a moment. It must have been a terrible memory for her.

"Then everything went like an avalanche," she said. "At first Daggoth moved, Taramis shouted to her priest, 'Kill her'. He raised the sacrificial knife, and at that moment Zela pierced him with her javelin, and Conan burst into the room. He defeated Bombaata before. Just in time. Daggoth woke up and on our astonished eyes he changed from a beautiful alabaster youngster into a terrible, one-horn monster."

She took another sip of wine and made her story:

"Daggoth wasn't an idol or even a living being. It was a monster designed for destruction and killing. No steel or arrows can defeat him. He punctured Taramis with horn and killed some of my servants with powerful paws."

"And how did you defeat him?" Iris asked.

"As the songs say," Jenna smiled. "Conan caught him by the horn and broke it off thanks to his superhuman strength."

"Interesting," I murmured, "and what happened then?"

"Well, that's interesting," said Zela, "because at that moment Daggoth was still, and after a while he broke into small pieces that melted into a fetid and a muddy puddle."

We exchanged instant glances with Iris.

"Oh, one more Your Highness," Iris corrected herself on her pillow, "it's said that when Daggoth returned to his cursed life, a terrible storm broke out over the castle, and at the same time the earthquake started..."

"Well, this is the legend added by the bards," she laughed delightfully, "the storm was later. And the earthquake was quite recent. Have you seen these wonderful statues when you leave the city? It was then that some of them were felled, literally felled by horizontal earth shakes..."

"And what next?" I asked.

"Then I managed to take over people from the Conan's team," Jenna smiled, "Mako is my hector, Akiro became an adviser, and Zela - is the commander of my guard. Only Conan went his way..." Jenna sighed and her eyes blurred for a moment.[2]

---

2   The story was based on the movie "Conan the Destroyer" (1984), dir. Richard Fleischer.

"I don't think there is anything to worry about," Iris said. "Conan has now ascended to the throne of Aquilonia and people said to be looking for a heir to the throne, and therefore, Your Highness, you've another chance to win his heart as Queen of Zamora."

"You comfort me," the queen sighed, "you've a good heart Iris. I won't forget this..."

* * *

We lay hugging each other, staring out the window at the stars streaming across the sky. A chill flew from the window, as if from the depths of the Universe. I embraced Iris and kissed her on the cheek. She turned and our lips merged in a hot, sweet kiss, but we did not want to do anything more. We covered ourselves with a thin blanket and we slowly fell into the first sleep. Suddenly Iris said:

"Listen, don't you think that Daggoth could have been the device, which Houg was talking about?"

"I'm sure of that," I replied. I did not want to sleep.

Iris turned to me and in the light of the stars I saw her bright eyes.

"So Conan defeated some... machine and not a living being?"

"Exactly," I put my cheek to her cheek, "you're absolutely right, honey."

"What do you think?" She asked. "How many such devices are there in the world?"

"Still a lot, especially in Stygia and at the East. It seems that there were two centers in which these devices were located. This is clearly apparent from the entries of the 'Book of Phuran' and 'Haggard Papyri.'"

"I don't know that, tell me about it," she said.

"'Book of Phuran' is a collection of old documents from the time of Atlantis. There are some strange information that we don't understand. We only know that wars are described there with the help of terribly devastating means."

"And the other one?"

"'Haggard Papyses'? This is a collection of Stygian papyrus from at least a thousand years ago. There are descriptions of means and devices reminiscent of what the Queen described - Daggoth was probably one of them. And that falls under the Brotherhood's interest."

"So it looks like there may be more such devices here?" She asked.

"It figures and I think I know what Stygian people are all about."

"For another copy of Daggoth and the horn?"

"You got it," I said, "for another Daggoth and the horn, which is the source of energy that moves him."

I embraced her and hugged her tightly.

VI

After two weeks, which we spent on sweet idleness and nights filled with love, a change came. It was precisely this hot afternoon that Zela brought the first news from the control carried out in Yezud. We were just swimming in the pool listening to music among exotic flowers when she came carrying a bundle of sheets of dense parchment in her hand. She quickly threw off her sweaty clothes, showing all the beauty of her brown body, and came up to us and sat on a cane seat. We left the water, looking for towels. Zela waved her hand, so we did not get dressed.

"Please, sit down," Zela invited us with a gesture. We sat down waiting for her words.

She spread the first page of the parchment.

"Listen," she began. She ran quickly through the page with the eyes. "Mmmm... mmm... mmm... oh, here: *at home I have not met anyone other than service and suppliers...*, interesting for Ishtar sake... mmm... mmm... mmm... oh, listen now: *...the interviewed service says that Stygians were here very briefly because after three days the caravans left the city, but where they were headed, nobody knows. There are rumors that two of them went towards the mountains - one to the east, the other to the west, while the others merged and went towards the south - most likely they returned to Stygia..."*

"So it looks like they got what they were looking for, but why did the two teams go..." at once I had the guess, "wait a moment! Maybe they went to look for something else in the mountains, about what they got tips in Yezud!?"

Zela looked at me appreciatively.

"It's logical," she said, "even very much. We won't find out now, because they are already in Khorai or Shemit."

"Besides, the Kothiyans are probably in league with them," Iris added.

"But wait," Zela read on, "look: *One of the servants by name... - no matter - when he was drunk, said that the Stygian car was loaded with something that looked like a cylinder in a polished metal mirror. This object had the shape of a cylinder and was ten feet long with a diameter of at least two. It had to weigh at least two mines. The Stygians put a guard on it and did not allow anybody to get close...*"

"I wonder where he got it from?" Iris wondered.

"Who? - ahh this Sarharadon? Most likely, he bought from someone from the north or the East."

"Rather, East," I said, "such artifacts have always been in the deserts and steppes. There are not many of them in the West, because they grow in the forest, but in the East... East is the same steppes and deserts..."

"And what's next?" Iris asked.

"Nothing special anymore. Well, we know one thing: they're looking for something that can be a powerful weapon after the Atlantean wars. Especially that it fits the descriptions contained in our books."

There was a moment of silence.

Zela thoughtfully paged the investigation report from Sarharadon.

"Oh, what is this?" She asked pointing at something with her brown finger. "I haven't seen anything like this before! Look!"

We looked. There was a strange object on the card, and a tree and a human figure next to it. I knew from experience that painters always place such 'figures' when they want to show the size of an unknown object. In this case, the strange resembling bowl with a turret on the upper part of the object was about twenty feet high and at least three times as large...

"What could it be?" Zela asked.

"It's flying? I mean, it floats above the ground?" Iris asked.

"Moment ... mmm... mmm... mmm..." Zela read the report, "yes, it's flying and it's high and very, very fast."

"And these characters?" Iris asked.

"They're similar to the writing used in Hyperborea, Vanaheim or Asgard..." I said uncertainly. "These two lightning strikes are two letters 's', but this cross, I don't know what it means. I don't know what the circle and the rest of these stamps mean. This isn't a letter I know..."

"Me too," Iris said.

"I saw something similar in Iranistan and these were numbers, but I'm not sure," said Zela.

"What did this thing do in Yezud?" I asked.

"Hmmm..." Zela read on, *"this 'something' flew several times at dawn over the city and even sat on the ground a mile from the city walls, then shot violently into the sky and disappeared heading towards the Little Guide."*

"That's really strange," I murmured. "But would anyone live in this orbital station, as our brother astronomer called it?"

"Maybe it's the gods? Zela thought.

"The gods don't need flying ships," Iris said, smiling and eyeing me, "the gods can fly by themselves without anyone's help..."

We all laughed.

"And what else is there?" I asked.

"And that's all, because the rest are specifications and similar trade and treasury information." Zela replied.

"Sure, we already know what we wanted to know," I said, "we're coming home tomorrow.

"If that's your will, you can go back, but we would be happy to keep you for another two weeks." Zela smiled.

* * *

The night slowly fell over the city. We stood in the window, watching as its buzz slowly fades away and the fires in the houses go out. Little Guide flew over our heads.

"What do you think, honey, what's there?" Iris asked, leaning her back against me.

I embraced her waist and dipped face into her hair for a moment. They smelled of herbs and the delicate smell of her sweat. She raised her head and kissed me.

"I don't know," I said. "Little Guide flew around the Earth for thousands of years. The same is true of the Great Guide, which can't be seen from here. Brothers-astronomers say that both should have fallen to Earth long ago, some six - seven thousand years ago..."

"But they didn't fall," Iris looked again at the starry sky.

"No," I replied, "and that's why they say that they aren't natural bodies, but created artificially and placed there, in a fiery ether..."

She sighed quietly.

"I believe..." she said finally, "because I have to..."

"Everything points to the fact that it really is like I said..."

"But there's one more puzzle that Zela didn't say a word about," Iris said.

"What honey?"

"Where has Gedrena gone...?" She answered quietly.

We had no answer to this question.

We paused for a moment staring at the stars. Again the chill drew from the window, as if from the depths of the Universe, into the abyss of the Cosmos. The warm Iris body warmed me more than the warmest plaid.

I abandoned the question of Gedrena.

"Iris," I said quietly, "do you really want to be my wife?" If so, we'll get married in Belverus as soon as we get there."

She turned back.

"Why?" She asked. "Of course, if you need it, we can. But understand Lestek," she looked into my eyes, "I'm your wife from the moment when in my defense you took out the sword and shed blood. These are the laws here. And I love you since I saw you. From the first moment, I won't leave you."

"I love you too, and I want to be with you, too," I said. "We both know that there are no gods and we can only swear to ourselves."

She nodded.

We kissed each other.

"So decided," I said, "we're with each other for better or worse."

We hugged each other.

"And what now?" She asked.

"Sleep, of course," I said, "and tomorrow. We will have to go quickly to Belverus, because what I heard here and saw looks very bad..."

VII

We left early in the morning. Zela led us out of the city gates. Farewell was short and after a while we moved south towards the Way of Kings. After two weeks of almost constant driving, we saw the gray walls of Belverus in the distance. Two days later, we were sitting in front of the Brotherhood and we were reporting on our trip to Zamora. This time, Master Brontosphoros interrogated us.

"Are you sure that Queen Gedrena left Yezud and went to Stygia?" He asked again.

"No, Master, we aren't sure of that," I said. "On the other hand, we're sure that something from Zamora has been exported as 'an extremely dangerous thing', and moreover, probably Stygians went to the mountains in search of more of these artifacts."

"I understand that only one caravan is the right one," said Brontosphoros, "and we don't know which one."

"Personally, I'm convinced that this is a caravan, or rather a search team that has gone east," I said in a tone of steadfast confidence, "because it was from there that this kind of thing was brought from the Turanian steppes and deserts. They were in clever hiding places on the shores of the Vilayet Sea and in the desert on the border with Hyperborea. Because it was there that the most intense combat operations during the Great Conflict were concentrated.

"Perhaps you're right," Brontosphoros rubbed his forehead thoughtfully. "Or is it that both teams are looking for two different caches with these things?"

"Master," I said, "let me make my mind that the mountains from the borderland of Zamora and Corinthia have already been thoroughly penetrated, described and mapped almost a thousand years ago. Until now, nothing noteworthy has been found there... Similarly, it's with the mountain ranges in Nemedia and the surrounding countries."

"Well," Brontosphoros said slowly, "I assume you're right, so what do you suggest?"

"I???" I asked, astonished. "Why me???"

"Because you're from the beginning in this case and you'll continue it. You and Iris. From now on, you've all the power to access the Brotherhood's information and all Brotherhood branches, wherever they may be. I know, it's a huge responsibility, but you both can handle it." Replied Brontosphoros.

"So what should I do, Master?" I asked.

"Now you decide about it, Master Lestek Vislanczyk, because now Iris is your Apprentice..."

We left the auditorium on soft legs. I did not expect this completely. I am a Master and I have my first independent case to attend to. And that meant that from all my actions I was responsible only to the Grand Master and sat in the Brotherhood Council. The downside was that now I had to decide for myself and take responsibility for all my moves. My and Iris. It is interesting that Iris was promoted immediately to Apprentice - it meant that the Council recognized her lower priesthood ordinations and immediately meant a promotion of two degrees in the Brotherhood hierarchy. But the worst thing was that I had no idea how to go about it and from which side.

"What we are doing my Master?" Iris asked, looking at me in love with her eyes.

"First, we'll go to the library," I replied, "because you've to see what we're dealing with..."

We went down to the basement of the Brotherhood's quarters. Our library and archive were located there. On the shelves there were scrolls, books and other materials that the Brotherhood gathered during its activity.

"What are we looking for?" Iris asked.

"First of all you need to get acquainted with 'Scrolls from Skelos' in an uncensored version." I said. "Then with 'Phuran Books' and 'Haggard Papyri.'"

"I think these books," she said, "are your only source of information about these things?"

"Among other things, because there're other records and even applications and legends, and historical facts, which are called the 'Nemedian Chronicles'. While the three sources I have mentioned are written in a rather vague and difficult language monĝo-llyn - already dead and originating in Atlantis, the 'Chronicles...' are written in a clear and contemporary Nemedian language."

"But there are translations to one of today's Hyborian languages?" Iris asked this question, wandering her eyes around the shelves.

"Of course, it has to be this way." I replied taking a thick volume from the shelf. "Here you have the 'Skelos Book'. The uncensored version is nearly three times thicker than the official, temple one. But we need something else.

I looked for another fat volume, which I pulled from a similar stack. I blew out a layer of dust.

"Well, I have it," I said, "you must read it.

I gave it to Iris. She opened it at random and began to read in her sonorous voice:

In battle, when this weapon began to shoot
The earth staggered, along with
the trees trembled
Rivers poured and the seas ruffled
Mountains and rocks crashed, wild winds blew
The fires extinguished, the solar rays dimmed -
Arĵuna! Arĵuna! - do not use miraculous weapons!
You can not use it like that because it is dangerous!
You can use it only in extreme danger...
After all, using this terrible weapon threatens to destroy
everything,
what is alive!...[3]

---

3   Fragment of "Mahabharata".

"Gods, what is it?" She was surprised. "And this? Oh:

Powerful Gurkha released from the deck of his vimana one,
the only arrow
against the passing Tri-City.
And he got up in
an infinite heat of a bright cloud,
m o r e   b r i g h t   t h a n   t o u s a n d   s u n s
and turned cities into ashes.
And when Gurkha left his cart toward the ground,
his cart became similar to
a shiny piece of antimony...[4]

"This is the 'Phuran Books'," I said. "You'll find here terrifying descriptions of what has happened on Earth thousands of years ago. And what else is in it and threatens us. That is why the Brotherhood was created to dispose of these terrible weapons... Now you understand this - Apprentice?"

She nodded.

"But the most important thing is," I reached for the book and took it out of her hands.

I was looking for the right paragraph for a moment, and when I found it, I put it back in her hand."

"Read." I asked.

She lifted the book to her eyes and read it lightly stammering:

It was a shiny arrow, burning, but not issuing smoke. It was fired at the enemy and everything was covered with thick fog. The venomous whirlpools swirled around. With a horrible roar the clouds rose and rose to the heavens. It seemed that the sun was swaying. The whole world was burned by the heat of an explosion, as if from a great heat. Thousands of wagons, ten thousand men and elephants turned to dust and ashes...

The only one arrow flew out. To the whiteness a glowing pillar of smoke, bright as ten thousand suns rose in a terrible roar... It was an

---

4   Ibid.

*unknown weapon, an iron arrow, a gigantic messenger of death who
turned into ashes the entire nation of Visnis and Andhaka... Their bodies were burned and impossible to recognition. Their hair and nails fell,
the clay pots cracked for an unknown reason, and the birds grew white.
After a few hours, all the food was contaminated... This strong weapon
has rejected a large number of warriors with their horses and elephants
and weapons, as if they were miserable leaves from the trees...*[5]

"Now you understand what we're dealing with?" I asked.

Her eyes widened with astonishment or terror.

"It's impossible!" She almost screamed. "It couldn't be that way!"

"It's possible," I said, "because it was."

I've looked for a different chapter.

"Read here," I ordered her, giving her the book.

Obediently, she reached for it and read again:

*And then came the day when the Sons of God stood before the
Lord, and Satan was among them, and stood before his eyes.*

*And thus the Lord said to him, 'Where do you come Satan?' And
Satan responded as he used to, 'I have circled the Earth and walked
down.'*

*And the Lord said to Satan, 'Have you looked at the simple and
sincere prince, my servant, the Name who hates evil and loves peace?'*

*Satan, answering said: 'Is the Name in vain fear of God? Have you
not blessed his land with great wealth and made him mighty among
nations? But take your hand out a bit and take it from what he has and
multiply the power of its enemy. Will he curse you in the face?'*

*The Lord said to Satan: 'This is all his fortune in your power. Just
do not touch him.'*

And Satan went before the face of God.

*Verily, the prince was not like the holy husband Iob, when his
lands were afflicted, and his people impoverished when he saw that his
enemy was growing in power, he felt fear and lost trust in God and told
himself: 'I must strike them, before the enemy will destroy me without*

---

5   Ibid.

taking the sword in their hand.' And verily it was in those days that the princes of the earth hardened their hearts against the law of the Lord, and their pride was immeasurable. And every one of them thought in a spirit that it would be better for everyone to get lost than the will of one prince would outweigh his will. Because the mighty of this land have struggled for supreme power over all. By stealing, betrayal and deception, they wanted to gain power, and wars feared and trembled, for the Lord of God allowed the wise men of the time to know the machines that could destroy the whole world, and in their hands they were given a SWORD of ARCHANGEL, which Lucifer was thrown to let people and the princes were afraid of God and humbled before the supreme. But they did not humble themselves.

Satan said to one of the princes, 'Do not be afraid to draw your sword, for the wise men have deceived you, saying that the world will be completely destroyed. Do not listen to the counsel of the weak, for they haunt you and serve your enemies, holding your hand raised against them. Hit, and know that you will be king over everything.'

And the prince obeyed the words of Satan and summoned all the wise men of the kingdom before him, and demanded that they advise him how the enemy could be destroyed so as not to bring God's wrath to his kingdom. But most of the wise men said, 'Lord, it is impossible, for our enemies have a sword that we have given you, and its heat is like hell fire and like the fury of the sun, because it took its flame from the sun.'

'Then you must make me another one, which would be seven times hotter than hell itself,' commanded the prince, for his insolence was greater than the insolence of the pharaoh.

And many of them said, 'No sir, do not ask this from us, because it is enough to smoke from such a fire, if we light it up for you, many would die.'

And the prince became angry at hearing their answer, and he began to suspect that they had betrayed him, and sent his spies among them, that they would test them and oppose them, and then the wise men became afraid. Some of them changed their answer so that his anger would not fall on them.

But one of the sorcerers was like Judah, and he gave a very devious testimony, betraying all his brothers, he lied to all people, saying *that they would not be afraid of the demon of Fall. The Prince listened intently to this false sage whose name was Miedzianoczol and ordered the spies to accuse many wise men from the people. The least wise of sorcerers fell into horror and advised the prince according to his desires, saying: 'This weapon can be used, so as not to exceed such and other limits, because then everyone will die for sure.'*

And the prince smote the cities of his enemies with that fire, and for three days and three nights his great catapults and iron birds were angry with them. Over each city the sun was brighter than the sun in the sky, and soon this city faded and melted like a wax in a torch flame, and its inhabitants stopped in the streets and the skin smoked on them and became like sparks thrown on glowing coals. And when the anger of the sun ceased, the whole city was burning and a huge thunderbolt struck like a huge PIK-A-DON hammer from the sky to crush it to the end. Poisonous fumes fell to the ground everywhere, and the ground flared at night from the secondary fire, and the curse of secondary fire caused scabs on the skin and made hair and blood fall out in the veins.

And the great stench has risen from the earth to the very heavens. The earth has become similar to Sodom and Gomorrah, and everywhere there were ruins, even in the land of that prince, for his enemies did not refrain from vengeance and sent fire to devour his cities, as did theirs. The stench of carnage has become annoying to the Lord, who spoke to Prince Name, saying: 'What burnt offering have you prepared for me? What is this fragrance rising from the place of burnt offering? Why have you made me a burnt offering of sheep or goats, or have you offered calf to your God?'

But the prince did not say anything, and God said, 'You have made a burnt offering from my sons.

And the Lord killed him with the traitor Miedzianoczol, and the plague fell to the earth, and madness overwhelmed the human race, so that the wise men and the nobles who were still alive were stoned to death.[6]

---

6   Here and further: Walter M. Miller, jr. - "Canticle for Leibowitz", in translation of Adam Szymanowski, Poznań 1998, pp. 200-203.

Iris paused.

"What is this?" She asked in horror.

"Shemit legend told before five hundred years ago," I replied, "read further my Apprentice, we will listen..."

From the confusion of languages, from the melting of the remains of many nations, hatred arose out of fear. And hate said: 'Let us stoner, tear and burn those who have done so. Let us put a burnt offering from all who committed this crime together with their naimites and wise men, let them die in flames with their creations, names, and even memory after them. Let us destroy them all and teach our children that the world has become new and that they can see nothing about things that have happened before. Let us make a great Rehabilitation, and then the world will start again.'

So it came to pass that after the Flood, Fall and plagues, madness and confusion of tongues, rage came a bloody revival, when some survivors tear apart the other survivors - a member by member, killing rulers, scholars, leaders, technicians, teachers and anyone whose leaders disorderliness fat recognized him deserving of death for helping the fact that the Earth became what it became..

"It's terrible ..." she whispered. "I didn't even realize that something like this happened here..."

"Not here, but where we'll go. We'll go to the Vilayet Sea and we'll look for answers to what the Stygian people were looking for there. Maybe they've already found it. If they found, let all the gods look after them..."

3

~

FIERY TURAN'S WELLS

I

"**A**re we there yet?" Iris woke up and picked her up from the makeshift bed.

"Two more days," I said.

We were traveling for the third month from Belverus to the easternmost edge of the Hyperborean desert, where it combined with the mountains and the Vilayet Sea at its northern end. It was still the territory of Turan, but in fact no one in his right mind would go there. And yet there was a Stygian caravan in the strength of fifty people to take over what was left of our Atlantean ancestors.

"I'm looking forward to the sea - finally I will take a bath and wash our rags," she said, "we start to stink."

"Not really, the Sea of Vileyet is very salty, and the Nezvaya River is far behind us. Besides, there are no human settlements here..."

"Well, but some streams are flowing from the mountains?" She asked anxiously. "And as for the settlements, it doesn't bother me somehow." She said with a wicked grin.

"Or there are puddles, like this one," I pointed with my chin towards a small pond, "on which the shore we camped."

"It's not bad," she said.

We were slowly gathering for the day's journey. Our horses grazed on lush grass. They too were tired of the long way. Fortunately, we only had mountains in front of us.

The next day, around noon, we saw the sea. At first, we felt a salty and fresh breeze, and then we heard all-encompassing sounds around the sound of waves crashing against the shores...

"Finally!" Iris exclaimed.

I sighed with relief. We did not go wrong. On the northern horizon, the huge silhouettes of the mountains were blazing. The setting was amazing. At this point, lasostep passed into mountain and coastal vegetation at the same time.

We went down a gentle escarpment to the sandy beach and dismounted from horses. Iris quickly unburdened her stallion and slapped him on the hindquarters.

"Go to feed," she said.

Then, without waiting for anything, she threw off her clothes and completely naked jumped into the waves.

"Come on!" She shouted. "It's wonderful!"

I unburdened my horse and quickly followed in her footsteps. I quickly swam to her and stood on a sandy bed. Warm waves caressed our bodies.

"So what?" I asked. "We'll give ourselves one day of rest?"

"Sure," she replied, "I'll soon wash our clothes, and then we'll get something to eat. You'll need to hunt..."

"The animals here are quite," I murmured, "forest steppe, there are subalpine forest..."

"But maybe you'll shave first?" She asked cautiously.

Actually, I was unshaven, like a pet. For half an hour we used the charms of life. Finally, we left for a warm wind that quickly dried our bodies. There was a quick stream near the sea. The bottom has also changed, the sandy has become stony. Apparently during the spring thaw it brought stones from the mountains and threw them into the sea. We washed our dirty and sweaty things and then spread them into the sun, which was still high in the sky. They will dry out in a while. I shaved in the meantime and became like a man. Iris ignited a small fire, on which she put a cauldron of water into which she threw a grated pelican and a handful of dried vegetables. Soon we had a pimiacant soup - not very tasty but nutritious.

I lay down to the sun. A shadow fell on me at once. Iris stood above me and watched in a special way. The sun was shining right above her head and it looked like her head was shining...

"You don't sleep?" I asked.

"No, I don't want to," she replied.

I looked at her and stood up. We stood next to each other. I looked at her clean, clear body and felt what she wanted me to feel...

"I'm going to use this time," I said, "and you?"

She nodded and I took her in my arms. First, gently, then more and more tightly clung to me with my whole body and kissed on the lips...

...Iris slumped in my arms. We were lying inhaling the smells of the meadow. I turned on my side and lay there to see her eyes. Still closed, and when she opened them they were still full of sweet insanity.

"My Love, it was wonderful," she whispered.

"Me too, are you a demon or a goddess?" I asked.

"Demon and goddess," she replied. "Do you want some more? I'm hard up for you. Those two months in this damn desert..."

"Very," I whispered, "but wait a bit..."

...And one day we had to go back to reality. The sun was already low above the horizon. We had to prepare ourselves for camping under the open sky. After bathing in the stream, we first collected our already dry clothes, but we did not want to dress. The wind was blowing and it was very nice. It was nice to look at Iris bustling around in our camp, at her nicely built body, which has been solidified in the hardships of travel, and I have just learned about his strength. She was beautiful because of her youth and health. I had a wonderful wife...

"What?" She asked. "Today we'll sleep good and tomorrow we'll go again?"

"We have only one day left," I said.

"Where it is?" She asked, meaning what we were supposed to find at the end of our journey.

"Even further to north," I answered.

"How do you know that it is there?" She asked.

"Think. Infer," I suggested, "you have exactly as much data as I..."

II

And yet, not everything went as smoothly as we imagined. The next day we set off early in the morning. We jumped into the sea in the morning and sailed side by side, when Iris's sharp vision spotted something on the bottom between the stones. She drew air into her lungs and dived. I looked down and saw her run down towards the bottom, then grab something and move up sharply. After a while she floated next to me, raising a strange object in her hand. We turned back to shore and after a while we sat on the sand watching the find.

It was a kind of one-and-a-half feet long, a broad dagger reminiscent of a dagger, but with a wide shield on a hand spiked with long spikes and a long, massive spike on the opposite side. It did not stay long in the water because rust did not seize it...

"What's that?" I asked.

"Stygian's dagger," she said, "it can also serve as a knuckle-duster. An extremely nasty weapon. Sometimes it is poisoned."

"So they were here and it was recently," I said.

Looking around we saw the remains of fires and traces of axes on the bushes. And that meant that the Stygian caravan was camping here before pulling north.

We dressed quickly and whistled on horses. They came running fast, and we saddled them and ladened them.

"I'll remember this place very nice," I said, kissing Iris.

"Me too," she said, giving me a kiss, "we must come here more often!"

And she laughed. We jumped on horses and headed north.

The trail began to rise and the vegetation thinned. We began to drive up to the foothills. The sea was behind us and now stretched out like a gray-haired tile cut by the crests of the waves. After fifteen miles, we saw something strange. It was a dome made of exactly matched stones - it resembled a structure of frozen snow I had seen in Hyperborea. But it was thirty feet high and it was about fifty. It looked awfully strange. It was covered with bushes, bare, almost leafless. It must have been very old, because their roots had squeezed into the gaps between the stones, and the moss itself overwhelmed them. But someone was here. Moss in places was frayed and traces led to the top of the dome. There must have been an entrance...

"Do you remember," said Iris, "'the Way of the Kings', a song about Conan and his duel with the skeleton?"

"Oh," I got it, "I remember. But I suspect it wasn't a skeleton and there was no..."

I jumped from the horse.

"What are you going to do?" She asked.

"Check the situation." I replied and began to climb.

After a few minutes, the vespers stood at the top of the dome. And here a surprise awaited me - there was a round hole on the very top, in which everything was black.

"Iris, honey, throw me a torch!" I shouted.

"Wait a minute!" I heard in response and heard the sound of sparks.

After a few minutes Iris climbed up to me with a fiery torch in her hand. We looked at each other. I slowly slipped the torch into the hole so that I could see what was inside the dome.

"Ugh!" Iris jumped away from the hole with a look of disgust on her face. "There... there are a lot of corpses!"

I looked down. In fact, in the uncertain light of the torch you could see some twisted skeletons lying on the floor.

"It's only skeletons, and only three," I said calmly, "but somebody was here. You can see the moss down. I'll go there. Please bring our bola.

Iris went down to ground to our horses, which indifferently grazed on blueberries and other forest bushes and after a while brought two strong ropes with a total length sufficient to descend to the bottom of the dome. I tied them together and dropped them down. Iris drove the Stygian dagger with a spike between the stones and tied the rope.

"At least it's useful for something." I thought.

"Okay, I'm going," I said and threw my legs over the edge of the entrance.

I went down and Iris dropped torch to me. I lifted it and looked around. There was nothing to be seen on the arched walls, except the roots of the bushes that grew the dome from the out-side. On the top of the dome, she slept in the best colony of bats. The lower moisture was shining in the firelight. I looked at the skeletons - they were old, faded. The bodies and clothing cover-ing them had break up. I counted - there were three under the hole, and the fourth one was lying against the wall and I did not notice it at first. I wondered what tragedy took place here many years ago, maybe even centuries ago? I was surprised by the lack of stone closing the shelter from the top, but I did not find a trace of the Stygian stay, who perhaps did not want to bother the dead or maybe they just did not find what they were looking for and gave them peace?

I scrambled slowly upstairs. Iris looked at me with a question in her eyes.

"There is nothing interesting there," I said, "only four skeletons."

"Who?" She asked.

I shrugged.

"Who knows?" I said, "but you aren't interested in the fact that there are no skeletons of animals, only people?"

"Are you saying that people came in through curiosity and the animals didn't want to enter there, despite the tasty scent of human carrion?" She raised her eyebrows.

"Yes, just like that: scavengers would have to be attracted by the scent of decomposing bodies," I said, "but they didn't get here, because they would have troubles to get out of it, or not at all... there was no other skeleton except human... But it's all looks like nothing, better tell me what Stygians were looking for there?"

For some time we have discussed this issue while going further. Suddenly the forest is over and an abyss has opened before us. We stood. It was very deep, actually it was a canyon of the river that flowed below us. Behind the abyss, a vast plateau with a mower and lush grass boiled in the sun.

"And what's next my Master?" Iris stared into the depths of the chasm.

"There is a bridge somewhere," I replied, "but where?"

Iris looked around and after a moment turned her steed to the right.

"Look," she said, pointing to the barely visible traces, they went here, almost on the edge of the abyss. She was right, after a dozen or so minutes we saw the bridge. We were amazed by its light, almost open-work construction. Our amazement increased when we rode in on it. The horseshoes of our horses rang on metal. I jumped off my horse and looked at the bridge structure - it was made of steel. And that's incredibly high quality! I have not even seen a trace of rust anywhere!

"Amazing," I said, "this is some super steel."

"Well, the bridge itself measures at least a mile," Iris added.

"Now imagine the amount of steel absorbed by this structure!" I replied. "How much of it would you be able to do such swords? A million or more..."

We reached the end of the bridge. Once upon a time there must have been a road here, but now only the mountain pine grew. Fortunately, the Stygians cut it and it was possible to follow the path along their tracks. Suddenly we went to the clearing, where there was a hole in the ground, fortified like a well. We stopped. I jumped from the horse and slowly walked to the hole. There was something strange in the middle that resembled a cylinder with a semicircular cap in silvery color, several dozen feet long. The diameter was at least seven feet. I heard Iris jump off the horses and came up to me.

"For Ishtar," she said, "what is it? It is...?"

"Yes, honey," I said slowly, "there is just one of the greatest curses of this world in front of you - *Brahmadanda*. A weapon striking with the strength of myriads of demons and poisoning everything around with the power of millions of scorpions. It was that, for which Gedrena sent her people.

III

Everything went silent. We looked around but nobody was around.

"What about them?" Iris asked, "they fell in the hole?"

"In a way, yes," I nodded, "each of these missiles, because it is just such a large self-propelled missle, such an arrow as from a bow or crossbow, but a million times larger and with a million times greater firepower, located in a well surrounded by a maze of corridors and underground pavements for its service.

"So what are we going to do with this... this... bullet?" She asked a bit helplessly.

"It can be disposed of by cutting off those ropes that connect it to the walls," I pointed to the thick bundles of ropes and tubes that connected the missle with the walls. "When they are cut, the missile won't fly, but you can die because sometimes the vapors of some poisonous liquids and/or gases emerge."

"Then what can you do to avoid poisoning?" She asked, dumbfounded.

"You'll see," I said mysteriously. "Look, oh, for Perun and Swarożyc!"

This last exclamation was justified, because I noticed that the outer cap was cut and its contents removed, which was the worst threat even if it did not explode. The missile was disarmed and could only fly without harming anyone.

"Professional work," said Iris, "do you think that..."

In fact, this person knew exactly where and what to look for and how to get to it. The missle head was accurately and expertly eviscerated from its lethal content...

"It looks like that," I said, and we looked into each other's eyes with one thought that could be summarized in one sentence: there was a traitor in the Brotherhood who had turned to Gedrena's side...

"We must find this caravan and dispose of the traitor, whoever he is," I said through my teeth. "This someone knows the methods of the Brotherhood and ways to recover dangerous materials. I wonder how much they gave him for this?"

"Certainly a lot," said Iris, looking at this little more cheerful. "So my Master..."

"We must catch the caravan and eliminate this..."

"How nice," Iris smiled ironically, "eliminate. Just kill!"

"Yes," I nodded, "kill him." Gedrena began a dangerous game that could lead to the destruction of life on Earth. There is no place for sentiments here. This knowledge in her hands is dangerous for the whole world. And we have to do it at the cost of our lives. There was no other way.

We found the second well with the same eviscerated missle the next day in the morning. And that same afternoon, we came across Stygians who were returning to their home after clearing out the entire starting field of these messengers of death - *Brahmadanda*. We heard them when they were one and a half staja away from us. The wind was blowing in our direction, so we were able to quickly get to a small elevation and watch the road from there. In fact, after a quarter of an hour, we saw four wagons and equestrians riding alongside them. We wondered what to do, and we had to act quickly, because at any moment they could discover our presence.

"Look there." Iris pointed to a group of riders following the carts.

I looked in the direction indicated. This group was within a thousand steps of us. A tall Shemit rode in the middle of it. I could not believe my eyes - it was master Arielles from Eruk. So he sold himself to the Stygians!

I remembered immediately that Arielles belonged to the Brotherhood of Aghrapur on the Vilayet Sea and disappeared a few months ago. Now everything was clear - he found the starting field and prepared it for the operation of obtaining warheads and transferring them to Stygia.

I loaded the crossbow and pointed it at Shemit's head. I had one shot and I could not waste it. I guided the weapon at the target, took a deep breath and pulled the trigger softly. The crossbow snarled briefly and the arrow dug into Arielles's left temple. There were screams and wagons stopped. Half a hundred robust warriors spilled out creating a cordon around the wagons. Arielles slowly slid from the horse to the ground. He was undeniably dead. One of our horses whinnied shortly and the Stygians rushed towards us with their swords. There was no point in hiding and we also showed ourselves first, and then our swords. We did not want to give up without a fight.

The Stygians were close, and we fell forward. The distance shortened rapidly when a commanding cry rang out at once. The Stygian horses stood still and the warriors left their swords and javelins. The warriors formed a cordon around the middle cart, leaving the others not defended. A woman came out from behind the cordon, whose appearance seemed to me familiar. She cried imperiously to her men who surrounded us with a ring, but did not betray their hostile intentions. Their swords went to the scabbards.

"Who are you and why did you kill this man?" She asked imperiously.

"People call me Lestko from Vislania and this is my wife Iris," I said, "and who are you?"

"I'm Gedrena, the queen of Stygia," she replied. "By what law have you killed this man?"

"He's a traitor," I replied. "He told you secrets that he had no right to tell anyone."

"Oh, the Brotherhood of the Green Dragon?" She asked mockingly. "You can't stop me from my plans. Take them!" She exclaimed.

A few of the Stygians fell on us and that was their mistake, because we used it quickly. Iris cut first of them over his head so that he ran into the other one and they both fell off the horses. I spurr my horse sharply and moved sideways, cutting the nearest warrior, then turned and stab under arm the man who wanted to get me in front. They both fell on the grass with blood.

Meanwhile, Iris parried two pushes directed at her breasts and she cut two more heads with one horizontal cut. I turned and attacked two warriors who swung at Iris's exposed back. I cut the first one by the head and cut the raised hand of other one with the sword.

Iris thanked me with a look and bounced off two blows, then she dug her sword into the throat of another guard.

Unfortunately. A wounded warrior lying on the ground stuck a pugin in stomach of my horse and I dropped to the ground. I took a few blows and cut off the hand of the one who killed my steed. Then the Stygians threw a net on us and they were tied up. I felt a strong blow to my head and lost consciousness.

When I recovered it, it was already dark. I sat bound and tied to the pile. My head ached terribly and my eyes was cloud. I was in a tent, in the middle of which a large olive lamp was shining. I felt that there was someone on the other side of the pile.

"Iris?" I asked in a low voice.

"Present, Master," she replied in a weak voice.

"How are you?" I asked.

"Pretty good, but I'm bound like a smoked ham sausage."

"Me too. And I probably can not break free. They hampered us good.

"They probably used up all their ropes," she laughed softly.

It was something I loved her for. Even in the worst troubles, she did not lose her sense of humor.

"They will torture us?" She asked.

"Well, they won't stammer us, he... he..." I also got her a hangman's humor. "How many of them did we kill?"

"it could be ten plus, of course, this Arielles skunk," she counted, recalling the events.

I laughed.

"Hmmm... Well, there are still forty and the Gedrena's waiting maid and she," Iris somehow did not care that we were almost naked, unarmed, and bound like rams.

"Somehow I don't..." I did not finish, because at once the wing of the tent leaned back and Gedrena entered with two women.

I wondered if I was still pretending to be unconscious, but I decided it did not make sense. It was necessary to accelerate the course of events and so I did.

"Oh, are you conscious?" She asked when I saw her. "That's great. How's your little one?"

She walked around the pale we were attached to, and after a moment I felt that she unseating Iris from it, and the two women immediately took her by the shoulders and brought her to the center of the tent. Iris was naked, there were signs of a fight on her body. She had her hands tied behind her.

"Are you silent?" She asked. "You don't like me?"

Iris shook her head.

Stygian woman went to the center of the tent and slid off her robe. I looked at her, she was nicely built and as limber as Iris.

"It's your loss. But I have something to offer you." She clapped her hands and one of the women brought a low table, which she placed between her and Gedrena.

"Sit down." She ordered.

Iris sat down and Gedrena sat down opposite her. The table was in between them. Gedrena took a figurine from a small bag and placed it on the board. Chessboard.

"Do you play chess?" She asked. "That's great. I'll play with you."

"And what when I'll refuse?" Iris asked.

"Oh, that's obvious," edrena smiled cynically, "I'll kill both of you and it give me a lot of pleasure.

Iris nodded. Gedrena clapped her hands. At her mark, one of woman cut her ties. She looked in my direction and our eyes met for a moment. I leaned my head a fraction of an inch.

"Now listen me, baby." The queen hissed. "This is the rules: you'll win - I'll play with you. You'll lose - I'll play with your boyfriend. Do you understand?"

IV

Iris nodded again.

"Don't expect too much from us," she said coldly.

Stygian laughed. She threw a dagger in me that stuck in a fraction of an inch above my head. She should not have done this. She made a serious mistake.

"You still don't know the power of Stygian magic... and mine," she said, smiling maliciously. But we play. You have white, get start."

Iris made the first move - a counter under the king. Subsequent shifts of counters and finally exchange. Second exchange...

I looked at them. Stygian sat less and less relaxed, because Iris began to push her to the wall. One castling, second one... I saw ironic smiles on the faces of both women. The figures began to fall from the chessboard. Finally, Iris said with an icy calm:

"Shah and mat. And what now?"

"I'll play with you." Gedrena made a gesture with her hand and two women entered the tent. They grabbed Iris and laid her on the bedclothes.

"Now listen to me, my little one," she said cynically, "you'll know the power of our magic. Do not be afraid, relax, oh yeah..."

Both women reached for the flasks with oily liquid and began to rub it into Iris's skin. She lay quietly letting herself anoint with fragrant oils. Their hands gently caressed the body of Iris, and Gedrena knelt down beside her, brushing her lips with her lips. She gave the sign and both women withdrew from the tent. Gedrena lay down next to Iris.

"And what, you don't feel good?" She asked in a dreamy voice. "You'll be better with me than with this man," she nodded toward me.

"Really?" Iris asked.

"Believe me, yes," Stygian whispered, hugging her and caressing her breasts. Her lips parted and she slid her tongue between Iris's lip. She gave in to her and for a moment they kissed passionately...

...

"So, what's up, baby?" She asked. "How you liked it."

"You're good," Iris said.

They lay there caressing and looking lovingly at each other's eyes.

Iris looked at me for a fleeting moment. I nodded slightly. Now.

"Can you call your servants?" She asked.

"Yes, baby," Gedrena nodded, "but why?"

"I want to play in foursome," Iris said.

"Oh, you got a little frisky?" Stygian asked with a smile and clapped her hands, "this isn't a stupid idea."

Both young women appeared immediately.

"Undress," Gedrena said.

The girls threw off their shirt and stood naked in front of their lady. Iris rose from her seat and took Gedrena with her. For a moment, they all giggled and stood surrounding Iris, who raised both hands up, presenting her breasts.

What happened later was like a small explosion, because Iris's body moved quickly like a spinning metal spring. The first girl flew on the bed, struck with a huge sheet in the chin and the second one got a powerful blow with an elbow on the bridge until I heard something like a crack of cracking bones. She fell to the ground, curled up in a pretzel. Gedrena did not regain her astonishment and a second later she flew on the bed after a massive kick-and-go kick to the jaw.

"And that would be enough, my big one," Iris looked with contempt at the woman lying unconscious. "Although I must admit, you're good in that stuff and I wouldn't throw you out of bed..."

"Good job, Apprentice," I said appreciatively. "And thank you!"

She came to me and cut my ties. Her hands embraced my neck and we kissed.

"Are we get out of here my Master?" She asked tenderly.

For a moment, I enjoyed the subtle touch of her smooth, fragrant and warm, heated by sex and fight body.

"Oh, no, we must first dispose of these warheads," I replied.

"Do you have any idea?" She asked, letting go of me and looking around the tent.

"Yes," I said, "first we have to do something unpleasant to your friends.

She giggled amused. I leaned over and shifted the naked limp bodies of three women into one place. Iris efficiently tied them in a stick and gagged. Our clothes and weapons lay on the heap against the wall of the tent, so we dressed quickly.

"We're going?" I asked.

I heard a small moan. The bound women woke and moaned. Iris was beating really hard and worst of all - painfully.

I leaned over them.

"Forgive us, dears. In other circumstances, we'd all have a really wonderful time, but we found ourselves in the wrong place and time on both sides of the barricade," I said regretfully. "But I give you a word, we will meet again, and then you will moan, but out of pleasure. So goodbye..."

Iris laughed, then we went out into the thick darkness.

V

The queen's tent was not guarded, which surprised me. It should be. After all, it was a ruling person, so even if this is the case, double guards should stand here. But there was no one. There were other tents about half a dozen steps, among which people were hovering here and there.

"What we do?" Iris asked.

"We'll wait for the moon to rise," I said in a whisper, "then we'll look around. "And for now we have to move away."

That is what we did. On the way, we came across a well, at the bottom of which stood a vertical missle.

"Let's stop here," I said.

We fell into the mountain pine and waited until it cleared in the east. The moon was rising and after a dozen or so minutes its dead glow brightened up the situation. We were at the edge of the plateau, some five miles from the bridge. The Stygian people in the camp have not yet discovered our disappearance, apparently they thought their queen was playing with us best. It was a very favorable circumstance for us. We came to the very edge of the well. I sniffed, but I did not sense any foreign smell. Some wells stunk with a characteristic, biting and bland concurrent stink of unknown origin. It was possible to overwhelm it, because inhaling this smell caused nausea and dizziness, and after a long time of inhaling this abomination made even loss of consciousness and death. There was nothing stinking here, so there was a chance that this missle could be disposed of, while at the same time scaring the Stygians and forcing them to escape. Then, along with Iris, we simply throw a deadly load into the canyon and no one will be able to bring out it... For a very long time.

The moon rose to two fingers above the horizon.

"We're starting," I said, rising from the ground.

Iris also rose and looked at me questioningly. I looked around and saw a few large boulders that could weigh about two - three minas each. We quoted a few to the roofing and struck a small fire.

"They won't notice us?" Iris asked anxiously.

"It doesn't matter anymore," I said.

I made a big torch from the pitchy log, which I smoked and threw it down. It fell and began to burn, shining even with a fairly bright though burning flame. In the light of it, I saw a handful of wires protruding from the wall and connected to the missle. The other wires were on the other side. We quoted the boulder and threw it in so that it would hit it. In fact, after a while, we heard a rumor and a sharp hiss. Pressed gas escaped from the entrained pipes.

"Alright!" I shouted. "And now the other side!"

We threw ourselves to the other side of the well and threw a second stone on the wires that cracked and a transparent liquid began to be emitted from them. A chill chilled from the well.

"Okay, now help me!" I got to the cover and pushed it towards the well hole, which went unexpectedly easily, because it was on metal guides. We closed the hole.

"Now run!" I ordered. "And quickly, because here will be a hell!"

We started running towards the Stygian camp. After about a thousand steps I looked back. At the same time, it happens what Master Hug taught me. The liquid and compressed or even liquefied gas merged into the closed well.

"Get down!" I shouted to Iris, quite unnecessarily, because a powerful shock brought us to the ground and a second later our eyes were smitten by a terrible orange flash of fire which grew from the place where the well was. A moment later we heard a roaring roar. The well has become a crater of an erupting volcano. A hundred-talented well's cover flew over us and fell near the camp, petrified by the terror of the Stygians. They did not wait for anything, but they fell into a disorderly escape, away from the cursed place.

"We could easily knock them out now," Iris said calmly.

"No," I murmured, "that would be a serious mistake.

"Why?" Her eyebrows rose high.

"Because, my Apprentice, they must bring news to the civilized world, about what they were dealing with here..." I smiled at her. "Besides, I'm disgusted with unnecessary bloodshed."

"Yhm..." she nodded, "you're right, Master. Excuse me."

"You're welcome," I answered. "We're starting."

We went towards the campsite. We did not come across any Stygian, apparently taken with fear, they run like hell. I whistled and our three horses ran to us. The fourth was lying somewhere on the battlefield, maybe the Stygian people ate him... We quickly saddled and laden them.

"Well, let's go." I commanded by fastening my steed. We set off slowly in the still faint moonlight and the raging fire. We took several dozen steps when Iris raised her hand. I stood.

"Do you hear?" She asked while listening.

"Over there." I pointed to the way from which a weak moan had come.

We came there and after a while we saw our old friends trembling with fear. They were completely terrified and confused. They looked at us with madness in their eyes, two girls were crying.

"I've told you that we'll meet again." I said.

They was silent. I searched Gedreza. She stood with her head down.

"You aren't Gedrena but her substitute, right?" I asked calmly. She nodded in response.

"You'll come with us," I said firmly, "here death threatens you at any moment. Now have you seen how it works?"

"Yes," she nodded again.

"Well..." I did not finish, because from the side of the interior of the plateau came a huge bang, which again covered us like a dome. It looked as if there was another explosion, or... The roar increased and passed into a roaring whistle. At the same time the sky in the north shone bright. The light seemed to rise and it was so strong that it illuminated the mountains visible on the horizon.

"OH! Osiris!" Stygians exclaimed and fell on they faces. "Don't punish us!"

"It looks like there's a system of launching these missiles," I said to Iris.

"That's probably what Master Houg called a "dead hand system," Iris smiled. "Bullets are flying up even when nobody released them or the system thought it was attacked."

"I hope they won't go far," I said. "Anyway, these eight thousand years... Some of the materials that were creating them had to grow old and just break down..."

Three women were whining and weeping at our feet. The view was very distasteful.

"I hope so too," Iris sighed.

"Get up," I shouted at the women wailing on the ground, "you see that nothing is happening!"

The second roar joined the first roar. And the third. Bullets like fire-spattering arrows were rising faster and faster into the sky. Earth from the horizon to the horizon was illuminated with this illumination.

"Do you remember how many of them was supposed to be here?" I asked.

"Twenty," Iris answered.

"There are nine in the air," I said, charging the luminous shots, "we has neutralized one of them, so ten, and another ten should fly, unless they are 'break down."

As if in response from the plateau there was a terrible bang.

"Eleven," Iris calmly counted out.

At once the sky burned over us. For a moment a fireball flared over us, which soon turned into a slowly extinguishing ring.

"Warhead explosion. There is no air there, so we won't hear it," I said to Iris.

The Stygians stopped whimpering and just stood hugging each other and trembling with terror throughout their whole bodies.

"And where is your Osiris?" Iris asked the question with a maximum hint in her voice. "Can you ride a horse?"

They nodded, sobbing and nodding.

"Well, saddle the horses, and take supplies for yourself." Iris commanded them with the skill of a warrior.

Something was still crashing up in the mountains, but that was the end of the fireworks. There was silence and one had to reckon with the fact that the Stygians could cool off from terror and return. We did not have much time.

"Go with them to the bridge, if it still exists, and I'll finish what we came here for," I started toward the camp. "We'll meet behind the bridge."

I moved and after a while I stood by the carts.

I went to the first one. I pulled the cloth back and looked inside. There were three conical objects long about five feet wide on the thick bedding of seagrass, wide at the base for two. I tried to pick up, each of them weighed at least two talents. But all Hell's power was hidden in them and it was necessary to neutralize them or at least create them inaccessible to people. Take away them a dangerous toys...

Such was the purpose of existence and mission of our Brotherhood.

VI

I looked around and quickly found the shortest way to the edge of the canyon. I quickly pushed all the carts into the abyss, they fell with a thud and crumbled, hitting the edge of the canyon. After a minute, a stone avalanche lurched around them, burying their remains under the tons of boulders. I was rubbing my hands - the work was done. I turned and froze.

Stygian warriors stood between me and the camp. And they did not have any peaceful intentions, steel glittered in their hands. Perhaps they were going to just slaughtered me, but I was probably sure of one thing - they wanted to take me alive. They had to somehow explain to the queen of the failure of mission and only the capture of the one who thwarted it, guaranteed them to avoid the wrath of Gedrena. That's why they were approaching me with furious flashes in their eyes. There were at least ten of them.

"We got you," the nearest of them nibbled.

"Not yet." I laughed in his face.

"We will also get your bitch and kill her," the second one told me.

I breathed a sigh of relief, because it meant that they did not get Iris and the women who accompanied her.

"Rather, she will do it with you," I said with a laugh.

It pissed them off. The exchange of courtesy ended and they rushed at me. I counterpunched two cuts and jumped back - both Stygians follow the carts in a hurry... The third one tried to push me, but I swiveled and my sword hit him perfectly between the eyes. I tore the sword from his fainting hand and took it to my left hand.

"Who's next?" I asked. Everyone threw at me. The first two repeated the mistake of their colleagues and flew after them a thousand feet to the bottom of the canyon. The next two tried to break through the shimmering curtain of steel I had surrounded. Five enemies, it was something that a single warrior could face when he knew Zipangian methods of fighting with two swords. Sparks flashed when I parried the punches and pushed their cords.

Stygians were furious because they still could not reach me. They lacked training in the art of fencing. Accustomed to the fighting of heavy swords, they could not play this duel with finesse and speed. I do not know if their stupidity or determination was so great that they did not bend their colleagues to hit me in a larger mass. Suddenly something broke up behind them. A rider approached us at great speed. When he equaled with us, he set his horse, who stood prancing annoyantly and his hooves slammed into the back of the Stygian warrior who stood in his way. A sword flashed and the man fell to the ground with his head banged. A second blow fell on the shoulder of another, who for a moment stared in amazement at the scarred cut of his hand and a fountain of blood, black in the moonlight that spilled from the cut arteries. The other three did not wait for death, only having abandoned their weapons, they were retreating to escape into the bosket.

"Hop in, what are you waiting for?" I heard the cheerful voice of Iris.

"You better go to these girls," I said. "I will catch up with you!"

I whistled loudly and my steed ran to the call. I jumped on the saddle and we moved trotting towards the bridge.

* * *

We drove the rest of the night to escape the damned plateau as quickly as possible. It was only in the morning that we allowed ourselves half an hour of rest. Around noon we stood on the seashore. I breathed a sigh of relief at the half-mile-long swaying ship with the flag of Turan on the gaff and the flag with the Green Dragon - the coat of arms of the Brotherhood on the coffers.

An hour later, I squeezed the hand of a young man dressed similar to us.

"Hello Master Lestek from Vislania," he said in greeting, "and you Iris from Ianthe, I'm Wolfer from Kordava."

"How do you know about us?" I asked. "After all our mission was strictly secret."

"Hmmm..." Wolfer smiled "We just saw it at night... And besides, we have a Belverus cipher on your operation."[7]

"But you're not here because of us?" I asked.

"No," he sighed and replied, "unfortunately not only because of that. We're here to capture and arrest Master Arielles from Eruk on charges of treason."

"Master Arielles is dead," I said. "I killed him when he conspired with the Stygians."

Wolfer raised only his eyebrows and the cloud flew through his usually cheerful face.

"I didn't think it was true," he said, "I believed in his innocence. But when we revised his cell on a Belverus order, we were surprised to find receipts and other documents proving his guilt. And almost the talent of gold... And he was my Master!"

"Sometimes it happens, gold has already charmed many people," I said, "but there is also a bright point here. And even two: now you are the Master and you embrace the vacancy."

---

7   The Brotherhood uses to its purposes solar telegraph along the Way of Kings, whose station near Belverus has a connection to its Headquarters.

"Yes, yes," he nodded.

"And one more thing: we'll have to interrogate these three women who are with us," I said, "one of them is a substitute for Queen Gedrena and the other two are her servants. They are so terrified of what we have done there that they'll testify and voluntarily. And I think they'll have a lot to say to us!"

After three days of sailing we arrived happily to Agrapur, where the Turanian Branch of the Brotherhood was located. A surprise awaited us here. We were sitting just at dinner, when a novice slipped into the refectory and with a low bow gave me a folded several times card.

"Cipher to Master Lestek and Apprentice Iris," he said with a low bow.

I unfolded the card. I read a few lines of the script and gave it to Iris. She read it and looked at me.

"Bad news?" Wolfer asked.

"The best, Master Wolfer," I said. "Your appointment has just arrived and what is more, you are taking the position of Commander of this Branch. However, we must go back to Belverus as soon as possible."

"Will there be an answer?" Asked the novice with a bow.

"Yes, of course." I wrote a confirmation of receiving the message with a lead rod and ended it with the statement that I will bring copies of the information from the interrogations of prisoners whom we took during this escapade.

"So what, Commander," I turned to Wolfer with a nod, "you'll let us interrogate our wards."

We went to the guest rooms, where we put all three women. First, we asked for bringing the one that was the substitute for Gedrena. She entered with astonishment in her eyes and looked around with interest. Her fear had passed and she had almost returned to her normal behavior.

"Will you torture me?" She asked.

"I don't see a need. If you'll answer questions, nothing bad will happen to you." I replied.

"And if not?" She replied.

"Of course you can not answer, it's your right," I said calmly, "but of course you'll bear the consequences. We'll find out what we want to find out, and you... hmmm... well, you're Stygian and, in addition, a woman. Even quite attractive. I'll get a silver mina for one like you in a slave market. And you'll go to the brothel or - with luck - to a patrician's house as a concubine... And here women are treated as something to work and to give birth to children. Exactly in this order. Do you want it? Think about it. You are free and you can be free, albeit with a changed name, but alive.

And I left giving her a quarter of hour to think about.

I returned in exactly fifteen minutes. She sat at the table, supporting her chin with her fists and looking at the wall. Tears glistened at the corners of the eyes.

"And what?" I asked. "Will we talk?"

She nodded. I called the clerk.

"We're starting. Ready?"

"Yes."

"Then please give your real name and titles."

"My name is Ami and I'm the daughter of Ed-amma and Ellenira from Luxur. My father is a senior assistant in the nomarch of Luxur."

"Who you were at the court of Queen Gedrena?"

"I was the queen of Gedreza double."

The first interrogation took four hours. I left with a parchment file in my hand. From the neighboring rooms the interrogating ones of two women came out and handed me the card files. It was evident that both were very talkative...

The reading of these parchments was extremely interesting. It resulted from it that Gedrena had great appetites for power and that in her intentions she would do anything. Testimonies described various court intrigues that aimed to remove some politicians who did not share the course of politics of the prevailing and even moderate in their views. It seemed that Gedrena, supported by a strong priesthood lobby, intended to introduce dictatorial governments and, in her speeches, increasingly demanded a living space for Stygia. It sounded very dangerous. But even more interesting was the fact that the queen was fulfilling the will not so much her own, but black demons, with whom she contacted using the talking stone with the strange name 'hanau'. The warheads were meant for them. Again, instead of solving one puzzle, we had a whole chain of consecutive ones.

VII

Night was falling, the cool wind was blowing from the sea, seared with salt and seaweed. We lay in a huge, comfortable bed, listening to the dying sounds of the city.

"What exactly will the Brotherhood do with these women?" Iris asked, hugging me.

"We'll change their identity. We'll create new memoir and get married," I replied.

"Really?" She asked in astonishment. "I thought you'd make them members of the Brotherhood."

"It's about people like you. For example a priestess, a warrior. These women will be good wives and mothers, and at the same time... our eyes and ears." I said. "Our agents."

"But..." she thought for a moment, "the Brotherhood isn't interested in such things as who is sleeping with whom and why...?"

"Yes, you're right, but don't forget that information is also a good and you can sell it well or exchange it," I answered, "this is what the Brotherhood's power and activities are based on. We know everything about everyone, and this knowledge is the guarantee of its existence. That is why it's above all divisions and its branches are found in all countries of the civilized world. This allows you to maintain a political balance in this world.

"Does it mean that you'll marry these girls with the Turans?" She asked.

"First, they must undergo training in our convent of the transition in Numalia - this is the preparation for marriage, but also for taking up our business. These women are valuable agents in our service. And they've to go through this because Gedrena will want to hunt them down and kill them, of course. Do you know what the highest trick in this work is all about?"

"Turning agents over and releasing them to our site?" She said in a tone of utmost certainty.

"You've done your homework, my Apprentice," I said appreciatively.

She smiled with satisfaction. Our eyes met. She turned me on the back and she lifted herself on my hands, still looking me hypnotically in the eye.

"It doesn't work for me," I said.

"I know." She smiled.

Her smelling of some herbs hair, fell on my face and tickled nicely. Iris moved her head so that it would be the most rousing. After a while she lay down on me and our lips met. First we gently stroked our lips, and then harder and harder, until finally we crushed them in a passionate kiss...

I admit that I was the one who envied them - this so vivid experience of fulfillment. This pure pleasure of sex, which they experienced as lively as a storm, like a hurricane, which then slowly calmed down to finally go into a peaceful sleep.

Her breathing slowly calmed and her body relaxed and got wispily. She opened her eyes and looked at me.

"And you?" She whispered.

"Don't be too quick," I said fondly.

I lay down next to her and listened to her breath, absorbing the warmth of her body.

"Do you have any idea?" She asked.

"Maybe?" I teased her.

"Oh no!" She breathed in my ear.

...

Her hot lips made a big hickey around my neck... And then we fell into a warm depths of sleep.

When we woke up, a slightly bitten moon was shining high in the sky. We shivered from the cold night. I got up and threw a huge bear pelt on Iris and lay down again. Iris hugged me and clung her body to my side. After a moment I felt her breathing calm down and leveled out. She slept sweetly like a child.

But I could not sleep. I was tormented by the thought that during the expedition to the plateau I missed something very important, some small but significant detail. I digested the events that we experienced in our minds and became more and more convinced that it concerns us - Iris and me. The sky began to glow when, finally, I fell asleep when can not figure out nothing more.

4

~

SHADOWS FROM VALUSSIA

I

I had the sound of sea waves in my ears , cool, soft sand under me. I lie on it embracing a hugged to me woman. We kiss cuddled naked bodies into a small armpit. Above us, the flaming sun rises, marking the fiery trail on the water of the Vilayet Sea. Shouts of gulls spread over the beach and waves, and for me the whole world focused on the pink curve of her lips. We planned to finish the morning bath and walk on the beach where we started it - in bed. I just lifted my head to propose it when we heard a grunt and a young girl's voice above us:

"Forgive me Master, I've an important message for you."

We looked this way. In front of us stood a young, still sixteen, maybe seventeen-year-old Schoolgirl dressed in a short navy blue tunic with the Brotherhood logo between nicely outlined breasts. She held sandals in her left hand. She had slender long legs and small but very shapely feet. She must have been thoroughly confused by what she saw here, because her blush was darkened on her cheeks. Maybe she did not expect our nakedness, or maybe she would find us in such an intimate situation. She lowered her dark-haired head and waited.

I kissed Iris quickly and we both jumped into our clothes.

"We're listening to you," Iris said, shaking the sand off her long hair. "What do they call you?"

The girl bowed.

"My name is Tia and I come from Agra. I'm a personal messenger today and I'm serving the Commander. You, Master, and you, Lady, are asked to Commander Wolfer in a very urgent matter," she said and curtsied again. She was very well-behaved.

"Please, follow me," she said with her sonorous voice and moved toward the city. We smiled to each other.

"This little one is funny," Iris said.

At the edge of the beach she put on sandals and she was proud of the task entrusted to her. It was also why I liked working with women, they were just accurate, conscientious and approached each task as if it were to be the one that depended on the existence of this world...

The Commander's office was in a mood of expectation. Also, Commander Wolfer could not hide his nervousness. Tia introduced us and quietly left closing the door.

"Hello, Commander," I said and with Iris, we bowed our heads.

"Stop it." Wolfer waved his hand. "I don't like this drill. Sit down, please!"

We sat down.

"You've really lovely staff, Commander!" I said to slightly unload the atmosphere of tense expectations.

"Ah, this chit?" He smiled unexpectedly. "This is my niece. She's got sixteen and a half years, her mother's beauty and a great head for mathematics. She'll be educated in the Brotherhood and when she turns twenty, I will send her to Belverus. She'd just wander here."

We laughed. The mood of the tension disappeared.

"Can we know why you called us?" I asked.

"Of course," he answered, reaching for the table, where a whole lot of parchments and papyri lay, from which he pulled one out and handed it to me.

"This is a letter I received yesterday afternoon from a messenger from Khorala. This is a letter from Emperor Vendhia," he put emphasis on the word 'emperor', "to our Grand Master. Read it, please."

"But he..." I started.

"... it's about you and you too," the Commander said to Iris.

I smiled. It was absurd, because from where Emperor Vendhia could know about us. They sang songs about Halidor, Conan, or Kullu Atlantis, but for us at the moment no one sang any songs, and our names have not been recorded anywhere in any chronicles, except for Brotherhood documents...

"Read!" Commander said.

I unfolded the papyrus and ran a line of plain, calligraphic script. I felt Iris breathing on my ear, which was peering over my shoulder. The papyrus clearly states:

...I am asking you with a discreet request, because the matter is extremely delicate. For some time now, on the south-western edge of our country, in the province of Goa, there have been rumors about the return of the snake-men from Valussia. The investigation into a dozen or so people who died in strange and still unexplained circumstances indicates that they were attacked and bitten by huge snakes and it was extremely poisonous - death occurred almost immediately or after a minute. Everything points to the fact that these people were attacked by a huge cobra, but... nobody has ever seen them in this area.

It occurred that people in this province are afraid to leave their homes after dark, although it is known that they were also attacked - or, most importantly - in homes. People are afraid to talk about it, there is a strange conspiracy of silence, because they consider it a punishment of the gods hanging over the province. From what I have learned to my administration, it is known that in areas where dead bodies of people with bite marks were found, strange people were seen, at the sight of which all dogs howled and other animals showed crazy, panicky fear.

Psychosis of fear has already led to the fact that my employees are unable to control a situation that is increasingly out of control and threatens with unpredictable consequences. What is more, there may be religious riots and this is what everyone is most afraid of in this province, because they can come after religious clashes and national scarcity will come for sure, because, as you probably know, Vendhia is conglomerate of many different nationalities and beliefs.

So my request is as follows - if you can and are able to, send to me someone from the Brotherhood who would be able to put an end to this dangerous situation, track down and kill the monster that is murdering my subjects in Goa. The matter is very serious and I do not know anyone in this world who would be able to help me. Of course, you will be well rewarded for that, the Empire of Vendhia can reward you with all your hardships and any sacrifice that you will suffer in your mission to my Empire, you can not worry about it. ...

I finished reading and looked at Commander Wolfer.

"What's that got to do with us?" I asked, though I already knew what the answer would be.

"You'll go to Vendhia by order of the Grand Master," said Commander Wolfer and gave me the second piece - this time a parchment. I took one look at it and freaked out. It was written with a mixture of letters and numbers. After a moment I understood - it was a personal code, to which I received the code with the nomination for the Master. I had to decipher it using a small disk of baked clay, which was covered with a spiral pattern containing the key of the cipher.[8] After a few minutes, I deciphered the cryptogram. It was a confirmation of the order to go to Vendhia and investigate the mysterious deaths.

"Are you doing it?" The commander asked us a sacramental question.

"Yes," we answered in unison. I could refuse to do the task and in that case someone else had to take it, but nobody has refused yet - it was a matter of honor and more. Either I would have to leave the Brotherhood or agree to the disgrace of returning to the novitiate as a Student. We looked at each other. Iris was deadly serious, but her eyes said something else. It was trusting and loving. I realized that

---

8   A few thousand years later, archaeologists will discover it in Crete and name it as the discs with A and B linear script.

having such a woman by my side I have nothing to fear. She will not let me down.

"So," said the Commander, "your mission began. There's not enough time, so we'll toss you by sea to Yuetshi at the mouth of the Zaporoska influx, then on horseback to Fort Ghori in the Ghulist Mountains and then straight on to Khorala. From there it's five hundred staja, maybe less, to Goa. They have quite good horses out there, so you'll be there in a month."

We spent the rest of the day preparing for the road. The worst part was that we could not count on any support from the Brotherhood that did not have any Branch there, and in case of what we were only relying on ourselves. We did not count on the local authorities if they could not deal with panic among the local population. We were traveling blind and unknown, but the Brotherhood was most interested in this task, because in the case of dealing with the matter, the rulers paid their obligations and kept the agreements. And we could also earn money on it and have security in old age for us and our relatives. We both realized that youth does not last forever and someday we will stop putting our necks in the noose.

If we survive this adventure...

II

We left Fort Ghori paying no attention. It was an old habit resulting from the absolute secrecy and discretion of the Brotherhood. In such cases, it only guaranteed us success. We headed south, where the gloomy and mighty wall of the Himelian Mountains rose. However, the route led safely through the valleys and only in one place - on the Me-lha pass it rose above the snow border, which we quickly crossed and on the seventh day the green and sunny plains of Vendhia appeared to our eyes.

After three days, we finally stood at the gates of Khorali. It was late afternoon. The rider in the front Iris let go to the ground of Arus, who barked happily a few times and then jumped off the horse with a great grip. A man ran out of the inn, shouting something to her, but when he looked at her he realized that he was dealing with a warrior woman bowed to her, inviting her inside. Iris moved ahead and though she wore only her travel outfit: a bright shirt and a leather tank and short pants that did not cover her bare slim legs and shoes with wide uppers half-calf, she moved with the grace of the queen. Arus ran after her, scenting the smells coming from the kitchen and dining room. I followed them.

The inn got busy, as always in such places. We came to some local rice-eaters with some additions that we were not able to identify. We ordered to give something to eat and soon we were brought a huge portion of roast ram poured with an incredibly spicy sauce with crumbs and fruit. We ate everything on a company with Arus, which fell under the table, and then we asked about free rooms. They were inexpensive. We could stay there for a few days. The room was simple: a table with four chairs, a huge bed and a dressing table for women. Iris clapped her hands.

"Excellently!" She cried. "At last I'll be able to get out and look like a woman!"

Meanwhile, the servants brought our luggage. There were not many of them. I gave them a few pieces of silver and I told them to leave. They went out bowing to us, like the owner of this inn.

When we finally got settled for good, Iris closed the door and jumped into a huge bed.

"Gods!" She cried. "I'm going to sleep and death to anyone who will disturb me!"

She kicked off her shoes and then stood up just to take off the rest of her clothes and she slipped naked under the thin sheet.

"What are you waiting for?" She asked. "Undress and come to me."

I did not give twice to ask and did the same. I embraced her waist and after a while we both slept with the sleep of a just man.

When I woke up, it was almost dark. I lifted my head and my gaze met Arus, who immediately ran to me and began to ask for go outside. I opened the door and the dog sneaked into the courtyard. I returned to the bed where Iris lay with her eyes open. I lay down next to her.

"Are you awake?" I asked and kissed on the cheek for good morning.

"Yes," she replied, "I've already slept enough."

"It will be clear soon," I said, "these are the tropics. And it'll be hot and stuffy. I don't like such climates. Man sweats like a pig."

"Me either, but..." She turned to me and wrapped her arms around my neck. "We took it our own will..."

"And I'm glad that we can finally stay together in one bed." I laughed taking her in my arms. Our lips met. We kissed first, gently stroking lips, and then harder and harder. Iris lay back and I kissed her face. After a while she also started kissing my neck and shoulders...

...

We slowly returned from the seventh heaven. The sun was already two fingers above the horizon.

"I'll bite you the next time," Iris said as she lay down next to me and exposed her body to a cool breeze coming from the window.

"I'll choke you," I retorted. We looked into the eyes with love.

We were lying for about half an hour resting and absorbing the view of our naked bodies.

"I'm almost grateful to this Kothij man," I said.

"For what?" Iris's almost black eyebrows went astray under the line of her dark-brown hair.

"If not him, I wouldn't be here with you," I said.

She smiled.

"We wouldn't be in seventh heaven now," she said, stretching herself. "Now we've to wash and eat something. Such love stocks increase appetite, I would eat an ox with horns and hooves... What kind of game plan do we have on this day?"

"We'll get over and go to ask for an audience with the Emperor. I hope he won't keep us in the antechamber and we'll find out what we need, and tomorrow we will go on the road."

"So, let's do it." Iris stood up and looked around for the bucket.

After two hours, washed, perfumed and full, we headed towards the imperial palace. At its gate, we were stopped by a guard who, however, let us in when we showed them a letter of recommendation. We were directed to the Grand Vizier who received us immediately. He was a powerful man with dark skin and a penetrating gaze and clashed clearly with our image of the local officials.

"Are you the envoys of the Grandmaster of the Brotherhood of Demon Destroyers?" He asked. We chimed in.

"Perfectly, so I'm asking you for your weapons," and in response to our stunned looks, he added, "this is the protocol and custom procedure here. We've had a few assaults here, so I hope you understand that."

"Of course," we answered in unison, placing our swords and daggers on the desk of the vizier.

"You'll get them back after the audience," he said, "and now here, to the private apartments of His Imperial Majesty. And please, call our Emperor , let he live forever, in that way. Is this the degree of discretion that suits you?"

"Yes, of course," I answered."

"Then please go inside." The Grand Vizier took a thick bundle of papyri from the desk and opened the door and entered the long but bright corridor.

And we follow him.

III

We walked for a few minutes and finally a kind of patio or even a cloister garth opened before us. There was a small fountain in the shape of a boy pouring water from a huge shell and an armchair, on which a richly clothed man sat with his back turned to us. We came closer to him.

"Your Imperial Majesty!" The Grand Vizier said in a low voice. "I brought the Grand Master's envoys.

The man rose and turned to us, and the Grand Vizier leaned forward in a deep bow. We also bowed.

"Welcome to Vendhia," said the emperor.

We were silent.

The Grand Vizier straightened.

"Sire!" He said," let me introduce Master Lestek from Vislania and his Apprentice Iris from Ianthe.

We inclined our heads.

I looked at the Emperor. He was a tall and thin man with a dark skin of Vendhians. He had raven-black hair cut short and a completely gray, short beard. Dark penetrating eyes and an eagle's nose completed the picture. And like most of his countrymen he smiled. I was not surprised that most of the inhabitants of this country liked him. He made a very nice impression. Unlike his vizier, who had the appearance of a good, competent and efficient clerk and was simply him.

"Please, sit down," the emperor pointed to the armchairs. He sat on a small stool. The Great Vizier spread his papyri. "So you have come to free us from this plague?"

"Yes, sire," I answered with a nod of my head, "may you live forever!" I added quickly remembering what the vizier had told us.

"You don't look like the heroes of our myths," he smiled slightly at Iris."

"Because we aren't them, until we do the task," I replied.

"And then?" The emperor bowed his head. "When you do it, will you change in them?"

"Your Majesty, may you live forever, it isn't us who become heroes." I replied. "It's our deeds that create them, but when nobody knows about them, we're nothing to the indifferent crowd...

"Good answer!" The emperor was pleased. "I like it, could we ever meet and discuss privately?"

"If it's your Imperial Majesty's wish, may you live forever," I said with a bow, "I'll gladly take part in this meeting."

The Grand Vizier cleared his throat.

"Gracious Lord." he said loudly, "I'm ready to report to our guests the latest reports."

Then refer to the Grand Vizier," the emperor graciously nodded.

We improved on the seats and the Grand Vizier took papyri in his hand and began to read. These were reports of officials, local notables, reports from military units and security services and, finally, requests made by ordinary citizens. There were about fifty of them and they concerned fifteen cases of mysterious deaths in the area of the province of Goa. The general scheme of events was as follows: people living alone in huts on the edge of the village were lost. In one case, a person died when went alone to the forest for brushes. The corpses were usually found in the morning, as if these people were murdered at night, again except in one case, when the corpse was found in the evening. All corpses looked the same: a change in the color of skin layers and raindrops indicated the use of very strong venom infecting the heart or brain of the victim. There were traces of snake bites on the body of the dead, except that the cobra's bite left two wounds located half to three-quarters apart from each other, whereas in the cases described it was one and a half to two inches!

"If it were a king cobra, it would have to be at least twenty feet long," said the Grand Vizier. "And as far as we know, they haven't been seen there!"

Unless it would be a sign of the Yig's action - snake people," the emperor chimed in. "But the Yigs were exterminated over a thousand years ago by Arjun during the Bharata wars for the succession of the Emperor Amitta III, infamous memory, because his name has been forgotten and is mentioned only in our chronicles..."

"For the pardon of your Imperial Majesty, may you live forever," I said, "can we know what he deserved for such a sad fate?"

"Of course," he said sadly, "it was he who led to the secession of Kosala in the west and Uttara Kuru in the east from the Vendhian Empire.

"Well," I thought, "I'm not surprised that the local rulers have such a traumatic memory after that..."

"I've a question for Your Grace," Iris asked the vizier, "can I?"

"Ask," said the yonder.

"What is known at all about Valussia, from which they, the Yigs are supposedly derived?"

"What are you getting at?" Grand Vizier's face was astonished.

"To determine what Valussia was at all," Iris said.

"'Skelos Scrolls' say that it was one of the kingdoms created after the Cataclysm." the emperor replied, "but little is known about it. We only know that the main deity was Yig - the Old Snake," he pronounced it like Jig, "and his people then spread out all over the South - from Iranistan to Cambudia."

"But Akira, the author of 'Kings Way', says Conan the Cimmerian killed one of them about thirty years ago in Nemedia," Iris replied.

"It's a fact, but this individual was brought to Nemedia from Stygia," the emperor replied, "you know, as it is with written sources, during the rewriting the individual authors of the editorials added something and Akira's dry relationship created a whole poem..."

"Personally, I'm of the opinion, Sire, may you live forever, we're dealing here with clever criminals and this matter should be entrusted to the police," the Grand Vizier once again said.

"Can you prove it, my Amitabh?" Asked the emperor with his inscrutable smirk.

"No, Sire, may you live forever," said the man with a bow, "because I've no direct evidence.

"Besides, Your Grace," I put in a conversation, "in such cases there should be a motive: revenge, profit or something else. These reports don't follow from these reports."

"And now I'll ask you directly: are you taking this case?"

"Your Imperial Majesty, may you live forever, we didn't go here for three weeks to turn back now," I said, "it wouldn't make sense. And besides, we're fulfilling the order of the Grand Master, and therefore..."

"I understand that you agree," said the emperor.

"Of course Your Majesty," we confirmed.

"So you know that an award awaits you for solving this puzzle?"

"Yes," I said, "as far as I know, a contract has been made between Your Majesty and the Grand Master."

"Yes, but something else is entitled to you personally."

"But what?" We asked in unison.

"That's what always in such cases," the emperor laughed cheerfully, "half of the kingdom and the hand of the imperial daughter in addition. I don't have any daughters anymore, but..." he paused for a moment, "I have the vacancy of the viceroy of the province of Goa, so..."

"Your Majesty is too kind," I replied. "Let me take care of the Walusians first, and then we'll think about the prizes. By the way, what happened to Goa's previous viceroy?"

"I ordered to string him," the emperor said in a calm voice, "because he escaped from the provinces as one of the first. I close my eyes to rackets at tributes, corruption and minor sins, but I don't tolerate cowardice. This is unworthy of a high official in my administration and a general of the Vendhian army!"

"Thank You, Your Majesty, for this honor, but I'm a warrior, and there I need a gifted administrator from what I see."

"And you, Iris from Ianthe?" Asked the emperor. "Would you like to be a Vendhian viceroy in Goa?"

Iris just smiled sweetly.

"My master is my husband and my Master," she said in a sweet voice, "and I'll only follow him. And if he doesn't want to be a king, I don't want too."

"Glorious loyalty!" Said the emperor, and turned to the vizier, "have you heard? Gods! - if my officials were like they... So what are you going to do?"

I thought about it for a moment.

"We'll go to Goa first," I said, "and then we'll look around. Of course, first of all in the villages where people were attacked. Then we'll find out where they can be, we'll set up an ambush and... we'll take the language, or at least try to get along with them.

"Maybe it's best to kill them right away?" The Grand Vizier looked at the emperor, as if expecting his master's acceptance.

"No, Your Majesty," I said, "you don't need to arrange for a bloody massacre. This is the last thing you need in this country. Either way, they are yours, sirs and you can't do it. In addition, Your Grace," I have turned to the Grand Vizier, "it must be taken into account that it isn't known who we really are dealing with."

"Well, Your Grace," Iris said, "tell me, have foreigners ever shown up in Goa?"

The Emperor and the Grand Vizier exchanged instant glances.

"Oh!" I thought, "She hit the sensitive point..."

"Yes, there appeared a group of about fifty Stygians, who brought there goods from Stygia and Punt," said the Grand Vizier. "But is there any connection between..."

"Did they come before these strange... hmmm... deaths or after?" Iris inquired further.

"As far as I know," the Grand Vizier began cautiously, "these accidents took place after they left the territory of Vendhia..."

"Oh, that's interesting," I said in turn, "and when and how they left your country?"

They sailed from Goa by ship and sailed westwards... It was a Stygian ship adapted for ocean and river navigation..."

"Has anyone followed this ship?" I asked.

"No," the vizier replied, "we didn't see such a need. Do... do you have any suspicions?"

"A suspicion!?" I looked at Iris, "we're sure that they are somehow involved in this matter. And I guess what they mean. If I'm right, we are all in serious danger. The Stygians are concerned that as many people as possible leave Goa!"

"But why for Indra and Varuna!?" The emperor cried.

"Because Queen Gedrena wants to match what is in this province and is related to Valussia, and may be a weapon of unimaginable power of destruction. So we have to hurry up, because the every moment is important..."

IV

The next day we were going to Goa along the sea coast. Our guide was Adjai, a centurion of the Vendhian army, who rode ahead and we followed him. Adjai, even though he was a low grade officer, he was probably the trusted one of Grand Vizier who sent him with us not only as a guide but also as his eyes and ears. He was a small Vendhian with unobtrusive appearance and lost in the crowd in a flash. The perfect agent for secret tasks.

We traveled under his guidance, although in truth it was difficult to lose the way, because every now and then we encountered groups of Goa refugees moving along the coast to the north. There was sadness and fear in the eyes of the refugees. Adjai tried to talk to them, but he did not find out too much. Everyone at the sound of the word 'snake' fell silent and looked around fearfully. That something, whatever it was, had to scare them seriously. And the most interesting we have learned from children who have little worried about the fear of adults and behaved as usual - they played joyfully and play a prank.

Adjai walked between them and began to talk to them. At first they were slightly frightened, but after a while they began to look at us and after a moment they were laughing at us. Adjai talked to them in Vendhia, so we did not understand much, but a moment later he translated the content of what they were talking about and it came out that some strangers were seen around the villages of Goa - men and women who looked like 'snakes'. Asked what their unusual looks were, they told us that their skin was unusually spotted like a snake's. Hence they were called their snake-men. When asked what the people were doing, the children answered in a chorus that there was nothing wrong with them - they stood behind the trees and watched the people from the village. And how many of them were there? - two or four were seen, there was no agreement about this. They had black eyes and black hair. They were almost completely naked. They moved silently and said nothing, only smiling.

It was interesting. Smiling murderers. We have already met such ones on our way, but why the Yigs would have to smile, we did not know that.

"As you can see there is no connection between them and these mysterious deaths.." Adjai summed up the conversation.

"For that, there is a relationship between them and Stygians." I replied.

"Oh! But what can Stygians have to us, who don't even border us and have never bordered?" Asked Adjai.

"The Stygians used the old legend of the Yigs to scare the people of Goa," I said, "and as you can see, they have succeeded."

"So what are you going to do, Master?" Asked Adjai.

"Take one of them and just find out who they are and what they want from people," it is obvious. "And of course, find out if they are as dangerous as people saying about them..."

"What about the Stygians?" asked Adjai, "What will they do now?"

"Stygians are pursuing some kind of plan whose purpose we don't know. I suspect they'll be looking for something in this province. Are you a native Goan, centurion?"

"Yes, Master," replied the officer, "I was born in a village near Goa, I even have my shirttail there."

"It's great!" I was glad, "You'll be able to visit them and we'll look around discreetly."

We drove on, stopping for the night on the beaches and sleeping under the open sky. After four days we managed to reach the border of the province. It was a beautiful country where life was concentrated in a coastal belt about twenty miles wide, beyond which the evergreen and rainforest forest was dozing. The city of Goa was located on the coastal plain and the most magnificent building was the viceroy's residence. Houses in the city were built in the Atlantean fashion of black, white and red bricks. They were wide, comfortable and gave the impression of being cozy.

"How do you like it here?" I asked Iris.

"Sympathetic," she replied, "it's nice here."

"You think so?" I asked.

"Yes," she said, "all year warm, the sea is close... Are we going to get old here?"

"You read in my mind," I raised my eyebrows.

"Honey, I can see it," she laughed, "you have such a dreaming sight..."

The head of the local police took us and immediately went to the point. Again, there were two deaths that interested us - an elderly woman died in a palm grove, where she collected brushwood and dried organic for firewood and a young boy was murdered almost at the entrance to the house where he lived with his parents and younger brother. In the latter case, there were witnesses who saw a figure in a dark clothing and mask on the face escaping from the crime scene. Despite the immediate pursuit, the murderer managed to escape. Both of these events took place in a village at south of the city of Goa, about half a day's drive.

I asked the warden for a map of the area with places of corpse finding. The headman put a papyrus sheet in front of us with colored points on it. I looked at it and something dawned on me.

"Look, please," I said, "it looks as if these murders were concentrated around this place." I pointed to the map where the geometric center of the figure designated by these points was. What's up there..."

Adjai and the police chief exchanged glances.

"Cursed Malabona," Adjai said quietly.

"What is this?" We asked in unison.

"A complex of ruins that everything that is alive bypasses." Said the head of the police. "They say it is ten thousand years old and the one who enters - is killed. Nobody walks right now, people are even afraid of that name..."

I looked at Iris, who nodded.

"It seems to Master that we have what Gedrena is looking for," she said in a tone of absolute certainty.

"What can she look for there?" Adjai and the police chief asked with astonishment.

"Weapons. A weapon so horrible that kills invisibly, but its power is unparalleled." I said in a serious tone. "We can't allow her to get into the hands of the Stygians or anyone else. Everyone who comes in contact with it will suffer death in terrible torments." I finished, because I did not see the point in describing their radiation sickness. I was afraid of one more thing that they could be some pathogens that caused the Black Plague, and many indicated that it could have been them. Therefore, it was necessary to act quickly before the plague spread by Stygians spread to the whole world. So we left there immediately.

The passed villages had a sad and deplorable view. Solitary and fear was everywhere. We rode through them trotting the horses from time to time. We still had a few miles to the ruins of Malabona, when night fell and we were forced to spend the night in one of these ghostly villages.

"It's even better," I thought, "we'll have a great opportunity to lay for these snakes..."

We took saddle off the horses and we started to prepare the accommodation. We chose a hut the nearest to the forest, that is, the one whose residents were most threatened by the potential attack from the Yigs. The sun has gone over the ocean and darkness has fallen, which was illuminated by a small fire lit to cook some food.

We ate supper in silence, listening to the sounds of the forest, but we did not hear anything suspicious.

After dinner, we decided to go to bed. We were tired of all-day riding and we wanted to rest. Iris curled up on her bed. My eyes also began to close. I agreed with Adjai that I will be watching until midnight and he will be there until morning. So I sat by the fire, tossing dried branches and dry masses of manure from time to time and listening to the sounds of the rain forest. There was a drizzle outside, which from time to time struck the reed walls and roof of the house with a stronger wave. Around midnight, the moon appeared, greeted with the screams of animals, and the sky cleared. I was about to wake Adjai when Arus, who was lying by the fire, raised his head and growled.

Iris woke up and listened too, and finally she lifted two fingers up and circled them. So there were two of them and they came from two sides circling the hut.

"Are we going?" I asked, gesturing.

She smiled and nodded. I got up and she too. We escaped quietly from the cottage, under reed walls, crawled silently to the nearest trees and sank into the forest. We have not noticed anyone yet.

A few minutes passed. The moon came out of the clouds and its greenish glow fell to the bottom of a rare forest in this place. I watched the nearest surroundings of the cottage, and the village that looked ghostly in the moonlight. A few steps up from me, a fragment of the palm tree trunk moved and turned into a small man who began to sneak in its direction. I did not wait for anything, carefully stepping bare feet across the damp earth, stood behind him and whistled softly. He turned quickly and then I punched him with a huge blow to the jaw, and then I jumped into him without allowing him to fall to the ground. A moment later, I heard a quiet "uh!" And the sound of the falling body. I threw a man on my shoulder like a pig and went towards the cottage. A moment later, I saw Iris carrying her prisoner similarly.

We entered the hut. Adjai was not asleep anymore and with arms in hand he looked around with anxiety. Arus jumped out to meet us.

"Light the torch," I said calmly but firmly, "and let's see what we have here."

Adjai filled the command without a word, lighting the torch and the olive lamp. Iris calmly bound her victim. After a while, I did the same with my prisoner. We planted them so that their faces could be seen in full light.

V

Adjai whistled softly. Iris said only something that sounded like 'oh-oh-oh-oh?'. Two young, charming faces of people with a beauty slightly different from the Vendhians looked at us. But I did not mean beauty. I leaned over and lifted the upper lip to the man revealing a beautiful suit of teeth. They looked normal and the upper three almost did not protrude beyond the others. Lower the same. They could not leave such traces as on the bodies of those killed. I took one look at the palate. There were no poison bags. Normal mucous membranes. No discoloration - nothing.

"And she?" I asked Iris.

"Same - nothing..." she answered, looking closely at the woman's lips.

"So it's not them, certainly," I said.

Adjai looked at them for a moment.

"Who is it then?"

"Murderer," I said, "merciless, sly and cunning. You have to revive them."

I patted their cheeks. After one more attempt they opened their eyes. Their irises were dark, almost black like pupils. They moved and their pretty faces twisted in terror.

"Can you talk with them, Centurion?" I asked. "I'd like to ask them a few questions."

"I'll try Master," he said, he has asked them in Vendhian.

The snake people answered something and Adjai raised his eyebrows in surprise.

"No, it's unbelievable!"He said after a long exchange of words.

"What's unbelievable?" We asked a harmonious chorus.

"They speak a very old dialect of the Vendhian language," Adjai replied incredulously astounded. "It was used here some two thousand years ago, and maybe three... In fact, it is the Vendhian language, from the Acheron hegemony..."

"It's interesting," I thought, "since when the centurions of the Vendhian army are linguists and still with knowledge of ancient dialects from the times of the mythical Empire of Evil...?"

I gave Iris a short look. It astonished her too. She nodded. We understood each other without a word.

"Ask them what they're doing here?" I asked the officer.

Once again, there was a short conversation, as a result of which Adjai declared that they were looking for missing members of their tribe who were captured by some sea humans. But their description did not match the Goans, and it matched the appearance of the Stygians.

"Okay, let's solve them and let go," I said to Iris and Adjai and, seeing their astonished eyes, added, "tell them to go to their own and keep away from the coast and the ruins of this Malabona."

"I don"t understand," Adjai was a picture of amazement.

"Well, you see that it isn't them!" I said with emphasis. "They're painted like snakes, but it's their protective painting in the jungle and protection against mosquitoes." I pulled my hand over the man's shoulder and a trace of paint remained on the skin. "They don't have any scales! Besides, one has to reckon with the fact that a massacre and unnecessary bloodshed may occur."

Adjai cut the two bonds. We helped them to get up. They were still a bit dumbfounded and shook their legs a bit. Adjai clarified them what to do. We looked closely at them - they were really beautiful with Nature's children, and their bodies were harmoniously but strongly built. They stood for a moment embracing each other, then left the hut and melted into the forest thicket. We returned to the cottage and spent the rest of the night sleeping.

In the morning after a modest meal, we went on the road. We drove around looking around and in two hours stood at the ruins of Malabona. We were expecting something more monumental, meanwhile we were blocked by a pile of huge basalt boulders with monstrous dimensions. The whole thing was like a pyramid, which a giant kicked with a leg, so that it crumbled like a sand woman. A strange thing, because the individual stones and the ground on which they stood was smooth and glazed. The sand was greenish, and some of the stone solids were covered with bubbles, as if their surface was boiling, and then it was cut off by sudden frost. The lush vegetation near the plate of vitrified sand was wasted, and no moss matted with the stones. The ruins were black and they were hot from them because the sun was heating up that black debris...

We toured this pile of black stones and realized that the building had the original shape of a pyramid with a pentagon base, whose side measured at least six hundred feet, and the height of the pyramid had to be the same. It was unusual because all the pyramids I know in Stygia and Shemit were based on squares. The area of the vitrified sand had a roughly elliptical shape, one and a half to two and a half feet, and the ruins were more or less in the middle. I jumped off my horse and examined the thickness of the glass cover - it was about half a foot. "There must have been an incredibly big bonfire here," I thought, "or that was the weapon that Gedrena wanted to have..."

I said it out loud. I saw disbelief on the officer's face.

"Now, do you understand, centurion, the purpose and sense of the existence of our Brotherhood?" I asked.

He nodded.

"Any war using such terrible means of destruction will be synonymous with the destruction of humanity and all life on Earth." I said emphatically. "Look, this pyramid was destroyed by one single missile that exploded over it and melted sand and stones with its heat! But the heat and the breeze is just a fraction of its energy that killed everything that lives around a mile away."

"But..." Adjai began.

"But we don't know what is hidden in the ruins, which although seem dead, it kill." I said. "I suspect that this pyramid is the source, among other things, of the recurring scourges of the Black Plague that haunts your country. The missle that exploded eight thousand years ago did not destroy it, and quite the opposite - it made it even more virulent."

"How do you know that?" On the face of the centurion the most genuine amazement was presented. "After all, only our priests and some high officials at the imperial court know about it?"

"The Brotherhood examines the appearance of the spread of these scourges around the world." I replied. "And in a dozen or so cases the source of their origin was in Vendhia and in the province of Goa. We stand before him.

Adjai tried to understand this message for a few moments.

"You're right, Master," he said finally. "You have to destroy it once and for all, but how?"

"The effects of the explosion of this missile called brahmashiras are extremely long-term," I replied, "and our calculations show that it will last for thousands of years. There are no ways to neutralize them. It's enough, therefore, that no one should enter the site of this ruin, so as not to spread this second plague."

"What do we have to do then?" The centurion asked for the second time.

I was amazed at his inquisitiveness. It did not fit to this grade officer. I took a chance.

"First of all, Your Majesty should be repelled by those who want to match what is hidden in these ruins and want to turn it against all people on Earth." I said emphatically accenting the words 'Your Majesty'. "And I think that this is a worthy job for the heir to the Vendhian throne!"

"I looked at his face. It got gray.

"How do you know?" He asked in amazement. "How did you guess who I am?"

"You ask too many wise questions and show concern for your people," I replied, "and these are the glorious qualities of the future ruler of such a great country as Vendhia."

"We have guests," Iris said, listening intently for some time. She was right - from behind the trees we heard sounds of squeaking of wheels, yells of coachmen and other sounds of coming people and animals. And after a while, Stygians appeared on our view.

VI

They spilled out of the forest and unexpectedly saw us. They stood amazed. I raised my hand.

"Stop! Stop!" I shouted.

"Why is that?" Their commander shouted back.

"There is an invisible death!" I shouted. The answer was an arrow shot from one of the Stygians. I took the crossbow off my shoulder and loaded it. Two further, but equally futile, flew in our direction.

"Your Majesty, we shouldn't risk," I said to the Archduke, "we must retreat."

Before I finished, Iris parried her sword with two more arrows flying on us. I shot towards the first archer, who grabbed the breast and loaded the crossbow again, and then sent an arrow towards the commander.

The Archduke straightened in the saddle and picked up a small whistle, then whistled a few times. At this signal the forest behind us moved and two hundred armed soldiers stood. Their commander approached Adjai's horse and gave honor by the sword.

"What will Your Majesty command?" He asked.

"Chase them back where they came from," the Archduke ordered peacefully. "And of course take captives. And of course, don't let them go to ruin!"

The Vendhians rushed to them and after a while they chased them back towards the sea. We followed them and to our amazement, we saw a ship that rocked on the waves perhaps less than a quarter staja from the shore. It was a large unit with a flat bottom, adapted for landing people and horses on the banks. Thanks to them, several battles were won, in which the decisive turned out to be a seaside attack of military units, which were attacked on hostile banks and at the right moment a sudden and unexpected attack tipped the scales of victory.

The Stygians were allowed to swim to their ship and sail to the open ocean. Within a few miles I noticed the formation of the merchant ships, which watched the situation ready to sink an unwelcome guest at any moment. Meanwhile, Vendhian soldiers were preparing to retreat and transport prisoners who were to be questioned in Goa. In addition to the wounded Stygian archer, three more marauders were caught.

"Well, it would be end Your Majesty," I said, "people can go home, and as for Malabona, I think it would be good to raise a high wall near it and not let anyone in."

"A good idea," answered the Archduke, "I'll give the orders right away and the new Goa's Viceroy will do the job. It is a pity, because I see you in this position, but as you are foreigners, I can not order to you..."

"Thank you, prince, but it's a great honor and responsibility for us..." I replied. "Besides, we also have our commitments. But I've a thought that I present to you for consideration of Your Majesty."

"I'm listening," he nodded encouragingly.

"We like Goa and your country," I said, "would you mind if a Brotherhood branch was established in Goa? The benefit of this is measurable, because you would always have good advice for your services and security from the various misfortunes of this kind in your country. And what is your Archduke's wish for?"

"The thing is worth thinking about." he said.

We went all the way back to Goa in silence.

We stayed for a night in Goa - the Archduke put us in one of the wings of the Goa's viceroy palace, where there were chambers and - most importantly - pools with hot and cold water, which especially pleased us. But the most important thing was the bathroom.

"Well, I'll finally feel like human!" Iris cried at the sight of a huge bathing pool with hot water and fragrant soaps and other cosmetics, which lay on a small, richly inlaid table. After a while, she threw off her clothes and went naked into the warm water. She purred like a cat and stretched out. As I knew her, she could splash in the water for a very long time, like a little girl.

"What are you waiting for?!" She cried. "Come on!"

And she began pouring in the water different fragrant ingredients, whose pleasant smells spread all around. I did not let to beg me for long and quickly sat down in front of her in the water. For a few minutes we were lying in this warm, fragrant water, not thinking about anything, and then we began to wash ourselves to get rid of the dirt and dust of the roads. Iris turned her back on me and handed me the sponge.

"Wash my back." She asked.

I did what she wanted by gently rubbing her back with a sponge. Then she washed my back. I kissed her.

"You're scratching," she said. "Sit down, I'll shave you."

She reached into the table and sat on my thighs with a razor in hand. I felt the warm touch of her hot body and I felt very hot for a moment. Meanwhile, Iris soaped my cheeks and gently - almost caressingly began to gather a few days beard.

"Don't be afraid," she smiled, "I won't be depilating you."

And she laid the razor on the table and then embraced my neck...

... We sat next to each other embracing and still trembling with effort.

"It's sooooo nice..." she said dreamily in her voice

"...but a bit tiring." I finished.

We burst out laughing and then we hugged each other again.

We looked through the wide open window. A Little Guide fluttered in the dark sky. I put my arm around Iris and she clung to me sideways. The warm touch of her body gave me strength and self-confidence. She sighed fondly and I kissed her on the lips. We were happy…

VII

Our stay in Goa lasted a week. During this time we participated in interrogation of prisoners, but we did not find much information. It was confirmed only that Gedrena sent merchant journeys in all directions, which in fact were only camouflage to places of reliance on ancient weapons of mass destruction or devices that were carriers for these weapons. The goal was obvious - power over the world or at least a significant part of it. On the seventh day, we were surprised. It turned out that the prisoners died in their cells. The reason was the bite of the king cobra...

"Shucks," said the governor, "that would mean I have a spy in my close surroundings!"

"Unfortunately, Your Majesty has right," I replied, "moreover, we should be worried about the life of Your Majesty."

"Maybe yes, maybe not," said Adjai, "don't forget that you are also involved in it..."

"Yes, but who cares about our death?" I asked. "Rather nobody or almost nobody, but the death of the heir to the throne may cause a serious crisis or even a civil war. I advise you to increase Your Majesty's security measures."

"Yes, you're right," he answered and ordered the doubled guards.

Anyway, we also stopped feeling safe. Admittedly, we were not someone great, but the knowledge we had was very dangerous to someone, as we saw the next night. We lay hugging each other. Iris slept sweetly at my side, and I could not sleep. I felt a thickening atmosphere in Goa and waited for something that could happen. The death of the Stygian people made me watch out. It was obvious that there was a Stygian agent in Goa and it was only a matter of time before another attack aimed at us or the Archduke.

It was already past midnight and I felt the dream begin to dawn when I heard a murmur and a dull thud at the same time as if some vessel had been broken. It was dark, but I burned the fire and lit the oil lamp. Then the second and third one - it got bright. Slowly walking quietly on the cool floor with bare feet I went in the direction from where I heard the suspicious sound. Suddenly, I heard a soft hiss. I stood and it probably saved my life. A gorgeous cobra was crawling around my legs. Immediately afterwards, the second and third. There were about a dozen of them. They crawled out of a broken pitcher, which was wrapped in a piece of matter. If I was sleeping, I would not hear the sound of its break... I put the lamp on the floor to have it fully lit.

I slowly sat down and then made a quick jump back. The snake hit the place where I stood by a fraction of a second. I got to the sword and got rid of it from the sheath. I decapitated the nearest cobra with a quick cut. A moment later, I heard the patter of legs and the swish of a sword behind me. Iris stood next to me naked with a katana in her hand. We quickly dealt with the other snakes.

"We'll have to clean up here," she murmured, hiding her sword.

"I wonder what bastard threw it to us." I was thinking about picking up corpses from the floor on a piece of a porter, which I unceremoniously cut off and made a makeshift sack out of it.

"Whoever he is, he likes a solid job," Iris said, "and he knows his stuff. He's a professional assassin."

"I'm going to bet that the next will be scorpions." I murmured.

"Anyway, we'll have to get out of here," she said, "someone is out the window," she added quietly that I barely heard her.

"Yes, honey, of course," I said loud, "we'll leave tomorrow, but we have to do something."

We jumped out of the window onto the window terrace. Iris was the first to reach the figure huddled under the window and spread it on the floor with one blow. I brought a lamp in which light appeared the cute face of one of the servants who served us.

"Oh, yes," Iris looked at her, "she is just an executive, but the real agent is somewhere else."

"How do you know?" I asked.

"It's obvious," she murmured. "She just dropped a pitcher of snakes into our mansion for someone's order. I can't imagine that she had time to run through the forest and catch the cobras."

"Well, you're right." I admitted. "In that case, she might not even know what's up there..."

"Okay," said Iris, "give her here, I'll talk with her."

I picked up the unconscious girl and brought her to our chambers. I put her in a chair and Iris patted her cheek. The girl sighed and opened her eyes. A grimace of terror appeared on her beautiful face.

"And what now?" Iris asked, putting on shirt and pants, " what's your name?"

"A... a... a..." Her eyes were getting more and more round with horror.

"What!!!???" I cried at her, "are you talking or should we help you?"

"Athirai," she said quickly, "my name is Athirai!"

"What were you doing here?" Iris said in a soft tone, but it sounded ominous.

The answer was silence. Athirai dropped her head.

"Speak, because I'll do with you what my grandfather did fifty years ago," I growled, taking my horsewhip, "so?"

Athirai looked at me with horror in her eyes.

"I'll tell you everything," she said quickly.

"We're listening." Iris's voice was warm and sweet, but there was a murder in her eyes.

From the story of Athirai, it appeared that yesterday afternoon commander Raghaul had called her and gave her the jug with the command to throw it through the window into our quarters. He told her that it was a joke and she believed him. She dropped the pitcher, which crashed, but when she saw what it contained - because as the curious woman looked inward - she petrified with fear, because she understood that it was about an attempt on our lives. Not knowing what to do, she crouched outside the window and waited for further developments. We caught her there. After throwing in the pitcher, she was supposed to meet with Raghaul in the palace park.

"Who is this whole Raghaul?" I asked, because a nasty suspicion dawned in me."

"It's the commander of the guard of His Imperial Majesty, which is in the service of the Archduke..." she did not finish, because we exchanged instant glances with Iris. We understood it quickly.

"Do you want to live?" I asked the terrified girl. She nodded. "Well, run away from here and this as far as possible. Do you have someone here?"

"Parents," she whimpered, "and my sister."

"Do you have any friend?" Iris asked.

She nodded.

"Then go to her and ask her to hide you. You can't stay here, you are in danger of death here at any moment," I said. "Come on!"

"But Raghaul?" She asked, sobbing.

"For Swarog and Sviatovid!" I shouted. "You don't understand yet that Raghaul wants to murder you? You know too much!"

"Oh, gods!" She moaned in horror and ran away like hell. For a moment I listened to the clatter of her sandals. I dressed quickly and took my weapon with me.

"What now?" Iris asked. "Are we going to catch Raghaul?"

"No," I said, "we're going to the Archduke. It's a military putsch and maybe even a coup d'état!"

We ran through chambers and corridors to the Archduke's chambers. It took half an hour for us to get to our feet from the moment Athirai escaped, during which time everything could have happened. The strange thing was that we did not meet anyone in the corridors, no servants, no duty attendants. Even castle guards. We came to the part of the palace where the Archduke was sleeping. There was also empty, only at the door there were two guardsmen.

"Open it!" I shouted. "Archduke in danger!"

They both took out their swords from their scabbards and without a word rushed at us. I understood that they also participated in the attack.

I did not wait for further intellectual conversations and discussions. With a powerful cut, I laid out the nearest guardsman and then cut the second one in the half-turn. They both tumbled like sheaves of grain. I opened the door and ran into the room. It was dark, but I could see the dark flesh of snakes on the floor of light marble. We have disposed of them with quick cuts. I ran to the bed. Archduke Adjai lay on his back. He was unconscious. It could not be underestimated - they had to give him something in food or drink. It took a few minutes to get him unconscious. He sat on the bed and looked around with unconscious eyes.

"Your Highness!" I cried. "We must escape."

"What happened?" He asked, rolling his eyes around. "What are these snakes?"

"This is a coup d'état!" I shouted. "You're in danger!"

"Gods!" Archduke immediately came to his senses. "My father!"

VIII

"What about His Imperial Majesty, let he live forever?" Iris asked.

"I don't know." The Archduke was having difficulty getting up, the drug he was given was still working. "Help me to get up."

We supported him from two sides and immediately moved to the corridor.

"They also betrayed," he mumbled when he saw the dead sentries. It was a statement.

"Unfortunately, yes." I replied. "From what we've learned, this's the fault of commander Raghaul."

And we told him about the events that took place in our room that night. He listened with a gloomy expression.

Finally, we descended from the first floor and headed for the exit to the palace courtyard.

"Someone is lying there," Iris whispered as she saw the stretched body on the stone flagstones. We came closer. In the moonlight, we saw a young woman lying down. There was a long dagger between her breasts. Blood tinted her bright robe in a dark color. I put my fingers to her neck. I did not feel pulse, her body was already cold.

"It's Minna," the Archduke whispered. "And she betrayed me too?" He sighed heavily. I felt sorry for him.

"There is also the second one." I heard the voice of Iris.

I looked in her direction. She leaned over the other woman lying down. Athirai lay on her stomach, face to the floor. Death reached her at the moment of escape. Someone gave her a merciless blow with a sword to the head and shoulder.

"They haven't betrayed you, Your Highness," I said. "They were only passive tools in the hands of a very clever and dangerous murderer. And it was you, Lord, you were his goal. And we too."

He sighed again.

"Please, answer me, Your Highness," I asked, "if in the event of your death, someone becomes a contender for the throne?"

"I don't have a younger sibling, except Princess Lilli, but she is already married to the heir to the throne of Hyrkania and..." he paused and fell silent as if struck by some sudden thought.

"And...?" I asked. "And what's next???"

"For all gods, Raghaul..." he said thoughtfully, "no, that's impossible... Raghul?"

"Who is this Raghaul?" We asked.

"This is the Grand Vizier Amitabha Arataśvimara's confidant," said the Archduke slowly. "For Varuna, in the event of my death, he becomes the ruler of Vendhia for the period of interregnum, that is, it covers the full power! As a regent he can stay on the throne and de facto and de jure be Emperor of Vendhia! Of course, after the opposition was liquidated."

"I admit," I said, "that makes sense, but I don't understand why he wanted to kill us? We didn't interfere with his plans, he could have killed you, Your Grace, and made us scapegoats..."

"He could, but in that case it means that it isn't just about me and the throne," he said calmly, "it's also about high treason! Working for another country!"

"So the Grand Vizier betrayed Vendhia and sold himself to Stygia," I said.

"It looks like..." said Adjai. "We're going!"

We started the run, because every minute of loss meant the advantage of the conspirators. There was no guard in the palace, but all entrances were guarded by Raghaul's guards. We were in a trap.

"He cleverly figured it out," I said with admiration, "you can't refuse him the ingenuity. I don't understand what he is waiting for, he should start assaulting."

We stood on the top floor and watched what was going on in the courtyard. After a moment, we understood - service was being carried out and murdered by blows of swords, axes and ice axes in the head. Quick and precise. Men and women, young and old, without exception. Raghaul did not want to have any living witness.

"Do you have a B plan?" Iris asked calmly.

"I have," I said, "we'll kill them as much as we can."

She smiled happily despite the nasty situation.

"Well, it's really a genius plan," she said with a laugh, "at least we'll die with a weapon in hand."

"Pst, pst!" We heard behind us. We turned around with the katanas in our hands.

An elderly man was standing behind us and gesturing for silence, then he motioned for us to follow him.

Not seeing the way out of the situation, we relied on him and after a moment we followed the old servant.

And it was about time. On the ground floor of the palace, there were footsteps and voices of rebel guardsmen. The old servant led us through some enfilm of chambers and rooms, towards the eastern wing of the palace, where there was a hole in the shaft, masked with a round stone. The old man pressed a siphon and the stone moved silently away revealing the stairs going down. We moved them blindfolded. After defeating two hundred winding stairs, we found ourselves in a tunnel with which we went in an unknown direction. I counted the steps, but after the third hundred I stopped counting. Our guide ran calmly and confidently. Finally, something hit and a moonlight shone in front of us. We quickly left the tunnel.

"Where are we?" I asked.

The Archduke looked around quickly.

"In West Suburb on the outskirts of Goa," he replied. "How did it happen that I didn't know about this passage?"

"Excuse me, Lord," the old man said in a clear, bright woman's voice, "but the secret of this passage is known only to trusted people protecting His Imperial Majesty and you."

The old man straightened up at once and ripped off the gray wig, beard and mustache that covered the beautiful face of a young woman, almost a girl. She could have been about five years younger than Iris.

"Who you are?" Asked Archduke in astonished voice. "How did it happen..."

"There is no time for explanations now," she said firmly, "I'm an agent of your protection and my name is Aisha.

"Where's the rest?" Asked Archduke.

"They secured the palace and hid," Aisha replied calmly. "It was my job to take you, Your Majesty, from the palace to a safe place."

"Do you have any horses nearby?" Adjai asked.

"Yes," she said, "they are waiting for Your Majesty and for you too." She smiled for the first time. She was really beautiful.

We followed Aisha. She led us to a suburban detour where we found horses ready for the road.

"What are you going to do, Your Highness?" I asked. "I think that it would be wisest to withdraw to…"

"No!" The archduke exclaimed. "It can't be. I've to hit them right now. Two staja from here is the Seventy-fifth Horse Division of the Vendhian army. We'll take them and hit the palace while the conspirators take to plundering and drinking. It's easier to break them and bounce the palace. And then we will catch Raghaul and bring him to justice."

We got on horses and we went with walk.

"You're right, Your Highness," I said, "but I'm afraid that Raghaul is only a pawn in a game played by someone more powerful than him!"

"Yes, of course," said the Archduke calmly, "we'll get to Grand Vizier before he can take over the full power after murdering my father. And I give you a word that he will feel that he is dying…"

"There is another aspect of this matter," Aisha said, "namely, that Stygians are involved in this conspiracy. From the information we have, the Grand Vizier has repeatedly contacted the Stygian ambassador in Khorala and we're almost sure that they're behind the attack."

"But for what purpose?" He asked.

"That's what we don't know," Aisha said in a worried tone, "we assumed that there would only be a coup d'état and that the Arataśvimar clan would take over the throne, but there is more to it."

"We'll answer that," I said. "Vendhia is to become the base of aggression for all countries outside of the Himelian Mountains. By the way, all the artifacts found here after the Empire of Atlantis will be taken over and used in wars against the whole world, because Queen Gedrena has enormous ambitions and great appetites."

"Well," said Aisha, "now I understand why the Stygians were so interested in our province, they wanted Malabona… And I know why you are interested in it. You'll help us and we'll help you - agree?"

"We have no choice," I replied. "Of course, it all depends on the governor or rather the regent, assuming that His Imperial Majesty was murdered by the conspirators."

"That's why you must first take Goa from the hands of the conspirators, and then we go to Khorala," said the Archduke.

And he chased his horse by a trot. And we rushed after him.

IX

Our fears did not check out and the 75th Horse Division was not involved in a plot. Its commander handed over the command to the Archduke and by midday we all moved to Goa. We drove into the almost deserted city and headed to the viceroy's palace. Guard posts that were on the tombs were disarmed and replaced by soldiers.

It was easier to get the castle than I expected, because the guards at the sight of Adjai laid down their arms, and the agents in the castle captured and arrested Raghaul and his supporters. Goa was acquired virtually without bloodshed. Regent pushed the deliberate to Khorala to learn something about the emperor's fate and take further steps. The envoys returned with the news that the Grand Vizier had made himself Emperor of Vendhia and that some of the court and officials had gone over to the usurping party.

Guests came to Goa together with them.

In the courtyard we heard the hoofbeat of horse hooves and five riders rode upon it. I looked and saw five students in navy blue short tunics who jumped down from the horses and looked around curiously. Two boys and three girls, among them I saw Tia from Agra, who saw me and waved her hand friendly. I called them and after a while the five of them entered our chambers.

"Greetings to the Master," they cried merrily and leaned forward in courteous bows.

"What brings you here?" I asked a bit surprised.

"We have been put at your disposal," Tia replied. "My uncle sent us to you. We have a practice here.

"Well, I forgot that the students have to go through the two-month practice four times before becoming Apprentices."

"We already know you," I smiled at her, "and the rest?"

I looked at the pair on the left, which looked like siblings.

"I'm Avan, and this is my Beryl," Avan introduced them. They both had curly auburn hair and a fair complexion. "We're from Brythunia."

"And you?" I asked the second pair.

"I'm Marhita and this is Sirdar," a fair-haired girl introduced herself. "I'm almost your countryman, Master, because I came from the Duchy of Tories from the Kingdoms of Borderlands, but Sirdar comes from the Himelian Mountains. We've met in Aghrapur, we've come to love and... we're here."

"You're tired of the road?" I said.

"Oh, no, we slept and we're ready for action," Beryl said, "and the accommodation was pointed out here."

All five of them in their tunics, with swords slung over their backs and soft riding boots, looked militantly. In addition, the girls had arched bows and quivers at the saddles, and the boys had short but dangerous javelins.

"Well, let's see what you can do," I said and walked out with them into the courtyard where Iris was already waiting, with whom they also greeted briefly but cordially.

"So who starts?" I asked.

"Maybe me?" Avan said shyly.

He reached for the saddlebag and took out a few daggers, which he took for the blades. Meanwhile, Beryl stood on her back against the wooden wall. Avan walked away from her twenty paces.

"Attention!" He called and waved his hand.

Dagger sizzled and stuck an inch from Beryl's left ear, which did not move, she must have steel nerves or maybe she knew the possibilities of her beloved brother... Then the other stuck in an inch from her other ear. Then the third and fourth struck her by her shoulders, and the fifth and sixth dug into the wood at the height of her hips.

Our hands gave them applause.

"It was easy," he said, tearing the daggers from the wall.

Beryl stood up against the wall again and Avan began throwing two daggers in both hands and at the same time. And again they dug precisely in almost the same places.

Applause rang out, which sounded louder, because several of the service and urban crowds joined the spectacle.

"Who is next?" I asked.

"That's me," Sirdar said, taking out his sword. His girlfriend threw a bundle of rope into the air. What happened next was very fast. Serdar was cutting the withers with a few quick blows from the wrist and after a few seconds the rope fell to the ground.

"What in this extraordinary?" I asked.

"Pick it up, Master," Sirdar said.

I went over and picked up. To my surprise, the rope was cut into eight parts perfectly even and clean... I showed it to the gathered - there was applause.

"Perfectly," I praised him, "and I thought I knew almost everything about having a katana...

He smiled, pleased with the praise.

"Master," he said with a bow, "don't forget that the world is moving forward.

"Where you learned this?" I asked.

"In my homeland, in mountain," he replied, "before I joined the Brotherhood. Now look!"

He reached for the war ax strapped to the saddle, swung powerfully, and let it drop. The flying missile hit one of the shields about half a step from us and hit it with the blade cutting it into two perfectly equal halves. If a man stood there, he would be dead. There was a loud applause, and Sirdar bowed low to the audience.

"Now, ladies of your's hearts," I said cheerfully, "what will you surprise us with?"

Both girls smiled and winked. As expected, from soft leather cases, they pulled out arches - beautiful Hyrkanese, compact arches made of gazelle horns, with the power of destruction surpassing the class of the famous Gunderland arches. They hung quivers with arrows and looked at me. They were ready for the show. I nodded.

First, each of them dropped five arrows into the shield - each of them hit the red circle in the middle.

"It was easy," said Beryl. "Now there will be a higher school."

She released the arrow, which was stuck in the center of the shield. She gave way to Marhita, who drove her arrow into Beryl's arrow. In turn, she fired an arrow that hit the shield next to Beryl's arrow and Beryl dug her arrow into the Marhita arrow. There was applause. They chilled politely.

"Now try to be brave," said Merita. "Come on, Tia!"

Tia bowed and stood against the wall. Both girls made eye contact and quickly drove five arrows into the wall an inch from Tia's body. Thunderous applause showered. All three curtsied politely and began to pull arrows from the wall.

"What will you show us Tia?" I asked.

"A little horseback riding," she announced.

She jumped on her horse and walked the walk, then trotting. She gave us a great show of the horse vaulting. She took the javelin at once and threw it in full motion, hitting the shield that the girls had used as a target. Then she dropped two javelins with two shields, which also hit center. There was applause. Then she jumped from her horse and threw the javelin with some device she held in her right hand. The spear flew through the whole courtyard and drove into the target located on the other side of the square. A whisper of recognition went through the crowd of onlookers.

Tia stood before us and curtsied.

"What is it?" I asked, pointing to the object held in her hand.

"It's an gavelock-pitcher, *atlat*" she said. "Its effect is to multiply the power of the throw by extending the arm of the javelin," she explained kindly.

"Where did it come from?" I asked.

"As far as I know, it was brought from across the West Ocean where local residents use it." She explained.

"You can see the changes here and there," I said, "please, let's go to dinner."

The horses were unweaned and brought to the stable, the saddle was repaired and the weapon was taken to the headquarters. And then we went to our chambers.

In the evening, we all sat on the terrace looking at the stars, among which the Little Guide was slowly moving. We talked about the travels and plans to dispose of Malabona. When it was dark, the two couples went to rest and only Tia sat staring at Iris, which was lit by a small lamp.

"Can I ask you something, Lady?" She finally said in a tone of praise.

"Of course, ask," said the other, astonished by the tone of her voice.

"Can you be my Master?"

"Not yet, but maybe in the future?" Iris replied. "I'm just an Apprentice. We'll talk about it tomorrow, it's late."

But it was not given to them, because everything went different...

X

We traveled yet three days through the jungle to Khorala - the capital of Vendhia controlled by the usurper. According to Vendhia officers, there were about ten miles left to our destination. But before we left, it was the same evening that I deciphered the cryptogram from Belverus, which the apprentices brought to me. It was the appointment of Iris for the Master in extraordinary mode and the command for two of us to create the Commander of the Brotherhood in Vendhia. After completing the two-month internship, the Students arrived, with the exception of Tia, who was still too young, promoted to Apprentices and were at our disposal. And Tia herself remained in the care of Iris, who became her Mistress. Iris was moved and Tia was happy. They embraced each other and kissed each other heartily. They were similar to each other, that they could be see as sisters. Now they rode next to me, looking around vigilantly, for at any moment we were threatened by the attack of the rebel guardsmen of Grand Vizier.

During our march through the jungle road, individual military units joined us, which we passed along the way. That is how the 2nd and 3rd Brigade of Combat Elephants and XI Orissa Infantry Corps joined us. From the north-west were heading for the capital city VIII and IX Frontier Corps also faithful to the Emperor. Against us, we had only a capital garrison of four divisions: two cavalry and two infantry, and the Imperial Brigade of the Imperial Guard, which was selectable in every respect of equipment and weaponry. It promised to be a bloody battle, because Khorala was an open city and its siege was out of the question. The Archduke's plan assumed an attack on the eastern districts of the city and blocking the city from the north and south so as to force the usurper's forces to retreat to the west and go straight to both Frontier Corps. He needed four days for it, because such great masses of the army could not be regrouped in a shorter period. However, meanwhile the Regent wanted to negotiate with the usurper before the assault and the general battle took place.

"Master," he said to me, "I have a petition for you."

"I'm listening to Your Highness?" I answered.

"Could you mediate?" He asked.

"If Your Majesty expresses such a wish," I said, "I'd gladly take it. I'm asking for a guide and I'm on my way. Oh, and one more thing: why me?"

"Because you're a foreigner and a Master," he replied calmly, "and I can only trust you... So you agree?" He asked again.

"Yes." I confirmed.

"Well, Master, so we'll do like that..."

I returned to our camp. Iris was waiting for me and anxiety was on her face.

"What were you talking about with Adjai?" She asked straight out.

"He asked me to be a representative," I replied.

"And you agreed, of course?" She said more than she asked. How she knows me well!

"Yes," I nodded.

"Well, I'll go with you," she said without thinking.

"You can't," I said, "only one member can go there, because you can become a hostage, so you understand... And secondly: you are already a Master and you have your student, whom you can't leave alone during the battle. Because it will come, I feel it through my skin. And then you will need each other."

How prophetic my words were!

I was traveling along with a pair of guides who brought me to the Khorala hornpost, where the Imperial Guard station stopped me. I announced that I am a parliamentary and I want to face the Grand Vizier. So I was led to him. I presented him with the terms set by the regent. He thought for a moment.

"So I just got an ultimatum: either a death at the hands of a hangman or death in a battle with a gun in my hand?"

"Yes, Your Grace," I nodded. "Regent Adjai promises in the case of capitulation that you'll be judged fairly by an independent court and you'll have a fair trial. In the case of a main penalty, your family will be spared and its property preserved. You know the law of Vendhia, so you know that in such cases, no one had mercy with convict and his family too?

He nodded.

"What do you think about this Master?" He asked me suddenly.

"Me?" I raised my eyebrows. "I can't think about it, I'm just an representative here."

"And privately?" He did not give in.

"Privately, I think that this is a very good proposal, given the circumstances." I replied.

"And if I reject it?"

"A lot of innocent blood pours in and many good young people die," I replied, "the country will be weakened and it will be a long time before it returns to glory. Think about it, Your Grace... You played high and lost. Civil war is the worst evil that can happen to this country..."

"I've heard these words already," he remarked harshly.

"Then what should I say to Regent Adjai?"

"I won't give him the throne and life, Master" he said slowly, "let him come here and pick it up by himself.

He nodded. The hearing was over.

I bowed and left the room. The officer who brought me here escorted me to the gates now and after a while I moved from the hoof to the regent's camp. He waited for me in front of his tent surrounded by the generals. His expression was cloudy. I did not have to guess too much, it was already decided - the assault would take place and it would be bloody. It took only a mere formality to say the matter from my mission. The orders were issued and the troops moved to their starting positions.

The attack began at dawn - the first formations of the raids set off first for reconnaissance and then the rest of the forces that were to attack the eastern districts of the capital. We drove through rare palm groves and small villages that were deserted. When we passed through one of them, shots rang around us. I looked around and could only get out of the huts that were on both sides of the road.

"Ambush!" I shouted. "Go back!"

The shots flew again. I saw several of them flying toward Iris, who took out the sword. But she did not make it, because Tia jumped in front of her and took them on herself. Two of them hit her a little higher above the left breast and thigh. The girl shouted and slumped from the saddle, thankfully Iris managed to catch her and pull her back - she quickly wandered and this saved her life, because the next shots flew in her direction. Iris also staggered because the arrow hit her left side. Then they disappeared from my sight.

I took out the sword. I hoped their wounds were not as dangerous as they looked. I waited for the next salvo of arrows and bolts to fly in our direction and when they flew, I swung my sword towards the huts.

"Forward!" I ordered. "To attack!"

And I started galloping. I counted on the fact that before the archers set up new shots and take us to the target, we will make our way to the huts and send them with our swords and axes. Crossbowmen who had more dangerous weapons did not count in this game, because the rate of fire of the crossbow was much smaller than the arcs. My Vendhians did not ask for anything, but they followed me. In a few seconds we got to the first huts. I jumped off the horse and ran into the first of them. The archers were completely surprised when I ran into them with a sword. I sprinkled the first of them, which stood in my way - the other three threw their weapons to the ground and fell on their knees, raising their hands over their heads.

"Take them!" I ordered.

My students quickly and efficiently (where and when did they learn it???) tied their hands and led them out of the cottage. Other archers were less fortunate. Troopers spread their swords on them and only a few of them remained. We waited for a moment for the regent's coming forces, to whom we told about it and then rushed in search of Iris and Tia. Anxiety about their fate squeezed my heart...

XI

I found them quickly in a field lazaret. Iris had only a superficial wound on her left side - the arrow slipped over her ribs. Tia had two wounds. The first arrow punctured her thigh, fortunately it did not violate the artery. The second hit her badly in the shoulder, just under the clavicle. Then she fainted in pain and almost fell from her horse.

"She'll getting out of it," the military medic said, "he has a young and strong body. She has lost some blood, but will recover it quickly. The main thing is that there are no disturbed arteries and will not bleed.

Iris was shocked, her eyes were red with tears. She was sitting in the stretcher, immersed in thoughtless thoughts. She stood up at my sight. She had a bandaged side.

"She saved me from death," she said in a wooden voice, "these were shots for me..."

"Let's hope she survives," I said. "Unless there will be no disease," I was referring to the rotting fever, which decimated the wounded after all the battles played in the countries of the hot South. I was worried whether the shots that hit both women were not poisoned or infected, but I will find out in a few days when the disease process develops and gives the first symptoms. And for now, Iris was completely depressed and Tia was weak and in traumatic shock.

"Take her to Goa," I said, "and we can't leave from here. We need to stave off this damn crisis while it only has a local range. And I will try not to get killed..."

* * *

After two days, the campaign ended. Imperial Guards laid down their weapons and moved to the regent's side. The Grand Vizier, seeing that his closest comrades leave him, committed suicide, asking in his last letter for mercy for his relatives. Regent accepted this request. The troops returned to the barracks and the confusion began to slowly begin in the country. The Stygian crisis in Vendhia has come to an end.

I quickly returned to Goa and after two weeks, both women were in better shape, though Tia still had a slight paresis of the right hand and Iris was scarred on the left side, where the arrow reached her. We set about organizing the Commandry, for which we had permission and in a short time everything was prepared. I took command of it and soon around Malabona, a wall erected a hundred and twenty cubits grew, securing it from the curious people. At least this case was settled until the end or at least enough to stop worrying about it. Around it was a small fort with a permanent crew that would guard it. The soldiers were tasked slowly to heap over the ruins a mountain of sand and stones, which would neutralize the negative impact of what was in the basement of the black pyramid.

Tia recovered and took up the horse vaulting again. But there was a change in it. She was not as happy as she used to be. Darn near death made her more mature and serious. But how she used to like being in the company of Iris, which she treated more like an older sister or even a mother and not like a Master and a mentor. I told Iris directly that we would recognize her as our daughter.

"Thank you dear," I heard in response, "that's what I expected from you."

And from that time on we have become a real family. Her uncle was not at all worried about it, at least he fell in the care of an adolescent girl... Iris and Tia were happy, because each of them could be fulfilled in their own way. One as a mother, the other as a daughter.

And so time passed slowly until the letter sent by the intentional came to us. It was an order to leave the Goa Commandry under the temporary care of Master Haneda and I was supposed to deal with the matter of the composition of strange objects on one of the islands of the Foggy Islands archipelago. As the letter from Belverus reported, recently a strange disease appeared that affected several fishermen fishing there. Three or four of them have already died and therefore more deaths were to be expected. It was necessary to go there and explain this matter and take some countermeasures. Interestingly, this information was obtained by a circuitous route from sailors from Messantia in Argos. So I was waiting for a sea voyage - short, because only three days away from Goa, but dangerous because of the problem that I had to face...

And it was like that...

5

~

THE ISLAND OF INVISIBLE DEATH

I

Farewell with Goa was fast and nervous. The cruise on the Isles of Mist did not seem to be a holiday getaway a bit because of that I did not know that area of the ocean and a bit because I was disturbed by news coming from this corner of the world. As far as we know, none of the members of the Brotherhood has been there since the beginning of its existence. In turn, we were slowly aware of the fact that the entire Vendhia is *terra incognita*, on whose territory there may be many deadly surprises, at which Malabona seemed to be a piece of cake.

We were also troubled by the other side of the medal, namely that Gedrena knew exactly where it was and we were groping... We guessed that some documents probably came up in her hand about where she was or someone helped her. It was rather obvious. In this context, weird news that some flying devices in the shape of discs with a dome and strange markings were seen over the deserts of Stygia gave a lot to think about... and worried even more.

Master Haneda appeared the same day that I received a letter announcing his arrival. He was young, thin as a Zipangian who, as it turned out, had to practice in front of the Brotherhood Commandry in the Far East, in the land of Khitayan, in Shu-Chen or Paikang - two cities near the Dead Marshes, from where the magicians used poisonous herbs and lotus to its stocks and mixtures. According to the Brotherhood's documents, in the Swamps could be found constructions called *vimanas* and *rakśasa*, which the former gods used to fly and which these swamps preserved very well. The idea was that we have not had a complete plan and model of these machines so far. There was a chance that we would finally extract a complete *vimana* or *rakśasa* and we will be able to learn about their possibilities.

In the meantime, we had to face something much worse - which was invisible, untouchable and terribly dangerous, and confirmed by the foggy news coming from this nomen-omena of the archipelago... So far we have dealt with only one kind of these deadly toys - fire-spitting giant 'shots', that flowed into the sky with a terribly loud, whistling roar and howl. Sometimes they exploded at great heights and sometimes they fell into the sea or land to the accompaniment of terrible thunders. Sometimes we found only the tops of these 'shots' (if the tip could be called a creature five feet long) - people died in terrible torments, when they were too long in their vicinity... - I was afraid that we could come across the composition here types of corroded, broken 'arrowheads' called 'warheads' from which a deadly venom of an invisible, untouchable, imperceptible death escaped, which, however, was so infernally real. Of course, we met with many other copies of the old weapons, but they were not as dangerous as those that we neutralized.

So I passed the command to Master Haneda from Nara and within two days I arranged for myself a sailboat cutter which I could take a sea trip from Goa to the archipelago of the Mist Isles. What's most interesting, they were not exactly mapped. On the best Vendhian maps, they were marked as a few dots on the west coast of the subcontinent and on others as part of a land bridge between the southern tip of Vendhia and the shores of the Black Kingdoms. Even Conan the Cymmerian was not there and the imperial officials were very rare. Nothing was mentioned about them in 'Skelos Scrolls' or 'Kings Way'. So we went completely blind and great unknown. Therefore I intended to make the first reliable description of these islands. I sailed there with my whole family - Iris, Tia and I with Arus.

We went on our way early in the morning to reach the destination as quickly as possible, which was the northernmost island of the archipelago. In fact, after two days of sailing to south we saw it in all its glory. It was only a small atoll quite overgrown with coconut palms and completely uninhabited. We only gave it an hour or two, because there was no reason, especially because in the south we noticed the contours of the next island, much bigger.

The second island turned out to be a collection of several atolls, with a shared lagoon. It was also uninhabited and the palm forest grew over it. Only turtles and seabirds that nested there used to live there. In total, there was nothing interesting there, but Tia found out at the bottom some strange items that we considered a shipwreck that once sailed there and it will remain there forever. We tried to dive into the wreck, but it turned out that the depth of the water was over a hundred fathoms, but the transparency of the water was so good, that it seemed to us that these objects are only a short distance away. I quickly drew a fairly accurate map of the second atoll and that is how the third day of our trip ended.

On the fourth day we set off together with the sun and with the still-favorable wind in the early afternoon we reached the third island. Unlike the previous two, it was the tip of a volcanic massif protruding above the surface of the sea. The tip of the volcano itself was invisible because it was covered by a tropical jungle, while black volcanic beaches were inhabited by people who behaved peacefully at our sight. They were calm fishermen and goat breeders and other animals which was a lot in the local forests. The island was more or less in the shape of a circle and measured over twenty miles in diameter. The volcano was its central point. The fertile soil was used by people to a small extent - they fed almost only what they extracted from the sea.

We went to a small marina and immediately we were surrounded by curious people who were watching our clothes and weapons with interest, which surprised us so much that they themselves walked almost naked. Besides, heat was pouring from heaven and we did not marvel at them too much. Work on and in the water did not encourage dressing, so it was understandable for us. I talked to them in a Hyborian, but they did not understand. I went to Vendhian and I was able to talk with them. They were a bit tense, but when I assured them that we were not imperial officers, they calmed down. I asked them to lead me to a local hakim or doctor. They did not know what it was.

"That is *aśipú*," I said in Iranistanian.

"Oh!" They exclaimed. "You mean *temoaa*!?"

And it turned out that it was a kind of priest and healer in one. I was led to the hut of an elderly old man who was holding on very straight.

"Hello, *temoaa*," I said, "I'm Lestko from the Brotherhood of the Green Dragon, and I've come to ask you for some information," I said, with little hope that it would say anything to him at this end of the world.

The old man looked at me sharply, raised his eyebrows and smiled.

"Hello, Master," he said. "The fame of the Demon of the Past Poverers even reached us here.

I understood.

"Was it you, O Venerable, told sailors from Messantia about what was happening here?" I asked.

"Yes, it's me and as I see the Grand Master treated the matter seriously sending you and your wife."

I decided solemnly not be surprised.

"Emperor of Vendhia, Adjai I also," I replied, "we're also acting on his power of attorney."

"Oh!" The old man was surprised. "There was the change of the ruler? Why so fast?"

"Yes, and his son ascended his throne." I replied and briefly told him about what was happening on the subcontinent in the last two months. He listened, staring somewhere at himself. When I finished, he shook off his thoughts and said:

"So the world won't be the same anymore, because the destiny of the Old Lord has been completed. But it doesn't seem that you wanted to talk about it with me, Master."

"You're right *temoaa*." I said. "I would like to know more about what is the reason for this visits. Tell me about these poisonings. Because I'm sure it was poisoning, am I wrong?"

The old man looked at me sharply again.

"You aren't mistaken, Master," he said slowly. "It was poisoning and some sort of violent means that nature we couldn't determine."

"We? So who?" I asked.

"Oh!" He said, waving his hand. "There are some healers in this archipelago. We are absolutely sure of one thing," the word 'absolutely' he pronounced with a clear emphasis, "that these are not any known plant or mineral poisons. We are also sure that they work equally well in contact as well as inhalation or gastric. It means lethal in any case. Mortality is one hundred percent. That's why we decided to get one of the Masters of the Brotherhood of Green Dragon here..."

"How did you get me here, Venerable?" I asked.

"Old Atlantean religion," he smiled again, "or the extraordinary possibilities of the human mind. We both know that the gods don't exist, but in man there are such possibilities that make him equal - let's say almost equal - invented by him gods."

"Strange," I thought, "they could bring people here from a distance of thousands of miles and at the same time they could not determine the cause of the deaths of people a few hundred miles away..."

"That's because, as I said, this cause isn't natural. The whole world and the Universe permeates the field of energy produced by everything that lives. In one place, there are more of it, in another it is less and therefore constantly strives to achieve a balance between two opposing and simultaneously complementary elements. Man and woman, white and black, good and evil... - you know the elements of this philosophy?"

"I know, but on the other hand... Forget about that. Tell me, Venerable, how and when did it start?"

"Three weeks ago, the first cases of disease occurred on the South Island. And from that time on whoever escaped from it - he died."

"How did it manifest itself?" I asked, intrigued to the highest degree.

"Different, but the effect was always one: death."

"I understand, but where did it start?"

"Usually from foot burns, which quickly transformed into open wounds. In a few cases, these were burns on the hands or other parts of the body. Death most often occurred as a result of general poisoning of the body or paralysis of the lungs and respiratory system..."

"And it isn't known under what circumstances these people succumbed to this..." I thought for a moment, "...paralysis?"

"When they were brought to us," the doctor said slowly, "they were mostly unconscious and we could not help them at all... There was nothing left than help them to die, as the book 'Bardo' recommends."

"So there is nothing else to do but go to the South Island, because there is this demon, which I must defeat." I said, farewelling the *temoaa*.

On the same day we went on our way...

II

South Island has grown up like an emerald from the malachite ocean. Like the other islands, it was part of a volcanic cone with black beaches and lush tropical greenery that grew over it. And yet there was something disturbing in its view that made us be on our guard. Our flat-bottomed boat approached the wide strip of the beach minimally and the wide beak brushed against the small stones. Tia skillfully jumped with an anchor on a long chain and drove it into a vulnerable floor. I looked at her with delight. She was just as agile and skilled as her adopted mother and dressed the same - leather tank top, white shirt and leather short pants and boots with short upper. She no longer had to wear the Student's tunic and as an Apprentice she could dress according to her own taste. On her head she wore a wide-brimmed hat. Dark wavy hair tied back into a ponytail. I was not surprised that the Vendhian boys were crazy about her. But their enthusiasm quickly cooled down her simple, Zipangian sword strapped to her back, which she could use extremely cleverly. Although this has changed recently, since Dravi, the son of one of the local notables, began to show up in her company, who was not discouraged by her approach to the boys, and he took lessons with the local school with her. It allowed to hope that Tia would moderate her irrepressible temperament...

Iris jumped after her daughter and both women found themselves on the black beach. I quickly followed in their footsteps and we all started looking around. We still could not understand what was disturbing us so much. After a moment, Iris found out as the first one.

"There isn't even one bird here!" She noted with astonishment, "I didn't notice even one..."

"Oh, don't overreact mom," Tia pointed somewhere in the east, "and that, what is it? A dog?"

In fact, a great frigate lay on the sand a hundred feet from us. The span of her wings must have been at least ten feet. We set off towards her. The caution at the origin was superfluous - a large, beautiful bird was undeniably dead. The body was dried by the sun.

"Don't touch!" I shouted, because Tia has already reached out her hand.

"Why daddy?" She asked.

"This carcass can be dangerous," I explained. "The factor that killed this bird can now kill you. We don't know what it is. Leave it!"

She left it. We looked around again. The beach was a huge cemetery of marine and terrestrial animals.

And people.

The human corpses dried like mummies lay here and there, where people reached death. The dried skin - especially the hands and legs was covered with bloody blisters. The bodies were twisted in a deadly contraction.

"What does it remind you of?" Iris asked.

"It looks like death from asphyxiation, not poisoning. Well, but these blisters..." I murmured.

"There're no fresh bodies," Tia looked around. "What will we do, daddy?"

"We'll look around, of course," Iris said. "We'll go down the beach around the island, maybe somebody else live here?"

"You'll have to go twenty miles at least," Tia murmured.

"Not more?" I asked. "The diameter of the island is some fifteen miles. Her circuit will have?...

"Wait," she thought for a moment, "it'll be, it'll be..."

"Two pi times semidiameter..." I suggested the undertone in a low voice."

"I know," she snarled, "I wanted to give you the result..." she thought for a moment. "No, it's over 47 miles! My legs will fall!"

"We have time," I said, "and that's why we came here to find out what killed those people and animals..."

"Do you have a plan?" Tia asked. "Are we improvising?"

"Plan A is like that," Iris said, "we are going along the coast looking for someone who is alive. If we don't find anyone, we start Plan B."

"That is, we are going to the interior of the island and we do what was in plan A," I added, "we're looking for the living ones.

"And what when we won't find no one?" Tia frowned.

"Then we continue the plan A," I said quickly, "we're looking for a cause and we'll try to neutralize it."

We have already gone a long way off the coast, when we were blocked by black rocks looking like high towers, chimneys or towers.

"We'll have to get around or circumnavigate," Tia said and after a moment she began to undress.

"What are you doing?" Iris cooled her enthusiasm. "We'll go overland."

"Eeeee..." Tia's beautiful face was showing disappointed. "I'd like to bathe so much..."

"Not in the sea," I said.

"Why???" Both women asked in unison.

"This water is so clean?" Tia noted abruptly.

The water was actually clean. It's too much for my taste.

"Think," I said, "you have exactly as much data as I do..."

Iris raised her eyebrows slightly.

"Sea animals," she said, "look how many of them are here. And they're all dead."

"And they don't even decay and they should," I added, "and therefore the lethal factor is not in the air or on land, but just in the water, did you understand, sweetie?"

A blush erupted on her cheeks.

"Yes, daddy," she said quietly, "and I'm sorry..."

"Don't apologize, just think," Iris said. "It'll increase your survival by at least twice or even three times as much."

"Let's go on land, then," I said, heading for the rocks.

It was the forehead of a lava stream that had arrived here thousands of years ago and frozen in contact with water. Now the jungle has claimed its rights and colored plant grew from every slit of the lava's iundisturbed soil and pressed grass. After half an hour of climbing, we finally entered the black cliff, from which a view of the whole was spread. At the bottom, the waves hitting the coral reefs. In contrast to the strip of the beach, a thriving life flourished here, insects and chirping birds were buzzing.

"Well, it's as we expected," Iris said, "the seawater is contaminated."

"But by what?" I was wondering. "That's the question!?"

We walked on and after halfway through, Tia leaned over the abyss pointing at something with her finger.

"What is that?" She cried.

We looked in the direction indicated. Near the shore on the sharp reefs lay the wreck of something that was once a ship. The wreck was fresh, sharp rocks ripped its sides from which some large objects resembled short thick cylinders. Some of them showed signs of damage others seemed intact.

"If I'm not mistaken," said Iris, "it's our friends from Stygia again."

I looked closer. What at first seemed to me as stack of some rags or bales of wool was a horribly crippled corpse scattered randomly on black and gray rocks.

"You're not mistaken," I said in a sinister tone, "that's them. And the worst thing is that they won't answer any of our questions. They are dead..."

III

"You sure there's no mistake?" Iris sounded surprised.

"No," I said, "those lying stack of rags are their corpses."

"We'll have to watch them?" Tia asked.

"No," I said, "we don't have the right outfits to protect against contaminated water, as firstly and secondly..."

"How do you know that there is a source of contamination?" Tia asked with exorbitant astonishment in her voice.

"Well, look more closely at the rocks and water," I said, pointing to large spots of brown liquid with a tar-like consistency that were located on the bottom and which were the rocks around the wreck.

"This is that..." Tia slowly recovered from her amazement. "That..."

"Without euphemisms, please," I said, "this is the poison from the group of *tasthra*, not the *mohamastra*, which are described in 'Dhrona Paarva'. Who knows, maybe it's *samarra*? Fortunately, it dissolves poorly in water. Otherwise we would have been dead... and fortunately that they had put a ship on these reefs, otherwise there would be even more contamination of water and air."

"So the end of the mission?" Tia asked hopefully. Apparently, she was terrified by the thought of going past 47 miles...

"No, sweetie," Iris said, "it seems to me that this is a secondary source of contamination and we don't know where it is primary. In other words, we don't know where they got their load. There can be much more there. And there is probably something that dissolves well in the water and works by contact and inhaling mingled with sea aerosol..." Iris looked at me and I nodded in agreement.

"You're right, honey," I confirmed, "these brown spots, it certainly is this substance that acts contact and inhalation on land. The fishermen poisoned by it when pulling out the nets, but the rest? It couldn't, and therefore must be one more strong poison that also works through water. We must go and find its source and maybe even the sources..."

"Where can we expect it?" Tia asked.

"My daughter, everywhere," I answered. "Let's hope this is somewhere on the coast..."

* * *

We spent the night in the vicinity of the wreck and I do not have to say that we did not sleep much, because every moment we were waked up by shout of various animals living in the jungle. But the morning rose so beautiful that we wanted to live. And interestingly enough, we did not see any trace of the fog from which these islands were famous... We ate a modest breakfast consisting of some of the supplies we took with us. We descended from the forehead of the lava stream and went on a black, rocky beach where we could find dead animals from time to time. This view was moving and squeezing the heart...

At once the road was blocked by a rushing torrent that came out of a deep crack in the V-shaped rocks. A fragment of a rising valley was visible through the crevasse, the upper parts of which resembled a glacial penalty, but were not there because there was a volcanic lake with which this stream flowed. All this was immersed in lush greenery. For a moment we were thinking and then we decided to go there and see what the interior of the island looked like. Judging by the sounds of the animals living there, life was going on there best without caring about the massacre that met the animals living in the sea and on the beach. So we entered a crack that widened after a mile into the valley, with the bottom of the stream flowing with water. It was mineralized, as in volcanic areas, but clean and drinkable. It was not contaminated. After traveling half a mile horizontally and several dozen feet vertically, at once our eyes opened a paradise view: before us was a lake with transparent water, to which fell a powdery waterfall from the lake, which was above. On the rocky shore there were brown and black, round and polished rocks that looked like the backs of some monsters from millions of years ago... the vegetation here had a faint bluish green shade, which meant that the sun was very strong here.

"Here is wonderful!" Tia called.

She was right, after what we saw on the beaches of this island, this corner seemed to be a paradise.

"I know, I know," I said, "jump into the water..."

Like Iris, Tia loved water and bathing, and she could splash for hours whenever she had time.

"And we'll go to that upper lake," I said to Iris.

"Sure - we have to see this island from above." She replied by making an eye to me.

So we went up, and Tia quickly jumped out of her clothes and the nude stomped into the water, where she began to swim around the lake, regularly cutting water with her strong arms.

We traveled another three hundred feet of height, sweaty and squinted, we stood on the bank of the second lake. Brown and gray rocks surrounded them, but without a trace of vegetation. I understood - from time to time the volcano would let know about itself by washing away everything that lived by the streams of hot geyser waters and a pair of fumaroles. Even the water of the lake was strangely warm compared to the cool wind that prevailed at this altitude.

"I've enough climbing for today," I said.

"Me too," Iris replied with a glint in her eye.

I took off my rucksack and my weapon from my back, then threw off my clothes and jumped into the water. It was as warm as soup and so I hoped for a refreshing chill. The lake was small and I swam through several dozen quick wavelets of the hands and legs of the crawl. I reached the steep rock ledge and turned away, leaning against my back against the wall, polished by the action of the water, which at this point reached me a little higher up the waist.

Iris followed in my footsteps and jumped into the water, after a few vigorous arm swings swam up the place where I stood and stood in front of me. Her breasts touched mine gently. She tilted her head, gazing flirtatiously at me, then with a vigorous motion she threw back her wet hair. Again her breasts with swollen strawberries touched my torso and her hands touched my shoulders. She closed her eyes and opened her mouth slightly.

I did not wait for further invitation. And she neither....

I turned around and leaned against the rock wall, and Iris slowly let me out and trembled again and again, hugging me. We breathed breathing like two blacksmith bellows. We kissed again, but it was a word of thanks for the wonderful impressions we gave to each other.

"Lestek?" I heard her voice.

"Yes, baby?" I answered.

In her eyes I saw astonishment and something like anxiety.

"Turn around, but slowly," she said.

There was something in her voice that made I had to listen her. I slowly turned my head.

In the field of view I had a gray cliff and the blue sky shining above it. And something else, something that frightened Iris, who embraced me tightly and breathed hard.

About ten feet above the surface of the lake hung in the air a big orange ball that had thirty or forty feet. Actually, it slowly moved towards the outlet of the waterfall, which fell to the lower lake. It floated through the air and finally found itself on the edge, and after a while it sped up and drifted away towards the north while hovering.

In one moment we came to our senses. We quickly got to the edge of the waterfalls.

"Tia!" I shouted. "Tia!!!"

"I'm here!" We heard her voice somewhere from the side. Her slender figure appeared on the approach and a moment later the girl stood on the boulder on which our clothes and weapons were lying.

"What happened?" She asked in astonishment at the sight of our mines. "Why are you scared?"

"Did you see that?" We asked in unison.

"I saw what...?" she answered the question with a question.

"A huge, orange sphere that flew in the air," I explained, "from here," I pointed to the middle of the lake, "to here and then to the north."

"Mom?" Tia turned to Iris.

"Exactly, it was like father says," Iris said calmly.

Tia's expression expressed everything she thought about us.

"Well? And what?" We asked one for the other.

Tia followed us with a look of extreme amazement."

I'm absolutely sure," she said calmly and firmly, "*that I didn't see any flying orange ball...*"

IV

We were silent for a moment.

"Are you sure?" I asked.

"Yes, daddy," she replied firmly. "It was not there. There was nothing in the air here. Even birds."

We looked at each other.

"For sure?" Iris asked again. "This is a very important matter!"

"I'm absolutely sure," Tia said firmly. "I didn't see anything in the air. What's up with you!?"

"Well, we've another problem," I sighed.

"That's how it is," Iris smiled at me, "when one problem ended, the next one appeared..."

We dressed quickly. We have not commented on this matter because we have more important things.

"So what, we'll look into the volcano's crater now?" Tia asked.

"Of course," I answered, "because something seems to me that it starts to wake up..."

"Is it?" Both women looked at me in disbelief. "How do you know?"

"*Temoaa* told me that the earth has been shaking regularly for two months," I replied. "And besides, such not very strong quakes always herald a volcanic eruption... Besides this lake - this water is suspiciously warm for this altitude and location in relation to the sun..."

"Yes..." Iris nodded. "We're going. I hope we won't see any flying oranges..."

And we moved. After an hour of climbing, we found ourselves on the edge of the crater. And finally, we saw the whole island in the harsh midday sun. But only its northern and eastern extremity. From the south and west there was an impenetrable mist coming out of the crater. It looked like the fumes coming out of a huge boiler. The landscape of this part of the island was gloomy and reminded all the worst descriptions of Hell. Gray and black in combination with the gray white steam and colored outbursts of gases and sludge of sulfur and other minerals that did not revive this unpleasant human sight, and even deepened it. At that altitude, the wind was strong at this height, from time to time it revealed the bottom of the crater, on which stood a huge dome, spitting a pair of fumaroles. That's where the central volcano chimney was located, waking up from sleep.

"When can this happen?" Tia asked.

"Today, tomorrow, maybe in two months..." I shrugged. "I don't know. Eruption can happen anytime. It'll be a really big 'boom"!"

"Well, why don't we go?" Tia asked. "I prefer to be down when it happens..."

I took farewell to gloomy landscape and we headed back.

"Daddy," Tia said with a slight blush on her cheeks, "you know, when you and mum, you know... you made love, I saw something strange on the beach in the east, about ten miles from here. Something like a landslide and a dome.

"Did you look at us?" Iris asked. "Oh, bad manners, bad manners!" And wagged her finger at her.

Tia blushed to the roots of her dark hair.

"Just a little," she said with a sly smile, "but you did it so... nice and passionate that I couldn't stand it and look at you... And I assure you that it was for what! You're also perfect in this!"

I want to laugh. Iris also gave me an amused look. After a moment we came back to earth with a bump.

"A parasitic cone?" I asked. "Such a small volcano?"

Tia shook her head to say no.

"No, this is something else. As if the building..."

"Lead us there," I said. "Maybe this is what we're looking for?"

Again, we walked along the beach on small black stones. My feet ached, but I was hoping that we would get there until the evening. Along the way, we experienced a light earthquake which was a very unpleasant feeling. We heard a stone avalanche fall somewhere, earth and rocks fell apart in a hurricane somewhere. From the forest we heard a scream of monkeys and voices of frightened birds whose keys flew over our heads flying east towards the mainland.

"They also feel the upcoming cataclysm," I thought.

I said it to Iris, who muttered something about poor animals and we went further. And after three hours of walking on the rocky beach, we finally stood before *this*...

It looked like a grounded dome protruding from the slope, which at this point fell to the beach creating a ramp. The slope itself looked like an open wound - there was a huge, rectangular room built in it, which from the bottom up to the ceiling was filled with something like metal barrels. They were not loose, but in the sand that filled the space between them. The earthquake ruined the wall from the sea side and there were several hundred barrels on the beach - one almost shiny despite the passage of thousands of years, others again corroded. It was from them that a jelly-like oily gooey smelled of garlic or grated mustard seeds. This odor irritated the eyes and forced to cough. It must have been thousands of talents. Fortunately, the wind blew from the sea and carried it into the forest.

"But this is something from the group of tasthra poisons," Iris said.

"Probably, the smell of garlic indicates it." I said. "I'm curious about one thing, namely - how did the Stygians know about it?"

"Gedrena's notes." Iris raised her eyebrows.

"Or Brotherhood documents," Tia said.

I was about to reply, but I remembered the betrayal of former Master Arielles from Eruk and I bit my tongue.

"Arielles?" Iris looked at me questioningly.

"It could be," I replied.

"Do you remember what those who we took from under Malabona said?" I asked. "Well, we know what they were looking for here. Probably Malabona and the South Island are warehouses of the *tasthra* weapons. I wonder how many such warehouses are on the territory of Vendhia?..."

I knew from experience that the toxic substances from the group of tasthra were not very volatile, which was a favorable factor, but their vapors could be poisonous and after they were absorbed, people died due to paralysis of the lungs. *Temoaa* was right, their higher concentrations caused skin burns and contact through the skin causing poisoning of the whole organism and a fatal descent. Apparently, they were stored without any means of neutralizing them here and in Malabona, except that in the latter there must have been some pathogens that caused epidemics of the Black and Red Plague, decimating the population of the South from time to time.

I was just wondering how to dispose of the terribly grave cemetery, when the monkeys were torn again and the ground under our feet swayed for a few seconds. We looked into each other's eyes.

"I think we're lucky," I said.

"How's that?" Tia looked at me with amazement. "Lucky?"

"Sure!" I shouted. "Oh, my incredulous and doubter women! The volcano will take the worst job for us! As it spits lava here, it'll bury all of them forever!"

I rolled a triumphant look at them.

"And how do you like it !?" I exclaimed.

Iris smiled warmly.

"And didn't I tell you that he's really genius?" She said to Tia and winked to her.

V

For the sleep we chose a place at the edge of the forest, sheltered from the sea by a rather tall stone wall. We found traces of the Stygian camp there, so we did not see any obstacles to take their place. The night passed us quite restlessly. Again, we felt underground tremors, and from time to time, grim murmurs reached us from the womb of the earth. The volcano woke up and it was faster and faster. We managed to sleep only in the morning.

We were awakened by another earthquake, much milder than what was on the previous day, but I was not fooled - it could have been the silence before the storm. We were returning quickly towards the boat. It was necessary to slowly leave this dangerous place...

"I'd like to take a look at these lakes and the crater," I said to both women. "Go to the boat and get ready to sail away, and I'll go there alone."

"Are you crazy?" Iris looked at me with a twinkle in eyes. "Do you want to die?"

"No, but maybe I can determine the time of eruption," I replied, "and this in turn will allow to determine its strength and direction."

"Well, I'm going with you." Iris shook her head, cutting off all the discussions. "If we'll die, we do it together."

"What about me?" Tia asked.

"You're going to the boat and if something happen you'll leave," I said.

"No!!!" Tia shouted. "I won't leave you here!!!"

"You'll leave and go to Goa, to report what happened here. It's an order," I said firmly, "paternal order. And also as a commander, and as a Master, I have a responsibility to turn my neck, but not someone else's, just my - clear?"

"And I as your Master, I'm telling you the same thing." Iris said it so firmly that Tia looked at her with astonishment and fear. "It's your task, independent, as if you didn't know. Do it!"

Tia did not say anything, just kissed us and headed to the boat.

We looked at each other.

"You spoiled her rotten," I murmured.

"She was always recalcitrant," Iris bit back immediately.

We looked into each other's eyes and laughed as if the danger did not exist. I was afraid for our and Tia's life, but the presence of Iris calmed down and encouraged, it let to pull myself together. I sighed with relief.

"Let's go," she said in the meantime and moved ahead, and I followed her.

And again, we went along the stream. It waters were not as crystal clear as when we were here for the first time. The water had a bitter aftertaste. Another sign of the upcoming eruption.

The lower lake was quite muddy. It waters were bitter and warm.

"Will we bathe?" Iris suggested.

"I'm afraid that after a few minutes only skeletons would be left from us..." I said, pointing to the bodies of animals floating here and there, scalded terribly by the water in which various minerals were dissolved.

"I'm afraid they'll even dissolve in this," Iris said, indicating what had once been an adult sloth.

The air was saturated with the bitter-sour smell of burnt sulfur and something sharper, which caused a tiring cough. The vegetation looked like it was chewed up and discolored. Breathing was difficult.

"Are we going higher?" Iris asked.

"We must," I replied, "I'd like to see the upper lake."

Again we went walking along the steep mountain path towards the upper lake and after exiting the ridge we breathed a sigh of relief. The wind blew steam and gases westward.

Suddenly, we heard a loud pop and a slight shock shook the mountain. There was a dead silence in which we heard a loud hiss that whistled and a howl. The noise was terrible, Iris clapped her ears with her hands pressed flat on her head and she looked around with open mouth. I did the same and felt a certain relief. It lasted for about five minutes, then the roar stopped at once and a velvet silence fell... Probably the water vapor and gases collected somewhere over the lava reservoir and found an outlet and broke out with a roar outside...

The upper lake was covered with a veil of fog. We entered it and after a while we stood on the bank. The water boiled, emitting the unpleasant smell of bad eggs. We were coughing immediately. The eyes were burning. I felt nauseous and a headache. A delicate scent of bitter almonds joined the hideous smell of the braces.

"We must run away!" I spluttered and pushed Iris to the perch, and then pulled where the wind was blowing. After a while, we stood on the ridge, ventilating the lungs with fresh air. The earth trembled sharply under our feet again. The frequency of shocks increased, which heralded a close explosion.

"Do what I do," Iris said. She made a deep bend of breath from the lungs, then straightened up, pulling in the maximum amount of air to oxidize the lungs. I understood and started doing the same. We had to quickly pass through the contaminated area at the second lake. We could stay here forever. And none of us wanted it. Going back to the beach was a nightmare. I only remember that we were falling a few times, we were getting up with difficulty and we were walking on, and at the end we were running almost on apnea, exhausted to the ground on the pebbles of the black beach.

Quickly - as soon as we were able - we trotted in the direction of the boat, which we found in good condition and ready to be pushed to the water. The sun started bowing to the west, when with a powerful push we dropped our barge on the water and, working furiously with oars, we swam away half a mile from the shore. Our heads ached and we felt exhausted - this was the result of the impurity of volcanic gases. I set sail and started to sail north - just away from the accursed island. After an hour we managed to sail for about five miles and we could see her vapor-covered cone in the distance. The sun sank more and more and finally came into contact with the horizon. South Island sank behind the horizon. The sun went beyond the horizon and thick darkness fell immediately. The moon only dawned around midnight, so we were only stranded at the stars.

It happened suddenly. In the darkness of the night a bushy orange flash appear. A powerful cloud of fast-drying volcanic ash has emitted a sky-high altitude by extinguishing the stars, like a huge black hand. After a while, its interior illuminated the blue-violet light of lightning. The volcano has finally exploded. After a while, we heard the horrible roar of a monstrous explosion that passed from the constant murmur of the continuous stream of smaller explosions.

Around midnight, the moon would rise, but we did not see it, because the entire southeast horizon was drowned in the darkness illuminated only by lightnings shooting furiously in the womb of a black cloud. At sunrise, we saw the shores of the third island where we left Arus. We came to the marina, actually what was left from it.

The whole quay was carrying traces of a terrible cataclysm. A huge wave of tsunamis had to hit the shores of the island, ravaging everything for two miles into its interior. We landed and our legs sank into a mule, which layer lay at least on the one foot. We were looking around with horror at what was left of the village. And there was not much left. The impact of tsunami waves must have been horrible, judging by the traces it left. Waves about at least a thousand feet high hit the land and broke into the interior of the island for two or even three miles. All villages of the settlement were destroyed and covered with mud with a thick layer for one foot or even three. A wide strip of palm trees was overthrown, the trees were broken and their trunks were crushed by the terrible strokes of water masses. I thought that the waves that hit the coast of Goa must have been a little smaller and my heart was squeezed by anxiety over the command office and the people who were subordinate to me. Nevertheless, we have found out that more valuable objects have disappeared from the ruins and there have been no corpses of people and animals. And that meant they were able to evacuate...

And that was indeed the case. After an hour from the interior of the island, we heard the voices of people and the barking of dogs and the bleating of goats, and after the next five minutes we saw the locals coming out to the beach. Everyone was safe and healthy, which we noticed with relief. Arus threw to us and hopped to lick us in the face. I thought that if he was with us on the South Island, he would have died there - volcanic fumes would kill him undoubtedly...

But that was not the most important thing now. I got to *temoaa* and asked him for a moment of conversation. He agreed willingly. We sat in the shade of a tall palm tree. I gave him a brief account of what we saw on the South Island. He nodded sadly.

"However, we were right." He said at the end. "It was not from this world..."

"At least now you are not in danger. But tell me, oh Venerable, how did you save from the tsunami?" I asked, because curiosity did not give me peace.

"You don't know how, Master?" *Temoaa* raised his eyebrows in amazement. "And I thought it was obvious... Where are you from?"

"Vislania in the Kingdoms of Borderland, and my wife from Brythunia. However, a foster daughter from Agra."

"Then you couldn't know about it..." he said thoughtfully.

A flash of understanding flew through my brain at once.

"Earthquakes?" I asked.

"Of course!" He replied. The behavior of birds and terrestrial and marine animals..."

I nodded. I opened my mouth to ask a question, but he was faster than me.

"Are you worried about the fate of your relatives and colleagues?" He asked. "Unnecessarily. They live and are healthy."

"How do you know, Venerable?" I asked with astonishment.

"You said, Master, that Master Haneda is with them. Judging by his name, he is a Zipangian, and they live there on volcanoes, so he should read the signs of the impending cataclysm correctly..." he said with a smile.

"Let it be so..." I sighed.

"And so it will be," he said with unshakeable certainty in his voice. "You have my word for it."

VI

And it was like that.

Goa suffered to a large extent, but thanks to Master Haneda, it was possible to avoid losses in people. We breathed a sigh of relief as we saw our people making their way around the reconstruction of the ruined city. The tide was already weaker and lower, but it still measured about a hundred feet high and ran into the land at a distance of one staja.

Master Haneda foresaw the cataclysm and managed to convince the city authorities and persuade people to evacuate, which was so easy that most of them had confidence in the new authorities and the Brotherhood, which enjoyed the authority. I was thinking about opening the university under our auspices, but the situation has not matured yet. Master Haneda thanked us for hospitality and escorted him through the crowd of Goans, he boarded a ship that would take him to Khitaju. We stood for a long time on the pier waving goodbye to him.

We returned to the commandery, which had to be repaired in general, which was possible within a month. And the days once again flowed in a steady and calm rhythm. Until one evening a runner from Yuteshi came to the commanding party, bringing a letter from Master Haneda and a letter from the Grand Master. I dismissed him and eagerly broke the wax seal with the image of the green dragon's battle, and opened a letter from Master Haneda written on beautiful, drawn paper. Master Haneda wrote to me like this:

Master Lestek,

I'm asking you with an extraordinary request for help in our research. As you probably remember, I organized a Brotherhood Commando in the Far East, in the land of Khitay, in its largest city of Paikang, which lies about 110 staja from the vast area of swamps known as the Mires of the Dead or simply the swamps of death. You probably also remember that we expected to come across the preserved in the swamp and well-preserved by the mud flying Vimana and Rakśas vehicles. In fact, during the first test we managed to find two copies of some metal structures sunk in the mud and a few others in a worse condition. The thing is, some people have had strange wounds during these tests, reminiscent of burns, but also poisoning with some poisonous substances, very similar to those that you came across in the territory of Vendhia and the Fog Isles.

Currently, you are the Master who has the most experience in dealing with them and I turn to you for help. Come as soon as you can, the matter is serious and I can count here only on you.

Haneda

I raised my eyebrows touched by the letter. Master Haneda did not belong to people who panic or cause false alarms from just about anything - anyway, you do not become a Brotherhood Master for beautiful eyes and you have to make specific achieve-ments to become one of them - or, as in my case, confirm your appointment to the Master with deed. So a new Adventure was being prepared?

The second letter remained. This one was on a piece of parchment and was extremely laconic:

Master Lestek,

If you're able and recent events haven't strained your health, then I'm asking you - go to Khitay. Consider one thing - please! This matter is very serious! We are dealing with something that exceeds our current knowledge and there are no links to knowledge from the archives of our Brotherhood, and, as far as I know, all temples known to us. You enter literally and metaphorically into an unknown and very dangerous area. So if you can go, and for the time of your absence, the Goa Commander will be joined by Master Iris of Ianthe - Your wife. She has all the powers of the Brotherhood to perform in your and her name.

Under the authority of the Grand Master -

- Brontosphoros

So it was the request of the Grand Master and his deputy, Master Brontosphoros. Such requests were not denied. Such a request was a directive and its fulfillment became a matter of honor.

Underneath I noticed a postscript, which I did not at first recognize as intrigued by the content of the first letter. It sounded like this:

P.S. Be careful! Brother Houg sends you instructions on how to behave, but you're only dependent on your reason and experience! Let Brain lead you! Good luck!

B.

I knew so much alone, but apparently Master Brontosphoros wanted to have a clear conscience. Unnecessarily, because the puzzle has already interest me and I decided to go after reading the letter from Master Haneda.

I stood with both letters in my hands and wondered about the consequences when I felt a touch on my shoulders. Iris's warm body clung to my back for a moment and I felt her teeth dig into my right ear. She usually let me know in that way she wanted something other than work or leisure. I turned around holding both letters in my hand. Iris stood clothed in almost transparent greenish saris that more emphasized than concealing her lovely figure.

"What's new?" She asked in a voice in which curiosity and anxiety quivered.

I gave her letters. She read both, and a cloud flew through her clear face.

"Of course, you're going?" She asked tersely.

I nodded.

"I'm leaving my Commander," I said.

Her eyes flashed.

"I knew, I knew, I knew!" She exclaimed.

"What did you know?" I asked, slightly astonished.

"That you'll go!" She answered. "I'll stay here and don't worry, it'll be like you being here. You can't worry about it! When are you moving?"

"Tomorrow," I replied, "as soon as possible. There can actually be hot!"

"Three months by caravan or a month of sailing," she said. "I'll miss you, my love!..."

"Me too..." I answered, realizing at once that our relationship was now just before the real test. "I'll try to get back to you, baby, as soon as possible..."

Iris slipped into my arms.

"I must farewell you," she whispered, "come on..."

She pulled me into the bedroom. I sat on the bed and she sat on my lap. I felt the warmth of her body through the delicate material of our clothes. I embraced her and she hugged me. We sat in silence. For the first time, we will have a long separation. I have always had support from this beloved woman who will now be missing from my side. I sighed.

"You are worried?" She asked. "Unnecessarily. I'll be here and you're needed somewhere else and to someone else."

"I'll miss you," I whispered. "You. Your presence, your body, your arm and support in need."

"You will be fine," she said calmly, "I'll miss you terribly."

"Me too," I said quietly, kissing her hair.

She raised her head.

"So what are we waiting for?" She asked, and her eyes lit a playful sparkle...

...

...We lay side by side breathing and slowly calming down. I looked into Iris's eyes, gray and luminous in the light of the lamp.

"Thank you," I whispered, "I'll have something to remember in the light of the camp fire.

She smiled.

"Me too," she said.

"You'll feel alone..." I said.

"Don't be afraid," she smiled again, "I like to make love, but I'm faithful to you."

"Aren't you afraid that I'll betray you with another woman?" I asked surreptitiously.

"If I don't find out, so no," she said.

"I won't betray you," I said, "I'll lose too much losing you."

We were lying silent and looking into the night sky. I could be calm about us - we survived so much, we will survive and this parting. And with this blissful thought I fell asleep embracing Iris, who was hugged to me.

And in the morning I went alone to meet a new adventure

⌐

6

FIRES ON DEAD SWAMPS

4. Ahau 16. Pax – morning

The hot sun slowly climbs into the sky. We stand on an almost treeless helmet[9] over a kind of infinite green plain overgrown with low, limp trees and lush grasses. Their bright color immediately warns against small pools with rust-colored water, in which the depth lurks. Overwhelmingly fragrant smell with beautiful flowers that grow here and there to form colorful clumps on a monotonous, furiously green background. During the day it is quite nice here, but at night there is no courage man - except for a few witches and sorcerers who derive significant benefits from their profession - who would dare to venture into these swamps. Formerly there was a delta of a great river here, which disappeared as a result of the Cataclysm, or maybe changed course... - it does not matter. Only the delta remained, which from the north adjoins the Eastern Ocean, and from the south to the plains of Crimea.

The swamp area takes a roughly rectangular size of two hundred to fifty miles. And this is where the remains of *Viman's* flying

---

9   A low hill with a round shape and gentle slopes.

machines and space-sage *Rakśiases* are to be found in this area. Some of them might have lethal weapons on board, which had to be located and, if possible, disposed of. Unless they first activate themselves and dispose of those who have come to seek them...

"Where will we camp?" I asked Master Haneda who was accompanying me.

"On top of this helmet," he replied. "It's the best place. We'll have an insight into the whole area, wolves won't come in here, and mosquitoes won't eat us alive.

It's true, mosquitoes. I forgot about this scourge completely. These was beyond measure here.

And mud.

"Tigers also stay away from this place. Wolves too," he added, "and animals are rarely seen here at all and it is only by chance. Even birds."

"They are afraid?" I asked. "But what?"

"That's why we're here to explain it," said Master Haneda indifferently and moved slowly toward the top of the helmet.

"Since when did it start?" I asked. "It wasn't always like that here?"

"Three years ago, after an extremely strong earthquake," he replied.

Yeah. I knew the rest. A few people went into this mud searching for rare plants and mushrooms, which were later sold to local pharmacists for miraculous potions. They were later sought after and found - the wretches lay horribly burned in the swamp, but this was not the cause of their death, but rather a kind of poisoning with substances that got into the body through the lungs. Approximately twenty of them were killed when the Emperor Czi became interested. He ordered his son to conduct a delicate investigation into this matter, because the local police could not do it - these areas remained under the control of the Crymatrians clan, who were reluctant to look at the envoys of the Jasper Palace. However, the investigation was carried out when the Crymatrian khan turned to Prince Czhien on the mysterious death of several of his tribesmen. The old grudges were forgotten and the Crymatrian people, together with the Han people, found a dozen more victims of the mysterious phenomenon. In all, thirty-two Hans and twenty Crymatrians were killed. The swamp was considered cursed and people avoided it. Also animals. And yet the Dead Swamp enjoyed a bad reputation also during the times of King Culla of Atlantis, that is at least for two thousand years. How many people died there, Sviatovid and Viśnu deign to know...

It turned out that the Jasper Palace decided to finally end this situation of uncertainty and fear. Emperor Czi decided to establish a lasting peace with the Crymatrian people and at the same time to drain the sinister swamps and populate these previously unpopulated areas, which gave a chance to get quite fertile rice fields and for the cultivation of millet, sago and wheat and vegetables. And now somewhere in these swampy backwoods there was something that killed people in such a strange and painful way... Finally, someone advised the emperor to bring representatives of the Brotherhood of the Green Dragon to put an end to the evil of the swamps. The imperial envoys first came to Master Wu Traketraj who trained us in the martial arts of katana, and who directed them to the Commander of the Brotherhood in Yuetshi in Hyrkania. And then it went quickly - from Hyrkania the request was directed to Aghrapuru and from there by solar telegraph to Belverus, from which on the same day there was a departure order for Master Haneda, who first went to Vendhia, and from there by sea to Khitay. After my adventures on the South Island of the Isle of Mist Archipelago, I sailed there and after three weeks of sailing I got to Paikang, where Master Haneda was waiting for me. And now we were both looking at the strange land at our feet...

At the same time my thoughts were interrupted by the thirst of a dozen or so horses behind our backs.

"It's a Crymatrian patrol," Haneda said calmly. "I'll talk to them."

We turned slowly and we saw a view of maybe twenty armed horsemen. They did not betray hostile intentions, but their numerical advantage seemed so devastating that they did not draw their weapons.

They came closer and the soldier nearest us told something in an unfamiliar to me language. Haneda answered and the stranger saluted him with the sword.

"This is the patrol of the Great Khan of the Crymatrians," he said, "asking what we're doing here and who allowed us to enter here. I said that we have permission from the emperor Czi and dzara[10] from the Great Khan.

The commander said something else, and Haneda nodded.

"We have to follow him to the Great Khan," he said with a slight surprise in his voice, "this is an invitation to the Naadaam festival, one of the most important holidays here. We must go with them. Remember, here the rejection of the invitation is the greatest insult..."

And he followed the leader and the rest of the unit behind him. Without thinking, I followed them.

4. Ahau 16. Pax – afternoon and evening

After two hours of driving, we reached the capital of Crimatria, if a few hundred yurts and tents, set on a relatively level place at the foot of a dozen or so hills that protected them from the cold winds from the sea in the winter, could be called the city.

The yurts were large and round. Their walls were white, red and black. In the largest of them was visible the great Khan's bunchuk. We were introduced to it without a large pump and the whole Eastern ceremonial, which apparently was only valid for the show, but there was a category of people that it did not apply, including us. After a while, we entered to see face of the Great Khan.

"Welcome!" He said in Hyborian, without a foreign accent, "Master Haneda and you, Master Vislanian!"

However, after a moment he went to the local dialect and Haneda explained to me half-arsed content of the conversation, which showed that on the occasion of the Naadaam festival we are special guests of the Great Khan and invites us to an evening feast.

I watched him closely because he did not look like a Crymatrian or even more like a Han man. He was tall at least seven feet and with a massive carcass. He was not fat but muscular. He was maybe forty

---

10 Type of letter of recommendation or permission for, among others passage and stay issued by lay rulers and spiritual leaders in Mongolia and Tibet.

years old, but no more. Black hair cut short above the forehead, blue cold eyes and a complexion lighter than the average inhabitant of these region. He moved with the dexterity of the tiger approaching his prey. He had a thundering voice and the laughter of a carefree child. He reminded me of someone, but I could not associate him with any character I knew - already alive, already legendary.

"So, I invite you to Naadaam Square," he cried with his powerful voice. "Follow me!!!"

And he went outside.

"Remember," Haneda said hastily, "at the feast you must not refuse anything. You must eat and drink even a small nibble or drench your lips. Besides, you can't...

He did not finish, because the Great Khan cried out and his subordinates almost put us in his powerful form. We had to admire the displays of warriors and civilians, and there was something to admire.

Great Chan introduced us all as his illustrious guests. Probably, because he mentioned our names, or maybe he said something else, enough that his speech to the people ended with a stormy applause, and then began to show off.

First riding horses and a horse vaulting, and then riding bulls performed by both men and women. Actually, it was not riding, but something like a vaulting, dance or something like that. The dancers ran up to the enraged animal from the forehead so as to jump and hit the feet in between the horns, and when the bull raised his head - they jumped into the air making the flippers and landed far behind his tail. Any mistake threatened death at the horns and hooves of the bull, but nothing dangerous happened. Fortunately.

The next was shooting with great compact bows. Shooting for immovable and moving targets. Also shot to large turnips thrown into the air. They were rarely missed. Then they were shot again from the speeding horses for shields and moving shields and pendulums. And then a group of riders fired at a large pumpkin placed on a twenty-foot wooden pole.

The next point of the program was a competition like our chasing a fox or a brythuan fox hunt. In this case, they were fighting for ram leather. All winners were rewarded with applause, beaten by laughter and whistling.

Next were the traditional battles of inventory masters - similar to Western stocks and Far East sumo. The players similarly liked the latter - powerful men and women weighing at least two or three times the average weight of the citizen of this land. Impressive clashes, powerful panting of these giants aroused the amazing emotions of the viewers. Also Great Khan, who also was passionate about this sport and maybe he did it when he was younger...

I watched the people around me. It was an amazing collection of various races and human types. There were completely white individuals resembling Aesirs or Nordlanders from Asgard and Vanaheim. There were also a few black Kushyts and residents of the Black Kingdoms. And everyone was treated equally. It was very interesting, because it meant that the Crimatrians had extensive relations among the nations of the world, but how could they have lived in these steppes? - that's what I was not able to find out now.

With the sunset, a general feast began. The whole valley was filled with the smell of roasted oxen and rams. We were invited to the yurt of the Great Khan, with whom we had a feast until dawn. And in fact - we sat in a circle and a feast began for the sign given by the Great Khan. The colorfully clad young women brought huge smoked bowls of meats in a spicy sauce and cakes of *czaparati*. The revelers took pieces of meat and divided them deftly with daggers and manipulated them with chopsticks, eating spicy rice with fruit and pineapples. There were sweet honey cakes and fruit. And many other very good things that I had to taste. What tasted the most to me was something that looked like our stewed cabbage, but the role of cabbage in it played onion, garlic and huge amounts of hot and mild peppers. The dish was spicy and woke up thirst, which was quenched with beer or drink from fermented milk.

The hum of chatter lulled and I felt lumbering. Around midnight, I took a nap while sitting on a pillow. The number of impressions exceeded the possibilities and I fell into half-sleep. After some time I was awakened by a powerful clap in hands and thunderous laughter. Great Khan looked at us warmly and when he laughed to the end, he said in a Hyborian:

"Master Lestek, don't sleep, because now you'll have to check up!" He cried. "Am I saying good?" And he handed me a cup of some fragrant drink.

"Good!" A whole bunch of revelers roared.

Great Chan raised his golden mug.

"Then Master," he said thunderously, "to the bottom! Here's to you!"

"Same to you!" I replied and tasted the liquor. It was sweet with a bitter note, but pleasant and warming the stomach nicely. After a while I felt a wave of heat - it had to contain a significant amount of alcohol and something else from which my heart moved with a sharp rhythm...

I drank all and I felt pleasant excitement and dizziness. This night promised to be more interesting than I imagined.

5. Imix 17. Pax – night

"Go for it!" The troop shouted.

I did not want to oppose the drunk people and moved from my place. A few people grabbed my arms and led me from the yurt of the Great Khan to a smaller one, standing on the sidelines. Gently, but firmly pushed me inside. I walked in and stunned for a moment.

A beautiful young girl lay on a large fluffy bed. She could be seventeen, maximum eighteen. Despite the haziness of a drink containing a drug, I understood two things at once, namely that I was supposed to be the father of her child, what was expected from me and what the Great Chan expected from me. In a short moment I remembered Akira's "Way of Kings" and a passage about the youth of Conan the Cymmerian, in which when he described his youth, he had similar episode... In an instant, I realized that the Great Chan is the son of Conan and some local beauty. Everything was right, the age of the Great Khan and...

I looked at the girl. She had the features of a typical Hyborian, long dark but not black hair with fringes trimmed above her eyes, which were shimmering with green. She was nicely built, her young body was velvety smooth and promised a lot. Unlike the women here, she wore rainbow sari and refined sandals on delicate feet. She was beautiful. She had little in her of the Han people, except for the charm that distinguishes Eastern women - here the blood of father turned out to be stronger.

She looked at me and smiled temptingly.

"Come to me," she said in a pleasant, girlish voice.

Perhaps at other times, I would not resist her and use her invitation, put my face in her hair and hug her, kiss her full pink lips and drown in the green of her eyes.

But not here and not now. There was a game going on, there was a test.

I bowed in front of her.

"Welcome granddaughter of the great Conan of Cymmeria, and today the king of Aquilonia." I said calmly. "What's your name?"

I felt the hellish drink slowly evaporate from me and my mind regains its former efficiency.

Cute eyebrows rose up over the girl's eyes, which in amazement resembled frightened saucers. She did not expect that. Not this.

"How do you know who I am?" She asked surprised. It's a secret... My father doesn't show me to the people..."

"You are like your father, first of all," I said, "and secondly your father is almost a copy of your grandfather. It is impossible to confuse them."

"Father told the truth," she said quietly. "You're indeed a great priest whose mind is able to penetrate everything. My name is T'ao, like my mother."

"I hope I don't have to make love with you, T'ao, although to tell you the truth I feel like I want it, I think it's because of this drink," I said, "and by the way, you have an interesting way to prevent some nasty diseases. Your women made love with foreigners and in this way you have a constant supply of fresh blood. Very clever!" I praised.

"You're right, Master Lestek," T'ao replied, "it was a test. "You'll feel better soon and your mind will be free of lust... Although truth be told... I also want to make love you..." She smiled.

"It won't happen," I said, "I'm married and have a daughter of your age."

"Really?" Her eyes was shining, "tell me about her!"

"But…???"

I smiled.

"Tia is a foster daughter," I said, "she comes from Agra, her parents are dead and she has only her uncle. And she is also a member of the Brotherhood of the Green Dragon. Incidentally, she saved our lives a few times…

"Master," she said in a humble voice, "please…"

"Perhaps at other times, T'ao," I said, "and for now I'd like to know what this test meant. Because, as I understand, your father should appear here soon…"

I felt a slight breath of air on my cheek and realized he was here. I turned around and T'ao jumped off the bed.

"Father," she said with a bow, "Master Lestek passed the test."

Of course. If he could only trust someone it would be his loved ones.

"Master," he said in a deep voice, "sit down and I'm asking you for a short conversation. It has a connection with what you'll do here."

I noticed that Haneda had slipped into the yurt quietly.

"So, it's like thia?" I thought. "That's why he didn't tell me everything."

I wanted to laugh but I could not laugh, because the moment was inappropriate.

"As far as I understand, Great Khan, this attempt is connected with our mission, am I wrong?" I asked.

"You aren't mistaken," he replied, "and to hell with the titles, these are just labels we stick to, to add seriousness. I'm Tengiz aka Arima son of Conan from Cymmeria. And T'ao is my counselor and confidant, I trust her only. And now to the point." He looked at us.

He had a way of being identical to his father.

"We are listening, lord," Haneda said.

"Go to sleep tonight, and tomorrow I'll introduce you to something that has a direct relationship with what really happens in these swamps. This test was necessary for Master Lestek. I don't trust anyone and I had to find out if you can influence and whether your mind controls the body even in such situations, I realized that yes. And that I can trust you - I can. I wish you a good night."

He got up and left with his daughter.

I fell on the bed and fell asleep like a gopher. Haneda too - we were both really tired of the day and the feast, and the action of the hellish aphrodisiac also did its job. So we slept until midday.

5. Imix 17. Pax – afternoon

Tengiz called us immediately as soon as he was informed that we were up. We were introduced to his yurt where he was waiting for us in the company of some people. We bowed to him and he introduced us without any further ado.

"Noble Masters!" He said. "These are the family members of the victims of these treacherous swamps. They would like to know the truth about what killed their relatives."

"Lord! Let me correct your words. "And in response to the astonished gaze of everyone I have added. "Because you can't say what about it, but who killed them."

"How can I understand your words, Master Lestek?" Great Khan asked me with a slight astonishment in his voice.

Haneda looked at me and raised his eyebrow slightly.

"Exactly as I said," I replied, "they weren't killed by swamps or animals living on them, they were killed by people and their products left here since the last war of the gods of air and darkness. I'm sure of that."

I paused for a moment. I gave Great Khan and the people some time to cool down, then I continued:

"Our investigation has shown that in the swamps there may be war machines and unknown types of weapons, which from time to time become active and become dangerous for people and everything that lives within their reach... And in our world also live people who want to get to them, because they dream of power over the world, won with these terrible weapons. Can there be something worse? I don't think so - isn't Great Khan?"

"I understand." The latter replied.

"I'd like to ask these people a few questions, if you allow the Great Khan." I bowed towards him. "Can I?"

"Ask, Master." He replied.

So I asked these people about where and when their relatives died. It turned out that there was no specific place in the swamps that would be highlighted. There was no point here. As for time, it was not known when death reached its victims - most often found after two or three days, when an alarmed family began to seek out with their own or neighbors or the imperial police. There was also no point here. The only common point was the state of corpses - they were covered with cruel burns that were still made during the victim's life, as if they were thrown into a campfire alive...

"Have you noticed something strange, unusual," I asked the next question, "something that has never been seen here or in the swamps?"

The reaction of people was interesting. The muttering crowd fell silent at once, as if from a silent strike of lightning. A thought came to my mind and I went all in. I went to the white wall of the yurt and drew the shape of a flying object, with the charcoal from the hearth, about which was told to us by interrogated Stygian prisoners captured in Goa. Beside it, I drew a sign of double lightning and cross from angles. I looked at the audience closely. Their reaction was unambiguous - they knew about it or saw it...

"Did any of you see anything like flying over swamps?" I asked.

The silence was deadly. But it spoke more than a thousand words uttered.

"Do I should understand that no?" I asked another question.

"Tell the truth," said the Great Khan, clearly agitated, "nothing will happen to you!"

The Crimatrians muttered something between themselves until a grandfather with a beard turned up.

I looked at him.

"Speak freely," said Tengiz-Arima.

"Great Khan!" Said the senile but strong voice. And you Master! Some of us have seen something like flying over swamps, always on the day or three days before finding these unfortunate people. We were afraid to talk about it so that we would not be taken for lunatics and expelled from the cluster..."

"These are the laws here," Haneda said explainingly.

I understood these people and their fear. On the other hand, I also understood this grim law. The cluster's interests were always above the interests of the individual...

Suddenly a young boy appeared from the cluster. He could be about fifteen. He bowed to the Khan and looked at us.

"Great Khan and you Masters," he said in a calm voice, "as you know, I was with my friend in the swamps. I didn't tell the whole truth because I saw Karim die."

"Who are you and where are you from?" I asked.

"I'm Ulisay-baatyr, son of baj[11] Hmalla-batyr, and I come from here...

"How did this happen?"

The boy shuddered at the memory of the terrible event. He cooled out and started his story:

"I and Karim went this morning to the swamps for the roots of sain-fhanu, it's a plant from which the root is used for various medicines. Apothecaries pay well for it, 2 gold drachmas for each root cun. But it's hard to find. A lot of it grows in swamps, but getting to places where it grows is dangerous..."

"To the point!" Chan interrupted him. "And what next?"

The boy looked at him without fear.

"We have just arrived to the island of d'Bu-Phü-Andrëre, standing at the edge of the swamps," he continued, "when we noticed at once this... this object. It was coming from the sea towards the land. Suddenly a thing like a cylinder sprang up from it and hissing next to us hissing. I was scared very much and escaped to the shore, and Karim stayed there..."

He fell silent as if gathering strength for a further tale.

---

11 Baj – rich man, rich merchant.

"And what happened next?" I asked. "Has there been a strong flare of a great fire and a bang?"

"No, sir..." The boy opened his eyes wide with astonishment. "No Master," he repeated.

"So what happened?" I asked with more and more astonishment.

"This item hissing more and more. Karim laughed that I was stupid, that I was running away, and then... then..." he was stuck again.

We were silent waiting for the next part.

"And then flames shot around him. It was strange because only the air around his feet was burning. Then he shouted and I jumped in to help him. He staggered and fell. He was covered in flames. I came too late, because when I bent over him, he was dead. His body looked terrible. Suddenly, I felt that I was weak. My head was dizzy, I felt nauseous and fell. When I regained consciousness it was already dark. The moon was shining. In the light of it, I sought out this mysterious object and took it with me. And in the morning I managed to get to the place where we camped, from where I went to my parents and my father's people. You already know the rest..."

"Do you have this item here?" I asked the boy.

"Yes Master," said the boy. He reached for the backpack he had brought with him and took out a mysterious bottle from it. He gave it to me, then bowed and returned to the cluster.

"Great Khan," I said, "this boy is worth for a reward."

5. Imix 17. Pax – evening

We were finally alone and we could think about it all. The most important result of our trip was that we had an object - a concrete proof of action from someone outside our world. They were not old, scarred artefacts that crumbled at the first touch. We had written accounts of witnesses and material evidence of the existence of these beings and their machines.

We watched the bottle from all sides. Undoubtedly, it was brand new, made the most the year before. It was made of light metal coated furiously with sulfur yellow varnish, on the surface of which we saw a string of black characters arranged in the following inscriptions - because the fact that they were inscriptions was more than certain:

GFCG-87
IG Farben Süd Amerika
Mod. A/2012
№ 0000147

And some strange drawings depicting a skull with crossed crossbones and a burning piece of wood, a black line drawn on an orange diamond-shaped background...

"What do you think about this, Master?" I asked Haneda.

"It's completely new," he said, "and it's done just as well, and maybe even better than what we've already seen."

"And these characters? Haven't we seen anything like this before?"

"I didn't, and you?"

"Me either. So we're dealing with someone new who entered the game and on the opposite side..." I said.

"Gedrena and her priests?"

"Exactly. And this is the worst thing that she's manipulated by them, or everyone is manipulated by these..."

"...others," Haneda prompted me.

"The Hyborians don't have such machines, also the Hyperboreans. Similarly like the Picts."

"There are no such here either," Haneda murmured, "so Lemurians and the people of Mu remain, but I doubt it. We'd know something about it. Similarly, Black Kingdoms and Zembabwei. And Vendhia with her neighbors."

"Vendhia is out," I said, "Iranistan, Kosala, Uttara Kuru, Kambudja - it all are out, because here you need completely new technical solutions, and they don't have it. Anyway, no one in modern..."

I fell silent because a thought dawned on me.

"And what's next?" Haneda looked at me waiting for the next words that did not occur, because I was touched by a sudden but mistaken guess.

"In the modern world, but who will warrant me or in the Past or... Future," I said, because at once I saw that something in the shape of a gate to look at the world differently opens to me.

"Do you think they... that they... came from another..." he searched for an appropriate term, "from another point in time?"

"Do you have another explanation?" I answered the question with a question. "Look, this object - it's new. It was done with an incredibly precise method that we don't know. It's covered with varnish that we can not make ourselves and are covered with inscriptions, if there are inscriptions, that we can't read. This container contained a gas that is not only flammable, it is still poisonous."

"The products of it burning are poisonous," Haneda said.

"You're right," I said, "that's how it is with it. In a word, it works on the principle: "if you don't use stick, use club". We didn't meet with something like that. So the conclusion is one..." I hung up my voice.

"We're dealing with newcomers from the Future..." Haneda said quietly.

"You said it Master..." I finished.

"Belverus will have to be noticed before they know that we know too much," I said, not knowing how close I was to the truth. "Send intentional man?"

"No need, the emperor has good mail, its couriers travel the country to 30 miles a day. Two weeks and the courier will reach the commandment in Yuetshi and then to Belverus, the message will be directed by the telegraph."

I sighed. Two weeks was a lot of time and accidents were starting to gain momentum. Suddenly, I heard something strange. An unusual sound coming from behind the corrugated wall of the yurt. I pointed his sword at Haneda and I took the crossbow and loaded it. With one blow I turned off the lamp and the yurt became dark. I heard sneaking steps on the side of Haneda, who, without waiting for anything, pushed his katana into the wall of the yurt. I heard a moan and the sound of the body falling.

The night exploded in a moment with muffled claps and holes appeared on the wall of the yurt, and the air was blown away from something invisible. We fell to the ground by reflex. One thing was certain - someone wanted to kill us. I crawled towards the wall and picked up the warp to look outside. And outside it was relatively bright, and in the light of the stars I saw black figures that pointed long black pipes to the yurt. After a while, I heard the muffled cracks again and the walls of the yurt covered with holes. I did not wait for the next string, I just crawled out of the yurt and got to the next one by one jump. Its round walls did not give any defense, but they gave shelter from the eyes of the aliens. I did not wait for the next string, but fired towards the nearest black figure. There was a moan and a grunt. The bolt stuck in the neck breaking the spine. I eliminated the second opponent. I charged the crossbow and decided to deal with the other two.

I did not manage to, because Haneda jumped from behind a different yurt and knocked down the third striker with one blow. The fourth turned to him and at the same moment I stuck a bolt into his neck. I looked around quickly, but there was no one in sight, but I saw something that at first I took for a big yurt, but it was not it...

On the ground stood this mysterious flying object, which was seen by the locals over the swamps.

"Haneda! Torches!" I shouted.

After a moment Haneda brought two torches that gave so much light that it was possible to look more closely at this object. It was shaped like two bowls joined together with a low dome on the upper part. Its color was black and so did not reflect the light, and the shape of the cross was visible on the dome with four white angles, two lightnings and two marks - 04. That was all. We heard some voices behind us - it was lured by the fight and lights that people from the neighboring yurts came out to see what had happened.

I turned to warn them, when out of the corner of my eye I noticed that one of the people I had shot (because I was sure that the Aliens were human) moved and slowly took out of the pocket on the sleeve a small box from which he took out a half-foot silvery rod. Something sparkled with a ruby red. The man looked at me for a moment with a terrible hatred in his eyes.

"*Auf wiedersehen im Hölle...*" He whispered and pressed on the red button. At the same moment something terribly flashed behind my back. I turned my head and saw the object turn into a blazing ball of fire that darkened and flowed. I turned around and, instead of four people, I saw only four dents in the grass straightening slowly. I understood that the man had activated some self-destructive mechanism, but at the same time he escaped - perhaps he returned to his time..."

"What did he say?" I heard Haneda's voice behind me.

"I don't know," I answered, "I think he said something about Hell, if the word *Hölle* is equivalent to the Hyperbornian helle, because it sounds identical. Does he wish me Hell?"

It was quite possible in his situation," Haneda murmured, smiling crookedly. "In his place, I'd like to wish you exactly the same..."

6. Ik 18. Pax – morning

We could not sleep that night. The awareness of the fact that the murderers threatened us with a dangerous machine gun did not give us peace. The only consolation was that we could fight and win with them. Our advantage was that they were too confident and it downfall them. We lay on the bedding and listened to every night noise.

June nights are short, so when we saw the first light of the day through the holes of the yurt, we breathed a sigh of relief and managed to fall into a nervous dream from which we were awakened only by the messenger of the Great Khan who called us to him. However, before we went to his yurt, we looked at the place of the night shooting.

The walls of the yurt were riddled with a series of small holes, which were the effect of alien weapons. Watching exactly the wooden frame of the yurt structure we found a dozen or so holes in which strangely regular pieces of metal were stuck, after the extraction of which we found that they were pieces of lead in steel, covered with golden tombac shirts. They all had sharp tips and flat backs. Besides, in the grass we found a lot of metal, brass sleeves that emitted a sharp smell from inside. Their blinded parts were again bearing signs that we did not know. Brass sleeves and pieces of metal embedded in the yurt wood construction matched each other. The diameter of the holes after these pieces of metal was some 1/3 of an inch...

"It's a kind of vartaĝarata weapon," Haneda said, watching our findings. "Something like this has already been found in the Stygian deserts."

"So what are we going with it to the Great Khan?"

Haneda nodded and we went.

A surprise awaited us in Great Khan's yurt. Above all, there was a Khitayan office and his footstools. Great Khan sat pensive on his throne, and next to him T'ao. We noticed concern on their faces.

"Hello," he said briefly to our welcome. "These are our masters from the Brotherhood of the Green Dragon, who are investigating the known accidents in the Swamp of the Dead, and here too..."

"My name is Feng," the Khitayan introduced himself unceremoniously, "and I'm the Imperial investigator delegated to this case. On behalf of emperor Czi, who is most eminent, let him live eternally, and whose name is known in all corners of the world, I'm asking you to tell me about what happened last night, please." He said, emphasizing the word "please", which in Eastern satres extremely rare.

I briefly summarized everything that we were able to determine and we agreed without going into the details of the night fight with four men in a flying vehicle. It seems Feng dealt with what had just happened to the flying structure, which he called the chariot, though he did not remember it in the slightest. He regretfully took note that the object so desirable by the emperor, would he live forever, the object disappeared.

"Can you go to Paikang with me and repeat all that personally to His Imperial Majesty, would he live forever?" Feng asked pleasantly.

Haneda nodded.

"Well, then tomorrow morning we're going to Paikang." Feng said. It seemed that he was very relieved. At least it guaranteed that his head would stay in place in the near future.

We have already exchanged a few polite nonsense with Feng, and the hearing ended. I got the impression that the Emperor became interested in the matter of a flying vehicle, which would greatly raise its prestige, which depended on him, like every mighty of the world and least concerned with the fate of his subjects, which did not bode well. As far as we are concerned, the goal of the mission has been achieved in so far as it has been explained - if a combination of such crazy events could be called an explanation - cases of strange and mysterious deaths in the Swamps of the Dead. We did not find what we were supposed to find, but from conversations with local people, Han and Crimatrians, we learned that there is nothing unusual in the swamps, and if it is, it is under a layer of mud and peat thick for several dozen feet that practically would not be possible bring it out without draining the swamps. So nature itself has made sure that dangerous artifacts do not get into the wrong hands.

Only the worst thing was that after solving one problem, the second problem appeared - far more dangerous and real. The problem of *strangers* from flying machines, which solution most probably was among the sands and temples of distant Stygia...

"Father is asking you Master," I heard T'ao's sweet voice behind me.

I turned around and saw her in a green-blue sari. There was a smile on her face and something that was a delicate blush. She hid it quickly, dropping her head.

"Come with me, Master," she said quietly and moved forward. I followed her. We entered the yurt which is a private apartment of the Great Khan. He was already waiting for us.

"Master Lestek, I have a private request for you that concerns my daughter," he began without preamble.

"How can I help you, Your Highness?" I asked.

"I'm concerned about T'ao's security," he said with a worried voice, "if it is as you told this Feng, this means that at any moment we are in danger of being attacked again by *those creatures*."

"Han people?" I asked, though I guessed who he meant.

"Theirs too," he said, "I don't trust them, that's why I'm asking you to take her away from here, as soon as possible, to my mother's family in Rou-Gen. I can entrust my daughter, the light and the pupil of my eyes, only to you, because only you can defend her and deliver her to her destination."

I raised my eyebrows.

"Who did they consider me to be a miracle worker?" I thought.

"If I can cope with this task," I said calmly, "I'll face it. The noble-man's word."

"Are you from a noble line?" He was surprised. "It doesn't show on you at all, Master!"

"Yet I am, like almost everyone in the Brotherhood," I smiled, "but it doesn't matter now."

"Then go tonight and let heaven lead you," he said, hugging his daughter. "I trust in you, Master."

"Thank you for trust," I answered with a nod, "I'll do everything in my power so that your daughter will come to the family."

7. Akbal 19. Pax

We drove in the darkness illuminated only by the faint flames of the stars. Initially, I was afraid that T'ao could not cope with the horse, but it turned out that he rides perfectly and can take care in the dark. She dressed like me - mid thigh pants, riding boots with short upper, a leather jacket and a masking cape. For this perfect local compact bow soft cases and quiver with twenty arrows. She could pass as a member of the Brotherhood. And that was it.

Later that same day Haneda would go with Feng to Paikang to report to Emperor Chi and deal with the issues of the commandery he was developing.

We left the campsite and headed not on the Paikan Route, but on the seafront, where we were after an hour of drive.

"We'll go along the seashore, that is much closer, and besides, we'll miss Paikang," T'ao said.

"Aren't you afraid to go on an unguarded road?" I asked.

"No, and in some aspects this route is the safest and... the most interesting," she replied enigmatically, "we'll go about five days.

And we drove along the sandy and pebble beach. There were one and a half urtons from the estate of the Great Khan to Paikang, that is one and a half days' drive, to Rou-Gen three times that, because the coast was longer - at least five urtons.

I was even happy that we were going this way, because I like two things: the sea and the stars overhead and the mountains and the stars overhead. There is no more beautiful view and there is nothing more subdued and allowing to think about infinity, like a starry night in the mountains or by the sea...

We drove silently next to each other and watched the flames of stars flying across the sky. A breeze blew from the sea, which heralded a storm. After traveling twenty miles, we made a bait at the foot of a strip of bizarre rocks that resembled ruins in their shapes.

"These are actually ruins," T'ao said, jumping off her horse. "I wanted you to look at them, because they should interest you."

I understood what she meant by speaking about certain aspects of this tour.

"What is this place?" I asked.

"Han people call it City of Ghosts," T'ao laughed at showing beautiful white teeth, "because it's supposedly haunting here. Incidentally, such cities on the route we will have more..."

"Really?"

"They are spoken like that to scare, but there is something in this, because such flying spheres have been seen here," I have turned up my ears, "such flying oranges."

I did not tell her about our adventures on the South Island, that is I said, but without mentioning some details. Observing the orange ball I carefully omitted...

"Really?" I act courteously surprised, "flying oranges?"

"Well, they're huge, at least ten to fifteen feet in diameter!" She cried enthusiastically. "If we succeed, maybe we'll see some of them!"

"I'd rather not," I thought, but on the other hand I was tempted by the riddle. I wondered if it had any connection with my would-be assassins.

We unsaddled the horses and set up an impromptu camp. We ate some of our supplies and drank water from a nearby stream. The sun was warming and the sea was rustling lazily, so not thinking much, we lay on the sand and fell asleep.

The awakening was brutal. The thunderbolt had ushered us to our feet. A shaft of black clouds was coming from the sea, above which a characteristic "anvil" was burning with a blinding white.

"A storm is coming, we'll take shelter in the ruins," T'ao shouted, shouting over the roar of the wind and pointing to the rocks.

We set off to this side and soon found a cave formed of a few flat plates that were broken at different angles and formed a large space closed on three sides in the rock - or rather in the ruins of some huge building. Inside, there were stalactites and stalagmites, which suggested that thousands of years had passed since it turned to the ruin...

Lightning bolts were thicker and thicker, and after half an hour darkness, interrupted by lightnings, came out. The roar of wind and waves went better with the thunder of a thunderbolt. T'ao was looking at the terrible game of the elements with complete phlegm. Nature's madness lasted until the night, and when it was over, the crystal web of constellations flared over us again. We fell asleep to the dead sleep of a just man.

8. Kan 0. Kayab - forenoon

The next day promised to be beautiful, but in the atmosphere you can feel a stuffiness. The night was quiet. I left the cave and I took the pleasure swimming in the sea. After yesterday's storm, the sea has washed up many strange things made of something like an amber mass, only in different colors and shapes. I gathered a dozen or so specimens into a bag made of a shirt, which I then intended to put into the bags. Kneeling, I was digging out of the sand next ones when a shadow fell on me.

I raised my head. T'ao stood over me. Her naked body and hair glistened with moisture in the morning sun. Small feet were drowning in the creamy sand.

"Good morning," she smiled at me, "I also took a bath. Wonderful water. And what did you dig out of this sand?"

I stood up, dusting my knees and calves from the sand. Our nakedness was a bit embarrassing, but I quickly went over it. T'ao was really beautiful. Her light skin contrasted nicely with the blue of the morning sky and dark hair and matched with the creamy whiteness of the sand. Her small girlish breasts were still lifting in the breath beat. A delicate blush filled her face...

"These pieces of colored material. They're so strange," I said, "I've not met them in such numbers anywhere."

"There's a many of them here," T'ao looked around, "you can collect it in many baskets. What exactly is it?"

"Some artificially made material," I said.

"Where do you get that confidence?" T'ao raised her eyebrows.

"Because in Nature there is no such thing." I replied. "So someone created them artificially."

"Who?" She asked with a sigh.

"They," I nodded at the ruins. T'ao's bare shoulder touched my arm. It was a very nice touch, which took me in a pleasant thrill... T'ao did not step back and we stood shoulder to shoulder looking at the ruins covered with shrubs and grass.

"It's horrible," she whispered with a serious face, "there must have been a populous city, big houses, streets, vehicles... And all at once turned into rubble."

"Don't think about it," I stroked her cheek. "It's gone like a bad dream."

She lifted her face and looked into my eyes. Her face expressed sadness.

"Lestek, they are gone, but memories remain," she said quietly. "Maybe a few thousand years ago there was someone like you and me in this place. Maybe they loved each other and... And there isn't any trace of them except for the pieces of this... something."

I put my arm around her and she hugged me, and her arm wrapped around my waist. I felt a wave of heat, but only for a moment. And for a moment I terribly missed Iris, I felt lack of her smile, her voice, a warm kind presence. We have not seen each other so much time...

"You miss Iris, don't you," T'ao asked quietly.

"Sure," I nodded, "she's alone there, I'm here alone..."

She raised her head and looked into my eyes. Her eyes had love and lust.

"It isn't as bad as you say," she said slowly. "Tia is with her, and I'm with you..."

She turned around and at once her arms wrapped around my neck, and a warm, delicate body stuck to me. I felt her rapid breathing on my neck and the brush of hot lips. I was gathering in a flash because it could have gone too far. I gently pushed her away and took a deep breath.

"So, what? We'll visit these ruins?" I asked.

T'ao also snapped out of it and mastered the emotions that she felt, but her eyes said something else...

"Oh, yes!" Sshe said. "I'll show you something right now."

We quickly put on our clothes and went towards the ruins that gave us shelter during the storm.

"Have you been here?" I asked.

"Yes, and several times," she said, "every time I discovered something new. Now I'll show you what is the most interesting.

I took out two torches and struck fire, after a while they flamed brightly. T'ao pulled my hand toward the nearest ruin complex. It must have been a huge building, because the slabs that formed it were now lying idly on a pile at least a hundred feet high. Despite the fact that it was overgrown with grass and pine trees, here and there was seen a complicated structure of what once housed people and their fate. T'ao guided me, striking me between huge rocks, which upon closer inspection seemed to be some columns or pillars, from which iron or steel rods, thick as my fist, came out. I tried to imagine a cataclysm that could break or break them, but I could not. It was beyond my imagination...

"It's there," T'ao pointed to a darkening, irregular hole seven or eight feet high. We went to it. After passing several dozen yards, the sidewalk began to fall down at a gentle angle. T'ao illuminated the wall and showed me a sign - a large white circle crossed diagonally with two lines.

"You were here?" I stated more than I asked.

"Yhm!" She replied. "A year ago. This corridor extends to the entire system of corridors running underground. Some of them are collapsed, and it runs for some four miles in the south-west direction.

"What's up there?" I asked with curiosity.

"Nothing, actually," she said. "Interestingly, that there are always thick metal rails in the shape similar to the Taj's ideogram." T'ao drew a vertical line that had a perpendicular bar on top. "And some of them had huge metal boxes. And skeletons. People and animals, a huge amount. Some rooms are simply littered paved with them.

"And this is why you know that this is ghost town?" I asked with a sneer.

"Probably..." She nodded, "those who were here believe that in the ruins are scaring ghosts of those people."

"So it'll have to be examined, and this is already a job for the Brotherhood."

She turned to me.

"Lestek," she said pleadingly, "could I belong to the Brother-hood?"

"You can, but on condition that you must be an adult..."

"...I'm adult," she replied. "Lestek, please!"

"What about your father?" I asked. "Don't forget that you're a princess and you're to take power over the Crimatrians."

"It doesn't threaten me," she smiled. "In Crimatria, a woman can't be a Great Khan, and I don't want to marry a sleazy savage or Han's swell... Now look!"

She pointed ahead.

A small hill protruded from the gloom. I lighted it with a torch and, despite my will, I shuddered. It was the mountain of bones of at least two hundred people. The skeletons lay without order and composition. Some of them fell apart, but some remained in quite good condition. The terrifying pile of bones lay at the very end of the corridor or tunnel, as it seemed to me, in fact, where it fell into an even wider and larger tunnel.

"Now look there!" T'ao went to the opposite wall and lit it with a torch."

The light fell on multicolored pebbles walled up in the plaster of the wall, so that together they formed a drawing.

"Mosaic!" I exclaimed. "No, it is...!"

"Exactly," T'ao smiled with triumph, "this is this city..."

8. Kan 0. Kayab – evening

And again, we sat at the blazing fire. There was a storm outside. We sat by the fire, warming in his warmth, and our clothes were drying on an improvised dryer. The rain caught us when we left one of the tunnels. Not wanting to go back through the stacks of bones we decided to go back to the beach. Our clothes were soaked in a few minutes, and when we got to "our" cave, we also were soaked. This time, we did not have fun in the performance and started a big fire, then we undressed and hung our clothes to dry on an improvised firegrate. T'ao sat down next to me and hugged me again. We were silent, because each of us was in our own way taken over by what we found in the dungeons of the Ghost Town. It got late, the storm died down, only the rain poured continuously, steadily and perpetually.

"Is it always here like that?" I asked.

"Yes," she nodded, "especially in the summer months.

"Do you know what I came up with?" I asked.

T'ao moved. In the light of the fire her body was pink with the heat of the flames.

"No, what's that?"

"That this city is connected to the Swamp of the Dead."

"How do you know?" She was surprised.

"Because, one of the largest tunnels runs towards them," I said, "and that could mean that there could be a port on the Swamps for the Chariots of Fire - as the Han people call it."

"But after a mile..." T'ao fell silent at once. "Indeed! You can be right!"

"Will we investigate this tomorrow?" I asked.

T'ao nodded.

"We got it," I said, "and now we go to sleep."

I spread the blankets for T'ao by the fire and the other at the entrance for myself. I wrapped it around me tightly and fell asleep listening to the noise and splash of rain.

* * *

I stood in the middle of a huge city. Houses the size of rocks surrounded me from all sides. Smashing vehicles darted down the smooth roads, flying vehicles in the shape of huge birds was flying above my head. It was a bright, sunny day. People were hurrying somewhere. Somewhere the voices of playing children were heard. People would come in and out of the ground, from where rumble was heard from time to time. Looking around I noticed that at once I rose into the air and see the city from a great height. This time my eyes went to the northeast, where the Swamps of the Dead should be.

They were not there. Instead of them, on the coastal plain, I saw something that resembled a cluster of huge towers that aimed at the sky. At once at the base of one of them flames flashed and the tower began to rise up. There was a horrifying, continuous thunder of higher and higher tones as the tower rose above me. I knew this phenomenon - Brahmasziras flying arrows were flying like that. So it must have been *Rakśias*... Suddenly a fragment separated from *Rakśias* and began to fall down. I thought that it would fall to the ground, but at the same time four canvas canopies blossomed over it, slowing down its momentum and allowing it to fall gently, and that time Rakśias flew on, dragging a streak of something like smoke or steam behind it.

The sun was higher above the ocean, and I was looking at it again. At once in the sky I saw a burning dot that was coming from the east. It speed was huge before I could count to five, a burning dot fell into the ocean maybe two or three miles from the shore. After a while the water in the place of the drop of this *object* brightened with an extremely strong glow. Before I could be surprised, a ball of fire sparkled from the water, sparkling with all the colors of the rainbow, which turned into a spherical cloud of steam...

The second same luminous spark fell into the ocean near the Swamps of the Dead. And there were identical phenomena. More balls and pillars of steam and smoke rose from the ocean. But this is nothing compared to the monstrous waves that arose as a result of the explosion. They moved from the epicenter to coastal cities and before I could say anything they fell. Under their terrible pressure, the walls of the houses burst, forming and falling down, burying everything and everyone under their ruins. Those who did not perish under the rubble drowned in the murky waters of the stormy sea...

I cried out in terror and horror.

* * *

And I woke up. Nearby, thunderbolts were thundering again. I was drenched in a cold sweat and my heart was beating in my chest like crazy. In the light of the lightning and the dying bonfire, I saw T'ao's worried face. I sat on my pallet.

"What was that?" She asked anxiously.

"Bad dream," I said.

She blew to my face.

"It's over now," she said. "It was just a stupid, bad dream. But I'm the only reality and understand it finally!"

In her eyes I saw love and lust again.

She sat on my lap. Before I could say anything, I felt her arms around my neck and lips on my lips. Her hot body clung to me. Small nipples dug into my torso.

"I love you, Lestek," she whispered hotly between one kiss and the other, "I love you... take me..."

That night I was faithful to Iris of Ianthe, but I could not leave a woman hard up for me to be unsatisfied. I could only do one thing...

...after a moment she shouted sharply and hung in my arms, breathing heavily. I understood that she had achieved her *nirvana*...[12]

9. Chicchan 1. Kayab – morning - noon

"Will you tell me what you dreamed about?" T'ao asked.

We finished eating breakfast, which consisted of pure water and dried fruits.

I shuddered at the memory of that dream. She noticed it.

---

12 In many cultures, continency is conceived as *coitus sine seminis eiaculatione*, and therefore Lestek *de facto* and *de iure* did not betray Iris and did not deeflorify T'ao.

"Tell me." She asked.

"All right," and I told her what I had seen in my dream.

She listened with half-open lips and very much taken over. Finally, I finished and breathed a sigh of relief as if I had throw one hundred pood weight off.

"It wasn't a dream," she said intently, "it was a vision. You have the gift of seeing the Past."

"No, not a gift," I murmured. "It just worked out the imaginary fancy after what we saw in the underground and in a dream made a synthesis of the images seen with my knowledge, just like that. And the rest is a matter of imagination."

"Yeees?" T'ao asked. "And then how did you know how the space port looks like, how did you call it? Where did you get the term 'space port'? Also from the imagination?"

"Hmmm... yeah, you're right," I nodded.

We did not discuss this subject further, but we did not want to stop penetrate the grim tunnels below the city. We decided to commit one more day to it.

Equipped with a torch beam, we went down the familiar corridor deep into the underground of the Ghost Town. We quickly passed the heaps of human bones, trying as little as possible to disturb the peace of their tomb. This time we went to the south-west, where the second part of the largest tunnel ran. It seemed that people lived on the surface, and their factories and other workshops were located under the surface. The tsunami caused by explosions in the ocean reached them just when they were underground. The two elements conspired against them and died, every single one... Because the fact that there was water here was surely one hundred percent - in the light of the torch, we saw all the rubble of sand and sludge applied here.

The tunnel ran south-west and after one and a half miles, it ended at the same time. It was not collapse, it was just the end of the tunnel. For a moment we looked around helplessly. All at once our attention was caught by what looked like a regular block of metal in the wall of the tunnel. We came closer to it and then it turned out that there are really thick doors. In the light of the torch, the gray material from which they were made could be seen. I tried to open them wider. They started, but they were incredibly heavy. A thought flashed and I tried to scratch it with a knife. It went amazingly easy, a silvery soft metal flashed under the gray layer.

"It's lead!" I said, surprised. "We must be carefull. Usually, hazardous structures are lined with lead."

We tried to open the door and after a lot of effort we succeeded.

We entered the dark interior. It was a kind of a vestibule or a lock, from which three doors led. In contrast to the tunnel and despite the open door there were no traces of water...

"I don't understand something here," I said aloud. "How is it? The entire tunnel was filled with water, and here there are no traces of it. And yet the door was half-open..."

"Maybe someone was there and after the resignation of water just left?" T'ao gave thought.

"But in that case his footprints would have to remain in the sand and slime," I replied, "and we haven't seen it..."

"It's really strange," T'ao said after a long reflection, "but I'm sure someone had to be here before us and after the waters from the tunnels and corridors had disappeared..."

We tried to open the other three doors and after a long struggle we opened one of them. To our surprise, a bluish-purple glow blazed behind them. We looked behind them and stood amazed. It did not shine any specific source of light, but the space itself where some (probably???) devices were located. We looked at it literally in a second, because I knew from experience that such a light was deadly. I pulled away T'ao's from door and closed it not without difficulty.

"What is this?" She asked, surprised.

"I'm not sure," I replied, "but it is probably some energy center, label or storage room, weapons warehouse..."

"Perhaps," she said unconvinced.

"Besides, I think I know why this city was attacked," I said, realizing that I had guessed something that bothered me from the very beginning, "precisely because it was in that, or rather under, that central. It is still working!..."

We were returning to the surface rather pleased with what we discovered, but nevertheless, a spoonful of tar in this honey barrel was the fact that someone in front of us in this central, or what it was, was staying. And we did not find any traces of this 'someone'. It was interesting because we found traces left by T'ao during her previous trips and they were perfectly preserved.

We broke camp and after an hour we rode south-west towards the city and port of Rou-Gen, avoiding Paikang from the south.

12. Lamat 4. Kayab - noon

Farewell with T'ao was short. We stood facing each other with our hands in our hands.

"I will miss you," she said.

"Don't exaggerate, princess," I replied looking in her almond-shaped eyes, "you'll forget me faster than you think. You'll find a prince and marry him. You'll rule your country through him. And the stupider he'll be, the easier it'll go.

She laughed.

"I will miss your dirty humor."

"You'll also can handle with that."

"Lestek," she said at once very seriously. "If something had happen to your Iris, you know... Than I... I'll be waiting here for you. You can always come to me."

"I don't promise you anything," I replied, "and now goodbye, because we're just bouncing off the pier."

We kissed each other and after a while I was aboard the junk, which bounced off the pier and headed towards Vendhia. I was going back home...

3. Eznab 14. Cumhu – noon and evening

Junk was berthing to the port of Goa. Two women in identical sapphire saris stood on the stone flagstones of the pier. I had no idea how they knew I would come today on this ship, but I did not care.

Mooring came to an end and merchant and clariners came in on board. After a few minutes, my feet again touched the ground, a terra firma. I walked towards the women and after a moment I embraced them both.

"You are here my beloved." I heard the voice of Iris.

"You are finally here, daddy." Tia added. "Welcome home."

For a long moment I embraced them enjoying their presence.

* * *

A fast blue twilight fell over the city, which soon turned into a night. We lay side by side on a wide bed on the patio of our house. I told Iris about what I experienced in the Swamp of the Dead and in the dungeons of the Ghost Town. I was wondering whether to tell her about T'ao. I could tell her or not - in the first case I would hurt her, in the second one I would feel bad.

"Iris, dear," I said slowly, "I must confess to you."

"What honey?" She looked at me in amazement." "Are you and T'ao..."

"I nodded."

"I caressed her and..."

"And she?"

"She got the orgasm and fell asleep."

She sighed.

"Well, I didn't expect that from you," she said reproachfully. "How could you…"

"I know, I'm sorry," I whispered.

"Do you know what pisses me off?" She asked.

"No." I looked at her with amazement.

"That you didn't fuck her!" She shouted. "And I don't even know, idiot, do I want to make a fuss about it or not!"

I was speechless from amazement...

⌒

7

THIRD DIRACA EQUATION

I

"Correspondence to you." Tia gave me a packet of papers and parchments. After my return from Khitay, she became the secretary and documentarian of our Commandry in Goa. In spite that she has twenty she fulfilled this function excellently - she was conscientious, calm, discreet and, above all, extremely diligent. In half a year, she was able to organize the library and the office of the Commandry, and with the knowledge of four languages, she was able to quickly establish contacts with people and - most importantly - to work them out extremely quickly. Her intuition and ever-deepening knowledge and organizational talent allowed her to believe that in the future she would take governments here.

These were four lists. First from the local governor with an invitation to the fiesta. I did not want to go, but it was necessary to have friends in the circles of power, so with a sigh I decided to go.

The second was a copy of a report on the progress in securing the ruins of Malabony, which could still threaten people with its very existence. The black pyramid was still dangerous, so we decided to cover its ruins and cover them with sand and clay. The robots were slowly moving, but the wall around the ruins was already standing, and now it only took them to fill up. I hired all the Students and Apprentices for this work, so we only three of us was in the Commandry: Iris, Tia and me.

The third letter was from a distance. It was visible after the seal of the Commandry in Messantia. I have not heard from the other side of the world for a long time, so I was intrigued to break the seal and open a letter. And the following was there:

Master Lestek!

I'm addressing you with an intriguing affair. By ordering the local library, I came across an amazing document written in an incomprehensible language. This isn't a manuscript, but a print that contains writing marks somewhat similar to those used in the Hyborian countries. So far, all attempts to read have come to nothing, because we have no idea in what language it was written. There are many indications that the most important expression is the one that is written with much bigger characters than the others and it looks exactly like that:

$$\gamma^{\mu} \left(i\delta_{\mu} - eA_{\mu} \right) \psi = m\psi$$

Perhaps it's the name of the author of the document or person or something else that this document concerns. But that's just my guess. It may be a document preserved from before the Cataclysm, but... as you know, this cataclysm took place 8,000 years ago and this paper is no more than 20 years old...

*Therefore, I have a request - come to us and see this find in person. Each your opinion may be valuable, because I suspect - just like you - that our Reality is penetrated by someone **outside** our space and time.*

I greet You and Your Loved Ones!–

Ewran from Messantia
Commander
Messantia, 10.0.0.3.1. 7. Muluc 0. Uo

I read it again and felt a familiar thrill. The letter was written in mid-August, and therefore when I was already in Goa. The fact that again there was another proof of the penetration of our planet by someone outside our time was already interesting and intriguing in itself. The suspicions I made in June slowly took on shapes and blushes.

"What's with you, daddy?" I heard Tia's alarmed voice. "Did something happen? Bad news?"

No, sweetie," I answered, "only..."

"Only???" Her beautifully drawn eyebrows rose slightly.

"Only, I have to leave, and with your mother."

"Daddy!!!" She stamped her feet in a delicate sandal. "Where now!? We have a lot work with this Malabona???"

I handed her a letter. She read it and her face darkened.

"Are you going to leave all because of some old paper?" She asked in a pathetic voice, but I saw that she was furious.

"This is a request," I replied, "if I want I can stay."

"Yeah right!" She exploded. "I can see it already! You are both so intimidated that if I know you, you'll go without me..."

I also saw it in dark colors.

"I'm afraid it's worse than we think," I answered, opening the fourth letter with the seals of Belverus. I unfolded a folded piece of paper and looked at her face.

It was empty.

I turned it into a verso - the same. We looked into each other's eyes.

"That's some stupid joke, daddy?" She asked with suppressed fury in her voice.

"No, honey," I answered calmly, "this is a confidential-letter. Bring a candle, please."

Tia went for a candle and after a few minutes she came carrying a silver candlestick with a lit candle. She put it in front of me and waited for what would happen.

"Honey, take a pencil and parchment and write," I said, gently heating the letter from Belverus. Under the influence of a flame on thin parchment, numbers and letters appeared. I began to dictate them, and Tia wrote them laboriously on piece of parchment.

"And what came out?" I asked.

She was silent for a moment.

"It's some nonsense! It doesn't make sense!" She replied.

"It does, it does," I said, "now take this disc."

I gave her a ring of baked clay covered with alphabet signs and numbers.

"Find the characters on the external disc and see what characters are on the inside. These are the right ones and write them down, did you understand?"

She nodded in response, then took on the decryption. The matter must have been very serious, since Master Brontosphoros applied such precautions.

"I got it!" She exclaimed after a few minutes, "but... it also doesn't make sense!"

"It makes sense, we only have to make a effort." I replied. "Tell me, what numbers open the record and close it?"

"8 opens and 7 closes." She replied. "Well, write this text on a matrix of 8 lines with 7 characters each," I ordered.

"Done," she replied after a few moments, "and what next?"

"Now read from top to bottom.

She reads it.

And I felt a sudden chill despite a hot day. And I understood why the Master Brontosphoros used three levels - the highest security for this information.

II

"I can't believe it," I said, referring all this matter to Iris. "It's probably impossible..."

The Grand Master and his advisers may be wrong," she said, looking at the evening sky sliding through the grenade.

We stood looking at burning of the city's fires. Night was coming to the continent and we were hugging each other waiting for it to come.

"I don't believe that someone from Messantia has sold itself to Stygians. They aren't Shemits or Kothyans..." I murmured. "Besides, it's the front commando right now, so they're probably more careful than ever."

"They have no evidence if they've commissioned you to investigate," she said."

"To us," I said. "You and me. The Brontosphorosa's command is clear. Tia will rule Commandery, who was nominated to the rank of Master and commander *ad interim*.[13] Incidentally, this creates a precedent, because it still has not happened that such a young Apprentice was appointed to the Master even ad interim and was entrusted her Commandery. This is the first case in the Brotherhood's history!"

"I'm afraid of her," Iris whispered, "she's still so young and inexperienced..."

"But I'm not stupid," I said, "and I believe I can handle it. Anyway, besides filling up Malabony has nothing to do. Well, maybe going to banquets on our behalf and collecting data. And she's the best in it."

"Banquet?" Iris smiled contrarily.

We laughed.

Tia was proud of the distinction when Iris attached her a round silver brooch with the image of the Green Dragon to her sari. It embraced the commandery, and this in itself was quite a distinction.

"Go in peace," she said through tears, "and come back as soon as possible..."

"Don't worry, we'll be back as soon as possible," I said, "in three months and not longer."

"I'll be fine," she replied, "and don't worry about me. Anyway, Dravi will be with me and Arus, so I'm safe."

Dravi was her official fiancé and we were expecting a wedding ceremony any minute. But somehow we both were not in a hurry, in our opinion rightly so. In this profession you should not be in a hurry...

* * *

---

13 Temporarily acting.

We left behind the banks of Vendhia. I will not describe our sea voyage, because apart from the two violent winter storms around the South Islands of the Black Coast, nothing interesting happened to us. Even the pirates avoided us. Anyway, after destroying the Red Brotherhood and the death of Bêlit - Queen of the Black Coast, they were not here at all.

When our ship finally arrived at the harbor of Massantia, it was the beginning of December. In Argos it was already winter - from the north there was a bitterly cold wind and a cold rain of leaden clouds that hung low over the harbor. The first thing after going ashore was to stock up on warm things, which came to us without difficulty. Just one of the brothers from the local commandery was waiting for us on the quay, which immediately imposed a warm cover on us. Then he invited us to his covered vehicle, which allowed us to avoid rain.

We moved quickly and after leaving the city we had to defeat eight more versts, after two hours we would be in Commandery of Messantia, where the Commander - Master Ewran welcomed us at the gate. He was a huge, great hulk of a man of about forty, a height of at least six feet and three inches and weighing at least two hundred and twenty pounds. The thick head was tangled with tusks of powdery hair, and a short beard surrounded a husky face with ruddy cheeks and a red nose. He had the appearance of a provincial peasant from Aquilonia, from where he came from. But it was enough to look into his blue eyes to be on guard. They betrayed lively intelligence and behind their veil hid a stout mind.

"I'm glad you came," he said after exchanging initial bows and politeness. "Our prayers have been heard."

"So, Master, is so bad?" I asked, astonished.

"Yes and no," he replied enigmatically.

"Belverus informed me of a very dangerous leak of our secret information from your Commanderies," I said, "that's why I'm here. And yours, Master Ewran, a message about this piece of paper that you can't read..."

"Yes," he confirmed, "but we'll talk about it after dinner."

But that was not the biggest surprise this afternoon. When we entered the dining room, it turned out that the Master Brontosphoros sits at the top of the table. Not tall, slim and against his name, he did not carry lightning[14], but hardly anyone could match him in the fight with short spears and *katana* swords. Wrapped in his gray-green cape, he did not look like someone who could cause political upheavals or falls of the monarchs, and he had the world's best machine for extruding the information he was interested in. In spite of his sixty-two years, he stuck straight and gushed with life energy like a twenty-year-old. He greeted us as eloquently as Ewran and in the mood of restless expectation we sat down at the table. Dinner was served shortly and it was not too exquisite but tasty. Bean soup with fried bacon and stuffed calamari for exchange with roasted turbot and boiled vegetables. For this was excellent, dark and thick wine, for which we refused. We drank water, which we only slightly stained with wine.

"You don't drink both?" The host was surprised.

"Master Lestek is famous for his sober head," Brontosphoros smiled, "thanks to which he avoided many nasty adventures and met his wonderful wife," he bowed his head towards Iris.

She gave him her most charming smile.

"Is it that?" Ewran was surprised. "Soon they'll probably start singing songs about them, like the king Conan and Valeria from the Red Brotherhood or beautiful Bêlit - the pirate queen of the Black Coast!"

Everyone laughed and we too. The mood became more direct. While eating, we talked about the weather in the ocean and the approaching winter. It was such a talk for the use of other confreres of both sexes who feasted with us. The official part was before us.

After dinner, we went to the Commander's office, where we sat back in the armchairs comfortably. The commander sat down behind his desk, Brontosphoros with us took a seat at a low, eastern lacquer table.

"We're all now, so it's time to start," the deputy of the Grand Master gave a sign to start the conference. "Master Ewran, we're waiting!"

---

14 Brontosphoros – from Greek, carrying lightning.

III

Master Ewran sighed, then scratched his disheveled head at the words:

"The whole thing began more or less in the spring of this year, when after the celebration of the Spring Equinox, we started the spring cleaning in our Commandory. As you can see, it's located in the old castle from the time of the Pictish Wars. It is actually a small fortress that King Argos gave us. It was almost completely destroyed, but after a year of hard work, a nice place was created here. At the moment, only the north-east wing is closed, but maybe next year we'll finish renovations there. For now, it isn't inhabited, but there is a library and archive of public records. The secret archive and the office are located here."

"To the point, please," said Brontosphoros impatiently.

"I'm already passing ad rem." Said Ewran. "At the end of March our librarians and archivist noticed that someone is reviewing our archive collections and data sets contained in the library, both archives and the office."

"How they got to know it?" Iris was interested.

"Good question," Ewran smiled to her, "someone who was browsing through them didn't put all the reviewed materials in their proper places. At first, we thought that it just happened through oblivion or distraction, but when the documents from the archive were found in the library and vice-versa, we found that the case is serious."

"And what did you do?" I asked in turn.

"Librarians and archivist were beyond all suspicion. In May, we conducted a query as a result of which it was revealed that no document has disappeared or been lost and everything was in perfect order. But…"

"But?…" I smiled, "there was some excess."

"Well," said Master Ewran, "there was a small superata of documents in the number of pieces one."

He extended his hand to us with the incriminated document. It was a card made of yellowish paper resembling a thick paper, but stronger than standard tissue paper and not as absorbent as it was. On both sides it was covered with tiny black stamps that actually resembled some of the typographic characters of the Hyborian alphabet. On one of the pages you could see the inscription I already knew:

$$\gamma^\mu \left(i\delta_\mu - eA_\mu\right) \psi = m\psi$$

...which was surrounded by a frame resembling a Stygian cartouche, but in the shape of a rectangle. I looked more closely at the black stamps and, to my amazement, I found a few familiar shapes: 0 and 4, which I saw on the hull of a flying machine of strangers who tried to murder me and Master Haneda and similar or identical signs to those on the flame-poisonous gas can, found in the Swamp of the Dead by a crimartian boy.

"What does Master Lestek Vislanian say about it?" Three pairs of eyes rested on me.

"Maybe later," I said and turned to Ewran, "and what happened next?"

"In May, after completing the query, someone was still browsing our documents. And interesting: when people were sleeping in the library and archives, everything was in the best order, but when people stayed in their own apartments, that person came back again."

"Do you suspect anyone for this?" I asked.

"No, nobody," he replied.

"So there is the possibility of third parties acting?" Iris asked.

"Hmmm... I'd like that it could be so simple," Ewran sighed, "unfortunately, no, because there are still sentries and dogs outside the locks who sense the presence of strangers wherever they hide. We also carried out a series of attempts to penetrate people into our secret rooms and in all cases these people were located by both."

"Sure, I understand," I nodded, "and now a different matter: who and for what purpose could do that?"

"When you look after recent events, it could be Stygians or Kothians," replied Ewran.

"Picts?" Brontosphoros suggested.

"Excluded." The Commander shook his head vigorously, and the haystack, which he had on his head, was even more disorganized, if it was possible, "I'd say straight out, the Picts are dangerous, but too primitive to use complicated technologies from the Past or Future."

"Well, but you all remember the case of Zohar-Saga and Jhebbal-Saga, which the Cimmerian tried to cope with?" Brontosphoros asked in his polite tone.

"It's certain that they were some products left over from Atlantis," said Ewran, "but this is known only from 'The Way of Kings' and 'Songs of the Arch and Sword' by Rommanus of Pirrice."

"Rommanus was a poet, not a historian," Iris said, "I know his songs and romances. Truths in them as much as dirt behind the nail…"

"Sure," I said in a summarizing tone, "so the Kothians and Stygians may be involved."

"Of course," said Ewran, "our commandery is frontal, because it is located between Stygians nationalism, Kothians revanchism and the Pityitan wilderness."

"But Zingara and Shemit are a buffer against the Picts and Stygians," Iris argued, "only you should be afraid of Kothians, who are sharpening their teeth at Argos and access to the sea for a long time…"

"That's why I'm so concerned about the alliance of Stygians and Kothians," said Brontosphoros. "Besides, the Zingarians are weak, for what an army of 5,000 infantry, without the support of cavalry and engineering troops? Empty laughter overwhelms me! As for Shemits, the Shemits were, they are and will always be corruptible. They are capable of everything for gold. I wonder if I can't abolish the commandery in Messantia and move it to Kulalo even…"

It has been coming for a longer discussion.

"OK, let's come back to Messantia," I said, seeing that things were moving in the direction of a political and military pre-dawn, for which I had neither time nor inclination. "And what happened next, Commander?"

"Actually, nothing more, except that the commander is haunted…"

"What?" Iris asked, thinking she had misheard, and her face expressed disapproval, "haunted?"

"Exactly," replied Ewran undeterred by her skepticism, "several strange figures were seen in the corridors of the unused part of the commandery, sometimes a large, orange and shining sphere appeared over the commodities... I suspect that there were more such facts, only people are afraid to talk about them..."

"Something like?" I asked. "Like sphere?"

"Orange and flying," said the Commander, "I'm already saying it."

We looked with Iris to each other and to Brontosphoros. The man nodded.

"We met with this sphere," I replied, "on the South Island in the Foggy Islands archipelago off the coast of Vendhia."

"Oh, it's interesting," Master Ewran has come alive, "tell me about it, please!"

I told about it.

"And you say it was before the volcano erupted?" He asked.

"A few days before the eruption," I replied. "But I've also heard of flying oranges in Khatayu. Exactly over the Swamps of the Dead and the Ghosts City..."

"Ghosts City?"

"Yes, that's what this place was called," I confirmed, "it's far from inhabited places in this country. It is evaded by the Crimatrians and Han people who are afraid of these places. Moreover, there in the Swamps, a gas cylinder with amazing properties was found: flammable and toxic gas. Or rather, the products of its burning in the air were highly toxic. It was used against people who ventured into these swamps. And they were used by people flying with the help of such vehicles." I quickly swiped the drawing of an alien vehicle on a piece of parchment. They have a high-speed weapon with quite a large range and accuracy. But they can be beat, which I proved with Master Haneda."

"Haneda?" Ewran raised an eyebrow. "I don't know him. Zipangian?"

I nodded.

"Yes," said Brontosphoros, turning to me, "you've thanks from him for the wonderful high-class student with great wisdom."

"Oh, T'ao," I said, "and how is she?"

"Perfectly, and in the spring she goes with Haneda to the Ghosts City."

"So, we greed," said the Grand Master's deputy, "act here and enjoy yourself. I have to get back before the snow."

We were silent for a moment, and then Master Brontosphoros began to say goodbye - he still today was moving the Way of Kings to Belverus. The meeting was over. After an hour we were alone.

IV

Outside the windows was an icy wind blowing rain and snow from Zingara and the Pictian Wastes. I felt sorry for Brontosphoros because of traveling in such a bad weather. One of the brothers led us to our room. It was small but very cozy, in the south tower overlooking the Tybor Valley, which here spilled over at least two miles creating an oxbow lake overgrown with trees and reeds. Now everything was graying and faint in the streams of rain and snow blown by the wind from the Rabirian Mountains.

"Look dear," I said to Iris, "if we'd like to, we can go up the river to Ianthe."

"I have no reason to do it," she muttered, "I don't have anyone there. Besides... Besides, I don't want to go back there."

I nodded and closed the window. It was already dark in the room, but the fire on the fireplace sent a wave of heat to the interior of the room and made us sleepy.

"Are we eating supper?" I asked.

"I don't want to eat," Iris said and yawned mournfully looking at the pallet by the fire.

"Well, then we're going to sleep."

The answer was a long yawn.

She quickly jumped out of her shirt and petticoat, and then she lay naked in front of the fireplace, exposing her body to the heat of the fire. I took off my clothes and lay down next to her. The elements were raging outside the window, in the chimney the wind was bleak and we were lying on the hides of wolves and bears, enjoying the warmth of the fire and their nearness. I embraced Iris, who hugged to me and we both slowly fell into the first sleep.

I woke up around midnight. A fire was dying on the chimney, but a pale lunar glow filtered through the window. The wind howled grimly and the clouds from time to time obscured the moon. Iris did not sleep either. I gently disengaged myself from her grip and threw on the embers two slags that slowly took over and after a few minutes they burst into flames.

"You can't sleep?" She asked.

"Not really," I said quietly. "What do you think about all this?" I asked.

"Interesting..." She sighed, hugging me in front and putting her back on the warm rays.

"I still have the feeling that not everything has been said," I said, "that we've overlooked something, something that is a small but significant detail."

"What detail?" She asked.

"Because I think," I said slowly, "there're strange things happening in the Commandory. Why exactly in this one and not another one?"

"What do you mean?" Iris pulled away from me to see my face.

"Well, look," I was drawn in a sudden inspiration, looking into her eyes, "this Commandory is located far away from the city. Actually, on some the woods. A cosmic boonies! There isn't even a decent road here. There is no sign of a living spirit within a radius of three versts. Neither settlements nor even home or cottage..."

"Well, so what?" Iris asked.

"That's it!" I almost shouted, because a flap in my brain has opened up, "think! All the Commandories in which I was, and I was almost all of them, are located in the cities. Only this one is located outside the city. Do you understand???"

"Eee... what should I understand?" She blinked her eyelids.

Drowsiness ran away completely.

"And that if it comes to contact with Them (whoever they are), it just happens here, in this Commandory."

"Do you think that...???"

"Oh, I'm completely sure of that," I said, "it's happening not without reason. We both know that there is no such thing as chance. You don't understand it yet?"

"But I understand," she smiled and her eyes became luminous, "who do you think they are?"

We embraced strongly.

"People, like us," I whispered, kissing her on the lips. "And I'm very happy that we'll meet them."

We looked into each other's eyes finding love and desire in them. Fatigue disappeared without a trace. We understood each other without words. A month of traveling by boat, which did not predispose for amorous frolics - we both felt that we wanted to reflect it. We were hard up for ourselves and when we saw our nakedness in the light of the bright flames, when our bodies warmed the warm rays of a living fire, we knew what we wanted. We wanted to love a ardent, crazy love. One look was enough for us...

...

...I fell to my hide and we both returned breathlessly back to the real world. Iris was looking at me. Her face was in partial shade. The breasts waved to the rhythm of a steadying breath.

"I love you," I whispered.

"I know," she smiled, and I love you too. It was worth to travel such a joke in the world to tell you it again..."

V

The morning greeted us with the first snow. During this time spent in Venhia, I saw snow only on the tops of the mountains. I missed his pure white, the sharp smell of frozen water and the bright reflection on the walls and ceiling. Argos was one of the warmer Hyborian's countries, so I did not expect that this snow would last a long time. Nevertheless, it was already for one foot.

After breakfast, we went outside to see the headquarters of the Commondory. We trudged in the fluffy snow in warm crakow, which we bought immediately in Messantia. We looked at the building that hung over us like a dark mass of stone and metal broken here and there by the sharp white of snow. It was a small fortress with thick walls and small windows that could be easily converted into shooting ranges. It was built on a square plan with four round towers at the corners. In addition, it was surrounded by a whole system of trenches and entanglements, which made it difficult to approach her secretly and the only way led to the entrance gate. There were no other entries visible.

"What do you think," I asked Iris, "is there any secret passage?"

"Theoretically, such small strongholds had a few spare exits," she replied after thinking, "one could be by the river and the other one somewhere in the forest. Such tunnels were even several hundred feet long."

"Well, that's a thought," I said. "We'll go to the library and the registrar's office after a walk. They should have some plans for this fortress.

As I said, we did. There were plans in the library, but the result was only that there was passage at the river. Two centuries ago, they were buried during one of the Pictas Wars. The Pictas found them and fell forward to get defenders on both sides. Pictas were repulsed, but the passage collapsed when they entered it. Or maybe it collapsed by itself when there was a fight in a narrow passage? - about this, story no longer spoke. One was sure - no stranger could enter the Commandery area - it was physically impossible for a human being.

And for *Them*?

Apparently, yes. I do not know why, but I had this wicked assurance that we'll meet them here. This meeting with the flying orange ball was not accidental. Nothing was accidental. It seemed that there were two types of Out-of-Time Arrivals: ugly guys shooting at us with pieces of iron and lead and luminous beings from flying orbs.

"What are you thinking about?" Iris asked, looking at me carefully.

"About the possibility of meeting with Them here." I replied. "I've the impression that this will be soon."

"Soon?" She laughed delightfully. "When?"

"Today at evening or tonight. And here."

"How do you know it?" Her eyebrows rose over eyes widened in amazement. "You say it with certainty that I'm inclined to believe you."

"I don't know," I replied, "but I have certainty."

The sunny morning soon turned into a gray and snowy blizzard. Around three in the afternoon it started to get dark and only the huge white flakes of wet snow gave a sense of unreality of what surrounded us. We went into the room. There was warmth in it and there was a merry fire on the chimney again. We dropped the cloaks, on which the last snow was melting and we sat in front of the fire. After a while it got warm to us.

I embraced Iris and hugged her. We sat looking into the fire. I turned my head towards her face and our lips met unexpectedly half way. Iris closed her eyes and I kissed her open lips. For a moment I wondered if I should go further, but I gave up. And good.

It was already completely dark outside - the short December day was definitely over. Dreamy, heated by fire, we sat looking into the flames. It was a moment of perfect happiness at the side of a beloved woman. And at once this moment was interrupted by screams coming from below. We looked at each other and got up in a moment. The intimate mood finished like a soap bubble. With swords in hand, we rushed down. The screams were heard at the entrance to the Commondatory, so we headed there.

We reached a huge, iron-wrought gate, which was half-open. Several brothers stood outside and watched something in concentration, shouting.

"What's happening???" Iris asked.

"Look there!!!" A few voices shouted back and the fingers showed us the direction.

We looked there. Over the battlements of the north-eastern tower, at a height of perhaps twenty feet, was a huge, shining orange ball. Actually, it was not orange, only orange-red, its colors changed from golden-yellow to dark-carmine. It separated itself from the sphere - it was the best word that came to my mind - a golden ray and touched the tower.

"I need to see it closely," I shouted.

I put a katana into my sheath and ran to the stairs leading to the upper floors of the fortress. Iris ran after me. After a few minutes we stopped for a moment at the entrance to the tower.

"Over there," Iris shouted, pointing to the top of the stairs.

There was a golden glow from there that illuminated scaffolding and formwork. It meant that They are still there. Silent silence surrounded us. We did not hear any excited voices from below, and we should... But we did not bother with that. I felt delicate pricks all over my body, like tiny needles, but I did not pay attention to it. Puffing like blacksmith bellows, we ran up the crooked stairs, risking to break the limbs. As it approached the top platform it was getting brighter. It was strange light - as if it penetrated through thick, stony and brick walls. We ran to the platform and stood as if we were breathing heavily panting. What we saw caused us speechless for a moment...

VI

The room was filled with golden light. Actually, it flowed from everywhere and... from nowhere. There was no one in the room except us, but we instinctively felt someone's Presence.

"Is anyone here?" I asked.

"I'm glad that we are finally meeting," an impersonal voice came to us, which came to us from every direction. We could not locate the sound source that came to us.

"Perhaps you would show up?" Iris spoke behind me.

"Of course, we only wanted you not to be scared," said the same voice.

The air at the opposite wall took on the density, it flashed with all the colors of the rainbow and slowly materialized in the form of three people who stood facing us. Two women and one man. Both women were dark-haired, the tall one was black-eyed, the other's eyes were green. They could be thirty or forty years old. Tall, slim, but not skinny. Dressed in colorful shirts and short pants, they had simple sandals on their feet. The man wore a colorful loose shirt and short, light trousers. His feet were in white, soft and shallow shoes. He looked forty years old. It has to be very warm in the place where they had to be...

"We hope you aren't afraid of us," said the man.

"No," I said, overcoming dryness of my throat.

"That's good," he answered, "but please don't come closer. We are a projection, a picture, not living people. You may experience a shock, and this is very unpleasant."

"Why are not you here, just your pictures, if I understand you well?" I asked the first question, "and why do you have such a strange voice?"

Those three smiled.

"It's about ours and your safety," one of the women said, "your diseases are deadly dangerous for us and vice-versa. So it'll be better for all of us if we only meet through television - that's why you see us. And as for the voice, you don't hear us, only the voice reproduced by the transducer, it is such a device that translates our language into your language and vice versa. If you wish, it'll have individual tone color for each of us.

"We do," Iris said. "Who are you?"

"The wish is accepted," the woman said again. She had a nice voice. "I'm sorry, we forgot to introduce ourselves. I'm Krystyna Zaleska, she is called Gemma Ruiz," she pointed to the second slightly shorter woman, "and he is Daniel Laskowski," she introduced the man.

"I'm Lestko, son of..." I started, but Krystyna interrupted me with a wave of her hand.

"We know who you are," she said, "otherwise we wouldn't meet with you. And we want to talk only with you."

"But why?" Iris said. "What about the others?"

"The rest are in a dead zone," Daniel explained calmly. "For them the time has stopped at the moment and only flows for us. And for the rest of the world too. Beyond them."

"Zone...?"

"Dead zone," Daniel explained, "is a zone out of the laws of the world you know. Turn around and try to get out of here."

I turned around and walked forward. I took two steps forward, but the third encountered an invisible, flexible but completely impermeable obstacle.

"Now you know how it works?" Daniel smiled at once like a little boy, "so no one will disturb us. Now listen to what we have to say to you."

"Maybe we'll ask you a few things?" I growled, because their patronizing volume made me nervous. "How much time do we have. And why did you imprison us?"

"Of course" Daniel said politely, "ask. And we have just enough time we will need. We haven't imprisoned you, but we've secured you and us against intruders. Of course, if you want to leave, it is enough to express your wish. But it'd be better if you'd listen to us. Here and now."

"Why?" Iris could not stand it. "Why is this conversation so important?"

"Because," a woman called Gemma said, "we'll explain a few things that are important to the existence of this world. Our common world that threatened serious danger. We need your information and we'll give you ours in return. You're in?"

We considered for a moment. I looked into Iris's eyes.

"Yes, we're in," I said, "and we have no choice, anyway.

Za daleko zabrnęliśmy, żeby tak po prostu skończyć. We'd come too far for them to just end."

"Who are you, anyway?" Iris asked.

"We come from various countries that were created on the ruins of your world," said Krystyna, "but our present day is year 2016 of our era, it means according to your time measures from year 10.016, therefore, the difference is exactly ten thousand years. We live on the borderline of the Age of Pisces and the Age of Aquarius - if it's more comfortable for you."

"On the ruins...?" Iris asked again.

"Yes, because the Earth will go through a series of geological cataclysms associated with the change of the zodiacal epochs, and also our plans. The change of Epochs has wiped Atlantis out, now changes also awaits you - Lemuria and Mu will collapse. Lanka will disappear at the shores of Vendhia - only Sri Lanka will remain. These changes are inevitable and irreversible. But there will be a new land in the West - its origins are already emerging from the ocean."

"Can we somehow prevent this?" I asked.

"Geological processes can not be prevented," Daniel said, "but you can alleviate their effects and save whatever you can. And in this we see your role."

"What you mean ours?" I asked.

"Yes, the role of your Brotherhood," Daniel replied, "it will get a new task. What you fought with is already over. It's actually over, because there are very few dangerous artifacts left after Atlantis. We'll provide you with instructions on how to find them and how to dispose of them."

"And you can't do it?" Iris asked. "You've more opportunities than us!"

"Yes, it's true, but at the same time we'll fight another battle," said Krystyna, "difficult, but needed to this planet. The battle for the unification of this world. Enough wars and woes caused by people to people. Well, we've to eliminate the biggest threat."

"What's your plan?" I asked directly.

"This is a long-term plan to reintegrate Humanity into one living and rational organism and direct its potential not on intra-civilizational fights, but on the conquest of the Cosmos." Krystyna replied. "It'll be the largest in the scale of this planet change of Reality and attempt to repair something that hasn't yet happened. In other words, we'll give Humanity a second chance of rebirth and peaceful coexistence and expansion into the galaxy. Into stellar system whose Sun and all the planets of the Solar System constitute only one hundred millionth part. And there are billions of such galaxies... And there are billions of alien civilizations like yours that also exist on billions of planets."

"But why is it that we are to take part in it?" Iris asked. "Why did you choose us for this job?"

Krystyna smiled.

"It's obvious," he said slowly and emphatically, "Gemma and Daniel are your next incarnations. And who you can trust more than yourself?"

VII

It was difficult to accept everything as the truth. And on the other hand, we had a tangible fact of their existence.

"And you, Krystyna?" Iris asked. "Who are you?" "I'm a Comer from other civilization," Krystyna answered calmly.

We fell silent for a moment, because it was hard to believe and accept the truth, and then a thought occurred to me.

"What danger you were talking about in connection with geological changes. For what reason are they supposed to happen?" I asked.

"It's related to what you call the Great Guide," Daniel replied.

Great Guide! We watched it with Iris throughout the cruise on bright days and nights. It seemed to be a ball suspended in the sky above the ocean's surface. The captains of the ships, according to its position, were able to determine the position of they units on the ocean - that's where the name of it comes from...

"This is the second largest moon of the Earth..." I said, "and the Little Guide is the third. In any case, this is an orbiter station, as Master Astrajos from Belverus called it."

"It's fact," said Daniel, "you are right that the Great Guide is the moon, it wasn't always the moon. It's playing this role only now."

"So what was it?" Iris asked.

"It was also an *orbiter station*," Daniel answered, "only that it's a *combat orbital station*. Built to prepare and conduct space war. A gigantic combat station designed to destroy targets on Earth and in space. It was controlled from Earth..."

A sudden guess lit up my confused mind.

"Oh my God!" I exclaimed, "it means that... It means that it was controlled from this headquarters under the City of Ghosts!"

Gemma smiled at me and then at Daniel.

"I told you so?" She said triumphantly. "They guessed it!"

"You were right, honey," the last one replied. Krystyna just smiled.

"We were in this City of Ghosts," Daniel said, "indeed, this Headquarters is also there. But most of all, weapons for this station were produced there. And also the source of the drive."

"Was it this thing what drives those huge arrows?" I asked.

"No, but you're close. It was also the same energy that liberation destroyed entire cities, as we have shown you before..."

"It was you???" I asked, "but how did you give me that vision?"

"Yes, it was us, but I won't tell you how we did it, because you wouldn't understand, Krystyna said softly, "this is a higher technique, or actually biotech, cerebroscopy, cerebrovision and everything..." she waved her hand. "Don't be angry..." she added.

"I'm not angry," I murmured. "But what was it? What did they produce there?"

"Antimatter," Daniel answered. "Same matter as the one from which we're all created and our world, but with the opposite electric charge. The combination of matter and antimatter causes them to annihilate with the release of massive amounts of radiant energy. We have given you something that was the key to understanding this issue."

"What is it?" I asked, though I already figured out what it was.

"A card from the quantum physics textbook," Daniel replied.

"So this boxed part of the text is...?"

"This is a formula that describes the behavior of material particles in the world around us," Daniel continued, "this is Dirac equation. Paul Adrien Maurice Dirac was the first man in *our time* who formulate it. The first and second equation, because they can be used in the description of both matter and antimatter. You don't know suach a math yet, but it was about intriguing you, showing you something mysterious and incomprehensible. You didn't read this equation, but you didn't make a mistake and you guessed who we are and where we came from."

"But what about this Great Guide?" Iris asked. "Will you destroy it?"

"We can't destroy it," Gemma replied, "because it would create a ring of tiny debris that would make the Earth similar to Jupiter, Saturn or Uranus, and that would change the amount of energy reaching our planet from the Sun and would result in even more disturbance on our planet."

"So what are you going to do?" I asked.

"Move it away from Earth and put it in orbit around some large planet," said Gemma, "preferably Jupiter or Saturn..."

"How will you do it?" Iris said.

"Gravitational impulse," Gemma replied, "we'll use the power of attraction to disconnect the Great Guide from Earth and place it in orbit around another planet. We have to do it, because this moon has become a huge antimatter depot. It's enough that it'll free itself and explode, and then life on Earth will simply be killed with gamma radiation."

I felt a sudden headache and weakness. I had to show it somehow because Daniel looked at me.

"I think it's enough for the first time. Lestek is getting a headache. Iris probably too," he looked at us with a tender and attentive look. "We have to finish, they have too many impressions for one day."

"So we'll finish and to the next meeting," said Krystyna. "We have to meet again, because there are several issues to be clarified."

"Goodbye," Iris said in a weak voice.

Honey light dimmed and then went out completely. Three figures disappeared, as if blown away. Only the dark room remained below the top of the tower.

On the stairs we heard the voices coming up and after a while a few people from the Commandry came up with a gun in their hands.

"Here you are!" Ewran cried. "Where are they?"

"They escaped," I said weakly.

I felt the weakness of my whole body, my head buzzing. Fighting the weakness and dizziness, we went down to our room and sat down in front of the fire. A hot broth and a huge bowl of boiled beef clad in vegetables was brought to us. The warm food made us feel a bit better.

Now we only felt the tension in which we were all the time and which was defused. Iris fell asleep over the bowl, I had to move her to bed and put her down. She slept like a child, she did not even open her eyes when I undressed her and put her under thick pelt. I did not feel any better either and just lay down next to her and fell asleep in a deep sleep without dreams or delusions.

VIII

When we woke up, it was already noon. We slept over fourteen hours! But we felt much better than yesterday. I opened my eyes and my gaze met Iris gaze. She lay on her side looking at me.

"Hello," I said.

She smiled.

"Good morning," she said, "how are you feeling?"

I felt great. I was rested and my mind was clear, like hardly ever.

"Perfect, and you?"

"Very well," she stretched tempting and a shiver ran through me. "What are you going to do with this nice day?"

"Begin it with you finally," I said, reaching out to her.

She laughed and jumped out of the bed, my hands catching the air.

"Catch me!" She shouted.

After a moment, we were chasing around the room - I wanted to catch her and she deftly eluded me laughing and scoffing. Despite the cold in our room, we were warmed up by the pursuit and the sight of our naked bodies... Finally, I drove her to the corner and caught her in my arms, and after a moment I lifted her up. She was hot and still smelling of sleep. I kissed her lips holding her by the chest and after a while she wrapped my neck around with warm and strong arms covered with delicate skin.

"Come on," she whispered fondly, "you caught me, now take your reward."

And she bit me gently in the ear.

"Maybe later?" I teased her.

Her eyes were dark.

"What???" She asked. "Oh no, what have we come to!"

She jerked and freed from my arms just to flip me over her hip to the bed. A second later she sat on my chest and pressed my hands to bed with her knees...

...

...We shouted quietly in a delightful spasm and Iris lay down completely exhausted. After a quarter of an hour our breaths calmed down and our muscles relaxed completely.

"I'm terribly hungry," Iris sighed as we finally cooled down.

The return to reality was always prosaic. We stood up and unclutterd our room. Then we washed, we put on clothes and went down to the kitchen. It turned out that we were waiting for a simple meal consisting of bread, meat and light Argosian beer, which we drank very fast.

"We go to Master Ewran," I said when we finished eating, "we've to tell him what happend yesterday and agree the strategy for today."

"Are you sure that *They* will also come today?" She asked.

"Yes, they have announced it to us," I replied.

But I was not sure at all.

Master Ewran took us in his office. We briefly briefed him on our impressions of our first contact. He lost his speech for a moment in amazement.

"That means they were here?" He finally asked, and he found a tongue.

"As we say, Commander." I replied.

"It is impossible, because we got there just behind you!" He exclaimed.

"And yet it's true," said Iris, "and this is proof that the dead-time zone really exists. You didn't feel it, because time stopped for you, whereas we talked with them for about half an hour..."

"What are you going to do?" The Commander asked.

"Wait for the next contact with them," I replied, "they're dealing the cards in this game, *They* and somebody else."

"Who are you thinikng about?" Iris asked.

"Those who tried to murder me and Master Haneda in Krymatria," I replied. "I'm almost certain that it's competition to rule the world..."

* * *

Outside the windows it was dark again. We lay down next to each other in front of a fire that was roaring on the fireplace, but this time we were not undressing while waiting for the meeting. I was lying with my eyes closed and I probably took a nap, because Iris jerked my hand violently.

"It begins!" She cried.

Indeed - the room was bright. Honey light was pouring on us from all sides. I sat on a bed of pelts. Krystyna, Gemma and Daniel appeared at the same moment. Only this time they sat on something like armchairs.

"Sorry, I hope we didn't wake up," Daniel said.

"No, we only took a short nap," I replied.

"So it's great," Daniel said again, "now it's time to explain to us a few things related to ours, as you described it, Lestek, competition.

IX

I raised my eyebrows slightly. He read in my mind?

"Yes," Daniel answered. "I read in your mind."

"How is it possible?" I asked in my mind.

"It's cerebrotronics," said Daniel, "a technology department that explores and uses the bioelectric potentials of the human brain."

"I don't understand," I shrugged, "let's move on to the merits of the case."

"Competition?" Daniel smiled humorlessly, "we have competition in the form of neo-Nazis. In our time, we had two wars caused by the sick ambitions of the leaders of the great and small nations. After the second of them, which was triggered by a man named Hitler, and his supporters were called Nazis. Hitler and his acolytes escaped justice to the mountains of the Taotooma continent - known in our country as South America and created there an underground state like Agarthy..."

"So it was they?" I asked.

"Yes," Daniel replied, "it was them. They disregarded you and thanks to that you managed to defeat them because you hit them with surprise. In fact, they are very dangerous. They made a plan to return to power and take over the world for themselves. To this end, they wanted to get an ultimative weapon - antimatter. They couldn't synthesize it for their own purposes, but they could move in time and knew that Atlantis had found the Third Solution for the Dirac Equation, thanks to which the Atlanteans produced antimatter on an industrial scale! And they produced another weapon of mass destruction - a D weapon - from the word disintegration, annihilation... It's able to destroy all other weapons. And Earth itself as an astronomical body too."

"Oh, Great Mother!" Iris groaned, "and what next?"

"And then it was that they decided to collect all the remaining, after the Great Conflict and subsequent Cataclysm dangerous objects and collect them in one place, and then transport them to our times and detonate in all major cities of the world on a strictly defined day and precisely defined hour - December 21, 2012, at 9:12 pm, time of the Yucatan Peninsula. That's how it came out of their calculations that one of the Mayan calendar cycles was about to end, which now begins to enter into use on Taotoom emerging from the depths of the Ocean... And then your Brotherhood stood in their way. You did a really great job by incapacitate this grunch!"

"Wait a minute," I said because I did not get something, "after all you're from 2016, how is it possible that you're alive?"

"You're right Lestek," Daniel said calmly, "we're from 2016, because we managed to prevent it."

"But how?..." I asked.

"As I told you, Queen Gedrena helps them to store on the territory of Stygia and Shemit their D warheads. These warheads are to be taken to the Future and detonated there. We managed to hinder them, but the price was terrible. In the area of Stygia there was an explosion, which resulted in the death of almost the entire population of the country and three-quarters of its territory turned into a desert. And that's exactly what started the geological changes."

"Who caused it?" I asked.

"One of Gedrena's priests," Daniel replied. "Unfortunately, through his stupidity and other priests, he accidentally detonated one of the warheads, which lost its stability and released antimatter. But it happened good, because it saved the world extra suffering. Gedrena was preparing for war with her neighbors. She currently has more than a million soldiers under arms and intends to concentrate her forces on the border with Shemit - go through Shemit where she has already bribed somebody there - and then strike from the east to Argos. At the same time, the armies of Koth will attack the Argos from the northeast. And from the north-west, the Picts will start, to get something from this cake - after all, Argos is famous for its riches...

We paused for a moment.

"Well, what about the Great Guide?" I asked.

"He'll slowly leave the Earth and leave the Earth - Moon system." Said Krystyna. "This is a very delicate operation, because if we did it violently, Earth would have an even worse cataclysm that would kill the remnants of life on it. It'll be embedded in a permanent orbit around Saturn, and in our time will be called Mimas. Antimatter from it will be shot in the direction of Jupiter, the largest planet of your solar system. This will create a second, smaller star shining at night..."

"And what is our role in all this?" I asked.

"And your role is," said Gemma, "take a quill pen and write..."

And she gave us something like a proclamation or appeal, not a specific action plan. When she finished, I put down my quill pen and looked at them.

"And only one more thing," I said, "who will do all this?"

Those three smiled only.

"You didn't guess?" Daniel asked. "You!"

"We?" I asked. "And how should I bring together Mankind, people from the underworld - Aghartians and Water People?"

"Don't worry about it, because you'll act according to a specific plan, and you'll always find tips whenever you need them," Gemma said. "As you can see, Water People exist because it's thanks to them that we're able to talk with you right now. It's thanks to their help that we can go back in time and make all significant changes and adjustments to our common history. Your task will be to establish contacts with them now and thus stop the process of their adaptation to the aquatic environment. Just like the Aghartians. In both cases, it's possible to return to their human form and return to the surface of the Earth. And here we'll need your help and your Brotherhood. These three main trunks of Mankind must unite again for humanity to enter the Cosmos for about 4,000 years from now."

"But why?" asked Iris, who was silent as of yet, "why is it so important?"

"That's why, darling," said Krystyna, "we want Humanity to enter the Galactic Federation as early as possible and join the Great

Plan of the Galactic Rebuilding and adapt it to the development of all forms of life that are living creatively on all planets."

"What will it give to us?" Iris said.

Krystyna smiled forgivingly.

"Nothing for you, but for your children and grandchildren and their children it will give a better life and the possibility of expansion into space. Of course, such a great change of Reality won't be unnoticed and in the moment of its implementation you'll lose your next incarnations, because the story will be completely different."

"So Gemma and Daniel...?"

"They will disappear," said Krystyna.

"Will they die?" I asked.

"No, no," Krystyna laughed, "they'll only disappear from your new Reality. They'll live in their Reality in the 21st century to the natural death with the knowledge that next to them is another - a better world. Your world."

It was difficult to understand everything. We felt a headache again.

"Are your heads hurt?" asked Krystyna, "good. This means that you're beginning to learn new data, new messages and new behavior patterns. It'll be a kind of *super memory* and *sub-knowledge* for you. Equipped with it, you'll be able to face what awaits you. And you'll take the position of the Grand Master and taking over the secret, but real power on this planet, because the emperors and kings will listen to your instructions. And follow them."

"What do we do now?" I asked.

"Now you'll go to Belverus and take over the Brotherhood into your own hands. They're already waiting for you there. A small modification of memory and the entire Council of the Brotherhood will stand behind you. And no one will die unnecessarily. The taking of power by you will be completely bloodless..."

We also hoped so.

X

The communication session with *Them* ended, and we lay tired by the fire. Iris took off her clothes and slipped under the pelts, and

I followed in her footsteps. I embraced her and she hugged me. She burrowed her face in my neck and after a moment I felt her even breath. I closed my eyes and absorbed the warmth of her body. After a few minutes I felt drowsy and fell asleep.

A chill woke me up. I opened my eyes and realized that Iris was not with me. In the chimney, they were only mainly firebrand. I got up and threw a few thick logs on the fireplace. And then I heard a sniff. I turned around and saw Iris standing in the window. On her light skin lay a vibrating green moonlight. The hair ran down the naked shoulders and back. I approached her and embraced her waist. She hugged to me by her back. Her body was icy.

"Honey," I whispered tenderly, "come to me, you will catch a cold."

Outside the window, the river slowly rolled its waters in an electric, moonlight. Single pieces of ice flowed. The first floe of this winter.

Iris turned to me and clung with her whole body. I felt the salty moisture of her tears on her cheek.

"You were crying?" I asked, "what happened to you?"

"I'm sorry my dear," she kissed my lips, "it's my fault. I felt apart."

"What happened?"

"I thought about Tia. She's alone there..." she whispered, cuddled up to me, "I'm scared of her..."

"She's safer than we are," I said calmly and firmly, "you know what the consequences of the explosion of this D warhead composition will be. There will not even be a radioactive fallout. Besides, the Decan Peninsula will be the least affected from all the world's lands."

"Wait a moment, what's Decan?" I thought in a panic, "Vendhia? Yes, India..."

I understood everything at once.

Iris nestled in me. Her body was slowly starting to warm up. I was massaging her arms from which goose bumps slowly disappeared. I turned her toward the fire and now her back warmed the warm rays from the burning fire. After a moment she raised her head and looked into my face. Her eyes were luminous.

"Actually, you're right..." she said with astonishment in her eyes. "How do I know that?"

"*Super memory* and *sub-knowledge*," I quoted Krystyna from memory.

I leaned over and picked up Iris, then took her in my arms. I kissed salty dampness from her cheeks, and then her lips touched mine and parted slightly. They were warm and wet. They invited and lured. I didn't let myself be asked for a long time.

I put her on a bed of bear pelts and wolf pelts in front of the already burning fireplace. We both liked to make love in the warm glow of the living fire. Her hands wrapped around my neck, and her strong and shapely body clung to me. She lay on top of me and her hair fell on my face. We kissed sweetly in the golden glow of burning logs. The warmth of her body penetrated me through and the touch of her lips caused something to feel sweet and overwhelming.

"I love you, Iris," I told to her ear, "you're the best thing that ever happened to me."

"You too, my beloved," she answered in a whisper, "we were destined for ourselves, do not you know?"

"Gemma and Daniel also met, although they waited a long time for themselves," I replied, "so we had to meet too..."

She raised her head and thought reflected on her face.

"Yes, indeed," she said and smiled, "but it's terribly complicated...

"She slipped off me and put it on the fire side. I put my arm around her and took her in, and she hugged me again and we lay there hugging each other, clasped together, cheek by the cheek. We were reluctant to have sex, each of us was lying to each other and sunk in our own thoughts. We were so good with each other that we did not need anything but our presence that made us happy. And so we finally fell asleep hugging each other.

The morning was cloudy and windy, but it blew warm from the sea. The snow dissolves quickly into a dirty white slush that ran with water. We sat in the Commander's office. The Master Ewran was clearly depressed. It turned out that the deputy Commander is his wife - Mirka, a pretty blonde girl with long braids. She smiled at us.

"Nice to meet you," she flashed a smile, "we're neighbors, because I come from the Duchy of Wagu. But I studied with you - in Posnania, in the Land of the Warta... And there I met my husband, with whom I went to Argos."

"Look, what a small world," replied Iris exchanging a hug with Mirka, "we also got in Goa a girl from the Duchy of Torysa... She is a phenomenal archer."

Iris talked for a moment about the talents of the young Apprentice.

We sat in armchairs. We told the story of the last contact with Krystyna, Gemma and Daniel, without hiding anything.

"That means you're leaving from here?" Ewran asked, worried at the news that we are going to leave the Commandory.

"Yes, we're going to Belverus," Iris said.

"And you're sure that nothing strange will happen here?" He asked anxiously. "I don't mean all these strange events with your participation, but a continuation. Are you sure that all these explosions, the departure of the Great Guide and transformation will not threaten us?"

"The departure of the Great Guide will take place in stages. Its mass is much smaller than the mass of the Moon, and thus the strength of its attraction is much smaller. You know, Master, that the diameter of the moon is two thousand, one hundred seventy two and a half miles, and the diameter of the Great Guide is only two hundred and fifty eight and three quarters of a mile, and its mass is sixty-two quadrillions, four hundred eighty-eight trillion, three hundred quarts of silver Argosian mines.[15] That is, if you will count in weight, the Great Guide is one thousand nine hundred and fifty-nine and ten times smaller than the Moon. The Earth will hardly feel it, because the force of gravity will slow down slowly. It would be worse if there was an immediate departure - then the system of tidal waves in the ocean would immediately change and as a result of this water could flood large areas of lowlands..."

"And what would happen if there was no explosion in this warehouse?" Mirka asked, "because as you say, it's to be a trigger for change?"

---

15 1 silver Argosian mine = 60.0 kg.

"A trigger that will only speed up what is inevitable anyway," I said, "and besides, Gedrena must see and experience what she has done and intended to do. And her priests. It's their fault the most. There is nothing worse than a Stygian priest who depraved gold, pleasures and a life of luxury...

We paused for a moment. We all felt fear of what awaited us and our world.

"So, I'm asking you, Commander," I addressed to Master Ewran, "to send this message to the Grand Master."

I quickly made the short note:

Messantia, 12. Ahau 5. Imix

VERY IMPORTANT
THE SECRET HIGHEST MEANING
To the Grand Master of the Brotherhood of the Green Dragon
(by hand)

I report that I carried out the task entrusted to me. I made contact with People from the Future, who gave us very important secrets about the future fate of our world and our Brotherhood, which has the next Mission to fulfill. Therefore, we must contact the Brotherhood Council and call an extraordinary meeting as soon as possible. Therefore, please send notices so that the Commanders can come to Belverus together with us.

With a fraternal greeting –
Lestek from Vislania
Commander of Goa, Vendhia
Iris from Ianthe
Deputy of Commander of Goa, Vendhia

- which I next encrypted and gave to be sent by a heliograph to Belverus. The dividing road of 2,500 miles will travel in two days, which we will pass in two and a half months...

We said goodbye to the Commander and his wife, lavishly thanking them for their hospitality, and then we went to our room.

Throughout the rest of the morning we packed and even at noon we headed east, onto the ancient Route of the Kings, which would lead us to Belverus and to the change of Reality, on the road to the Infinite...

8

STRANGE DAYS

I

The noise of the wind in the branches of the trees fell silent and the girl on the horse could hear what was happening in front of her and behind her on the winding mountain trail. Pines and spruces obscured the road and a surprise could be hidden behind each corner. It could be forest animals, it could be semi-human-semi-monkey Thaks - quiet and cruel, it could be some jete - even more blood-thirsty and cruel bandits from the border of Ghulistan and Vendhia. The girl listened, but her ears did not pick up any signals of lurking danger. Dark, sharp eyes penetrated the forest thicket. She did not notice anything suspicious and lightly hit her horse with her heels.

"*Hoc, hoc!*" She cried softly.

The horse moved slowly and carefully forward. The girl, calmed by the silence interrupted only by the sound of the wind and the chatter of the mountain stream, decided to speed up the ride and after a while moved faster heading for the mountain pass that was looming in the rainbow clouds. The trail showed relatively fresh traces of four horses and traces of camping at least two people. Man and woman, which she concluded from the traces left at the places of their camp. She thought that they were some wanderers going to Turan, and probably not missing too much for human company. They were probably two or three hours away from her, and probably they had already left the forest zone, entered the zone of the mugho pines and the alpine tundra. The worst part of the road. Unless they camped in the forest, gathering strength to pass the pass in one day. Behind the ridge was the village of Dropeks, where you could rest and refresh yourself. The jete attack threatened only here - to the forest border. In spite of their bloodthirstyness, they were afraid of going higher into the open space and attacking only among the trees where they felt safe. And unpunished.

The next half hour ride up the hill was calm and even the girl let herself whistle a melody. It was fun and she began to wonder where she would break up the camp, when her ears picked up distant cheers. She was not wrong - they were coming from the front. Her horses were restrained with their ears. There were shouts again. The girl hit the horse with her heels in the ribs.

"*Hoc!!!*" She cried, and both horses moved forward with a rapid trot as much as the steepness of the slope and obstacles in the form of roots and stones allowed. After a quarter of a crazy ride, she went to a rather large and flat glade, as if created for camping. Astonishing sight appeared to her astonished eyes: in the center stood two people facing each other by back - a man and a woman. Simple swords flashed in their hands. Twenty men armed to the teeth attacked them. Whatever it was, at least half a dozen of them were covered in blood and were lying on the beaten grass.

The girl released the reins and got a compact Turanian bow from the case, a long arrow from the quiver, and without waiting, she sent the first missile towards the nearest bandit - because she had no doubt who the attackers were. A second later, the second enemy knocked down by the arrow, and before the bandits realized what was going on, the third of them caught the throat in which the feathery bullet lodged. New forces entered the attackers and their swords found their target. Two more bodies fell to the ground. The girl spurred her horse.

"*Hesh! Hesh!*" She cried and crashed to the succor, drawing from a long, slightly bent, Zipangians katana sword from the sheath strapped to her back. She caught the first thug, bounced the spear aimed at her, and cut terribly through the head. A second later, slightly hovering in the saddle, she decapitated the second bandit and immediately, half-turning, cut the third one.

"Amazon!" There was a cry of terror. Attackers at the sight of loss with a young woman, who was wielding a sword and a bow like an experienced warrior, lost their spirit and went their backs. They thought they were dealing with a warrior from the merciless, valiant and cruel tribe of female warriors. The girl sent two more shots that found their target and two corpses rolled into the forest. The screams of the fleeing attackers were moving away. The girl drove up to two people she saved from oppression and jumped off her horse. She went to the first lying corpse and turned him over with one strong kick. With a phlegm, she wiped her sword against the filthy muster of the fallen thug and looked around her battlefield. She put her sword in her scabbard and snatched her arrows from her bodies and put her calmly into the quiver. Having finished her activities, she turned to those whom she had helped.

"Who are you?" She asked with arrogance in the voice, which is common at young age and with awareness of her own advantage. "And who attacked you?"

The man and the woman hid their swords and looked at her with care but without much submission. The girl looked at them more closely and amazed at her face. The man was under fifty, but it was obvious that he was very strong when he was young. Wide bars and powerful fists testified to the warrior's skill. His companion was as tall as he was and was armed with a long, simple hybrid sword like him. Her hair was the color of fire, but there was a gray strand here and there. But her gray eyes were young and full of boldness. The fair complexion betrayed the origin of the land of the North.

"You are…??? No, it's probably impossible…", the girl wondered loudly.

"Not too many people recognise us now," a man said, "not this epoch and not those times…", he ended with a note of melancholy.

At once the girl's eyes flashed.

"You are... prince Halidor!" She exclaimed, "so you're, Lady, Red-haired Sonja!"

"Indeed," said Halidor, "though the cursed duke is more suited to me."

"But I have heard the power of things about you!" The girl exclaimed. "All skalds, bards, fishmen and troubadours sing about you, from the Picts Wilderness to Zipango and from Asgard to Black Kingdoms and Vendhia! And your fame can match the fame of King Conan and Culla Atlantis!"

A pair of noble wanderers laughed carefree.

"And who are you, who are we to thank for help and perhaps saving lives?" Red-haired Sonja asked.

The girl bowed.

"I'm Ilva, the younger daughter of the master Lestek Vislanian, called the Crossbowman from Belverus."

Halidor raised his eyebrows.

"As far as I know, Lestko did not have children, and you..." he paused waiting for explanations.

"Well, sir, you have outdated information," Ilva smiled, "because a few years ago, Lestek and his wife Iris from Ianthe first accepted my older sister Tia and then me. And it happened when they were traveling from Argos to Nemedia to take on the position of Grand Master of the Green Dragon Brotherhood, they came across the Picts who made a trip to the Royal Route. The Picts attacked our village, they killed all men and took us in a slave. Crossbowman and his people took us back, and since I didn't have parents, they took me in and I stayed with them."

"And what are you doing here now, so far from Belverus?" Red-haired asked in astonishment.

"I'm coming back from Goa in Vendhia, where Tia and her husband live now," Ilva said. "She is now the Commander of the Brotherhood in this city. And I am the Apprentice of our Brotherhood."

"I heard about you and about your business," said Halidor, "you saved the lives of many people."

"Thanks, my lord, for a good word," said Ilva, "but our work is ending. At the moment there is only one, the only one problem that my parents are busy with." - "And me too," she added in her mind.

"I think we've the same problem," said Halidor, looking around the battlefield.

Ilva looked where Halidor and Sonja turned their eyes.

"These dogs aren't jete," said Halidor.

"Stygians," Ilva said more than she asked.

"Of course," Halidor went to the corpse and with one strong motion he stripped off jerkin and shirt. "Look!"

Some hieroglyphics were tattooed on the body of the dead man.

"This is a Stygian officer," he said, "a centaurion, if I'm not mistaken.

"You aren't mistaken, sir," Ilva nodded.

"Do you know Stygians?" Halidor was surprised.

"A little bit," Ilva nodded, "I've learned many things in Belverus. But I haven't graduated yet."

"I wonder one thing," said Sonja, "why they attacked us."

Ilva looked at her with a slight smile.

"It's obvious, lady," she said, "they wanted to murder me. A woman with a sword. They only made a mistake and attacked you. As they realized about the mistake, they decided to murder you so that there would be no witnesses."

II

Sonja looked at her in disbelief.

"So, they were going to murder you?" She asked in astonishment.

"That's what the logic law says," said Ilva. "You know how it is. Do you remember how your sister was murdered?"

A shadow of anger and hate flashed through the calm and pleasant face of Red-haired.

"Exactly. And the same person tried to kill her and tried to kill me."

"Gedrena?" Halidor asked. "But why? You're so young..."

"Gedrena," Ilva confirmed. "And why? And because I'm the daughter of the Grand Master of the Brotherhood of the Green Dragon. And Gedrena wants power over the world, and the Brotherhood is the only force that is able to resist her sick plans. Insane plans. For plans that are coming from Hell."

All three fell silent.

* * *

They came to the village at night. Dropeks accustomed to such guests indicated to them the tavern, to which they directed their steps. Ilva came in behind the majestic couple and made sure no one paid any attention to her. However, she sat down with Sonja and closely inspected the surroundings. There were a few Dropeks and visiting buyers traveling from the Hyborian lands to Vendhia. They behaved noisily, ate, drank and listened to an itinerant bard who sang songs from the "Road of Kings" accompanied by a kithara.

After a moment, the owner of the tavern came over to them, old Yorestes, whose face and clothing betrayed Shemits origins. He wiped the table with a dirty cloth and accepted the order. He stood at the table for a moment, then bent over Ilva.

"And a missy, maybe instead of roast from a mountain goat, wants his gonads fried in olive oil and pineapples with pouri mushrooms and honey?" He made eye for her and added in a whisper. "Three and fifteen..."

"No, thank you, I prefer decent food from this prrrr!" She snorted with disgust and immediately added a whisper. "Seventeen to one."

She felt cold sweat pour over her.

It was an alert password used only when Courier's life was in danger. It consisted of two numbers, which added to each other were the number of the day, as well as the response. The rule was that correct password had to first have a smaller number and then a larger number, and conversely in response. So everything agreed.

"Eat missy and we'll meet in a cell behind the kitchen for a quarter of an hour." Yorestes turned and walked toward the bar.

They did not notice that during their conversation a gray clothed man of a wicked stance slipped out of the inn. After a while, the servants brought a huge bowl of meat in a spicy curry sauce and large cakes of czaparatti, pieces of which dipped in a sauce and ate with a faint palm beer imported from Drujistan. Ilva took a small knife out, which she cut her portion of roasts and ate hurriedly waiting for the end of the quarter. After that, she got up from the bench where she sat and walked towards the kitchen, without stopping there, turning into the narrow corridor where the cell door was. A stream of light seeped from the crack near the floor, so there was someone. Ilva slowly pushed the door and looked at the cell in which there was only a table on which the candle was burning. Yorestes stood by the window and looked outside.

"I've fixed you up, Yorestes, and I'm here," she said in a whisper. He turned around.

"You can not stay here," he said in a whisper. "My inn is under the watch of Stygians, who hunt for you, the daughter of a Vislanian. Their driveway is standing some three stands down the valley and I think someone has already alerted them of your arrival. Who are your companions?"

Ilva shrugged. She expected something like that, so she showed no feelings.

"It's Prince Halidor and Red-haired Sonja," she said, "I joined them on the trail."

"Do you trust them?" He asked.

"Yes," she nodded. "We have joint rumble, so I can count on them."

"Then warn them too," said old Shemit, "and you'd better run away because there are at least fifty of them..."

"Sixteen per head," she thought, "and two more. It will be hard.

"I wonder why Gedrena cares about you so much that she has decided on such a massive intelligence operation so far from the Stygian borders?" Said Yorestes. "Don't you think that by sending a division of cavalry and henchpersons from her Royal Guards against you, she is afraid of something more than just one girl, even one who wields a gun like you?"

Ilva went to the old man and stroked his cheek.

"Yorestes," she said almost tenderly, "this is the secret that kills and my father only entrusted it to me. The less you know, the better for you. Do you know the rules of this game? So please, do not ask me anything."

She kissed him on the cheek, turned and left.

Entering the dining room, she looked at it intently. It seemed to her that in the corner, in a darker corner, it was missing one man. Nothing important, but all the warning lights came on in her brain. She went to the table, where a couple of famous slaughterers feasted. She sat down and leaned toward Halidor.

"Lord!" She said quietly, but with emphasis. "We aren't safe here. There are half hundred Stygians about three staja from here. I know it for sure."

"Those dogs again?" Halidor growled. "You can't even eat and rest peacefully in this country?"

"This is a borderland and there is no law outside the law of fists," said Sonja.

Halidor quickly took the rest of the meal and threw two pieces of gold for the bollard serving them.

"We're going," he said, "I wasn't used to fighting after dinner, but I think someone feel itching on his Stygians ass..."

"Halidor!" Sonja looked offended.

"It'll be better, my lady, if you get ready to play," he said going outside, "because it promises to be quite interesting."

Suddenly he turned to Ilva.

"And where are you so well-informed from?" He asked in a sharp tone. "Maybe you want to get us trapped? It strangely looks to me: we're attacked by Stygians in the guise of jete, and you appear out of nowhere, now we are behind the pass, and you're talking about the next ambush. Strange."

Ilva raised her eyebrows.

"Don't you trust me, my lord?" She asked in a cool voice.

"No," Halidor growled.

"I'm not surprised," she shrugged, "I'm the one for who I claim to be. And they," she nodded to the darkness, "are chasing me because of this."

With a quick move she removed a strap from the neck, on which a rectangular badge, five inches by three, was tied.

Halidor reached for it and examined it carefully. He weighed it in his hand and grimaced.

"Gold-plated copper," he murmured disappointedly, "and they're chasing you because of this... piece of crap? After all, it has no value?"

The plate itself is not, but what is written on it," Ilva said, pointing to the surface of the gold-plated tile covered with the Atlantean characters of the rongo script. "This is a table of activation codes, or as you prefer a key."

"To the treasury?" The prince asked with sudden interest.

"No," said Ilva, "to the instrument of destruction of many times greater power than I'm able to describe, at which the Talisman that you destroyed with your venerable wife is a funny firecracker."

III

They rode in the opposite direction to the continuation of the planned road, towards the mountain ridge, which loomed in the light of the stars with the white of eternal snow.

"Do you know what lies behind this ridge?" Halidor asked.

"I've never been there," Ilva said, "but, Lord, people says there is another valley, to which there is no road. I mean, the way exist, but the Dropeks are afraid to go there."

"Why is that?" Red-haired asked.

Ilva smiled sardonically into the darkness.

"Ghosts," she explained, "false fires and invisible hands pushing people into the abyss. And stuff like that. I don't believe it."

"Gods too?" Sonja's voice sounded mockery.

"Also," Ilva said, "so far I haven't seen any, but I've seen the products of people who can be considered products of the gods. But there is nothing divine in them, but rather they are devilish, because they serve mass killing people and other living beings..."

"Or they're maybe a Hell's products?" Sonja asked again.

"I don't think so, lady," Ilva replied.

They passed the next mile in silence. Suddenly a gust of night wind brought people's voices and hooves to them.

"They're following us," said Sonja.

"Will we stop them here or higher?" The girl asked reaching for the bow.

"Higher, when you'll have a wider field of fire and more steepness. They'll have no place to hide and they'll not be able to hunt us down, and you can shoot them like ducks on a pond."

They moved faster up the slope, which become more and more sheer. The trail ran ever higher and higher, until finally it went beyond the forest. The rugged wall of a rocky and snowy slope stood before the riders...

"Where are we going?" Halidor asked.

Ilva looked around. She did not have much choice.

"Right," she said in a tone of steadfast confidence.

They turned right and drove along the rock wall. The chasing voices were inevitably coming. Ilva slowly reached for a bow. She did not intend to sell her life cheaply. She was looking for a place where she would have the best field of fire when she saw something strange in the moonlight.

"Come here!" She cried softly. "There is a road!"

In fact - from the rock wall ran an ancient road from huge stone slabs so matched that no grass grew between them. It ran towards the forest and died between the trees, while the other end reached the rock wall on which the dark patch of the tunnel was cut off.

They moved rapidly. Whatever was on the other side of the tunnel was better than what was waiting for them here. Sonja came first, followed by Halidor, and Ilva followed them, looking behind her in search of danger. After a moment the fugitives heard a deaf groan and the entrance to the tunnel disappeared. Before them they saw a hole through which a dark grenade of the sky could be seen. The second tunnel opening was open - a patch of sky was visible through it. They drove half a dozen staja and left his dark abyss, which also contained a dull thud of a moving rock.

They were safe. At least for the moment, because they had no idea what is on the other side of the mountain ridge and where the road leads, which descended a few lines down, into a valley that was visible in the dark.

Ilva raised her head and let out a small cry.

"You can't see the moon and stars here!"

Indeed, looking at the sky, one had the impression that one was looking at a low-hanging dome that passed the light, but did not let it see the blue lights...

"How strange is here," said Red-haired.

"For now we have some peace," said Halidor, "let's go down the valley for now. You can see some lights and a tower there."

They traveled some time until the night passed into the day-break when the ground lay down and the first trees appeared instead of rocks and grasses. Cedars, spruces, firs and pine trees. The lower they have been, the vegetation was more luxuriant and more trop-ical. Finally, they entered the grove of date palms and the road led them between the ponds in which lotuses, water lilies and other aquatic plants grew. Finally it became brightly. The blue dome above the valley was first white and then blue. But the light that fell from all sides was just as white and warm as the sun. When it was completely bright and warm, they rode in between the first solid houses where people and animals lived. Dogs barked, some cats lazily basked on flat roofs. No human was visible.

"A ghost town?" Sonja asked.

Oh, people are probably still asleep," said Halidor. "Besides, there are dogs, sheep and cows here, judging by the sounds. So there are also people."

They went to a wide square, in the middle of which stood a huge tower reminiscent of an Iranistanian ziggurat. However, it was not built of burnt bricks but of huge blocks of hewn stones. Her height could be about a thousand feet and towered over the area.

Ilva jumped off her horse and looked around curiously. From all sides one could see huge rock walls, while straight ahead and against the direction from which they came there was a mountain in the shape of a four-sided pyramid, several dozen thousand feet high, and a few smaller ones next to it.

"What a strange place," she said almost in a whisper.

"Indeed," said Halidor, "I'm afraid you're right..."

He did not finish, because something extraordinary happened. People started coming out from behind the houses - men, women, old people, youth and children. Halidor's hand went to his side, but he withdrew it. The inhabitants of the valley were unarmed. They surrounded them with a close circle, Ilva quickly counted them, as she used to do that - there were about two hundred people.

"Hello people!" Said Halidor in a Hyborian. "We arrive in peace. And we won't stay here long."

He repeated it again in the language of Turanians and in Hyrkans. People did not speak. Sonja said this in turn in the Aesir and Vanir language. Without response.

"Now you," said Halidor to Ilva, who repeated the greeting in Vendhian language.

This finally triggered a reaction. People came to life and began to speak in their own language.

"What do they say?" Halidor asked and Sonja gave Ilva a questioning look.

"I don't understand them much, they say in some ancient dialect of the People-Snakes of Valussia, but they say they are happy with our arrival.

"Ask them, what's the name of this place?" Said the prince.

Ilva exchanged a few sentences with the people around them and looked at them with astonishment in her eyes.

"And what? and what?" Halidor was impatient.

"They say that this place is called D'Śanśung-bö o'śangśung-goł o'śangśung-tań - Land Of Which Time Forgot. Put it simply - Shambhallah in Vendhia language, or Land Ü in Han language...

IV

In the afternoon, when they finally rested after the hardships of the day and night, they were invited by the king of the village to one of the most splendid houses of this town. They went to him before it got dark, in any case in front of many houses lanterns were lighting, so the streets were relatively bright. They entered the one-story bungalow painted white. And it was basically the only difference between houses painted black and whose roofs were red.

The king of the village greeted them in a small but cozy living room. Without introductions and long greetings, he asked them to sit on large, soft pillows that lay on a thick mat next to his chair. They sat opposite each other - Ilva as a translator sat down next to a slim, maybe twenty-two-year-old boy with smiling, slightly slanted eyes and dark complexion of the East man. He spoke fluent in the Hyborian, so she did not have to pursue her not-so-good Vendhian. The king was accompanied by his wife and another man, dressed in a uniform, orange toga. His head was clean-shaven, and his slanted eyes looked sharply and intelligent. Ilva guessed that this is some priest of the local religion.

"Welcome, foreigners," said the king, "you, Prince Halidor, you Red-haired Sonja who knows no fear, and you Ilva, daughter of Lestek Crossbowman the Vislanian - Grand Master of the Brotherhood of the Green Dragon, Slayer and Tamers of Old Evil.

Ilva was surprised that the alien had accurately listed the names and all her father's titles. Everyone seemed to know him here.

"Why was this presentation supposed to serve?" The girl thought for a moment.

"I'm the king here, my name is Brahytma," he said. "This is my wife and the confidante, Mahytma, and this is Mahynga, the chairman of the highest college of Nam-che priests. We know what brings you here and in what circumstances you are here. You're being hunted down by the soldiers and guards of Stygian Queen - Gedrena. You are safe here. Outside you are in danger of death, and you," he looked at Ilva, "kidnapping and delivering to Stygia, where you'll be tortured to death. Anyway - the effect will be the same."

"Should we treat it as an invitation or an ultimatum?" Halidor asked.

"Friendly warning," Brahytma smiled lightly, "Gedrena can't let you deprive her Talisman and destroy her castle. You can stay here and avoid danger."

"Where's the catch?" The prince smiled as he examined his interlocutors.

"The catch is that you can't leave anymore," Brahytma said seriously, "of course you can go out, but you'll go straight into the hands of the bandits and die. These are the rules of this game. Here you enter and leave at the same time you entered. Don't forget, prince, that this is the Land of Which Time Forgot. Time isn't here, so looking at us with your eyes we are immortal to you. But this is only here - in this Valley and only in the shadow of Kharakhall." Brahytma pointed to the snow-capped peak illuminated by the night glow of the obscured sky...

"Kharakhall?" Sonja repeated unknowingly.

"...also known as Hailias in Vendhia." Brahytma. finished.

There was a moment of silence, which Ilva interrupted.

"What about me? Should I stay here?" She asked in a slightly trembling voice.

Brahytma nodded.

"Of course you can stay here, but your father asked you for an important mission to do," he said. "The fate of your world depends on this mission."

"But I don't understand something," despite her confusion, her mind worked soberly and quickly, "since the time outside stops and flows only for us..."

"Not in your case," Brahytma corrected calmly. "In your case, time is working for Gedrena and her crazy priests. That's why you should get out of the Valley..."

"...and let yourself be killed?" Ilva allowed herself a sarcasm. "Thank you, I know a few more interesting ways to commit suicide."

"No," replied Brahytma, "you'll be kidnapped and put away to the camp of Stygian forces in the Oasis of the Haunted Pyramids. There is what the key that is hanging on your neck is designed for. Please understand, this key must be there. Oh - your quit starts time, so Halidor and Sonja will be able to leave safely."

The three travelers looked at each other in amazement. Brahytma smiled.

"'That's your father's plan," he said, "and take my word for it, he knew what he was doing by entrusting you with this mission. He could only trust you. That is why you should leave here and give yourself over to the Stygian people. The sooner the better. And then you've to trust your enemy because you've to escape when the day is coming in the dark night. Death first visible and then invisible will be with you and you'll be safe only when you come across the great river for the second time. That's all I can tell you. Please, think about it. And make the decision as soon as possible."

Ilva thought for a moment. She felt sorry for her young life, but on the other hand, she had nothing to lose except it.

"I made a decision," she said, "I'm leaving tomorrow."

Brahytma looked into her eyes and Ilva felt a deep calm at once. Fear disappeared somewhere and only slight excitement remained, as before the fight.

"Are you sure?" Brahytma.

"I am," she replied in a tone of unshakeable certainty.

"Then, Ilva, see you tomorrow!," said Brahytma. "Kiri will take you to your accommodation and tomorrow he'll lead you to the Exodus from the Valley."

At the gesture of Brahytma, the young man rose from the cushion and gave her a hand.

"Lady," he said, "I'm honored to be able to take you to the Gate.

Ilva said goodbye to Sonja and Halidor, nodded to Brahytma and his wife and priest and, led by Kiri, left the king's house. Kiri led her to the house over a large pond and left her alone, wishing her a good night. Without thinking, she undressed and jumped into the water. She was cool and refreshing, but at the same time she caressed her naked body. She lay down on the water on her back and looked up to the sky - there was not a single star visible on the navy blue sky, only gleamed by the sharp white peak of Kharakhall. She swam through the pond several times and left the water. The warm wind quickly dried her skin. She wove her wet hair and dries it with a towel. She entered the house and threw herself on a large, comfortable and soft bed. She tucked her face into the pillow and after a while her breathing calmed down, her eyes sealed themselves, and she fell asleep with the peaceful sleep of a human who did not have bad dreams.

V

The sky was beginning to whiten as Ilva said goodbye to Kiri and plunged into the depths of the tunnel. She knew that she would return to the same point in time she had entered the tunnel the day before and when she came out on the other side she was ready to fight. She was not afraid - not anymore.

She left the tunnel and the rock closed behind her. Ilva looked at the moon hanging over the valley and on Stygian soldiers heading towards her. At their head was a tall warrior - their commander. At the sight of her, he stood up in the saddle.

"Take this bitch!" He yelled. "Alive!"

A few of the Stygians fell on Ilva, who remained motionless with a sword in her hands. She knew that having a rock behind her would not be easy to them. That's what happened. The quick exchange of blows, one, the second and two Stygians fell from the horses, shedding black blood in the moonlight.

"Dogs! Fleabags!" The commander boiled with rage. "Are you afraid of one girl?"

Again they fell on her and stepped back, and another three more bloody bodies spread out on the ground. Several soldiers took up bows.

"Hold on morons!!!" The commander has flipped out. "She has to be alive!"

"But...", someone objected, but did not finish.

"Fools, ahead!" The commander shouted. "Throw the net on her!"

Four guardsmen seized the net and galloped toward Ilva, who moved toward the first man, droving him with a sword. Unfortunately, the net fell on her and constrained her. She felt herself fall from her horse to the ground and felt a powerful blow to her head that rendered her of consciousness.

* * *

She suddenly woke up. Someone poured a bucket of ice water at her.

"She's alive chief," she heard someone say over herself.

She lay bound like a ham. The amount of rope that was used to bind her would be enough to immobilize the rhinoceros. When she realized that, she wanted to laugh. They must have been afraid of her - it comes to her aching head. Because the next impression was a headache. Someone had to hit her in the head with a club or a cudgel. She plunged into blackness again.

She opened her eyes.

It was already a bright day. A young, maybe twenty-year-old boy was leaning over her. He wore the uniform of a royal guard. He gently wrapped the bandage around her head. She shook her head. The explosion of pain caused dark before her eyes.

"Do not move," the guard warned her in a calm voice, "you have a wound on your head, it'll hurt. I dresed it, so you should not get infected."

He took out a bottle, uncorked it and put it to her lips.

"Drink," he ordered, "it's obnoxious, but you'll feel better."

She drank a few sips. The nasty, stinging bitterness spilled in her mouth, but after a few minutes the pain eased and she could think more clearly.

"Thank you," she said in Stygian, barely remembering her words. "Where am I? And in whose hands?"

"We're going to Stygia, and you're in the hands of commander of ten-thousand-man, Dacha."

She happily realized that she only had arms and legs bounded, which allowed her to move to a limited extent, but enough to be able to free herself and escape. They traveled north, towards Ghori and left the route on the Ghulistian Route. She sat down in the wagon that she was taken and looked around. Escape was basically possible, but she had no chance - at least a hundred people were surrounding her. Well armed, on horses and with the appearance of good warriors.

Dacha approached her at a stop. He did not beat around the bush.

"Where do you have it?" He asked without any introduction.

"What do I have?" She asked naively.

She got hit in the face. Dacha hit her not with anger or hatre. He did it as if he did not care much about it, and with a weariness written on his face. He sat down next to her.

"Key." Dacha said it in a bored tone and extend his hand. "Do you want one more time?" He asked almost politely.

"No, don't beat me," she said.

"Where do you have it?" He asked.

"On the neck," she replied. He took the strap and with the delicacy unexpected from him took off her key from her neck. He looked at it closely.

"I lost twenty-six people because of something like that?" He said with astonishment in his voice. "Not bad for a girl like you. You've been trained well," he added appreciatively.

"Thank you." Ilva snarled through her clenched teeth. "But you didn't kidnap me to make kudos here? Will you kill me now, or a little later?"

"I don't decide about it," Dacha said it with phlegm, "this will be decision of our lady, Queen Gedrena, may she live forever. I've an order to bring you in unhurt condition, and what's next with you is not my thing. You must be valuable, because she promised for you as much gold as you weigh."

He got up and jumped off the wagon.

"Annuar!" He shouted, "come to me!"

One of the riders turned back, rode up to Dacha and jumped off the horse.

"What will you command, commander?" He asked.

"You'll take a second officer and go to the Oasis of Haunted Pyramids, and give it to the queen, let she live eternally." Dacha said in a determined tone. "You've to urge the horses, but this plate is something very important to her, you are responsible for it with your head. And also say that we have a girl. Go on!"

"Yes, chief!" Annuar shouted back and mounted the horse. After a quarter of an hour, the two riders detached themselves from the convoy and raced off towards the north, towards the white towers of Fort Ghori.

After two days they reached the fork of roads, from which the north ran towards the Sea of Vileyet and the port of Yuetshi, while the western along the mountain range towards Zamboula, where fork goes to the towns of the western coast of the Sea of Vileyet. They turned west and drove the semi-arid plain with the sun-burned brown mountains to the north, and the gigantic peaks of the snowy Himelian mountains to the south. Ilva was coming back to herself and her wound healing quickly. She was looked by the same young guardsman who helped her after capture. His name was Kheram and he tried his best to make the girl have the least onerous conditions of travel. At the stops they talked often and when Dacha could not see, he brought her some better food from the kitchen. Two young people became friends, despite the fact that they stood on the two extreme sides of the barricade. Kheram came from Luxur, a city in western Stygia, and joined the Guard to improve the fate of his parents and siblings who were not doing well. Against the background of cruel warriors he seemed to be a misunderstanding, a man who was among them by accident. Ilva was perfectly aware that this was a chance for her to escape, and therefore she tried to talk to him as much as possible and to as many topics as possible. It operated in accordance with the principle of having it saw the weakest link in the chain separating it from freedom.

VI

Meanwhile, the two messengers of Dacha were approaching the Oasis of the Haunted Pyramids, which were exactly fifty-two. In their dungeons, Gedrena collected the world's captured nuclear, biological, chemical and disintegration weapons. However, she did it on commission of - a richly payed in gold - neo-Nazis organization from the Andean Fortress. These warheads were to be collected and transported using *Haunebu* and *Vril* vehicles to 2012 and detonated in an one moment on December 21, at 9:12 pm. That was the plan of the fourth clone of Adolf Hitler. Gedrena was to have the fact that some of these warheads were to be used to destroy several major Hyborian cities, allowing her to bow the continent to knees and then conquer the rest of the world. These insane plans were aroused by the greedy power and influence of the priests and prominent representatives of the army, and above all the Royal Guard, which acted as the secret political police, catching and killing all internal and external enemies of Gedrena. The real thorn in Gerdena's side was the Brotherhood of the Green Dragon, which consistently liquidated all sources of A, B, C, D and N and O warheads, thus making it impossible to carry out its designs.

The liquidation of one of the SS time-flying machine at the Swamps of the Dead showed her that she was dealing with consistent and very dangerous opponents. Therefore, through her spies and special services, she decided to give the Brotherhood a blow and a decisive one. It was reported that the daughter of the Grand Master of the Brotherhood - Ilva went alone to her older sister in the Goa, where her operative and subversive group had a miserable failure, and where she found a long-sought code table for the activation of weapons D - disintegration warheads. Without this table, its use would not be possible. The spies reported that the girl would be returning by land through the Himelian Mountains on the way to Yuetshi and then across the Sea of Vileyet to Aghrapuru, from where straight by the Way of Kings to Belverus.

This message was like a balm on her heart. She immediately called on the commander of ten-thousend-man, Dacha and gave him the order to capture the girl and deliver her healthy to the Haunted Pyramid Oasis, where the main depot of the weapons of mass extermination of Queen Gedrena and her neo-nazi accessories was located. That's what happened, and Dacha managed to take the position on her route. She now waited impatiently for the results of this action. She intended to force the Grand Master to submit and give her all the secrets in his possession. Of course, she did not intend to keep her word and decided to irrevocably kill the Grand Master and his family. Painful memory of events from several years ago, when she took over the first nuclear warhead, which turned out to be unstable and had to throw it into the abyss of the Fire Mountains and this caused an explosion of the volcano, which killed one sixth of Stygian citizens inhabited there, and disfigured her for the rest of her life. Her face wore ugly scars that she covered with a mask. There was also another wound inflicted on her by Red-haired

Sonja when she tried to take back her handsome Prince Halidor. The wound in the heart was still bleeding after the event... When she found out that Sonja and Halidor were in Vendhia, she decided to kill them too. She counted, that Dacha - her favorite - will deal with both of these tasks.

* * *

Meanwhile, a few hundred miles east of the convoy carrying Ilva to the Haunted Pyramid Oasis, the old innkeeper, Yorestes, instructed his son, who was ready for the road, was saddled his horse.

"Ari, my son," he said to him, "hurry up, because this news must reach Yuetshi very quickly. The sooner the better. Remember: you've to find Master Omahr and tell him that all the colorful birds flew out of the cage and have flown west. Repeat."

Ari repeated.

"Remember," said Yorestes, "you've to tell him that, and nothing more. And only in this way, because any change in the sentence will change its meaning. Remember: all colored birds flew out of the cage and have flown west." He repeated the message with emphasis.

The son nodded. He was eighteen years old and wanted to see a distant world. A brave heart was beating beneath the deer's cape. He took to the deed and for the first time he had to take the exam, complete the mission his father had given him.

"Go Ari," the old man said unexpectedly in a soft voice, "let your mind guide you. And come back..."

"I'll come back, Father," said Ari, jumping on his horse, "and I'll try to return, and if not, Beera is with you..."

Beera was Arie's older sister. Tall, black-haired, she reminded her mother. A mother who left when she died because of explosion of some deadly device in the mountains. Since then, Yorestes and his family have been bound with the Brotherhood for better or for worse, serving its Couriers as a stopping point in their path on the Himelian Trail.

"I'm not saying goodbye to you, because we'll see each other soon," said Ari, and spurred his horse, then went down the valley toward Fort Ghori. The old man and the girl followed him with eyes and then returned to the inn full of travelers.

* * *

Darkness fell over the Stygian camp. It was lit only by the bonfires. A gray shadow sneaked into the wagon, where Ilva slept, covered with thick blankets. After a while there was a quiet scraping in the boards of the vehicle.

"Ilva! It's me - Kheram!" There was a small whisper. "Ilva, are you still awake?"

"Yes," answered the equally quiet whisper from the depths of the wagon, "something happened?"

"We'll have to run away," Kheram whispered, "but the opportunity will only be in the desert."

"You want to run away too?" Ilva almost sat down in surprise.

"Yes, I'll help you escape," he replied. "I don't want to set my hand to your death."

"Dacha is going to kill me?" She asked.

"Not him, but more Gedrena. I overheard Dacha's conversation with Untan tonight, his deputy. Dacha said that Gedrena will kill you and your family regardless of the outcome of the negotiations. You've to be on the lam. And I'm with you, because if Dacha realizes I've helped you, he'll kill me too. I've enough of this service and these people." He sighed. "Will you take me with you?"

"What about your family?" Ilva asked. "Gedrena will not persecute them?"

"I don't know," he replied and he was frustrated. "But the most important thing now is to let you escape from here. You're in danger of death here. And I... I don't want to lose you..." he whispered in a tone of confession and Ilva felt warm at heart. Without thinking, she rose and kissed Kherama on the cheek and then on the lips. He blushed and was glad that the darkness was hidden his blush. He quickly recovered, this night outweighs his fate, because he just made a choice.

"Death with you and an invisible death after brightness at night" - meanwhile, Ilva remembered Brahytma's words. The first one is

Gedrena and Dacha, and the other one? Oh, and that's another: "your enemy will help you, you can count on him" or somehow like that. It's about Kheram, it's obvious. What is this brightness at night?

"When will we see the Great Guide?" Ilva asked.

"For about two or three days in the desert. It'll be visible in the south-west."

"Maybe it was about that?" She thought. "In that case, we will be able to escape in two or three days."

"Why?" Kheram was surprised.

"Because it'll be bright at night," she said uncertainly, "we'll see..."

The next day they rode the Ilbarian River and went to the steppe, slowly passing into a rocky and stony desert with still the unbelievable peaks of the Ilbarian Mountains still on their left hand. Two days before them, a view of the sea of fawn and yellow sands opened, and the mountains began to melt into the bluish haze of remoteness.

"How far do we have to the Oasis?" Ilva asked when Kheram brought her an evening meal.

"About three hundred miles in a bird's flight," he answered. "If we're to escape, it's only now..."

"So tonight," she said, believing they would succeed, though she had no idea how she would do it.

Meanwhile, total darkness fell.

"Do you know Ilva?" He said. "It's weird, but I don't see the Great Guide. It should already be in its place. The conclusion is that we are either further east than Untans visage, or..."

"...or the Great Guide has disappeared," Ilva finished.

They looked at each other in the light of the stars.

"Impossible," Kheram said, but it sounded uncertain.

Ilva kissed him gently on the lips. Kheram gave her a kiss back.

"Let's be ready at midnight, when the first sleep is the most powerful." She said. "Now free my hands."

Kheram untied her with one knife cut. Ilva began rubbing her sore wrists.

"Now go, so that they won't suspect anything," she said, "as soon as..."

She did not finish. Because something strange happened...

VII

Gedrena waited in her tent in the camp in the Oasis of the Haunted Pyramids. She was waiting for the envoys of Dacha, who were to bring her the long-awaited artifact. Then she will only enter the secret store, take out the black box, enter the secret code from the gold badge, press the buttons and...

Well, that "and" she could not imagine. Admittedly her allies from the flying saucers warned her about the possible consequences, but she did not care. She wanted to be the lady of the world and there was no strength to stop her from doing so. Last night she ordered the murder of the high priest Nem-mer-akhet, who resisted when she announced her decision to the High Priest Council. This morning his body was found among the dunes. He was strangled...

"Idiot..." The queen smiled sardonically to herself. "He thought his opposition would have some meaning. And besides, it scared off potential political opponents..."

A night fell slowly and the servants lit all the lamps. Silvery stars blazed over the dark dunes.

"Queen?" She heard behind her. She turned around, and the priest Moeru stood behind her.

"What do you want, priest?" She asked him haughtily.

"I wanted to tell you queen, may you live forever, that something strange happened in the sky," he said quietly, but with tense in his voice.

"What?" She asked.

"The Great Guide has disappeared," said the priest.

"Yeah?" She was surprised a bit, "so what?"

"That, queen, may you live forever, something is going on that we couldn't have foreseen," replied the priest calmly.

"So what?" She shrugged. "So what? It's just a moon there, the hell with him..."

"But..."

"Don't bore me, priest..." Gedrena waved a hand dismissively. "Tonight I intend to finalize my plans and finally end up with those who bother me to become the lady of the world..." She said slowly accenting these words and enjoying their sound.

There were voices and the sound of quick steps at once. After a while, in front of Gedrena grew up Shamari, who was her vizier.

"Queen, may you live forever!" He exclaimed. "The envoys from the commander of ten-thousand-man, Dacha, have arrived and they tell you that they have a girlfriend and send this..."

Vizier stretched out his hand in which there was a gold-plated badge on the strop. Gedrena greedily reached for it and after a moment her eyes rested on its surface, and her lips curved a cruel smile.

"Vizier?" Gedrena took the plate and put it on her neck.

"What will you command, queen, may you live forever?"

"Call Nikotrix out and collect the priesthood in the Pyramid of the Moon. Only discreetly. I don't want unnecessary traffic in the camp. Those man can't find out..."

Nikotrix - the queen's double appeared promptly. Both women quickly changed their clothes, then the queen came out of her tent heading for the high Pyramid of the Moon. She came to it within a quarter of an hour and immersed herself in the sidewalk leading to the base, deep into the mighty foundations. All the rooms of the pyramid were turned into warehouses in which there were almost two hundred A, B, C and the most dangerous units - D - disintegration weapons. It was possible to activate it only by connecting to the warheads of a special black box with sixteen convex keys. But that still did not guarantee its operation. You will need a key to press the buttons in a specific order. And that is what Ilva had with her. Without it, the entire arsenal of forty-four units of D weapon was only scrap metal.

The queen stood in the middle of the room. Silvery warheads, all 44 pieces laid under the walls. They waited for their time. And this one was running inexorably. After a moment, the first priest entered. Behind him, the second and third. That's how twelve of them came. Silently, they stood half-circle waiting for the words of the queen.

"We're all, Queen, may you live forever," said the eldest of them, "and what now?"

"So, we can start," she said. "We'll arm our warheads and then we'll become masters of this world!"

In her naivety, she hoped that the weapon itself would give her something. She did not know that the warheads had yet to be moved and detonated over or near the target... Her friends from the Andean Fortress did not share their knowledge with her or her priests.

"Give me the box," she ordered, holding out the hand in which the key was located.

One of the priests gave her a black object and was intrigued to see what she would do with it. Meanwhile, the queen approached the first silver cone and connected the cables to the socket on the casing. The black box at once glittered with a green light. Gedrena stirred. The light meant that both devices were operational and ready for use. She handed the plate to the eldest priest.

"Read the top first and when I tell you, the bottom one." She said.

The man only nodded.

"I'm starting." She said. "I'm entering the first sequence. Read!"

Her slender fingers touched the keys.

"First sequence: Ra, Osir, Beel, Ea, Ra, Thot, Loki, Ea, Sig, Num." The priest read slowly.

"I have it," said Gedrena, "now read the second one.

"Isis, Are, Ka, Isis, Ea, Ursa, Ursa, Isis, Tyr, Gimel... The end..." Said the priest.

"...the end..." Gedrena said, pressing the last key.

The moment of the highest expectation has come.

And nothing happened.

Mocking smileys began to appear on the priests' faces. Finally, they'll show her to the upstarter her place. At once the smileys went out as if blown away. The box in the Queen's hand first went out and then it shone with a sharp orange light. White marks flashed on its side. One of the priests recognized them.

"These are the numbers of Armamen!" He exclaimed. "18... 17... 16... 15..." He counted down looking at the display.

"Just a moment and I'll be the lady of the world!" Gedrena thought. A smiley poison like a cobra filled her mouth.

"10... 9... 8..."

"More..." she thought.

"4... 3... 2... 1... 0..." The priest said and fell silent.

The box in the queen's hand flashed for a moment like a photographic flash and crumbled into a fine powder.

"What the hell!" Gedrena shouted.

She did not know that she had entered the wrong code and that entering the wrong code triggered the warhead self-destruct mechanism. Its computer interpreted the wrong code as an attempt to arm it by the enemy.

There was only one option for this case.

One of the constructors of the atomic bomb said that the atomic explosion is a matter of three wags with the tail of a calf. The annihilation explosion was a matter of its fraction. In a second after self-destruction of the device entering the code, the computer of the warhead opened the valve causing the liquid helium to fly out of the container in which frozen antiprotons were found - the nuclei of the anti-hydrogen. In the next second, the temperature inside the pan adiabatically rose by five Kelvin. It was enough and one hundred kilograms of antiprotons combined with an equivalent amount of matter.

Neither Gedrena nor any of the priests saw the warhead burst under the influence of a powerful impact of gamma rays, which were released and spread at the speed of light, activating all the other warheads. People evaporated in a fraction of a second before the nerves leading impulses from their eyes to the brains managed to pass them on. Within a few tens of miles, all life has been voided by an avalanche of gamma rays. The terrible explosion of the remaining warheads caused the formation of a huge crater, and particles of radioactive dust launched into the atmosphere began to form a huge mushroom, which grew into the lower layers of the ionosphere. A terrible earthquake was felt by people who lived hundreds of miles from the place of the explosion. The volcanoes of the Fire Mountains, which spouted with lava flows, became active. The cataclysm that started the hand of Gedrena felt all the inhabitants of the Hyborian countries...

VIII

The western horizon at once shone with a heavy white-blue glow. Ilva reacted immediately.

"Kheram! Get down!" She cried. "Don't look at this!!!"

She dug her nose in the sand, covering her eyes with her hands. In spite of this, she could see the brightness through her hands and her closed eyelids. Kheram lay beside her with his eyes closed. They both felt a sudden blow of heat on their backs and bare legs.

Ilva, despite the panic that seized her at the sight of the phenomenon, understood that an uncontrolled outburst of Gedrena's ammunition and its supporters must have occurred. She mastered herself instantly. She already knew she had to run away now and that it was her only chance to do it. She heard the cries of people whose eyes were struck by unusual light.

She stood up and looked at the sky. In the west, a huge mushroom was slowly rising after the composition of the warheads exploded. Its underside was dark and the growing hat glowed with a gloomy glow illuminated by the sun hidden below the horizon.

"Kheram!" She shouted. "How far is it to the Oasis?"

"About three hundred miles, maybe a bit less," he shouted back.

And he did not say anything more anymore, because a powerful toss of earth beat them off their feet. The ground shook and trembled feverishly. At the same time, a huge wave of compressed air hit the camp and rushed farther into the desert, raising clouds of dust and sand. After a few minutes, the ground calmed down and dust began to settle. People's screams died down. Suddenly there was a horrible bang from which the eardrums could crack. It was the sound wave of the explosion that reached the camp, dragging behind a wave of radiation, a seismic wave and a shock wave in the air.

Ilva jumped to her feet and jerked up Kheram, who scrambled in the sand.

"We're running away!" She shouted. "Now!"

They looked around for the horses that were tied on the ground, snorting and snoring in horror. Ilva quickly found her accouterment and weapons. She sadly saddled her horse and ladened the other one. Kheram also took his horse and two others, which he ladened with supplies.

They jumped on horses and were about to move when they came out at once, not knowing from where the silhouette of a warrior with a sword in one hand and an ax in the other.

"Where you want to go?" They heard mocking voice of Dacha. "I've written your's death in my soul. For you, for having caused death of my lady, let she live forever...

Despite the threat of danger, Ilva laughed sneering.

"You must have been crazy, Dacha," she said mockingly, "finally you are free, you can go with us, you can go back to yours, but there is nothing, there is only death there..."

"And I'll kill you for treason," Dacha snarled, aiming his ax at Kheram, who was sitting motionless on the horse, as if hypnotized.

Ilva understood that Kheram was afraid and that it would be the cause of his loss. Dacha will kill him with an ax throw if she does not do something final.

And she did.

"*Hoc! Hoc!*" She shouted and her horse jumped towards Dacha. Dacha looked at her and made a mistake. For a moment he turned his attention to the girl and at the same moment her sword bite into his chest. Ilva simply threw it like a javelin with one powerful sweep of the skillful arm. She bedded her horse and jumped off him. With one quick move she unhooked the short ax from the saddle and jumped to the commander. She did not have to kill him. Dacha was dead now, her sword hit his heart.

"It's because you called me a bitch and hit me in the face," she said, "we don't forgive that in our place..."

She jumped on the horse.

"Let's go!" She cried. "An invisible death above us!" She pointed her hand at the sky, on which the huge mushroom after the explosion was still rising, clearly bowing towards the east. She knew that in a few minutes the radioactive fall-out would begin, and then nobody would survive here.

"How did he know that? She thought about the strange prophecy of Brahytma. "Everything has checked so far!"

"But where?" Kheram asked with a lump in throat because of excess of adrenaline. He was sick, his heart was pounding and his mouth was salivating. He spat in disgust and took a deep breath.

"Away," she said, "north-east, toward the Vilayet Sea. Here we can't stay longer."

"But why?" Kheram did not realize of the danger.

Ilva turned to him.

"Because of this cloud, poison will begin to pour into the desert," she explained to him so that he would understand. "It's invisible and has no taste or smell, kills slowly but mercilessly and has no antidote. First, hair and nails fall out of the man, then teeth, and the whole body is covered with ulcers. Then, vomiting, chills and diarrhea begin, and then the person weakens and dies in terrible suffering.

"Oh, Osir!" Kheram groaned.

"Don't moan, buck up and tell where the north is?" She said in a commanding tone.

That finally sobered him. He looked around and firmly pointed the direction.

"There, where these rocks are," he pointed to two rocks standing like a gate.

"So, let's go," Ilva said and spurred her horse.

Kheram silently followed her.

IX

They traveled two days, far away from the accursed place. They only allowed themselves a short break to give tired horses a break. They were lucky because the western wind pushed the radioactive clouds towards Ghulistan and further to the Kathai steppes, which became the plain of death. When the blood-red aurora burst on the third day, they noticed that grass and sand under the hooves of their horses had finally been replaced with grass and lush steppe grass. They breathed a sigh of relief. They were saved. They stopped and unsaddled the horses allowing them to eat. And they laid themselves on the grass in the shadow of some puny trees wrapped in blankets with saddles under their heads and fell into a nervous, exhausting sleep. They slept until the evening, and then they went on their way again, still heading for Thuban, which was finally perfectly visible in the dark blue sky, which was no longer obscured by a terrible explosion.

They slept all day. They woke up when the sun was in the west. The sky was saturated with red and orange color. The sun itself was hanging like a cherry ball with three fingers above the horizon. There was no cloud, but it seemed that the whole sky was shrouded in mist in orange and ecru colors.

"What happened to the sun?" Kheram asked uneasily.

"Nothing," Ilva shrugged. "It's only the explosive dust that changed the sunlight," she said, carefully choosing Stygian words.

"We go further?" He asked helplessly.

Ilva was not surprised. Everything changed in his life and he could not find himself in a new reality...

"If you want, you can stay here," she said with a contradictory smile, "but sooner or later you'll be hit by some jighit or jete and you'll have trouble. And they are much worse than Dacha, may he rest in peace... I'm going from here, anyway. Don't forget that we are threatened with poison from the clouds, and we'll be safe only when we cross the river."

"How do you know?" Kheram raised his eyebrows in amazement.

"Just because..." She cut off, because she did not want to explain obviously (to her) things. "Have you already packed up?"

He nodded. Ilva's erudition sometimes knocked him out.

"Where are we going?" He asked.

Ilva looked around at the stars that scarcely reddened in the sky.

"To the east," she said firmly, "to Ilbarians, there we'll be able to breathe."

And they moved on.

The road lingered hopelessly for them, so they shortened their time by learning the language. Kheram quickly mastered the basic phrases in the Hyborian language and the learning was getting better and better to him.

Around midnight the moon rose, its light was orange. They rode, heading for his huge shield, which decreased as it rose above the horizon. At once they gave out astonishment. Above the eastern horizon slowly raised the second light, smaller but more vivid than the Silver Globe.

"What is that?" Kheram for the second time amazed himself immensely.

"I'm going to bet that this is the Great Guide," Ilva said, "but why is it here, not by the Black Kingdoms?"

"I don't know," Kheram replied.

"Tell me, is he bigger or smaller now?" Ilva was thinking feverishly about something.

Kheram looked at the shield of the Earth's satellite. On it was a blur of the antimatter thrower, which resembled a large impact crater.

"It's clearly smaller," he said.

"How much?" Ilva was inquisitive.

Kheram covered it with the thumb of his outstretched hand.

"About half as much," he answered.

"For sure?"

"Sure," he answered firmly, "what's going on?"

Ilva thought for a moment.

"The point is that the Great Guide has come down from Earth orbit and is flying away from it on the tangent. That is why it is smaller and moves in the sky.

Kheram did not answer. He did not understand what she was saying to him. He shook his head.

"I'll explain to you as soon as we get to the river, and now..."

She did not finish, because in the west a great golden light appeared, which flew northeast to crash into thousands of rainbow sparks that faded away from it.

"What's that!!!???" They exclaimed in unison, looking at this spectacle.

A brightly glowing ball flew over them and after a second it splashed into a swarm of rapidly fading sparks.

"Falling star?" Kheram asked.

"Maybe, or..." She paused for a moment, because it seemed unlikely, "or... Little Guide. It was flying such a path..."

X

A wide, two-and-a-half-mile river Ilbarian opened in front of the travelers. They greeted her with shouts of joy. The horses broke into the water and stopped only when they could drink water. Real, not trapped in flasks or contained in hard desert-steppe grass. Ilva jumped off her horse and was delighted to be immersed in cool and clean water. Kheram followed in her footsteps and after a while they puddled each other like happy children.

"Catch me," she cried, taking off her tunic she had tossed ashore and plunged into the river. She was a good swimmer, so she swam several dozen yards with a few strong hand movements. Kheram also threw off his clothes and followed her. However, he miscalculated with his strength, and the cool water caused the muscles of his shins to spasm. He felt water cover him. He jerked hard and it lifted him slightly above the water.

"Ilva!!!" He shouted. "Help!"

Ilva initially thought she was playing, but there was so much fear in his voice that she turned back and after a few waves of strong hands and legs, she found herself beside him.

"Take in the air," she shouted, "how much you can and lie on the water!"

He obediently obeyed her command, his leg ached a lot. Ilva came up to him from the back and began towing him to the shallows, towards a wide sandy patch. Hissing in pain slowly, supporting on her shoulder, he went to the beach and fell on the warm sand. The contraction finally released and the pain drifted away. Nevertheless, he could still feel it in his muscles. He sat down. Ilva stood above him in the warm sunshine, like a bright statue of Isis - the Stygian goddess of love and beauty. She squeezed her hair, which she threw on her back. After a moment, she combed it with a horn comb and tied it with a strop in a "ponytail". She put the wet clothes on the grass to dry in the sun.

He looked at her with delight.

"Thank you," he said quietly, "for the second time you saved my life..."

She shrugged and sat down next to him.

"I didn't know that you are not a very good swimmer and that the water is so cold," she said, "it's my fault, I couldn't call you..."

He put his arm around her and kissed her on the cheek.

"Anyway, thank you," he said. "Now tell me what exactly we saw in that night? You promised!"

Her long and thick eyebrows went to the hairline. She lost her self-assurance for a moment because of amazement. She expected something different, a confession, a kiss or even a fondling, maybe even sex. At the sleeping stands, they were cuddled together, so they were tamed with each other. She counted on something more and here... She sighed.

"You can't have everything at once, it would be an excess of happiness," she thought.

After a moment she shook her head in amazement. She reached for a stick and looked around. She found a piece of even, damp sand and nodded to Kheram.

"Come on," she said, "I'll give you a small lecture."

He stood up and walked to her. She looked at him with appreciation - he was nicely, harmoniously built. Looking at him, she felt a gentle tickle in the bottom of her stomach and the tips of her breasts. Their nakedness was pleasantly exciting...

He sat on the sand. She knelt beside him to expose her breasts.

"You know that Earth is a sphere?" She began.

He nodded.

"And do you know that it orbits the Sun, which is a sphere made of glowing gases?"

Kheram's eyes widened in amazement so much that they resembled saucers.

"Re... re-really?" He stammered.

She nodded.

"And I'll tell you that it's about nine million, three hundred seventy-five thousand miles away from Earth. But that's not important. Around Earth, in the average distance of two hundred and forty thousand two hundred and fifty miles orbits the Moon."

Ilva drew a larger circle signifying Earth and a second circle, smaller, depicting the Moon. Then she drew the orbit of the Moon around the Earth.

"Understand?" She asked. "Now look. There are also other objects around the Earth: the Great Guide, which hangs over the Black Kingdoms, and also the Little Guide, which flies - or actually flew - around the Earth."

With quick movements she drew two smaller satellites of the Earth.

"Yes, that would be right," said Kheram, looking at her, "what's next?"

"Well," she said, "something must have happened that the Little Guide fell into the atmosphere and burned what we saw."

"How did it burn?" Kheram was surprised once again.

"Normally, like meteors," she replied, "everything there," she pointed at the sky, "moves with enormous speeds. When these bodies encounter the layer of air surrounding our Earth, then they burn from the friction of the air..."

"Impossible!" He exclaimed.

"You saw it yourself," Ilva said quietly.

"Yes..." he admitted. "You're right, and what's next? What about the Great Guide?"

"I don't know, but it apparently stopped circling the Earth at the equator and walked away from it on the tangent," she drew a tangent arrow into the Great Guide's orbit, "and that's why we see it like that night."

"But why?" He asked.

"I forgot to tell you," she explained, "that the Earth revolves around its own axis, and that's why we have night and day. Now you understand it?"

He nodded.

"Indeed, this explains a lot, but not everything," he admitted after a long thought.

"What do you not understand?" She asked.

"What caused one Guide to get into the atmosphere and the other flew away somewhere to hell?"

"I don't know, maybe people from Belverus know something," she replied.

"Let's go!" Kheram almost exclaimed. "What are we waiting for?"

"Let's have a rest first," Ilva said. "Our horses are tired and must eat something. Driving through the desert emaciatoned them. Perhaps we will move in two days?"

"Well, let it be," Kheram said reluctantly.

At once, he looked up and looked at Ilva. She sat on her heels in front of her drawings. Her dark hair ran down her bare shoulders and back. The steep breasts hovered to the rhythm of the accelerated breath. She closed her eyes and half-opened her lips. He understood. He stood up and knelt beside her. He gently touched her cheek with his fingers and raised her chin, then brushed his lips with her half-open lips.

"Finally," she whispered and her arms wrapped around his neck. Their lips were joined by a hot, passionate kiss. Ilva lay on the sand pulling him with her. His hot lips caressed her face and then her neck and cheeks. Her hands stroked his arms and then her back and sides of his body.

Kheram reached by the mouth her breasts, which were tumid with hot blood. She moaned softly with pleasure and he felt a tear break in him. He had a lovely, fresh like flower girl in his arms that loved him and now she was giving herself to him... He understood that he loved her from the first sight, from the moment when he saw her for the first time with a sword in her hand successfully fending off his colleagues' attacks. And then, when he cleaned and patched the wound on her head, he decontaminated her finer wounds, he looked after her and stealthily met her at night... And now, when she saved him from Dacha's ax and pulled him out of the currents of the river. He felt grateful for this girl who had invaded his life and showed him another world, better than he lived in. He raised his head and looked at her. He felt gratitude and love for her. She opened her misty eyes.

"Ilva," he asked in a low voice, "I love you, will you be my wife?"

The joy that flashed in her eyes was the answer. She smiled.

"I thought you would never ask me about it," she said quietly. "Sure, I want it. I didn't save you from death to let you go, just like that."

XI

They kissed again on the soft sand in the warm sunshine. Suddenly one of the horses snorted softly. But Kheram was the first one who felt danger. Driven by more instinct than by experience, he suddenly pushed Ilva away from him. Just in time, a short spear stuck in the place where they were lying.

"What a..." Ilva opened her eyes and then jumped to her feet only to take lying in the sun tunics.

Kheram glanced toward the river. At a distance of perhaps two hundred steps from the shore a long boat sailed, on which board stood some warriors not displaying any friendly intentions - quite the opposite... The warrior who threw the spear was just putting the second one on spear-thrower and took a wide swing.

"Let's go!" Kheram cried, hopping on the horse, thanking all the gods of Stygia for not having unsaddled their horses.

Ilva also jumped on her horse and shouted hesh! They rushed forward in the direction of the river. They jumped for about half a mile and stopped. The strangers landed and watched the place where they intended to camp. However, they did not intend to pursue them.

"Dress up." Ilva handed him the tunic, which he put on. "What are those people? They did not look nice at all."

"It's *ilbarskebutyri*, local river pirates," he explained. "They are good on the water, but on land they show little value. They are primarily deserters from the army - mainly from Stygian and other liggers. Recently, there were some free Zaporosian from Wlodymyr Zaporoski and Ilbarians"

"I think it's better to get out of their way." Ilva stared at the pirates charging back and forth. "There are just too many of them, for my taste."

"Oh, and mine too," said Kheram and slapped his horse on the neck. "Anyway, we'll go along the river and spend the night anywhere."

"Maybe there?" Ilva had been looking at the horizon for a long time and her arm pointed north-west. "Where the black spot is. Maybe there are some rocks or something where you can set up a camp and defend yourself if necessary. Desert Tribes do not really look here. Pirates, as you can see - too."

"So, let's go!" Ilva pulled on the reins and headed for the black spot looming over the steppe horizon. "It's probably some kind of śivet, a desert stronghold like many in this area..."

They seemed to have about four, not more than five miles to it. It soon turned out that it was a black tower similar to a thick minaret. The closer they got to it, the more they were amazed. Finally, they were standing in front of the entrance - because it was not just a gate, just entering the street, which ended like a cut - on one side there was a gray, burnt terrain of the sun, and on the other, pitchy black stone tiles on the ground floors or at most storey houses- boxes. There was no sign of life. The Black City was before them empty, silent and... somewhat scary.

"Black City," said Kheram, "the legendary Black City, where ghoul-corpse-eater and Jhill's Children live."

"I don't believe in the ghoul," Ilva muttered, shrugging her shoulders, "and Jhill's children are only vultures... They probably live here and that's why these stupid legends were created."

"I envy your confidence," Kheram said sourly.

"You'll learn, you'll know as much as I do," she replied calmly, "there is a university and our academy in Belverus, so you'll have a place to study. Oh, and military academy. Nemedians are good fighters and have experienced, educated leaders. Gedrena was afraid of them the most. That's why she was getting something extra for Nemedia and Brythunia. More than two million warriors and guards, plus Picts forces and Kothians - a total of three and a half million people."

"How do you know that?" Kheram wondered. "This wasn't even told us."

"Because it was the most secretive plans of Gedrena and her priesthood, who the Brotherhood has infiltrated, and that's why she hated us so much," Ilva said. "But for now, look around for some accommodation, the sun goes down."

In fact, the sun was setting in orange-gold glow and the Black City looked even more amazing in the stuffy, still air. Having looked better at the stone slabs, they noticed that they emanated a delicate, rainbow glow visible only in the shade and the walls of the houses were covered with some glowing bluish, glittering glow.

"Can you read this?" Ilva asked when they entered one of the buildings.

"No, this is an old, very old letter," he said. "Probably even before the Cataclysm." He added after thinking for a moment.

He meant the Cataclysm that had swept Atlantis from the surface of the Ocean. Like every Stygian he knew and used only demotic writing, and the hieratic priestly writing was something inaccessible to him. Only people from the peaks of power were using it. The highest and the closest to the Throne and the Altar...

"Where do we stay?" He asked. "I suggest here. It's quite spacious here and we'll all fit in..."

And there is a tight roof," Ilva added, "and it gathers for a storm."

They quickly brought the horses into the neighboring room, and they occupied themselves somewhat smaller, whose window looked out onto the street in the direction from which they came, because they assumed that they could be attacked just from the side of the river. They laid on saddlecloths beds and saddles under their heads. At first they wondered whether to keep the guard by midnight, but gave up and went to sleep listening to the roaring of the storm that was coming up from the Sea of Vileyet. They fell asleep.

They were awakened by a thunder. The storm center came over the Black City and a huge, multi-mile electric discharge struck the minaret again and again. The rumble covered them every now and then like a lid, and the rain covered the black slabs of buildings and streets.

Kheram stood up to look around. He looked toward the river - he saw nothing but the gray rainstorm. He went to the window overlooking the minaret and was beating with delight. Here was the thunderbolt that hit the top, and the whole structure and surroundings of the minaret lit up with rainbow colored multicolour light. Another thunderbolt and another feast of colorful light. And another...

"Ilva, wake up! Ilva, honey!" He shouted. "Get up and look!"

The girl stood up from the bed rubbing her eyes. She looked at him quizzically and went to the window.

"Look there," he pointed direction.

Four more discharges hit into the tower of the minaret that shone with rainbow light. Ilva cried out in amazement and delight.

"Beautiful, isn't?" He asked embracing her.

"Wonderful," she admitted.

They stood embracing watching an unusual spectacle. The city became something less unfriendly than it seemed to them firstly. And then, when the storm went away towards the Shemit desert, they went to sleep and slept until the morning, this time sleeping in young people sleep, without dreams and nightmares...

XII

They woke up when the sun was high in the sky. The entire steppe was covered with fresh greenery, which the water lured out from under the stones and sand. Kheram got up and went to the horses that were sleeping in the next room. He went in and rubbed his eyes in amazement.

The horses were gone!

It was impossible, he remembered exactly how he took them there and...

Suddenly he heard a familiar neigh and snort. He looked out the window and saw them grazing in the meadow. He breathed a sigh of relief.

"Did you expel them to graze?" Ilva stood behind him, hugging him.

"No, they went by themselves," he murmured, taking her hands that surrounded him. They stood for a few minutes enjoying each other in silence.

"What do we do next?" He finally asked. "Do you have a plan?" She raised her head.

"Yes, of course," she said, "we must get to the other side of the river. The only solid bridge is the bridge on the Zamboulian Trail to Samara and Aghrapuru. In Aghrapuru, we have a Commander of our Brotherhood and only there we are really safe. Admittedly, the trail is not very safe, because you can come across Shemit-Stygian patrols, and this can give us some trouble. Especially during the interregnum..."

"So?"

"So we'll only go along the river to the bridge and then in the direction of Aghrapuru - we just do not have a different possibilities."

"What about *ilbarskebutyri*?"

"Don't you have other worries?"

"Not for this moment," he said. "We will worry about them over the river."

They kissed each other. And then they went outside. Their sandals clapped on the matt-black flagstones.

At one point, Kheram knelt down for a moment and amazement was drawn on his face. He produced an inarticulate murmur and his hands began to touch the plates.

"What happened?" Ilva asked.

"They're cold," he said in astonishment, "touch yourself. Almost freezing."

Indeed, black plates lying in the full sun should burst with heat, but they were almost ice-cold.

"As if they absorbing heat," she said unknowingly.

"But that explains exactly why the horses ran into the meadow," Kheram guessed, "it was just too cold for them. We did not feel it because we slept on the blankets, and they didn't..."

"So this isn't a city, but some... some..." she was choosing words, "...a receiver, concentrator and converter of solar or atmospheric energy in electricity..."

Kheram's face showed astonishing amazement.

"What??? What is this... e... receiver, e... conce-something and that... elect-something-yet?"

Ilva looked at him with superiority.

"Receiver, it is a device for receiving something - in this case the heat of the sun or its light or thunderbolt power, the concentrator is used for their concentration, density - explained patiently - and the converter to convert them to electricity."

"For what?"

"For electricity." She explained. "The Atlanteans used it on a mass scale. They illuminated her headquarters, driven their machines..."

They temporarily stopped discussions, because they came to horses that came running to their whistles and waited, shifting from foot to foot and waving their tails.

There was no living spirit in the city, not even animals. Because this city was ruled by its laws. Kheram tried to chop off a fragment of a stone wall. It ended up with nothing and even after hitting an ax with a hat a blue spark of sparks jumped out. It was smelling of ozone.

"This is the manifestation of electricity," Ilva explained, who calmly stood at one side watching his actions. "You better not move anything, because you can have less luck..."

"Yhym," he muttered and put down his ax.

They saddled the horses and went on their way. Before leaving, Ilva wanted to place her name from the stones found in the square to prove that they were here. And then they experienced a second surprise, because there was not a single stone in the ruinous city. Also outside the City. It was another phenomenon they did not understand.

They traveled along the northeast, towards the Ilbarian River and towards the bridge forming a knot of routes from north to south and from east to west. On the third day, they found themselves on the Ilbarian Route, thanks to which, after a further two days, reached the bridge.

It was a gigantic structure boldly bent over the river, which measured almost four miles wide at this point. Both outposts and all the spans were made of huge boulders, while the upper part was made of light-burned bricks, which were bonded with strong and weather-resistant cement. It was unbelievably old, there were legends telling that the Atlanteans had placed it before they died in the flames of the war they had begun...

They went to the bridge, marveling at its vastness. Its width was almost half a mile and it did not change over its entire length. They were four feet fifty feet above the water level. What surprised them was that despite the rather late pace on the bridge, there was no living spirit. Both routes were also empty. Halfway to the road, some people appeared at the same time, but they did not follow the path, but jumped on it from the sides. Ilva looked back instinctively and to her horror she noticed the second group following them. She understood everything in one flash of thought.

"We have company," she said in a trembling voice, "it's *ilbarske-butyri*..."

"I see, he nodded, "we won't sell cheap our skin."

"Oh, no," she shrugged, "they don't have horses and besides, you said that they are weak on land, so we have a chance to break through."

"Let's get ready, it's still mile to them," said Kheram. "They revealed themselves too early and it was their mistake, because now we know about them."

"Are we charging?" She asked taking the sword in a hand.

"Not now," he said, "they count on it. We'll do this: you'll shoot some of them with a bow, and the rest will be defeated by swords, unless they have something extra for our horses, then we have to think about IPB."

"???"

"Instant Plan B."

"Do you have any?"

"No," he shook his head.

They rode for about two hundred feet and Ilva reached for a bow. Without waiting for anything, she let go of the first arrow, knocking down a big man. A second later the second one fell on him with an arrow in his neck. The pirates went all for them from two sides. They were confident of their advantage, so they did not hide. Ilva's arrow found her third target.

"Well done!" Kheram shouted. "And now hold on near to me and leap!"

The pirates did not expect this. They both fell between them, and they tried to sack them from their horses or reach them with swords, spears and javelins. Ilva bounced blows and, in the intervals between attacks, she handled short and terrible sword cuts into the heads and shoulders of enemies. Blood splashed around people and horses. Suddenly, the lasso thrown at the back fell on her, then the second one. With a swipe of her sword she cut the lines that bound her, before the loops tightened. Unfortunately, her horse slipped on intestines of Ilbarian or Shemit, and she fell down with him. The pirates tightened the circle around her and waited for the opportunity to attack. Kheram jumped on the saddle of his horse and jumped down to be next to her.

"Not good!" He said with difficulty, catching his breath.

"I see," she said, "we jump to the water?"

"This is your IPB?" She asked mockingly and laughed despite the nasty situation.

Her laughter acted like a lashing whip against pirates. They started to attack. Meanwhile, Ilva and Kheram tried to keep them away from each other. Their swords formed a veil of shimmering steel in front of them. Whoever entered it - he died.

"Surrender, you've no place to escape," said the bandit's leader, about the posture and appearance of Cyclops.

"Kiss my ass," said Kheram quietly, "if you can get to it."

"Boys, learn them good manners." Cyclops turned to his subordinates.

They started again and again the three bodies remained in place.

"What the hell!" Cyclops foamed. "Don't you have javelins? This isn't about them, just their pouches! So...!!!" The rest of the command remained in the throat. In the center of his low forehead, a short, fat arrow with a distinctive "wzzzzzt..." appeared in a second. Two long shots stuck in the breasts of two of his bodyguards. There was a massive throb of warhorses, to which the sound of pirates left the urge to fight and gave their backs.

Ilva looked back. A group of horsemen dressed in identical, gray-green masking capes rode at a distance of one and a half feet, and a man with a crossbow in his hand at the head of it. She felt her heart in her throat.

"Dad, I'm here!" She cried.

"Chase these bastards," said Crossbowman to his men, who were trotting after the pirates. "And take one or more alive!!!"

He jumped from his horse and walked over to the petrified Ilva.

"Excuse me, my daughter," he said in repentance, "I was late but I think we arrived on time..."

XIII

"Well, now it's time for you, daddy." Ilva improved on her chair.

They were sitting in the Aghrapuruan's clubhouse of Brotherhood commandory. The night had fallen past the windows, only the gentle glow of the evening mist above the sea, illuminated by the natural phosphorescence of sea plankton. Ilva told her father, Prince Halidor and his wife, and the entire team about their adventures on the trail, which in such a circuitous way failed her and her boyfriend to Aghrapuru.

Lestek adjusted himself in his seat and moved his eyes around the room.

"You had to Know, daughter," he began, "that all, almost all, your adventures have been carefully planned a year ago. And everybody, as we are here, we have become a chain of events in which you were the main link. And you did the most dangerous job. But I could only trust you absolutely."

There was a murmur of appreciation. Ilva flushed with satisfaction like cherry.

"Why daddy?"

"It's obvious," Lestek smiled, "you're my daughter, but not only. I needed girl like you: brave, strong, well-trained and clever. That's why I chose you. And, of course, my second daughter helped us - Tia, who found a year ago the key to the weapon owned by Gedrena. It was a gold tile five by three inches, with twenty Armamen marks. She found it in Malabony, during the next renovation and sealing of the local sarcophagus. She immediately realized the value of the subject and gave the news about it to Belverus. At first, I didn't know what to do with it, but our archivists and librarians quickly found the answer in the "Script of Velitrium". It describes the devices arming and firing all types of warheads known to us. Thanks to this we already knew what we have in our hands. The third element was missing.

"What kind?" Everyone looked at Lestek. He stood up and lifted the horn filled with golden honey from the slopes of the Tatrian Mountains. His face became serious.

"Though time is joyous," he said sadly, "we must remember the one that now allows us to celebrate triumphs. A woman who was braver than any man who lasted until the last moment with our enemy informing us of his intentions! I drink for the memory of the beautiful and brave Nefre called Nikotrix!"

They all fulfilled this toast, sipping a few drops on the floor, in honor of the goddess Dekerto, the patrons of the dead.

"And what's next, Grand Master?" Red-haired Sonja asked.

"Oh! Thanks to Nefre, we knew where Gedrena stored the found and extracted warheads. They were well protected inside the Pyramid of the Moon and guarded by the Queen's Guard and the priest's guard. They could not be deflected either with a frontal attack or a ruse. You had to find a different way. And with Iris from Ianthe we came up with it! Cheers, my great wife, wherever you are!"

He took a sip of honey and continued.

"So, through the Stygian spies in Goa, we heard that Tia had found the Key to arm the warheads. Before the news reached Gedrena, I sent Ilva for a holiday to Goa. Returning from her sister, she was to take the forgery of the intervening counterfeit with the changed sequences of characters. We knew that entering the wrong code could result in self-destruction of the warhead, but we didn't predict that there would be another nuclear ammunition set up by her companions from the Future to transport them to our future world and use there. We wanted to get Gedrena and her crazy priests.

Without them, the warheads were safe. Gedrena solved our dilemma by herself..."

He fell silent for a moment.

"Well, then it was easy. Through Gedrena's spies in Vendhia, we told her that the key goes with Ilva to Belverus through the Himelian Mountains. I asked my friend, Prince Halidor and his esteemed wife, to keep an eye on her. And of course they met in the most inconvenient place and time. Commandor of ten-thousand-men, Dacha was not stupid - he set up a dozen dams on their route. The entire Royal Guards Division! Ilva could not slip. But she went to Shambhalla and got additional motivation there. She let herself be caught and carried away to Stygia and Shemit. Meanwhile, prince went away from the valley for which time forgot a day after her and went to protect Ari son of Yorestes, who went with a report from his father to the Commander in Yuetshi. They rode there, as fast as horses let them, from where the news was passed to Aghrapuru, where I waited with the team. We left immediately and on the way we saw a terrible flash in the south-west. And that meant that Gedrena had activated a detonator in her stupidity and lust for power. You know the rest, Gedrena and everything that lived 100 miles from the place of the explosion was killed by radiation. The impact of radiation blinded the systems of the Little Guide, which fell over the Stygian Desert, and what saw Ilva with Kheram."

"Daddy, what about the Great Guide?" Ilva asked.

"It flew into space and it will soon become a satellite of the planet, which Stygians called Hor-ka, and our friends Saturn."

"And one more thing: how did you intend to take me back from Stygians?" Ilva asked, puzzled.

"Your escape was included in the action plan," replied Lestek. "In the land of D'Śanśung-bö o'śangśung-goł o'śangśung-tań (for Sviatovid, what is the name!) you got a clear instruction of conduct. And I would hang your's head if you did not understand it. I could count on Brahytma, besides he gave me some ideas that I used during this operation..."

"But why did he give it to me in the form of a prophecy?"

Lestek cried with a huge laugh.

"Ha! ha! And that's because I know you!" He cried. "I know that you love secrets and sooner you'll hear the prophecy than the factual instruction!"

Everyone laughed.

"Daddy!" Ilva shouted in a resentful tone.

Lestek patted her on the shoulder and kissed her on the forehead.

"Honey, don't be angry with the old one. Did you have some entertainment? - You had. Each of your friends would give half a life for such an adventure! And what was it like? - like verses from the "Road of Kings"! Your romantic imagination immediately began to create a plan of action before it became necessary. You couldn't do it without imagination, and you live like that and you're among us, so don't complain..."

She was still grumpy, but finally she smiled at Kheram.

"And what happened next?" She asked her father.

"We continued on to Samara by Ilbarian Road heading to the bridge, where we chased pirates."

"Well, where did Brahytma know what and when to tell me?"

"It's obvious I was with him and everyone received their instructions and played their roles. Oh, yes, my theater is huge!" Lestko recited it with pathos. "I only feel sorry for poor Nefre. Only consolation that she didn't suffer, she died in the blink of an eye without even realizing it..."

"She could run away?" Red-haired asked.

"She could, but she didn't want to," said Lestek sadly. "She wanted to be in the Gedrena camp to make sure our plan was successful. As a double she had opportunities that we could only dream about."

"Who was Nefre?" Kheram asked.

"Gedrena's younger sister," said Lestek. "But her character was completely different. When she realized what her sister was going to, then she contacted us..."

They fell silent for a moment digesting this news.

"I imagine her face when she realized she had introduced the wrong code," Halidor laughed.

"I'm afraid she got really angry," said Lestek. "But I don't think she knew she had activated the self-destructing mechanism. Anyway, it did not matter anymore - after twenty seconds she ceased to exist."

* * *

Meanwhile, Ilva and Kheram slipped out of the common room and went to the balcony, where they stood embraced and cuddled together in the evening sky.

"What are you going to do after wedding?" Ilva asked him.

"I'll study with you," he sighed.

"And then?"

"I don't know, I'll definitely work for the Brotherhood. It's, as your father says, so much to do. It's hard for me to believe that these aren't crystal lamps attached to transparent spheres, and balls of hot gas that shine on its own. I'd like to know why?"

"You'll find out," she said. "But first me, then our children, and they are next in queue."

They snorted a short laugh and looked up at the dark blue sky.

It was diamond-like from the stars.

⤷

9

BLACK TOWER OF NERGAL

I

The meeting was coming to an end. Gathered people in Consultation Hall of Green Dragon Brotherhood were already slightly tired of the long lecture of Grand Master Lestek Crossbowman from Vislania, in which he mentioned the merits and victories of the Brotherhood, which for more than two centuries sought and liquidated the murderous remnants of the Great War of the Gods, which swept from the surface of the Western Ocean the island of Atlantis and its Empire. Finally the Grand Master finished and reached for the cup.

"I drink for those members of the Brotherhood who fell during this godly work!" He said, raising a toast and rising from his ornate chair.

The other Great Masters of their Commanderies also stood up, raising their richly decorated mugs.

"Let oblivion didn't erase memory of those heroes," the chairman of the College of Elders, the former Grand Master Brontosphoros added, "let living ones honor their memory, let the troubadours and bards sing songs of their deeds from the ocean to the steppes and swamps of Kithia and the island of Zipangu! And from the ice of Asgard to the Black Kingdom and the backwoods of Vendhia!"

Everyone eagerly emptied their cups and stood up to go to the banquet hall, where a feast awaited them before departing to different parts of the world. Lestek handed Iris, his wife, arm and they both waited while the twenty closest associates forming the strategic brain of the Brotherhood would move into the second room and sit down at the set tables. However, this time something that was not provided for by the protocol of such solemn briefings happend.

"Master Brontosphoros," said Lestek, "I'm asking you, stay a little longer."

The chairman of the College of Elders raised his eyebrows slightly and paused, then turned to Lestek and Iris. Something like this happened for the first time and everyone stopped in amazement.

"Iris, please go with them and do the honors of the host." Lestko smiled at his wife, who nodded to Brontosphoros and left closing the door. Both Great Masters were alone.

They sat back behind the wide table.

"Is there anything you didn't say in your speach?" Brontosphoros asked.

When they were alone, they turned to each other by forenames. The Crossbowman nodded.

"Yes," replied Lestek, "and I'm tired of it."

"So, drop this weight," Brontosphoros smiled. "It helps."

"Yes, you are right," Crossbowman got up and poured water into the cup, "it turns out that our mission isn't over yet..."

He moistened his throat. Brontosphoros waited for his words, staring at his face.

"Not yet Crossbowman?"

"No," Lestek shook his head, then reached into the pocket from which he drew a wad of parchment covered in writing. In the headline there was the logo of the commanderie in Messantia.

"What is it?" Brontosphoros asked.

"A report from Master Ewran," said Crossbowman, "that's why he wasn't here today. Read it.

Brontosphotos unfolded the parchment. Dark brown letters appeared on its yellowish background. He followed them with his eyes. It was a decrypted typewriter.

Master Ewran from Messantia
Commandory of Messantia,
Argos

> **Grand Master of the Brotherhood of the Green Dragon**
> *Belverus, Nemedia*

> ### About rumors among black folks

*I inform the Grand Master that a few days ago one of the members of the Council of the Twelve Negotiates returned to Argos - a merchant **Anselmus from Poitania in Aquilonia**. This merchant leads a lively trade with the Black Kingdoms and during this trip he stayed in the port of Kulalo, from which he brought cargo from the Southern Islands.*

*During a feast, he told that the Blacks from one of the Kingdoms lying about two weeks of road through the jungle, going in the direction of Xuhotl, slightly to the north of the trail between Kulalo and Xuhotl, and called **Cono-oñañgho** discovered a huge tower in these ancient forests, or rather its ruins, in which strange things happened. And here the rumors differ. According to Anselmus, it is difficult to say something for sure. Some Black people say that it was a tower reaching heaven, which fell into ruin when the Great Guide left us. Others say that it has been like that for ages. However, all their accounts agree that these are cursed ruins and that only a few lucky ones managed to get out alive from them, and those who went out alive with these ruins tell things from which the hairs are bristling. The complex of these ruins is called by Black people as **Black or Bloody Tower of Nergal** and they have a mystical fear because of it.*

So they are talking about dead people coming out of the walls and murdering newcomers, cruel little predators resembling crocodiles walking on two legs and with three-fingered paws, about glowing balls in ruins that cause deaths of people and animals at a distance and many other amazing things that are there. These ruins are to be located approximately 600 miles in a straight line north-east of Kulalo, and you can only reach through the bottomless tropical swamps and other difficulties. We can not count on Black people help, they are seriously scared and they announced the place as a taboo zone, which they observe fanatically.

*According to Anselmus, he obtained all this information by feasting with his intermediary Bamulas **Kitanga Catombe from Kulalo**, which has a network of its suppliers all over the Black Coast. Everything indicates that in the Black Kingdoms there are remains that may be potentially dangerous for people and other living beings, and therefore I propose to send an expedition to this region of the world in order to locate and dispose them.*

Messantia, 7. Chicchan, 0. Mac

"What day today is?" Brontosphoros asked.

"Tenth Lamat," said Lestek.

The date was from three days ago. Brontosphoros finished reading and put the parchment on the table.

There was a moment of silence.

"And what are you suggest, oh Venerable?" Crossbowman asked after a moment.

"It sounds scary enough, and you can't leave this, Grand Master," Brontosphoros said slowly, "or at least put it on the shelf or sweep it under the rug."

"We once wanted to create a commandory in the Black Kingdoms, remember Master?" The Crossbowman got up from his place and started walking around the room back and forth. "But we gave up this plan, because so far we had no signals about the danger that could threaten us from that side. This document changes the form of things. We say that we win too early."

"Anyway, you have to send a reconnaissance expedition there," Brontosphoros murmured, "because if people penetrate those continents, soon there may be another Gedrena with twisted Seth priests or other god who will have power over the world and the ultimate weapon."

"You're right," Lestek smiled sardonically, "admittedly, only a crater of three miles wide and deep for half a mile left after Gedrena and her priests, but that doesn't mean that there won't be anyone in the world with an appetite for power..."

"So what do you want to do?" Brontosphoros raised his head and fixed his penetrating gaze at the Crossbowman."

"I need your advice, Master," he said slowly, but firmly, "should I bring all these revelations to light and throw all Brotherhood forces into action, or act secretly only through the Messanian Commandery?"

There was silence again. Behind the door you could hear the sounds of a cheerful feast.

"I think, that facts should be reported to the general message of the Brotherhood and act as before," said Brontosphoros, "with all the forces and means of the Brotherhood. Only this way you can be successful. As for now, we're eliminating headquarters in Belverus and commandories in the Hyborian lands, and thus we can limit ourselves to three Brotherhood institutions."

"Only three?" Crossbowman raised his eyebrows in amazement. "Only?"

"You don't need any more," said the old Master, "outpost in Messantia, Goa, and now the one we will create - in Kulalo."

"Personally, I would prefer Xuhotl," murmured the Grand Master. "Because we are closer to the area of our activities."

"But there is no connection with the sea and with Goa and Messantia we only have communication by sea and there is no other."

Lestek digested it for a moment, then nodded.

"You are right, and therefore we are moving from Belverus to Kulalo. I'm only surprised by one thing..."

"What's surprising you?" Brontosphoros asked.

"I'm surprised that our friends from the Future haven't told us about these ruins," said the Vislanian, "and that's what worries me..."

II

Everything went much easier than he expected. The Brotherhood Council approved their plan the more that everyone realized that these ventures are the sense and condition of the continued existence of the organization they served. The problem was that until now these people were operating in areas with a relatively livable climate, and now they came to serve in the hot and humid equatorial rain forests that are a breeding ground for various infections. Although the Brotherhood has the best doctors, nevertheless even the best doctor is powerless against a tropical disease, for which no drugs were known yet... But they were not thinking about it now. Everyone was hoping for a new place of work and activity - the younger ones wanted to satisfy the hunger of adventure, the elders of knowledge. Two days after the feast, the commanders went to their commandories to liquidate them and then bring their people to Messantia, where four large ships were already built to move them to the Black Coast...

* * *

"Get up you bludger!" I heard over myself. "Dommel! What are you waiting for?"

I opened one eye. Angus leaned over my bunk, he was the journeyman of Master Bearnës from Ashantia. And the superior of all students.

I got up as soon as the low *Argoisan's Siren* allowed me - our ship, which we sailed to the new commandory in Kulalo. I quickly put on the tunic with the Brotherhood logo on my chest and tied my sandals. I ran aboard. The sea was calm, but despite the bright sun, there was anxiety as if lurking beneath the long, oceanic waves. The solar shield touched the horizon, the red-orange glow lay on the white sails encircled by the north-west wind from the open ocean. I looked towards the bow and half a mile away I saw the three remaining ships sailing in a fan-like array.

Angus just appeared suddenly, like a specter from the Kesangian steppes.

"Go for breakfast!" He yelled over my ear, as if we stand each other at least a verst away. "And next to work! What're you still doing here!?"

He had the manner of Corporal of Stygian camel cavalry. Nobody liked him, but he was not here to be liked. His parents died somewhere in Koth when their car drove into the swamp. As luck would have it, that there was something terribly poisonous and corrosive in the swamp. Only the bones remained from their bodies, and there was softened by the action of a militant substance. From then on, he joined the Brotherhood and began training young novices. He had only one weakness. Her name was Ornella and she was the superior of novice. She was eighteen, red hair and a stubby, freckled nose. She even looked nice, but she was able to knock down a powerful ox with one blow of her fist. She was our melee instructor. Ideally suited for this job. And strangely suited to the surly Angus...

I went down to the galley, where I got a huge piece of salted fish and a big slice of bread. From experience I already knew that something like this was heralding a storm. The salted and dried fish filled the stomach and did not allow its content to be thrown away in case of torsion. It was hairpiece. An old fishermen's trick from the shores of the Vileyet Sea, which has come in handy now in this mission. It let survive even the biggest storm. I did not get sick when rocking, like many Brotherhood members, but I felt drowsy and lethargic. Rocking tormented me quickly and did not allow me to act effectively.

I ate what they gave me and along with three friends I went to the amidships, where Angus waited with buckets and brushes. It was known that he would run to scrub the decks. During the cruise, we had nothing to do anyway, so that we would not get bored, we grabbed the brushes. We knew that the deck was never clean enough for Angus, so we did not hurry up with the job. From time to time I looked to the left, where in the distance, in the increasingly thickening golden haze, the shores of Stygia were looming. After dinner, the wind began to become solid and the waves began to pile up steeper and higher. Heavy, leaden clouds appeared in the west. The ship swayed creaking with all the bindings.

"Everyone under the deck!" I heard the voice of an older officer. "But you, Dommel, stay on board!"

"Why?" I asked, astonished and at the same time glad that I would not have to look at my vomiting colleagues.

"We need your eyes," he explained, "where do you prefer: to go to the eye, or to the crow's nest?"

"I don't care," I shrugged , "maybe a crow's nest."

"Well, go up. Take care of yourself, fasten yourself well. In an hour, Kaeso and then Tito will change you. Do it!"

"Yes, sir!" I replied and quickly climbed the crow's nest. The jetty was on the mainmast, seventy feet above the deck of our ship. Puffing, I climbed the rope ladder and after a minute I stood on the observation deck. It rocked here much stronger than on the deck, so I quickly fastened myself to the handrail and looked around. The ocean has already been covered with foam crests. The wind was getting stronger. Our three ships were visible in front of the bow two miles away. It did not look scary from above. But our ship sank into the deeper and deeper valleys of the waves and climbed more and more to their peaks.

"What's up there?" Said Perinous, our captain.

"It's all right." I screamed. "All ships in sight, about two miles in front of the bow!"

"Don't lose them!" I heard. "And report every change you see!"

"Aye-aye, captain!" I screamed the place down. Pernous smiled under his mustache and entered the forecastle. And I focused on observing the horizon, where storm clouds were becoming increasingly thick. The wind rose again and it was blowing more and more from the west. Also in this direction the sky was covered with more and more navy-lead, ominous darkness. Suddenly a lightning appeared on its background, which brightened them for a moment with a ghostly yellow and purple glow. In the light of it, I saw something like a strip of land. I waited for another lightning...

"Ahoy! The deck!" I shouted. "Land on the horizon!"

"Where!?" I heard from below.

"On the starboard side," I shouted back, "about eight to nine miles!"

A powerful blow from the wind rocked our ship. I did not manage to say anything because the wind forced my breath back into my lungs.

"Get down, little man!" Someone shouted from below. "Immediately."

"I see squall," I replied, "from the northwest!"

And without waiting for further encouragement, I began to climb down the rope ladder, instead of using the rope to slide. And that was my mistake.

A huge gust of wind and wave struck the ship. I felt a monstrous tug pulling the rope of my ladder from my hands and realized that I was flying. A second later, the salty surge shut on me. I tried to get out to the surface and I was able only to feel a powerful blow to the head, after which I fell and the roaring darkness...

* * *

Sensation woke up as first. I lay on something soft and wet. Then I felt a headache when I tried to lift it. I moaned involuntarily and opened my eyes. At first I only had blue and white in them, then my eyes sharpened and I saw the whiteness of sand and the blue of the sky. And I heard the sound of the sea and the cry of sea birds. Gulls circled around me. They must have been furious that I was not dead, like a few crabs that jumped to a safe distance when I moved and now stood staring at me with their eyes on the posts.

I stood up, hissing in pain. I felt my head - I had a huge tumor on it, I had to smash my head with item washed away from the deck - I thought and a nasty reality came to me at once. I was completely alone on a white, sandy-coral beach. I did not see one sail at sea. There was a palm forest in sight, and more like a jungle, judging by the sounds that came from beyond the palm trees. Birds and monkeys screaming. That I knew from previous trips to Goa and Pearl Islands... However, this time...

I stood facing the sea. The sun was low in front of me, slightly on the right. So there was the east - I deliberated. And that meant that I could only be on the only larger island among the archipelagos of the reefs and coral atolls of the Black Coast. It could not be the

Snake Island or the Black Island - both were more west and north. I remembered from the lectures of our cosmographer, Master Nabonides, that apart from the reefs and atolls of the Black Coast, there is also the Kamroon island, where Conan the Cimmerian found his asylum with his beloved Bêlit, when they were kicked off by Stygians and Shemits from the shores of Stygia and Khem, which they plunder... They lived on it for half a year waiting for the case to dry up enough that the combined anti-piracy forces were withdrawn to their bases in Asgalu, Kemi and Luxura. I tried to remember the stanzas of "Song of Bêlit", but the increasingly burning sun and aching head were not conducive to any thought processes. This island has already been penetrated twice by the Brotherhood search and recognition teams, but each time they returned with nothing. It is simply, this is an island that has been uninhabited since the time of the Empire of Atlantis. It was not a point of resistance or attack for any of the belligerents at that time. And now it lay on the sidelines of shipping routes and no one even knew who it belonged to...

"But it's almost a paradise on earth," I thought aloud.

I looked more closely into the beach and walked in a direction, in which I saw some dark objects lying on the beach, on the border of water and land. I had about three quarters of a mile to them and I moved in their direction in no hurry. At first I walked slowly, saving my strength, but quickly returned to form and walked faster and faster. Along the way, I encountered a stream of cool but sweet water. I immediately took advantage of it by washing sea salt and drinking a lot. Then I moved towards something that at first seemed like a wisp of rags and seaweed thrown to the shore by the waves, and then I felt my heart beat faster. A few birds jumped up at my sight and I saw her.

On the beach lay an unconscious girl, dressed in the same short knee-length tunic with the logo of the Green Dragon on small but shapely breasts. She could be my age, also a fifteen year old. I quickly approached her and leaned in and then knelt beside her and put my ear to her left breast. After a while, I breathed a sigh of relief - the girl was alive. Her heart was beating weakly, but regularly. I shook her, and then patted her cheek. After a moment, she opened her eyes and took a deep breath.

"How you feel?" I asked.

She stared at me for a moment. She stood up on her elbows. I helped her sit down.

"How you feel?" I repeated the question.

"G... good... I think... good," she mumbled, trying to overcome the stiffness of the tongue.

"Something hurts you?"

"Everything, holy Mother!" She moaned, and then she got emesis. For a long moment she gulped the rest of the salt water.

I picked her up and slowly staggered like drunks. I led her to the stream. She drank some water and coughed again. But she was starting to feel better. Her beautiful, black eyes were already quite conscious. Her dark brown hair was running in her backs. A slightly sun-tanned face with a freckled nose made a nice impression.

"Who are you and where are we?" She asked in a normal voice, looking around her agate eyes. I felt my heart beat faster.

"I'm Dommel from Messantia, actually I'm from Numalia, I'm a Nemedian from the Commandory in Messantia, I was sailing in the *Argosian Siren* and this place is the coast of the island of Kamroon," I replied, "and you?"

She smiled for the first time. She was really very pretty.

"I'm Annala from Venarium, almost from the very foot of the holy Golamir mountain," she introduced herself, "and I was on the *Star of Argos...*"

It was the westernmost ship. Strange, I thought.

"How did you get here?" I asked. Annala looked at me and I felt a wave of heat at once.

"The wave washed me off the deck when I wanted..." she blushed slightly, "you know... I was sick..."

"Oh, I understand, and then you found yourself in the water and what next?' I asked.

"As long as I could, I was swimming, I shouted, but no one heard it. I lost consciousness and then I woke up as soon as you found me. Thank you..." she added more quietly.

"You're welcome, you were just lucky," I murmured. "I fell from the mainmast and hit my head, already in the water in some object, and then I woke up on the beach, about three quarters of a mile from you."

"So, are we at Kamroon?" She asked, raising her beautifully outlined eyebrows.

I confirmed by nod.

"Like Conan and Bêlit," she said quietly, "and there is no one here besides us..."

"I haven't seen anyone here, except you," I said, overcoming a sudden cramp in my throat, "but that doesn't mean that nobody is here outside of us. I wouldn't be so sure...

III

She looked at me with some astonishment on her face.

"What did you mean by that?" She asked, surprised.

I shook my head.

"It's strange that we are here. We shouldn't be here...

"You're oversensitive?" She said hesitantly. "What do you mean?"

My head ached, but the thought was clear and precise.

"Annala, think," I said emphatically, "we dropped out of our ships, which were at least two miles apart. Two miles!"

"Two miles..." Annala's eyebrows rose like wings of a bird to fly. "So what?"

"That we shouldn't be here," I repeated.

"But why!?"

I understood that it was difficult for her to understand it. She lived in a commandory inside a huge Hyborian continent and had no idea about sailing. I think she saw the sea for the first time, at least for the first time she was so far from the mainland...

"I'll explain it to you," I said, drawing a situational sketch on the sand. "These are our ships when the squall comes. The squall came from here," I drew an arrow from the northwest.

"Well, from the side," she said, "I remember that..."

"That's right, and now look: this is the island that I saw almost exactly in the west in the light of lightning. Do you remember where the waves were coming from?"

She wondered for a moment.

"Well, from the side of the squall," she said reluctantly, "the wind rushed at these masses of water and foam... They were terribly high.

"That's right, so there were two forces here: the wind force from the northwest and the power of the current from the east. That is why such high waves were created."

"Okay, so what?" She asked with fear.

"I've two messages: ships have been pushed by the wind and waves to the east and maybe now they are on the Black Coast. This is good news, because there they have a cover of reefs and atolls that flatten the wave. The bad message is that it's not known if they arrived there...

We paused for a moment. Annala toyed with a piece of shell, staring at the endless ocean.

"How are we get here?" She asked.

"That's what I don't know, because the resultant of waves, sea current and wind should push us into the open ocean. In the meantime, we traveled eight to ten miles from ships to Kamroon Island somehow and we left it alive. I hit in my head, you had a drink of water. And we should go to the bottom, or finish as sharks food. In the meantime, we landed very close to each other, at the source of fresh water. Isn't that strange?"

"Well, it is..." she admitted reluctantly. "A miracle?"

"You know that there are no miracles," I said.

"Fluke?" Her agate eyes rested on my lips, as if awaiting confirmation.

"Maybe, but I'm not sure. What we do?" I asked to finish this discussion.

She smiled delightfully.

"From two of us, you're a sailor," she said with a mischievous smile. She felt better and the inherent joy and youthful optimism took precedence over the fear and uncertainty of tomorrow.

"Well, we must first get the fire. I don't see flints, but it's a volcanic mountain, so there should be sparks. Fire stones[16]." I added,

---

16 It's about iron sulphide, pyrite, which - like silica - sparks when struck.

seeing that she did not understand what I was talking about. "We should eat something - there are coconut palms, so we have so much food as we need. I saw mussels and edible snails in the water. And oysters! Lobsters are here too. Just light a fire and yum, yum...."

We both laughed.

"Are we going up on the mountain?" I suggested. "We'll see what is visible from it and maybe we'll find something that will help us to survive."

She nodded.

We entered the forest. It was not a jungle, as I was afraid, but above all, coconut and perhaps date palm trees, some cycadales and strange feathery fern trees. There was no trace of grass on the sandy-stony soil.

"Interesting," Annala said, "it looks like *sigillaria* or *eusigillaria*, and that tree reminds me of *calamites*... And look, this is *lepidodendron*..."

"So what?" I asked.

"Nothing, except that they died long ago," she said thoughtfully, "at least that's what my Master Mimiko-san from Nakikawa claimed, who teach us botany and herbalism. I saw prints of their leaves and bark on the stones that were mined in mines around the world. Now I see them alive... This island is wonderful!"

I did not share her admiration. There would be more bananas than some prehistoric trees...

And then we saw the bird. It was not a bird or any other creature. This creature was similar to a bird and reptile at the same time. It had the size of a hen, a strong beak, a tail, and colored feathers, but the similarity to the bird ended, because it also had four gripping limbs, like a monkey. And it made roaring squeaks, it was not jumping, it was flying from tree to tree.

"O Mother of All Gods!" Annala exclaimed with devout admiration. "This is Archaeopteryx! I think I'm dreaming!"

"Is there anything more edible here?" I asked, feeling stomach growling.

Annala came to her senses momentarily brought back with my comment to reality.

"I'm hungry, too," she said. "We can go back to the beach for coconuts. Besides, if here are such an animals, some inferior monsters may come."

She was right. We returned to the beach. We quickly looked for food, not overly straining. A dozen large coconuts and oysters had to be enough for the first meal. We drank everything with water and looked at the world more optimistically. It was noon and the sun was scalding mercilessly. We lay down in the shade of a palm, enjoying the moment of sweet idleness. I fell asleep.

The awakening was sudden. Annala tugged at my hand.

"Look! Sails on the horizon!" She called.

I got up very fast and looked in the direction indicated. In fact, the white square of the sail was clearly visible against the sky. A ship was sailing from the north-east.

"What a pity we don't have a fire," Annala sighed, "we could let them know that we're here..."

"This isn't one of our ships," I murmured, "besides..."

I did not finish, because my eyes caught something on the blue of the sky. A few clouds of smoke hovered over the distant cape on the north side of the island. An unknown ship turned in that direction. After a few minutes, the clouds dissolved on the sea breeze.

"So, we aren't alone here..." she said.

"Yes," I said, "we'll have to see who it is and ask for help. By the way, we have ten miles to walk... We will go down the beach, but on the edge of the forest."

"Why?" Annala asked.

I shrugged.

"I don't know why," I said, "but I don't like it. This island is *taboo*, but as you can see, someone visits it and maybe that's why it's *taboo*? Have not you thought about it?"

She looked at me with astonishment in agate eyes.

"Pirates? From the Red Brotherhood?" She asked with fear.

"Probably not," I replied, "you know the "Song of Bêlit"? After her death, the black pirates fell apart. The same was with the Red Brotherhood when Valeria left them. Only the Free Pirate remains, but they don't go here. They operate on Styx and Tybor and rarely venture into the ocean."

"So who can it be?" She asked again.

"I don't know and we will have to found out," I said. "We'll go now and we need to sneak near them at night and see who is it…

IV

We lay on our stomachs on the overhanging rock looking down at the bay. Some shrubs sheltered us from above. Only the stars and phosphorescent water lit up the darkness. At the bottom, on the beach, a big fire was burning. We were distant from it with a shot from the bow and we saw exactly and we heard everything by being invisible. The aliens felt at ease and apparently they were sure of themself, because they did not set up a guard or even search the landing site. Two ships swayed on the phosphorescent water of the bay. In the last shines of the day, we managed to take a good look at them. The one we saw had a characteristic construction and was a two-decked rowing and sailing ship. It was more adapted to the cabotage and river navigation than the ocean. The flag of Stygia was on the mast.

However, we were most surprised with the second ship. It was long and narrow. It had one deck and a raised beak and stern. A sculptured dragon's head was visible in the bow. The classic, dangerous and very fast longship of Aesir's from Vanaheim. It was not amazing, but his crew consisting of a collection of people of different races and nationalities: there were powerful Kushis, small Shemits and Zamorans, red-skinned Pikts and tall, fair-haired Aesirs and several Blacks. Unlike the Stygian ship, no flag fluttered on the longship. However, it was not an accidental motley crew. These people looked like good fighters and they were just them. They moved quietly and with the cat skillfull. Seeing their movements, it was clear that they were perfectly trained assassins. But they also stayed on the beach without delving too much into the interior of the island.

"What are they so afraid of?" I was wondering. During our journey we did not see any dangerous looking creature. We did not see any traces of big animals. And yet, the newcomers clearly avoided entering the forest, stopping only at the penetration of palm groves.

As for the Stygians, there were normal soldiers and sailors. They were led by a good-looking man of just about six and a half feet, with a clean shaven head with sharp features. He was like an old vulture, but he could be no more than thirty years old. He was dressed in ordinary sailing clothes, but everyone turned to him with respect. We heard shreds of their conversations, but they spoke in some unknown language, so we did not understand anything. After some time, we fell drowsiness and gave up on watching what was happening on the shore. Annala fell asleep, but I could not sleep, just listened to what was happening around us. But nothing interesting happened - night animals romped in the bushes and crowns of palms. The moon grew, and in its splendor you could admire the bay and the ships standing in its waters. There was still nothing happening, so I was finally asleep with the impressions of the day.

It was already clear when I woke up. A fire burned in the camp on the beach and the smell of food was coming to us. Stygians were preparing to march into the interior of the island, which was evident after their equipment and bustle. The collection of differnet man remained in place.

"What we do?" I asked Annala.

"Maybe we'll follow them?" I suggested the thought. I did not want to sit in the bushes on the rock and I wanted to stretch out some bones and get to the fruit, which grew around.

"Good thought," she murmured, "we've nothing to do anyway...

Meanwhile, fifty Stygian people went deep into Kamroon. They walked in a tight cluster watching closely everything. A few of them went ahead as searchlights or scouts. They walked around the rock that was our hiding place and, still looking around, they went alert to the path that led up the hill - to the top of the volcano. It seemed to us at least. We waited fifteen minutes, and when we stopped hearing their voices we followed them.

We entered between the densely growing sigillaries and sneaking around Stygian people, we were still gaining height. The sun came out higher and it began to heat. It got brighter in the forest and we had to hide well to avoid being noticed. And that the Stygians were looking good, so we had to extend the distance a bit by following them. From tree to tree. Still up. Finally, after some time, the path ended with the entrance to the cavern, whose opening was five feet high and was vaulted with pointed.

"A mine?" I heard a hot whisper over my ear.

"You're the one in this company who knows about the mines," I replied.

I turned my head and we looked into each other's eyes. She smiled.

"This is a mine," she said, "you can believe me."

"But I don't question it," I replied, "I'm curious what they mine from it!"

"We'll wait, we'll see," she replied. "From what I see on the surface, there may be ores of various non-ferrous metals here. But it's weird..."

She hung her voice and looked in disbelief at the rock walls surrounding the entrance to the mine.

"What... what is strange?" I asked.

"Construction of these rocks. These are sedimentary rocks, not effusive." She said in astonishment.

"So what? What is the difference?"

"Fundamental," she said firmly, "understand, this mountain is NOT a volcano!"

"But it..." I said uncertainly. "But it looks like a volcano."

"Exactly," she smiled charmingly, "it looks. You're right. But it isn't a volcano. It isn't because there is no trace of lava. There is no fumarol and solfatar, and that should be here if it was a volcano! Understand???"

I nodded.

"So where does the strange shape of the mountain come from?"

"I don't know."

We still waited. After some time Stygians emerged from the tunnel. They carried small bags, which had to be heavy, because they were clearly difficult to carry. And again, taking all precautions, they began to coming down. A few of them crashed a hole with heavy stones.

"I don't think we'll find out what they're getting out there," I said, "we can't go in there."

"Then let's follow them," said Annala. "Maybe we'll find out something."

We carefully followed Stygians, taking care not to stare at their rearguard. In the middle of the road a tumult arose. One of the porters stumbled and rolled over, dropping his pouch from which something spilled. Someone, probably his supervisor, cursed him and this man took this thing back into the bag and quickly joined the rest. We waited a few minutes and go down. We came to the place where the porter spilled the contents of the bag. We looked around urgently for clues when Annala let out a small cry that sounded astonished.

"Come see," she said to me, pointing to something on the ground.

I looked and fumed. Among the remains of the leaves and scales of lepidodendron bark lay a shiny, bright yellow nugget. Annala picked it up and weighed it in her hand.

"Gold..." She muttered.

She gave me a lump. It was heavy and warm to the touch. I found a stone and made a scratch on it. It was soft and left a clear mark on the dark surface of the stone.

"In fact, it's gold, nugget." I added when I saw she raise her eyebrows. "So this is a bonanza. Now I understand why they are guarding themselves... Well, we know where the gold of Stygians come from. Not from the land of Punt, or Kush, but from Kamroon!" I said. "You realize that we've discovered the greatest mystery of the rulers of Stygia???"

"And it can cost us our lives," Annala said. "We'd better get out of here before they know we're here. They'll kill us as soon as they get us!"

"Where will we go? I think only up, because the coast isn't safe, as long as they are here..."

We began to climb the sloping slope of the mountain. The sun lazily moved behind us...

V

When we climbed up, it was already well past noon. Breathless and sweaty, we stood on the edge of a huge crater, whose wide view stretched out before us. It was a huge mountain circus with a diameter of at least five miles and a depth of about five hundred feet. At the bottom of it was a lake of turquoise blue and green. Annala knelt and looked at the rocks we had under our feet. At the same time, she made a quiet cry of amazement.

"Domek, listen," she said finally, "there has never been high temperatures here, and these rocks are sedimentary sandstones and shale slate. Dolomite and marl, and everything what you want, but there is no volcanic rock here!"

"So this is not a volcano?"

"Of course not," she said. "I see something like this for the first time!"

"Indeed," I murmured skeptically, "you saw it in good momment."

"Golamira is an extinct volcano," she said calmly, "and I was on it several times with my Mistress."

I looked at her, she had a sulky expression.

"I'm sorry," I said finally.

"Don't worry." She answered and smiled at me.

And I got warmer on my heart and I thought that if I had her at my side I could do great things. And this thought amazed me, because I never thought in this way of any girl in my life...

"So what is it?" I broke the silence.

"It IS a crater, but not a volcanic one," she said with emphasis on the word "is." "There's a bonanza underneath. This is pure gold. Assay 24 K. Native.

She took the lump from her tunic pocket and watched it in the sun. She burned yellow in her white hands.

"I'll tell you more," she said, "this lump has been forged, cut out or broken from some larger whole."

She gave it under my nose.

"Look," she ordered, "here you can see a trail of impact and shearing. Someone cut it off from something bigger. Maybe even cut pure gold from the pay dirt. If it was in the stream, the water would coat it and look like a pebble, and now..."

She was right.

"How many of it they could have?" I thought about it.

"There were fifty of them... each of them had a bag..." she calculated, "oh mother, at least fifty talents!"

"Fifty talents!" It was the sum for which you could buy half of the cultivated lands in the Messiantic province. "I'm curious, why these criminal types need such a lot of money? And from the Stygians. We have to inform the Great...

I stopped because I realized that we were just the two of us, without a weapon, on an island far away from shipping lanes... "Shucks..." I growled.

"Anyway, something must be done about it," said Annala, "and by the way I'm hungry like a mad dog."

"We're going down, but there," I pointed to the west side of the island. "We are relatively safe there."

"I think we're safe now," she said, pointing to the ocean.

I looked and saw two ships sailing towards the north-east. "To Stygia." I thought.

In silence, we started going down to the beach.

* * *

The ship swayed on a gentle wave. Help arrived in two weeks after the events described. It turned out that all of the Brotherhood's ships survived the storm and entered to Kulalo. We were lamented and even a symbolic funeral was carried out, when a fisherman came to the Brotherhood's office, who brought a large bottle to the Grand Master, and a letter in it containing information that we - that is Annala and Dommel - are on Kamroon Island and we ask for help. The Crossbowman, in spite of the doubt, sent Master Tomes and twenty men aboard the fast ship, which after three days reached the shores of Kamroon and we returned to our people.

Everything would be fine, if not for the fact that we could not send this message. We had neither a bottle nor a papyrus and a pen...

It was another link in the chain of puzzles in this trip. After three days of sailing, we finally found ourselves in Kulalo, where the new Headquarters of our Brotherhood was created.

We were given 24 hours to rest and bring ourselves to order, and the next day we received the order to appear in front of the Grand Master. In fact, I was waiting for this moment because I could see Annal again. These two weeks on the island have brought us closer together. First, our intimacy was intimidating, and then we got used to it. We stayed together and it gave us confidence that we would survive this adventure. Fate was kind to us and the search and rescue team of Master Tomes found us in good health and mental and physical condition. Now we had to report this to the Grand Master. We sat in the chamber and waited for the call. Finally, the door opened and Journeyman Romuus, his secretary and adjutant, stood in them.

"The Great Master is calling you," he said. "Follow me, please."

We entered the office of the Grand Master. The Crossbowman sat behind his huge desk. Romuus pointed to two cane chairs and he sat on a stool with a papyrus card and a cane pen in his hand. On the right, sat Master Mimiko-san - guardian of Annala, my mentor - Master Arietys from Numalia. On the left - Master Iris from Ianthe - wife of Crossbowman and at the same time the superior of the Archives of the Brotherhood.

"Sit down," said the Grand Master, pointing to the seats.

We sat down feeling the questioning looks of our superiors and teachers.

"Now tell me everything from the moment you dropped our ships. I'm asking you for all the details, because even the smallest detail can be important. Romuus, note everything as accurately as possible," and he turned to us again. "So speak. We listen!..."

We told everything we remembered, putting a special emphasis on meeting with Stygians and a jumble of warriors on longship. We talked about gold, and Annala about their observations about the topography and construction of the island. When we finished after two hours, we were completely pumped out and the Crossbowman ordered a break. After dinner, we again took seats in his office. This time we were facing a round of cross-fire of questions. We have not made a mistake.

"What that Stygian man looked like, who was the commander of this group?" My Master asked.

"A tall, stout, warrior," I said, "he was six and a half feet tall, shaven head, face of a vulture, a large, curved nose.

"Would you recognize him in the picture?" Asked Crossbowman.

"I think so," I said, "that face is not one that you could forget."

"Is this one?" Master Arietys put a few miniatures painted on thin boards on the table in front of us. I looked through them with Annala for a few moments. Finally, we found the right match. This time, the man was clothed in rich robes and on his head he had a helmet with feathers.

"That's the man," we said in unison.

"Are you sure? "Asked Crossbowman.

"Yes! Yes!" We responded in unison. "It's definitely him!"

Arietys exchanged glances with Crossbowman and Iris.

"Romuus," Iris said, "please call Master Alcinoos."

Master Alcinoos was the head of the Brotherhood Special Operations Department. And that meant that the matter was very serious.

Annala looked after them.

"Grand Master," she said in her polite voice, "who is this man?"

The crossbowman exchanged glances with our Masters again. They nodded their heads in agreement.

"You've the right to know," he said after a moment. "This man is the missing successor to the Stygian throne. Prince Menkaur."

"Or rather Set-Amner-Men-Kaure," the voice of Master Alcinoos came behind us.

"How is it missing?" Annala was amazed. "We saw him as we see you now..."

"And that's the problem," the Great Master sighed, "because we thought he was dead..."

I sighed heavily, with concern.

VI

There was dead silence.

"Are you sure you saw him there?" Master Alcinoos asked us in round terms.

"Yes," I said and Annala only nodded, "we're sure."

"Could you describe who was with him?"

Hmmm... it will be difficult," I replied, "although we watched them from a short distance, but we preferred not to show them. We saw him properly by accident. He simply stand out, and the Stygians addressed him with great respect."

"And *those* men?" Crossbowman asked.

"*Those*? Who?..." Annala raised her eyebrows. "Oh, those from the other ship?"

We looked at each other.

"We didn't notice that they was contacting him..." I answered uncertainly. "In the end, if it's a Stygian prince, he wouldn't talk with just anybody in person... They always say through someone."

"A proper remark," said Master Alcinoos, "and how were they armed?"

"Both to the teeth," I replied, "the Stygians, like their army, had standard weapons: war javelins, bows, swords and daggers, and slingshots. Those men," I used the Alcinoosa term, "they had everything: bows, crossbows, swords, clubs and gods are eager to know what else. That's why I think they were pirates. And it's devilishly well-versed with fighting in the field and guerrilla warfare and with martial arts in general. It's seen."

The Masters exchanged a quick glance, Alcinoos suppressed a laugh.

"For Bel's fingers, I like this boy," he said, "send him to me, Master Arietys, he will be useful to the Brotherhood in our service!"

Arietys said nothing, but nodded in agreement. Work in the most secret department of the Brotherhood was a great honor!

"What do you think about this Master?" Asked Crossbowman.

"There're two possibilities," replied Alcinoos. "The first of them assumes that Prince Menkaur joined the pirates after the death of

Gedrena and her priests and supported them financially, which would be very strange, as pirates, by definition, live from assaults and plunder."

"That's one option," Arietys said. "Where's the other one?"

"The second is that he was kidnapped by pirates and he just paid the ransom and regained his freedom. But no, that's also out."

"Why?" Annala asked.

"Explain it to her." Master Alcinoos looked at me.

"This is because Stygians were armed, and both ships sailed to the island at different times, and sailed away together. If that were the case, as Master Alcinoos says, it'd be the other way round, the ships would come together from one direction and float separately in two directions of the world."

"Exactly." Master Alcinoos supported my argument. "So we must assume that there was a third option."

"They weren't pirates, but mercenaries who interact with prince Menkaur," Annala said, "and he paid them for some work they should do for him or have already done. I think they'll just do it, or they wouldn't go away together in one direction... I'm sorry..."

It suited one to the other. Our Masters exchanged instant glances again. Their faces showed a token of appreciation.

"Bravo Annala," said Crossbowman, turning to Master Alcinoos, "it seems you'll have not one but two students. And don't apologize. You are smart and perceptive. And you can draw the right conclusions."

Annala blushed and lowered her head. I touched her hand and she took it gently and did not let go. Our eyes met for a moment. I felt how hot I was from this touch. And yet on Kamroon island we got used to each other by sharing a bed, bathing together and drying out in the sun, looking for oysters for meals and choosing what nicer pebbles amid the coral sand. Our nakedness was something natural and understandable. Now this touch made me feel a dry throat and a fast heartbeat, and confusion in my head.

"Probably in Stygia a coup d'état is being prepared," said Master Arietys.

"It looks like," Master Iris nodded. "Can we prevent it, Master Alcinoos?"

"Our agent hasn't reported us yet," said the other one, "let's not forget that now we've only the sea route. We need to build a thread of solar telegraph, but unfortunately between Kulalo and Messantia there is the territory of Stygia, and between Kulalo and Goa almost the entire continent and the South Sea. Admittedly, we have the territory of Vendhia all the way to Iranistan, but we have to get along with the kings of Iranistan and Zembabwei, and it won't be easy because the latter don't have friendly feelings for the Bamulas and Blacks from the Kingdoms. I hope that this will be achieved when we show them great benefits from the rapid exchange of information between Vendhia and the Black Kingdoms and countries lying in the path of the telegraph line. The problem is also in costs, because it's about half a million drahma, or some 200,000 lunas in gold. We don't have enough to cover costs alone. The move itself cost us a lot of money. Unless…"

Master Alcinoos paused for a moment.

"Unless, what?" Asked the Grand Master. I understood him immediately.

"Unless we borrow some money from Stygians…" I said quietly, but loud enough for everyone to understand.

"Hmmm… Wouldn't it be ordinary stealing?" Said Master Iris.

Alcinoos and Arietys shook their heads.

"How is that?" Wondered Master Mimiko-san, but after a while she realize. "Yes, the Numalian Treaty recognizes only the properties of those mines that are registered in his Executive Protocol, so it can be done…"

"Master Mimiko-san," said Master Alcinoos, "I remind you that Stygia signed the Treaty but did not ratify it."

"But it doesn't matter in this situation," Master Mimiko-san retorted, "so we can have all rights to this gold if we register this mine."

"But Stygians will get mad!" The Grand Master laughed, "Menkaur will bite his sword…!"

"Or he'll come to Kulalo with his team," said Master Alcinoos. "I suspect these are members of the clan of the Sons of the Night. The assassins of Tolos Doom are gentle lambs compared to them."

For a moment, it seemed that a typical dispute between theoreticians and practitioners would begin, but Crossbowman would not allow it. He looked at us and focused his attention on me.

"There is one more thing to discuss," he said. "Call the captains Perinus and Neviges here."

Romuus got up from his stool and put down the writing utensils, then left.

"What do you mean, Grand Master?" Master Alcinoos asked.

"There is one more puzzle to solve," said Crossbowman, "namely, how it happened that they both survived the hell of the water poles from which they landed happily on the island of Kamroon. Because this is a TRUE puzzle and we should start with it."

There were footsteps of both captains behind the door.

VII

They entered, preceded by Romuus, who gave them armchairs and took his own place with a block of papyrus and a pen in his hand. They bowed stiffly to the Grand Master and his wife, and then took their seats. There was an awkward silence for a moment, which was cut by the voice of Crossbowman:

"Captains," he said, "I've allowed myself to take you away from the duties, because there was a need to explain an incident that happened in the vicinity of Kamroon Island."

"Are you talking about these two students?" Neviges asked, "we think it's impossible for them to save themselves from this boiling wave. This is impossible."

"Impossible!" Perinus nodded. "We barely managed to get out of this with life, which I think is almost a miracle. We should all lie on ocean floor. This storm was terrible! We haven't seen such waves yet."

"Indeed," Neviges chimed in, "after the disappearance of the Great Guide in the heavens, the arrangement of winds and currents has changed, and yet there is no Sailing Directions here. And if it does, it's about sailing along the shore, not in the open ocean."

It was true - such a Sailing Directions, i.e. description of shipping routes and natural conditions prevailing there, at that time did not exist yet. All the sailors kept to the shores and only a few daredevils like Conan the Cymmerian or his companions from the Red Brotherhood or the Pirates of the Black Coast managed to sail out into the Western Ocean and return to the living and healthy of this adventure. If anyone has gone so far as to Kamroon or other islands, then just jump from the atoll to the atoll, from the island to the island trying to have land in sight..."

"So how could it happen that the two," the Crossbowman pointed at us, "reached Kamroon Island almost without any injuries? Can you explain it in some way?"

"No, Grand Master," the two captains said in unison, "this is impossible."

"And yet it happened," said Crossbowman.

"A fortune..." Neviges muttered.

"A proverbial stroke of luck..." added Perinus.

There was a dead silence for a moment.

"Please tell me your whole story again from the time you dropped from the ship until you reach Kamroon," the Grand Master ordered us. "You first."

Annala nodded and once again told how she had leaned over the rail at the moment the ship was hit by a huge wave. She dropped overboard into the foaming water holes and the water covered her. She tried to stay afloat, but the waves jerked and tossed her, and finally she gasped and felt the choking weight of the fluid in her lungs realizing she was drowning. After a moment she lost consciousness. She regained it only on the beach when I took care of her."

"Now you," ordered the Crossbowman.

I told my story. Everyone listened without interrupting me once.

"Where did you hit?" Master Alcinoos asked at once. "Show it."

I showed.

"Interesting!" He said. "He hit himself, or he was hit on the most sensitive point of the skull. A blow to this point must have deprived him of consciousness."

"What do you suggest, Master?" Asked Crossbowman.

"All indications are that Dommel was struck to deprive him of consciousness and then transferred to the beach or near the beach on Kamroon. And with Annala it was similar to the fact that she didn't need to be deprived of consciousness, because she was already unconscious after being choked with water."

Everyone silently processed this revelation.

"Who could have done it?" Master Arietys asked. "Is the legend of the Sea Nation the truth?"

"Do you want to tell, Master, about Syrens and Tritons?" The chief of special operations asked this question in a polite tone.

"Exactly, Master Alcinoos," said the other.

"Legends of my nation," Master Mimiko-san said, "they speak of intelligent beings living in the water. According to them, these are people who have cut themselves off from their roots and moved to the waters of the All-Ocean. Other legends say that they were Atlanteans, who were adapted to fight in the water. I suspect that other peoples also have their legends about Sea People. And what do our friends from the Future say about them?"

The Crossbowman smiled.

"They are those people and those from continents. They joined forces to finally straighten out a few things in the history of our planet. Our Brotherhood is a part, a significant part of their plan."

"So we assume that they were saved by the People of the Sea?" Said Master Iris from Ianthe.

"Yes," said Crossbowman, "that's what I think. Is anyone has a different opinion? Any suggestions?"

The answer was silence.

"So I think the meeting is finished. And tomorrow..." he thought for a moment. "And tomorrow we'll be discussing what to do in the coming month so that the Brotherhood can function again...

VIII

From what I found out later, the Brotherhood Council decided to send two trips - the first, by the sea, to the island of Kamroon for Stygian gold, and the second one to the jungle in order to recognize the possibility of building a heliograph station system and finding the Black Tower Nergal. I was curious to which team I will be assigned, although on the other hand I was sure that I would sail with Annala to Kamroon. And I was not wrong. After two days, I was called in front of the Crossbowman. In the waiting room I have already found Annala and her Master Mimiko-san. Both were chattering about something in the language of Zipangi and I did not understand even a word of that. But at the sight of me, Annala switched to the Hyborian.

"Hello." She said. "I'm really happy for this journey! And you?"

"Me too," I replied, "but I don't see my Master."

"He's already there," said Mimiko-san with her charming, disarming smile. Now I have noticed that she is young and very pretty. In general, I began to notice many things that had escaped my attention before.

As expected, we were assigned to the team running on Kamroon. The Grand Master assigned us tasks to do - lead the team to the place and be at the disposal of our Masters. An uncomplicated task, but it was so at first glance, because the trip was really full of dangers resulting from the necessity of sailing outside coastal waters and the possibility of encountering Stygians and their mercenaries. The goal was the gold, but also to penetrate the island in search of ancient artifacts from the Great War of Gods. Crossbowman and his council came to the conclusion that the previous expeditions did not complete the task one hundred percent and they missed as much as the bonanza gold. On the other hand, it was difficult to blame them - the entrance to the mine was masked and secured so that no outsider could even think about finding this tunnel. And for this trip to be successful, there were we: Annala and me.

* * *

We stood in front of a boulder collapse, seemingly no different from the rest of the boulders in the area. But we knew that under them is the entrance to the mysterious mine, from where it was possible to extract fifty talents of gold in just half an hour.

"These are the boulders." Said Annala pointing to two huge blocks of rock. "You have to take them away, and there is a transition behind them..."

Master Arietys gave the sign to several powerful Apprentices who stood firm and were ready to push one of the boulders.

"Attention!" Arietys shouted. "Three... four!"

The young men pushed and the amazing thing happened - boulders bobbed lightly and without sound, revealing a metal door fitted to the rock.

So it has that kind of patent?" said one of them, "these boulders walk very smoothly and two people are enough to close it or open it."

"You're right, Rufus," Master Mimiko-san said, "but how will we open the door now?"

"I don't know, my lady," said the other, "but there is someone who knows."

He said this because Master Arietys watched the door closed and after a moment he looked at it with contempt.

"A combination lock." He said pointing to something that covered the small hood. "This is an old Atlantean robot and a runic description. You have to enter the password and the mechanism will open the door."

"Do you know password, Master?" Master Mimiko-san asked with a slightly ironic smile. "Because I'm not."

"Me too," he said calmly, "but..."

Mimiko-san's slanted eyes glittered for a moment.

"But what?..." she asked.

I noticed that there was a sort of secretive and fierce competition between them. Each of them wanted to show their superiority in the field of knowledge and intelligence. This competition crank them and it was a guarantee that everything would succeed..."

"You can enter a hit-and-miss password," said Arietys, "but this isn't a method. The method of trial and error in such cases has to the point that it can lead to blocking the lock, launch defense devices or in the best case, it's fun to tapping the access code to the end of the world."

"So, Master?" Mimiko-san's voice was already a clear challenge, "what do you propose?"

"That's what always in such cases," said Master Arietys with undisturbed calm, "or I take a hammer, or..."

"Or what?"

"Or I run the imagination. One moment." He said and concentrated to the maximum. His eyes narrowed, and the fingers of his right hand rested on the keyboard. After a moment he closed his eyes and his fingers gently moved on the keys.

I looked more closely at the keyboard. It was sixteen square tiles with convex Futhark Waten runes. They were set in a four-by-four square. The master stopped touching the keys. He opened his eyes and looked at me. His eyes smirked.

"We will try?" He asked.

I nodded.

The master smiled and slowly and carefully pressed the keys: Sig, Eh, Sig, Ar, Man...

There was a small crack and the door opened.

Everyone was petrified for a moment.

"How did you do it to Master?" I asked in a voice trembling with emotion. I realized that I would have to learn more than one thing...

The master smiled.

"Think," he said, "you've exactly as much data as I do.

I started thinking. I went to the keyboard because I was sure that the secret was hiding there. Like my master, I began to gently run my fingertips on the keys. After a moment I understood. Runes Ar, Eh, Man and Sig were smoother and less coarse than the others.

"These keys were used most often," I said, "but that word? What does it mean?"

"The word *sesam*, or rather se-s'am, means in old-Stygian language as much as a *treasury*." Said my Master.

"So you risked, Master," I said contrarily.

"Yes, but I was sure that this is the right answer to the question," the Master shrugged, "as you know, the word Sesame is written differently because it changed Stygian writing, so here Futhark Waten was used, where there is no "z", it was by all means obvious that the "s" must be it. Simple my student?"

I nodded.

"Of course," I murmured, "NOW it's simple..."

He patted me cordially on the back.

"And what do you think that it was given to me?" He said. "I also learned, I'll tell you in secret that mainly on my mistakes."

And he smiled at Master Mimiko-san and her student. Master answered him with a smile, and Annala's face burned with a sudden blush.

"Well, maybe enough of these intellectual chit-chat?" Said Master Alcinoos, in command of the expedition. "We light the torches and go inside. Zenir and Alexa," he turned to the two journeymen, "you stay in the watch. The rest behind me. Oh, and please protect it." He pointed to the door and the stones. "I don't want to be trapped here."

I felt cold hearing these words. I remembered the dark and icy corridors of the frosty hell of Frigida - an underground city in the Hyperborea mountains, located some two hundred and fifty miles north-east of Haloga - the capital of this icy country. It was my first serious and non-training task that I did with Master Arietys. We were looking for devices left by the Atlantis, and which could contain some dangerous or even useful elements. We found nothing, except for the dead and perfectly preserved by the frost corpses of people, dogs and other animals that got here and did not come out, because Dekerto plunged them into their sleepless sleep. My Master came to the conclusion that these people died due to poisoning with an unknown gas, which escaped from leaking tanks of some energy devices. We have found rust-colored remains of some machines - on their basis it was difficult to determine what they were used for, but they had empty containers for liquid fuel - as my Master explained - that slowly evaporated despite the low temperature. I will not forget this view for all my life. Will I stand face to face with dead and cruel deaths of people and animals?

I looked at the Master and he patted me on the shoulder.

"Don't be afraid, there is no dead creatures," he said soothingly. "It's not Frigida."

How did he know? I must have had it written on my face.

Meanwhile, the Apprentices ignited the torches and disappeared with the elders one by one in the dark tunnel. We were alone. I took a deep breath and made my first step towards the black entrance. After a while her darkness surrounded me and I walked almost blindly towards the light of the torch burning in the hand of the journeyman in front of me.

IX

The tunnel corridor was so wide and high that we could walk freely without risking collision with the walls or hitting the head. The walls of the tunnel, the footwall and the ceiling were bright and, as Annala explained, they were carved into limestone rocks and soft sandstones. After a few dozen yards, the base became yellow from the light sandstone, and the walls became darker. Their composition has changed.

"That's strange," muttered Master Mimiko-san. "There are no even rocks in which there are usually gold nuggets. I don't understand it."

We set her opinion free immediately. There must have been a golden bonanza here, giving hundreds, if not thousands, of pure metal talents.

At once from the front we heard loud cries of astonishment, but not fear. We accelerated our pace and a wide excavation appeared to our eyes, whose front wall glistened with a sunny yellow color. People stood looking at this phenomenon with astonishment in their eyes. Master Mimiko-san had her eyes and mouth wide open for a moment.

"For all the gods of Zipang," she whispered in a loud, stage whisper, "I haven't seen anything like that yet!"

Sure, there were not thousands here, as naively I assumed, but at least two million talents of gold!

"We too," said the two Masters.

"Can you somehow... explain it?" Master Alcinoos turned to her.

Master looked around for Annala, but her pupil, not caring about the whole mess, calmly watched the rock bordering the golden wall.

"This rock was crushed, like after a huge impact and pressed again," she announced calmly. "And what's more, it's partially melted."

"And what's the conclusion?" Master asked her intrigued to the highest degree.

"The only solution is that once some cavity was cut in the ground and rocks, molten gold was poured in and without waiting for it to set in was covered with crumbled spoil..." Annala said uncertainly. "But why was it done? And by who??? It doesn't make sense..."

"Of course it's nonsense," said Mimiko-san. "What I say may sound... strange, but that's the truth. If there is a crater at the top, we are in the drift knocked out to its center. It looks like a meteorite made of pure gold - 24 K - has fallen here! And it has to be huge, the diameter of the crater is about five miles and five hundred feet deep."

"Or more," I said without thinking.

"Exactly! And this shows that it's a shock crater, not a volcanic crater!"

"Does this mean that gold has fallen from the sky?" Asked one of the Apprentices with astonishment.

"Yes, Fiona," said Master, "by the way, it's a similar formation - also striking - is Pathenia and Loulan Plateau. There also was a decline in a cosmic body that hit the Earth almost on a tangent flying from south to north. Only it was not gold but olivine."

"Okay, let's take that gold," said Master Alcinoos, and looked around. "They left here tools for forging metal from the wall!

Everyone voluntarily went to work. At the end of the day, we made so much gold that it would be enough to put at least two telegraph lines to Kulalo. We quickly transported them to the ship and the same day we took off from the improvised haven taking a course to the Black Coast.

Before we left, we closed the gates of the underground and carefully blocked with two stones, so as not to arouse the suspicions of the Stygians. I doubt if they realized that someone had picked up a little something of their huge treasure - there was so much gold that it would be enough for the whole world.

"Master?" I asked Master Arietys, when the island disappeared in the night-shift. "Why did not we take more gold more than we needed for current expenses?"

"That's obvious," said Arietys. "Think about what would happen if we circulated such a huge amount of gold that is on Kamroon?"

"Everyone would be rich? Or maybe only some of people?" I answered uncertainly, because economic issues were a complete abstraction for me.

"Yes and no," my master said mysteriously, "first of all, its value would decrease, because gold is a certain security of capital and is a universal conversion. Everything can be converted into an equivalent in gold, and if it was too much on the market, the economy of our entire world would be endangered by a huge crisis. That is why we are launching only as much gold as we need and no more. Stygians also realize this and don't use more than they must. However, I think that this is a matter of preserving the existence of this treasure in secret from the world, not economics. If Menkaure uses this treasure, we'll have trouble... Big trouble..."

"Why?" I asked, though I already guessed the answer.

"It's obvious," said the Master, "as you can guess, he could use this gold as an economic weapon destabilizing the economic order of this world. But he won't use it, because he isn't so stupid. Although..."

And he was deep in thought.

After three days of sailing, we reached the port of Kulalo.

* * *

"Well, that's it, dear students," said Master Haneda, putting a scroll of papyrus on the shelf covered with stamps of the ideographic ideological script, "read the third and fourth chapter of the textbook for tomorrow and get ready for the test!"

We got up from the floor and ran out of the lecture hall onto the sun-drenched square. I ran out with the others just to fall into Annala's arms, who was waiting for me at the bench. We sat together looking at the frisky friends and colleagues.

"Don't sit for long, my Master asks you to talk." Annala pulled my hand.

It was interesting. I got up and ran after Annala to the administrative building.

X

They were waiting there for us in Master Mimiko-san's office. We walked in and felt my heart beat harder. In addition to Master Mimiko-san, there was Master Arietys, Alcinoos and Grand Master Lestko Vislanian. He looked at me and stood up.

"Well, we are now all here," he said. "Let's get to the matter, because we have very little time."

He picked up a papyrus from the desk and looked at us sharply. Everyone stood up. Annala slipped her hand into my palm and gave it a small hug. I answered with hug.

"So listen, all of you," said Crossbowman, "this is the decision of the Chapter of our Brotherhood, whom I, Lestek from Vislania, give to you my Grand Master. The will of the Chapter is to complete your termination for your services to the Brotherhood and to become its Apprentices. From today and from now on you have all the rights and obligations of Apprentices. You have the right to bear the sword and the duty to take it in a just cause: to defend the interests of the Brotherhood, the weak and the oppressed. You have the right to vote and the duty to take it in matters important to the Brotherhood. You have the duty to participate in all the work of the Brotherhood and obey the Grand Master..."

And there was more, but I did not remember it. At the end, we were ordered to take off the navy blue tunics and put on the gray-green masking apparel of the Apprentices with the silver-green Brotherhood logo on the left shoulder. Then the Grand Master handed us our weapons - long, straight swords that could be worn by the belt or stuck on back.

"And finally," continued Crossbowman, "one more message. I think that it'll be good for both of you."

We're all ears.

"By the decision of your Masters you were added to the crew of expedition to the Nergal Tower. Your training has finally come to an end, now you'll need an internship in a specific mission..."

"As if the previous two missions were unimportant," I thought.

"...so get ready to leave, because the expedition is starting tomorrow."

"And who is coming with us, Grand Master?" Annala asked.

The crossbowman raised his eyebrows.

"You don't know?" He asked in amazement, "And I thought you were guessed. Of course, your Masters and Master Alcinoos. This is a special operation. You're going as a team to build a solar telegraph line in the direction of Xuchotl - this is the official reason for your trip given to the authorities of Kulalo, but you only reach the middle distance, because you turn north towards the equator. Well, you'll penetrate this... Tower of Nergal.

We left the office of Mimiko-san with a slight dizziness. We spent the rest of the day together saying goodbye to our friends. In the evening, I accompanied Annala to her apartment. Above the city's houses, the stars lit up, in a stuffy atmosphere they glowed with reddish fires. We stood under a huge baobab through the branches of which the orange moon shone.

"Tomorrow, we'll be about thirty miles away," I said.

"I'm glad," said Annala.

"That you are leaving?" I asked. "Don't you like Kulalo?"

She smiled in the semi-darkness and looked at me. Her eyes were big and luminous.

"Not only," she said, "I like Kulalo, but I'm most happy that you are coming with me."

Her face darkened with a blush.

I took her hands.

"Me too, Annala," I said, beating pressure in my throat. "Me too, very much."

We looked into each other's eyes.

Suddenly Annala threw her arms around my neck. I felt her body hugging mine. I was out of breath for a moment. I embraced her and she looked into my eyes.

"Do you love me?" She asked quietly and humbly, curtseying her head tenderly.

I took a deep breath as before jumping into the water. I felt pressure in my throat again.

"Yes, Annala," I whispered, quietly forcing the accursed intimidation and feeling my cheeks burning, "I was about to tell you that for a long time, but..."

"Me too..." she also whispered.

She put her head on my chest. Her dark hair was glowing in the bend of the moonlight and smelled something very pleasant. The smell was bitter but exciting. We stood with our hearts beating and we hugged each other. I did not know what to say. But that was not important, the most important thing was that we finally said what each of us felt subconsciously.

I looked at the moon - it raised another two fingers above the horizon.

"It's late," I said, "we've to go to sleep, we're going tomorrow."

"I don't want to sleep," she said, "I feel so good."

"Me too," I said, "but... but we'll have plenty of time for ourselves. All our life.

She raised her head and looked into my eyes.

"Really?" She asked quietly.

"Really," I said in a normal voice.

Suddenly, she tilted her head back slightly and closed her eyes, her lips parting slightly. I understood without words. I leaned in and touched her lips with my lips. The kiss was hot and sweet. I had never kissed a girl before, and I was grateful for the fact that my first kiss had just come here, in a lunar moonlight under a huge baobab tree, amid the darkness of the night equator...

In the foliage a night bird torn above us and we both slowly returned to reality.

"I must go now," she said quietly, "though, for Ishtar, I would rather stay with you here."

"Me too, but for now, we have responsibilities," I sighed.

We kissed again and Annala ran towards the door to her quarters. She turned and waved at me, then disappeared through the door. I stayed alone. And the next morning we plunged into the jungle growing over the gates of Kulalo. Another adventure has begun.

XI

The arrow whistled to the side of a good-looking antelope, which fell like a thunderbolt.

"Excellent shot," I praised Annala.

She smiled in response.

We hunted to supplement our food supply. For two weeks we have been dragging ourselves along the Xuchotlanian Route through the land of the unbelievably sounding name Cono-oñañgho to get near the Black Tower of Nergal. If we believe the measurements and calculations of our Masters, we were close to the goal - at most two days. The equatorial forest was over and the savannah began. There was many animals, we could hunt. And we were just sent to repair our depleted stocks...

Annala moved toward the hunted animal when something disturbed us. Nearby shrubs moved and two people appeared at once with tense bows aimed at us. I tugged the string back in a moment and took aim at the nearest one. For several infinitely long seconds we measured ourselves with eyes.

It was two young people, with brown skin, black hair and eyes. Girl and boy - probably our peers. They were both wearing colorful satchels, and their necks were decorated with amulets made of animal fangs and claws. In addition, they had bows and arrows and short javelins. Their bodies were agile, and smooth, economical movements betrayed perfect preparation for life in the wilderness and savanna. It would be a pity to kill them - I thought.

"Me either," I murmured, leaning down my bow and removing the arrow from the string. I put the bow in the case and the arrow into the quiver. Annala did the same. A few seconds elapsed. The others stood as if they were petrified.

Annala walked quietly to the dead antelope and leaned over her. She took an arrow from the wound and showed it to the black girl, then put it on the quiver and turned her back to her. It seemed to me that they also breathed a sigh of relief.

"We give them this antelope?" I asked.

Annala nodded.

"Of course, this is their prey. Poor antelope, she got shots from two sides…"

I understood. The other ones were also hunting and by accident we were shooting the same animal. And we hit simultaneously.

Meanwhile, both blacks approached the animal and watched it from all sides. They talked something in their own way. It did not sound hostile, but rather like a question.

"Do you speak Hyborian?" I asked.

Their gazes were all too eloquent. They did not understand. I asked in Stygian, then Annala in Brythuan and Nemedian. As we expected, they did not know these languages. We had impasse for a moment, that the black girl broke down. She came to us.

"Malou," she said, putting a hand on her chest, "Adân," she pointed to the boy.

"Annala," Annala pointed to herself, "Dommel," she completed the presentation pointing to me.

"They are probably siblings," I said, "they're very similar to each other."

She nodded.

"I think so," she confirmed my guess.

"How to explain to them that they should come with us?" I was wondering. "Maybe one of our Masters could talk with them?"

"Let's try this." Annala approached Malou and took her hand, then dragged her behind. Malou let to be lead, so I did not think much and nodded at Adan and went. Adân threw an antelope over his shoulder and followed us. After an hour we reached our camp. It turned out that one of our guides knew their language and was able to get talk with them. And it went on quickly. Malou and Adân, who were indeed siblings, took us to their Xatatatl tribe village. It was a tribe who lived in areas near the Black Tower of Nergal. At our request, the king of the village ordered the siblings to lead us to its foot, but not further.

"Why?" Master Alcinoos asked him.

"Taboo," the village king explained briefly, "we don't go there, because it threatens with death. The Masters exchanged glances because it was interesting to us.

"What death is there?" Master Arietys asked.

"There are various traps," replied the king. "Some of them are neutralized, because they killed those who went there. But some are still ready to kill. We stay away from these places, but if you're able to dispose them, then you have all our help and protection guaranteed. Just in case…"

"Thank you, chief," said Arietys. "Your help will be necessary, but for now we only ask for guides."

"It's done," the king clapped his hands and pointed to the siblings, "they'll take you wherever you want. They are young, but they know every place here."

"Who they are?" Master Alcinoos became interested.

A shadow passed through the king's face.

"They're my children," he answered quietly, "and please, take care of them, they are unpredictable…"

* * *

And the next day we saw it.

I imagined myself as something sky-high, soaring and inaccessible. In the meantime, it was a trapezoidal construction with gigantic dimensions whose side measured about five miles in length and a height as much. Its top was whitened by eternal snows. It was an amazing, incredible building. It blackness - deep in the bright light of the equatorial sun - has lost nothing over the centuries that have elapsed since its construction. But it was not the most interesting, but the path that led to its peak. It did not run directly, but inclined to the top of the periphery. And it was very wide - four cars could easily go side by side and there was still some space left. It was sixty feet wide over its entire length. But we settled it later, and for now we stood looking at it like spellbound.

"Oh, no," said Alcinoos, "I think I'm dreaming."

"Such a construction is impossible at all," murmured my Master.

"I think it's granite and basalt," Annala said from behind, "but where did they get that much?"

"And yet it stands," I said to her. "Someone built it."

"Come on," Malou said, "it's still safe here. The problems start only at the foot of the mountain."

"Problems?" I asked.

She smiled.

"Difficulties and traps," she said in a tone of explanation, "let's go."

And she moved towards the foot of the tower, and we followed her.

XII

Approaching the tower, we saw here and there skeletons and piles of human and animal bones located where they came across precautions. This object must have had a very special purpose, since it was so much protected. From what our Masters said among themselves, most of them were known to them and already met with them, but - as everyone admitted - not in such an amount and such a perfect quality, which is still dangerous even after so many centuries.

"Notice that these bones are still fresh," said Master Alcinoos, "this man had to be killed a year, at most two years ago."

"And what killed him?" I asked.-

"Look at the skeleton," he replied, "what do you see?"

I looked. The skull, chest and upper limbs were fine. The pelvis was whole, the spine also. But the lower limbs...

"He or she has no legs," I said uncertainly, feeling the saliva coming to my lips.

Alcinoos nodded.

"What's the conclusion?" He asked.

"He entered the anti-personnel mine," I replied.

"That's right," he nodded. "So we've to watch. These damn mines have it to themselves that they were made without using even played metal. The bodies are made of plastic material and sintered carbides or a super-resistant gelatinous material..."

"Claymore's mines," I suggested.

It was an extremely nasty weapon. A few pints of liquid explosive in a gelatinous shell, hidden half a foot under the ground. It was enough to cause an explosion that would break legs. There was a lot of them here. And not only people died, but even animals, and therefore both kept away from the Nergal Tower. We had at least ten more or less complete human skeletons in sight.

"Uhm..." The master nodded. "We're going, we came here for it..."

We walked slowly, marking the path traveled with small flags. It could have been useful in the event of a sudden retreat, when there would be no time to set a new route.

After several dozen minutes, we stood at the foot of an artificial mountain. This comparison was at least correct, because it was built of millions of elements cut out in black and gray granite and basalt. The powerful cubes were matched perfectly to each other with incredible precision - it was impossible to push the knife blade between them.

"Unbelievable," Master Mimiko-san whispered, " just unbelievable. How could they do it?"

"From what we know, they were able to control gravity," Master Arietys told her. "They arranged these stone blocks as a child arranges blocks or dominoes. Only the scale is breathtaking."

"And I've seen something like that before," Alcinoos interjected. "It's similar to Shemits *zuiggurads*. Only that those are round and, of course, lower. And they were built now, during this millennium."

We approached the entrance to the ramp surrounding the Tower. We had a few more steps when Master Alcinoos shouted for us to stop.

"Stop! There is something here." He said with a strained tone.

"What?" Master Mimiko-san checked out the visible part of the ramp. "I don't see anything here..."

"Because you're looking in wrong way," said Alcinoos, taking off his backpack. He took out a three-part folding pole that ended with a long, thin and sharp spike. Mine feeler - I immediately recognized this useful instrument for detecting mines. "Go back!"

Obediently, we went back fifty steps. The Master Alcinoos, step by step carefully pricking the ground, and after a while fell to it and began gently hewing something with his hand armed with a small blade. After fifteen minutes, he stood up and was pleased to put the extracted object in a safe place.

"Well, we can go now," he announced.

"What is this?" Arietys asked, looking at the extracted object from a distance. It had the shape of a one foot pot and was made of a porous material. It was the same color as the reddish savanna land. If not Alcinoos, we would probably go over it without noticing anything.

"Fugas, the chemical one," Alcinoos said. "Extremely nasty stuff. Its explosion throws out a cloud of poisonous gas that kills immediately, paralyzing the nerves and muscles."

"There's no more here?" Annala asked.

"No, there were a few of them here, but they exploded. This one is the last one. We'll leave it here and then dispose of it."

This kind of "pits" was disposed of by burrying them six feet underground. Due to the pressure of the earth's layer, the fugas cracked without exploding, and the released poisonous gases were pushed deep into the earth to the rock, where they slowly degraded.

"Ok, we're going!" He said. "We've five miles to go, to the first break."

We set off on our way. I expected further surprises, but no, they were gone, but the road was terribly boring - it was going uphill all the time. After one and a half hour we came to the first bend.

"We'll rest," Alcinoos ordered, "then we've to go to the eastern slope and spend the night there."

"Why is that?" Annala asked.

"In the morning the first rays of the sun will fall there and we'll go on the northern and western slopes and we'll make another 16 miles in the shade."

And indeed. We spent the night lying against the wall in our sleeping bags and when the first rays of the hot sun leaned against the wall, we moved on. Master Alcinoos was right. We walked all the time in the shadows and quenched our's thirst thanks to small streams of water that ran down the walls of the Tower from the ice fields visible above. We spent the second night in the middle of the southern wall. It was getting colder, because we were almost a mile above the level of the savannah. We still have seven more miles to climb. Going at such a pace we would reach the summit in two weeks. We did not have food for such an expedition, so we decided to penetrate the mountain halfway up.

Another night was much colder. At three miles we felt a strong night chill. I was sleeping close to Annala and yet I was waking up from the cold. Tired, I finally fell asleep and when I was awakened by the first rays of the sun and their warmth, I was ready to jump for joy. It was not possible because we were ossified. It was only after a long warm-up that I could return to that form.

In the afternoon we reached the zone of eternal snow.

XIII

A further path became impossible due to the prevailing freezing. None of us counted on the fact that we would come up with an artificial creation about the height of the Himelian Sagaramatha. The smooth plates covered the ice and the further road was impossible. In addition, the prevailing cold weather and thinning of the air causing problems with breathing forced us to retreat.

"This is the fourth pole of the Earth." My Master made a remarkable remark.

"But why was it built?" I canalized my amazement.

"You can't guess yet?" He asked with astonishment. "It's obvious!"

"Not for me," said Annala, "and it isn't so obvious to me, Master."

Arietys raised his eyebrows as if in boundless amazement.

"Oh, no," he said, "and I thought it was obvious to you!"

"It isn't," I replied.

He sighed.

"It's obvious," he said with exultation, "where are we? Geographically, of course!"

"At the equator," I said together with Annala.

"And the results of this is?" He asked further. "What was here? Above us?"

It flashed to my mind.

"Great Guide!" We exclaimed in unison. "So here it is...?"

He smiled.

"Yes," he confirmed calmly, "right here. And how do you think it was built, eh?"

"It was released... wait... is it from this Tower?" Annala's eyes looked like astonished saucers.

"Yes, exactly like that," said Arietys. "The Nergal Tower is a spaceport from which the Grand Guide's components were launched into orbit. Then they were only combined and the Grand Guide began its independent flight around the Earth. Of course, it hung over one place, just above it. Most probably, at the end of the conflict, one of the fighting parties decided to use it as a space combat station, to defeat the targets on Earth and in space with antimatter. It was supposed to be an ultimate weapon."

"And it hasn't been used?" Annala asked.

"Of course, yes!" Answered Arietys. "And the use of antimatter caused irreversible changes in the earth's crust, as a result of which Atlantis sank to the surface of the Ocean. In general there was a whole series of cataclysms that have finished off that civilization..."

It was difficult for us to accept this. One thing was to know about these cataclysms and other thing was to come face to face with tangible facts.

* * *

It took us less time to come down than enter, but it was just as tiring. With a shout of relief, we welcomed an even surface. At the foot of the artificial mountain our guides were waiting for us. They were whole and healthy. Now we only have to return to the village. After a dozen or so days we arrived in Kulalo, where we delivered report from our trip to the Grand Master and his advisers.

"So what you're saying here," said the Crossbowman, "is that the Black Tower of Nergal is basically inaccessible because of the icing?"

"Yes, Grand Master," answered Master Alcinoos. "Besides, there is still coldness and the progressive thinning of the air. We have reached about half the height and it's comparable to the height of

Sagaramatha, the highest known mountain in the world. So far, no one has managed to enter it. Everyone was dying of cold and lack of air..."

"In other words, is it safe?"

"Yes, of course, you have to clean up all the adjacent area from the mines and traps. There is still dangerous in this respect. The mines that were laid there are virtually indestructible and you just have to dig them out and detonate. In addition, there are still fugas gases, which must also be disposed of. But this is cosmetics."

"Do you have any idea for using the Nergal Tower?" Asked the Grand Master.

"I think we can put one of our telegraph stations there," said Master Brontosphoros, "from a height of two, two and a half miles, its range will increase many times."

"Can you specify how much?" Asked Crossbowman.

"One moment, Grand Master." Brontosphoros reached into the pocket for a stylus and for a moment sketched the numbers on the table top. The others waited for the calculation result.

After a moment, Master Brontosphoros looked up.

"About 180 miles on each side, which would be an stretch of 360 miles, and this is at least five or even six telegraph stations. We'll save money. Of course, we must ensure decent service conditions, but this is a technical matter."

The Grand Master nodded. The case was decided.

We were about to go to the next check-in point, which was the administrative matters, when the adjutant of Crossbowman entered the room and gave him a papyrus.

"This is a urgency matter, Grand Master," he said.

The Crossbowman spread the paper and his eyes ran through the text. He raised his eyebrows slightly. He read it again. There was deadly silence in the room. At once, he looked up from the papyrus and rolled it around.

"Masters and journeymen!" He said in a grim voice in which anxiety vibrated. "I've just received a report from our agents in Luxuru, Kemi and Asgalun. There was a palace revolution in Stygia and Prince Menkaure took over the power three weeks ago. Stygian troops leave Shemit and head towards the border with Kush. It all seems that Stygia intends to take Kush and, by the way, all the surrounding islands, including the island of Kamroon. We don't have branches in Kush, but we have to follow the actions of the Stygians, so I immediately suggest sending scouts to this land. What do you say?"

A discussion began as a result of which scouts were dispatched to the land of Kush to follow the actions of the Stygian usurper. But this is a separate story. Annala and I were transferred to a group whose task was to mine the area of the Black Nergal Tower and build a solar telegraph station. We left together with the whole team of journeymen and apprentices. We had, above all, the task of winning the trust of local natives, because their villages would be supply bases for us, so the mission was very delicate. We were hoping that we would be able to do this task.

And with this hope we set out on the road.

10

⸝

DAGGER FROM TURANU

I

The sun bowed slowly towards the horizon, reducing the strength and heat of its rays. Slowly, I drove up to the stone pool of the Minus Fountain - a place famous BY the bards and skalds talking about Conan the Cymmerian who had just fled from the greed of Shadizar citizens when he returned from his journey to the mythical, cursed and ruined Larsha. In his time, there were three arrows from the arch from the west gate of the city - today the city has absorbed it long ago and where it stood, there was a large square built around two-storey houses in which there were merchant warehouses. Traffic during the day was largish here, now it stopped in the evening, in the perspective of the streets reaching the square, only some children were playing.

I drove to the pool and the horse leaned forward and started to drink the water greedily. I jumped from the saddle and went to the pool, where the cool and reasonably pure water shone. I washed my face and neck, but I did not risk drinking it - I could get sick of one of many local diseases that medicine was powerless to deal with. Anyway, I did not mean to do it. I looked around, but nothing suspicious was visible. And nobody except screaming kids.

I took a look at the part from the east side, i.e. from the city side. There was a line drawn on it with one horizontal stroke of the arrow with opposite tips on both sides. Agreed sign. I leaned in and slowly, so as not to draw anyone's attention, I sat down on the fountain. I looked at the stones and reached to the fifth from the left. I hooked my fingers and jerked. It emerged easily from the fountain, revealing a black hole in which I slipped my hand. There was nothing in the cache. I quickly put in a piece of parchment with the date of the meeting with the agent, which was to take place within two days. I only knew about her that she wore the pseudonym of Arghalla and I took her from Master Agaton, who died two weeks ago. As his successor, I received the honor of setting fire to his funeral pyre and gathering ashes for the urn, which I sent to a family living in Belverus. Today I found myself at one of the contact points of his agent in Shadizar - the dead box at the Fountain of Minus.

I took out a piece of chalk and made a vertical line with two hooks at the ends, so that the whole figure resembled the Vendhian symbol of the sun... A sign for the agent indicating that there was a parcel for her in the contact box. The outsider would think that there were some Vendhians here who left their religious sign or had some children playing. No one should suspect that this is a contact letter with the most important agent of the Green Dragon Brotherhood in the capital of Zamora, the factotum of Queen Hybris, whose activities were interested in the Brotherhood due to its exuberant temperament and plans to expand its country to neighboring countries, which she wanted to implement by methods not so much political but brutal force. Strength supported by some technical novelties, and this already fell under the Brotherhood's interests, which eliminated and neutralized any remnants of war technique after the loss in history of the Empire of Atlantis...

After a few minutes, as if nothing had happened, I jumped on my horse and headed towards the city center. I heard the throbbing behind me. Four riders galloped next to me, heading towards the center. They had huge horses, sable and very resilient. They were clothed with black burnooses that were blown away from the momentum. Faces covered by hoods. They flashed past me and rushed on like the wind. They had to hurry. After a few minutes, I stopped hearing them, because I turned to the tavern where I intended to stand for a few days.

* * *

There was teeming and bustling in the tavern, which was very convenient for me. I entered the main entrance without paying attention to anyone. Because no one paid special attention to a man in his prime in a gray-green sheet with a monk's hood and a Zipang-ian sword strapped to his back. I went to the bar and demanded from a man standing there, with the appearance of Shemit, an accommo-dation for me and a place in the stable for my horse. I threw him two golden lunas and after a while the host appeared, offering his services.

For a moment I aroused the interest of some man who drank light beer, but when they saw a katana and a short dagger - a weapon tremendous in melee combat - they let go. They preferred not to mess with someone who was seasoned to fight with sev-eral opponents at once. Or maybe they were the spies of Queen Hybris. In his reports, Master Agaton mentioned a perfectly orga-nized queen secret intelligence that kept an eye on everything and everyone in her country. But they had the appearance of typical cutthroats from the suburbs, who were interested in my saddlebag, not my person. But who know... However, at all costs I wanted to avoid a fight or a fuss at all. I was on a strange territory with a del-icate mission and I could not jeopardize it with some ill-conceived move.

I ordered a supper to my accommodations and I wanted to have peace at least for the next night. Driving through tiring roads was hard and after a week of resting under the open sky, the body wanted warmth and cosiness of a comfortable bed. I ate the supper without even feeling it taste and threw myself on the bed to fall into a dead sleep, regardless of the fact that I was in the City of Villains.

The morning woke me with a buzz coming from below. Morning - it was already noon. I slept all night and a good chunk of the day. I was hoping that the agent did not take the news of the meeting and that I would have some time for myself. I ordered breakfast and then, after eating the salted sea cucumbers stuffed with sea-buckthorn seeds, I watched the dining room and the sun-drenched street in front of it, through which the daily crowd of residents of the capital and visitors like me was buzzing along.

It was noon and nothing happened. Hot sun rays banished passers-by - those who could go to siesta. I half-sat and half-lay on the bench, keeping an eye on what was happening on the street and inside. Some beer lovers drank beer, a few visiting nobles played cards or dice arguing lazily. It's time for siesta - I thought - it is time for slackers and drunkards.

An hour passed, then another. The sun has already descended from the top of its path and headed westwards towards the Corinthian mountains. I was taking a nap when a bent old woman came out of the street through wide openers. I looked at her and something awakened my vigilance. The old woman came up to the counter and with a hoarse-baritone asked about something the Shemit who had a nap there. This man pointed her out of the tavern. The old woman stamped her foot and threw him something that worked on him. He jumped up and showed her the first floor, where there were rooms for guests. The old woman, shuffling her feet, climbed the stairs and slowly disappeared upstairs. Puzzled, I got up and trying to ignore anyone's attention, I followed her. I only heard the door close gently, as if someone did not want to be heard. I waited for half a minute and silently approached my number. I carefully opened the door with my left hand - on the right I had a switchblade. Caution will never hurt - this was the first rule in this job.

She was standing in the center of the room with her back to the door. I looked at her, and she spoke first in her ghastly voice.

"Welcome to Shanizdar; Thuban and Mizar."

"I came in peace," I replied, "Dragon and Big Dipper."

It was a slogan and response. A perverse thought came to me at once. I put the dagger in my pocket and, without waiting for further conversation, I wrote down my favorite stanzas:

> *…there is not much*
> *Worth*
> *The Beauty hidden*
> *Before the world*
> *My love*
> *My sweetest*
> *My only one*
> *Make it appear…*

The old woman turned and lifted her head, then became a little miracle - at once she straightened her bent figure, with a quick motion she took off her big hat, which along with the gray, slovenly wig, fluttered on the bed. Followed by them flew a faded burka, under which appeared a golden-green, brocaded dress hung on thin, almost invisible straps. In front of me stood a pretty, maybe twenty-five-year-old woman and smiling, tilting his head flirtatiously on the right arm, she was looking at my character with green eyes. She shook her head and her hair, the color of a ripe chestnut, showered on her naked, swarthy and round arms. She smiled from the impression she had made on me. And then, she vibrantly recited fluently:

> *My beauty*
> *Since today is*
> *Yours*
> *My body*
> *Is only*
> *For you*
> *My lover*
> *My lover*
> *My lover*
> *Take me now*
> *In your arms…*

I was silent for a moment because I was surprised. I was expecting everything, but not that.

"I thought I knew Fernir Skald's poem well, but those rhymes..." I circled my hand "as if it was not there?"

She smiled.

"Because it's true, I have just made up them," she said with some pride, "after all, you know that there is no better poetic foot to improvise, than the Asgardian lijohåttar? And besides, I can also sing and dance."

I nodded.

So it was this mysterious agent with the pseudonym Arghalla, about which so many were said in the staff of the Brotherhood.

"Arghalla," I said, "you've been wonderfully characterized. But I've three reservations."

"What, my Master?" A shadow flashed through her pretty face.

"First: your voice. The old ladies talk rather with a screeching tenor, and not a drunken bass, unless you want to be an old whore."

She laughed.

"You're right, Master," she said, laughing, "I'll remember. What about the other one?"

"Secondly, don't throw coins to the tavern or innkeeper, because it betrays you right away. You can see at once that you are a young, temperamental woman who doesn't like to wait and repeat everything twice. You should give him to a hand looking at what and to whom you give... You're not court, it's an inn!"

She become serious.

"Okay, you're right," she said quietly, "what about third?"

"Your feet. You put nice, fashionable sandals. You have manicured fingers and varnished nails. Have mercy - show me an old lady who does that? You should put on some old, crumpled slippers covering yours - I admit - lovely feet."

She burned with a blush.

"Or maybe..." she stuttered for a moment "or did I do it especially for someone?"

"Perhaps," I have cut off dry, "but something like that in other circumstances could cost you life. By kindness I won't say anything about the tortures that would have been waiting for you before you died. The spy's life is balancing on the edge, on a very thin and tight line. One step and you fall forever!"

"I understand, my Master," she said quietly. Her face was still blushing. It must have touched her.

"Okay, Arghalla, what you say for a little dinner?" I asked to blow off awkward silence that fell.

"Thank you, Master Nertuss," she answered politely, "but I've already had my dinner. But if you aren't, I'll be happy to accompany you. And in general, call me Thalia. This is my real name. I'm Brythunian."

"I've already had meal too," I said pointing to her chair, "and anyway, I come from the Borderlands Kingdoms. I was born and raised in the Duchy of Vislania - just like our great master and your queen."

"How's our lady?" Thalia raised her beautiful eyebrows with genuine surprise. "Does she come from the Kingdoms?"

"Yes, she is really called Dobrava and comes from the Duchy of Torysy. It's neighbouring place. And Hybris is her Zamorian name, or rather Zamoran."

"Well, now I understand why the Brotherhood sent you here." I saw a flash of understanding in her eyes. "Do you want…"

"Yes, if it was possible," I replied, "the Great Master asks you to arrange a private audience for me. It won't be difficult, she knows me personally. You'll just tell her that Nert Vislanian wants to see her…"

She smiled.

"It's done, my Master," she said. "Is there anything else?"

"Nothing at the moment, anyway," I went to the saddle and the saddlebags that were in the corner. I untied the bellows and took out a thick pouch.

"What is it?" She asked, nodding at it.

"Two hundred gold tetradrachma, it is fifty lunas for the last information that greatly pleased our Grand Master." I gave her the sack. "And this is a gift from the Grand Master for you, such a bonus, the second two hundred tetradrachma. Total, one thousand six hundred drachmas. You might need it."

II

I gave her a second sack as heavy and bulky as the previous one. She put them on the table without even opening it. Her eyes were serious.

"What happened, are not you happy?"

She looked at me with sadness in green eyes.

"I'm happy," she said quietly, "very much."

"Well, why don't you smile at all?"

"Because I have no reason. What will I do with this money?"

I was in shock for a moment.

"Oh, no!" I cried. "A woman doesn't know what to do with money!? The world is ending!"

Despite the sadness in her eyes, she smiled. But also humorlessly.

"That's not what it's about," she said. "I've a lot of money and no friendly soul around me."

I understood.

"Do you feel very lonely?"

"That's an understatement..."

"This is our job, the loneliness of the spy. You knew about it by signing a contract with us. You could retire even after completing your training at Belverus."

"I knew, but one thing is to know and other thing to feel the hard way."

There was a moment of silence. We were both thinking about something - she probably about that she said too much to me. I wondered if Master Agaton also had such conversations with her.

"Do you have someone?" I asked.

She shook her head and her hair fell on her face. She threw off them with a determined movement.

"I have friends. Yes, I even had a few men, but it was not what I want. I even went to bed with a few, but they just wanted to sleep with me, and I only extruded information from them. There was nothing between me and them. No feelings. Such a job. And you, Master?"

I laughed mirthlessly.

"I can say the same as you. I hang around the whole territory, I meet the Brotherhood's field agents. I just work as a courier."

It was almost true. In the meantime, we performed some search and liquidation operations of the dangerous remains of the Great War of the Gods. No, not gods - Atlantis. Recently, we have neutralized the battery, especially the nasty missiles, thirty feet into the rocky ground of the southern end of Zamora. It was supposed to look like an out of focus volcano. We managed it, but not completely. At that time, in the terrible explosion of the last of them died Master Agaton, and I, as the oldest of his journeymen, was already liberated, I become the Master. A natural turn of things in the Brotherhood. I took over the agency in Zamora. Two officers from the local security forces in the garrison of Yezud and the mysterious Arghalla - Thalia, the manor and the trustee of the queen. My mission was to penetrate to the queen and probe her intentions, and more specifically, the means she intended to use to expand her country. Thalia had to take me to the queen - and that was her job. The information she collected was of secondary importance and could be used to acquire and place additional agents at the royal court.

"Well, you don't have an easy life either," she replied.

"Yes." I sighed. "But let's get back to the topic. I need your help in getting to the queen. Can you lead me to her?"

"Of course, even tonight."

"Perfectly." I said. "And one more thing. I'd like you to be with this conversation."

She looked at me with astonishment.

"Why is that?" She asked.

"Because I'll want to force her to change her plans, and it won't be easy. I'll need someone she trust. And we'll do it like this...

* * *

A warm twilight fell on the city when we left the tavern. Streets of the City of Villains - as Shadizar was called, thanks to several good measures of the queen's administration, became safe, brightly lit at night and busy after sunset. Only on the outskirts and slums of the city was crime, but none of us were going there at night.

We reached the queen's palace without any problems. The guards let us pass by without checking who we are - Thalia was well known there as the queen's bodyguard, which greatly facilitated my task. It made the task easier for us, because Thalia was also supposed to take part in it directly.

"We'll go to the queen's private apartment," Thalia said and pulled me with me.

We walked along some corridors of this labyrinth, which was partially hewn in limestone rock, partly built of blocks of limestone, which were excavated on the spot, digging through the underground storeys of the castle of Zamora's kings. We went through all the en suite rooms that were bright from lamps or windows. From time to time, there were three-man sentry guards in the passages blocking access to further parts of the building complex. We finally left the square, which was a kind of close and we went to the next pass. Thalia stopped.

"It's weird," she said in a changed voice, "where they are. They should be here."

"Who?" I asked.

She looked at me, she had anxiety in her eyes.

"Royal guards," she replied. "Here is the entrance to the queen's apartments and there are always three of them... For Ishtar!" She exclaimed, pointing to something that lay in the middle of the corridor.

I looked that way. A man lay on the stone floor. He was a guardsman in full weaponry. We reached him. He lay on his side in some strange position with his arms and legs scattered. He looked dead and he was dead. He did not breathe and there was no pulse in the carotid artery. But the body was still warm and the smell of fresh blood hovered over him. Death must have taken him recently. One could still feel her chilling presence...

"We're going to get help," I said to Thalia, who was worried in horror, "I need light, and maybe whoever did it is still here."

"You don't have a weapon," she whispered.

"I don't need this scrap metal," I murmured, "and if I need it, I'll borrow from him," I pointed to the corpse with a nod.

The guardsman was carrying a short wide sword and a spear. He still had a long dagger on his belt. It was just strange - it looked as if death surprised him suddenly, that he did not even draw his sword to defend himself.

Thalia ran out and after a moment I heard her scream. There was a dead silence from the royal apartments, which heightened the mood of horror.

Meanwhile, night fell and after a quarter of an hour guards with lamps led by Thalia appeared. They surrounded me with a tight circle.

One of them pointed with his finger.

"Who you are?" He asked.

Thalia stood next to me. She smiled.

"Aelius Rufus, let me introduce my husband," she said in a calm voice as if she were conversing at a courtly party.

"I didn't know you were married..." Aelius's eyebrows went up.

"Because nobody asked me," she said quickly, "my husband, Master Nertuss from the Borderland Kingdoms. He is an itinerant teacher and rarely happens to be at home..." She hung her voice looking at Aelius.

I nodded to him.

"It's you, Lord, you are... the Great Crown Guardian?" I asked.

"Yes."

"Well, it looks like you have one less subordinate," I said without a hint, "he was killed about half an hour ago."

"It's Obahl," one of the guardsmen said.

"How do you know that, Master?" Rufus asked disparagingly.

"The corpses didn't stiffen, and when we found him, he was still warm."

He looked at me with a slight surprise.

"Are you a doctor?"

"Among other things," I answered evasively, "I've several skills. And besides, I participated in the Second Assassin's War. I've seen many dead men..."

"Did you participate in the Assassin's War?" He asked in astonishment, and his men uttered a murmur of astonishment.

I nodded. I did not want to go back to those memories.

"Where are the rest of the guards?" I asked to change the topic.

Aelius looked around.

"Seek the rest," he ordered.

"One moment," I said, "if we're to look for them, it's only in the group. And let no one touch anything. You can erase the traces relevant to the case. And besides, they can still be here..."

"I don'ot think so, but... Maybe it's better to stay on guard."

We set off to the apartments. We found the second guard at the threshold of a bedroom-looking room. He lay on the floor like the first one. And just like the first one, he was killed with a single dagger blow between the shoulders. It looked as if the assassin was attacking his victim from the back, as if he was busy with something else.

"It's Flavius," Aelius said grimly.

"How many of them were there?" I asked.

"Today five," he said, "Flavius and Obahl at the main entrance and the centurion Gerinus and two at the entrance to the hanging gardens."

He meant the gardens stretching from the queen's apartments to the steep cliff at the northern edge of the palace complex.

III

"Where can the queen be?" Aelius asked.

"Usually, at this time of the day, she took a bath in the pool in front of the entering to gardens," Thalia said.

"Let's go," he nodded to us and his people. "Laertus, put three people at the entrance and don't let anyone in here and let anyone out, and the rest follow me!"

The three guards immediately ran to the entrance. Aelius turned and walked toward the gardens. We passed two more chambers. I looked there and at the same moment Thalia gave a small cry. A woman was lying in the room on thick Iranistanian carpets. Her greenish dress was disfigured by a scarlet stain on her back. Thalia got to her. I ran after her.

"For Ishtar, it's Ehoya," she whispered in horror.

"Killed in the same way as the others," I heard Aelius's voice behind me. "Push of the dagger in the back."

In fact, there was the same small wound on her back as in the two guards.

"Who was supposed to be here today?" Aelius asked, "I mean the waiting maids."

Thalia looked at us, her green eyes were full of tears.

She sniffled.

"Ehoya, then Avillea, Irleda, Chena and me..."

"It looks like your husband saved your life," muttered Rufus. "If you were here, then..."

He turned his thumb to the ground.

"Looks like we won't find anyone alive here," he concluded. "It looks like regicide, or a coup, a coup d'état."

I shrugged.

"If it was a coup d'état, then the supporters of the assassins would be storming the palaces and seats of the administration, and there is no such thing," I said, "so that was regicide."

"Anyway, we're screwed," Aelius growled, "my people have failed and died without a gun in their hands. Sons of the dog!" He said it in such a way that it was not known who he meant.

In the next chamber was a dark-skinned Chen. I think she was Kathanian, as her oriental beauty indicated. She was wearing only a thin, light, flowery paero on her hips. Thalia gave a small cry of pain again. Chena was her friend. She also had a wound on her back. Death reached her as she approached the bed on which the queen lay. Aelius walked to her body with a lamp in his hand.

"She's dead," he said.

It was predictable. Suddenly he let out a murmur of astonishment.

"Master and Thalia, come to me," he said in a tone that felt tense. And fear.

We approached.

Queen Hybris vel Dobrava lay on her back. She was wearing a silk bathrobe with some Kathanian patterns and ideograms. Under her left breast was a dagger stabbed to the hilt, which caused her death. On the face of a thirty-six-year-old woman, the calm of Eternity was painted. And something in the shape of amazement. Anyway, it may have seemed to me. Good bye my young years' friend - I thought maybe a little pathetically, feeling something in my throat. I used to love her like a native sister, then our paths went away, I went to Vendhia, and she studied in Paikang. Then she married the aged king of Zamora, and after his death she ruled the country undivided. As you can see, she had to get under somebody's skin, since he committed such a massacre...

"You're witnesses," said Aelius.

We nodded.

Aelius drew the dagger from the wound. It was long and narrow. In the glow of the lamp, the purple red of blood on his blade flashed gloomily.

"Turanian work," I said, pointing to the hilt on which the horse-shaped ornament was located.

"That's right," said Rufus.

"But they were not Turanian," I said, "because, as far as I know, you didn't have too much disagreement with them."

"That's right," he said a second time.

"Where's the rest?" Aelius had already recovered from the impression her lady body had caused on him.

We entered the chamber, from which there was a view of the garden.

"Avillea and Irleda," Thalia whispered again.

Both young women, the girls were still lying on the edge of the pool. Their naked bodies were still damp, like their hair. They probably bathed when the killers entered the loggia.

"Well, it's just missing the centurion and Hermios and Alfes."

After a moment, we heard the shout of one of the guardsmen. We approached and noticed both guards.

"It's strange," said Aelius, "they even took their weapons again!"

Both soldiers lay a few steps away from each other. In their case, they were killed with blows of the dagger in the heart and throat. The assassins obviously wanted to be sure that even dying ones would not call for help. The scent of the night flowers mingled with the stench of blood.

"Where's the centurion?" Aelius wondered. "Search the garden!"

The guards rushed to search. After half an hour they returned with nothing. The centurion's body was not found.

"Don't tell me that Gerinus betrayed," Aelius growled, "and that he murdered everyone and the queen."

A thought flashed me at once.

"Somebody give the light to the rock," I said, "maybe he just fell down and lies somewhere..."

The guards moved to the edge of the garden, which ended in a steep, overhanging trail, and after a few minutes we heard their screams. The unfortunate Gerinus fell from the rock, which was more than one hundred and fifty feet high at this point and lay at its foot.

"We have all of them," Aelius concluded grimly. "What do you think about that, Master?"

I shrugged.

"You'll have to take all the bodies and search the apartments and adjacent areas. Maybe the murderers have left some traces that will tell us more about them than what we've seen," I said.

"I believe that too," he answered. "We'll need to look after corpses. And... to inform the Regency Council and the heir to the throne, Prince Shadarr. Oh, and one more thing: please don't leave the palace. I want to have you at hand."

I smiled crookedly.

"Don't be afraid, we won't run away. And besides, it's my business now. First of all because my wife could also die here. Secondly..."

"What's the secondly?" Aelius asked, raising his eyebrows.

"Secondly, Queen Dobrava, because that is her real name, she is... she was my childhood friend in the Borderlands Kingdom and I want to avenge her death.

IV

We were walking through the maze of corridors through which Thalia led me. We were silent. It was not easy to pull oneself together after all this. The sight of the murdered men did not scare me. I've seen enough death in the war. There it was on the agenda. But murdered women were something I did not like. They could live, love and be loved. They could have husbands and children, be wives and mothers. They could enjoy life. Someone's criminal hand broke the threads of their lives and there was nothing in front of them except a funeral or rock tomb. I felt nothing but a terrible regret.

And a terrible rage. If I could get these criminals, I would do them every torture that I know. The grim senselessness of this crime struck me. I understood that the goal was the queen, but what did the courtiers blame for? Guards were killed so fast that they did not resist, nay! - they did not even reach for the weapon! There was something incomprehensible about it, but on the other hand it could only be one - the murderers did not want to be recognized. So someone could identify them. And be a very uncomfortable witness.

That's what I thought, following Thalia down a spiral staircase to the top floor of the castle where the servants' apartments were located. After a few minutes, Thalia opened the door and led me into her apartment. It was basically one room with two windows looking south. A silvery moon was in the blue sky and in the distance the snow-capped peaks were visible. The night wind carried the sweet smell of hay and flowers from the queen's gardens. I went to a window with a magnificent view of the foothills, now dormant in the greenish moonlight. Behind me I heard a quiet sobbing. I turned and saw Thalia lying on the bed with her face buried in the headrest. She was crying - she had been brave so far, now she lost her nerve.

I sat next to her and stroked her hair gently. She sobbed and hid her face on my chest. I embraced her and she hugged me. I could imagine what she was experiencing. What we saw, this bloody massacre, shook even experienced warriors, let alone her... We lay down and I cover her with a rug - it must have had a lot of heat now, which relieves the shocked experience. After all, she could have been there, at the moment when... I still had the compelling impression that we had overlooked something, some minor but the most important detail from the whole matter. Some key sitter. But the tired mind refused to be obey and fell asleep feeling the woman's body, which was warming up slowly.

I woke up when the sun was high in the sky. I looked around and my eyes met Thalia's wide open green eyes. She smiled at me.

"How did you sleep?" She asked.

"Thank you, fine" I answered, "and you?"

She smiled again.

"Almost wonderful," she replied.

"Almost?" I asked.

She blushed.

"I'd prefer to do something different with you, but let's just give it a start."

"Well, we weren't able to do anything yesterday," I said.

"Yes, you're right ," she sighed and her face darkened, "I still can't believe it. Poor Chena...-"

"Did you like her?" I asked a bit senselessly, because it was obvious.

"We lived together," she replied, "and I had no one except her. She also, and that brought us closer together. She taught me the Han language and we spent time together. A very clever girl. She was only twenty-one years old."

I felt that everything was boiling in me again.

"Beasts," I drawled with sudden passion, "I'll catch them."

Thalia took my hands.

"Master, my Master," she said quietly, "I swear to you that I'll help you with all my strength."

"Thank you," I said, "but I don't want to put you in danger. Besides, it's my business, the queen was my friend and..."

"...and mine too, Chen also," she finished. "As you can see, I've twice as many reasons for revenge."

I embraced her.

"Let's not bid," I said conciliatory, "we both have our reasons and we have to support each other. I also promise you that I'll do everything to get them and bring them justice."

I wanted to say something more soothing, but I was interrupted by a thud to the door. Thalia said that is open and a centurion entered the room with two guardsmen carrying my lapels.

"Here are your things, Master." He said without preamble. "Your horse is well-kept now in a palace stable. Oh, General Aelius Rufus is asking you to visit his quarters for inspection of the bodies."

I got up from the bed and threw quick glance to Thalia. She took a deep breath. She nodded. She was ready to look again at the dead faces of her friends. We followed the centurion and his men down to the ground floor, and then to the lower levels, the winding stairs that finally ended when I counted three hundred and twenty-six. We were in a dreary, cold dungeon in which lamps were rarely lit. It was probably about keeping the temperature low here, to prevent the rapid decomposition of bodies. Centurion ushered us into a large hall lit by bright light that came from the ceiling constituting some complicated crystal. It was sunlight, but strangely cool, not even giving a feeling of warmth. Apparently, the crystals that formed the ceiling retained the sun's heat by letting only sharp, white light.

Nine naked bodies of men and women lay on the long tables. Above each body was a tablet with the names: Obahl, Flavius, Ehoya, Chen, Avillea, Irleda, Hermios, Alfes and Gerinus. There was only a queen missing, which was understandable in that apparently the heir to the throne or the regent did not want ordinary people to see her nakedness.

"Hello," said Rufus. His face was gray and his eyes were red. He was getting the smell of digested alcohol. He had to get well drunk this night. But his gaze was already sober. "I put them all in the order in which we found them, going from the entrance to the royal apartments to the balustrade surrounding the hanging gardens."

"Thalia, you'll be doing the minutes of the inspection," I said after exchanging a few courtesies with Rufus and the doctor who was with him.

"For what?" Aelius asked. "Will it be needed?"

"Of course, because it can help us reconstruct what happened there."

"Oh, I think there is nothing to reconstruct," he shrugged, "I'm sure that the perpetrator got to the palace and then he got to the royal apartments, eliminating the persons he encountered in turn. It's clear."

I looked at him.

"But please, let Thalia do the minutes of all observations from the inspection, and then we'll discuss it at dinner," I said with emphasis on the word "dinner."

He thought about it for a moment.

"All right, Master, if you think so, so be it," he finally agreed, rubbing his aching temples. He must have had a good hangover, I thought.

"So, let's start." I said and went to the first table.

We finished after an hour. Thalia, shivering from the cold near fainting with joy, went on her way back to the real sun. She ran out into the courtyard and sat down on the bench with pleasure, exposing to the sun's rays. I pointed the place to Aelius and sat down.

"You want to tell me something, Master?" He asked in a slightly mocking tone.

"I've two questions for you," I replied without paying attention to it, "because you are local and you know the local systems. So the first question: who is in power after the murdered queen Dobrava? Because the heir to the throne is a minor, so he can't be. Am I wrong?"

They looked at each other.

"According to the law, during the interregnum period, the chairman of the Throne Council is elected. It's Severinus - the high priest of the Ishtar Temple in Shadizar."

It was a novelty for me.

"High Priest and Throne Council?" I asked, astonished. "How did it happen that the high priest became its president?"

"It happened after the death of Avienus Rufus the Elder," Aelius replied.

"About a year ago," Thalia added.

"Rufus?" I asked again. "Is this someone from your family, General?""

"This was my father," he replied. "I must add that his death was also unusual. Doctors say it was a heart attack, but he never suffered from heart disease, and besides..."

"What besides?"

"Besides, strange purple spots appeared on his body, as if..." The general barely inhaled. "As if he was poisoning some mushrooms. But he never ate mushrooms!"

V

There was a moment of silence.

"Your second question?" Thalia interrupted.

"Who will benefit most from the queen's death?"

They thought about it for a moment.

"Opposition in the Throne Council, but..." Rufus waved a hand dismissively, "they're only strong in their mouths, and would not dare to do anything like that. This is a handful of malcontents and ultra-nationalists who dream of the great Zamora. Complete nonsense."

"And the external enemies?" I did not give in.

"They didn't exist and they don't exist. We have treaties with all neighboring countries and kingdoms, so I don't think anyone will let that happen. Although this Turanian dagger gives you a lot to think about... What you're up to, Master? Do you think it's me or my people? You're wrong. It's not me, because the only man in the queen's life was me. And she will confirm it." He said sadly, pointing to Thalia.

Thalia nodded to indicate that the general's words were true.

"I confirm." She said.

"And Severinus?"

"You accuse the second person after prince in the state, now the first one, beware!" Said Aelius. "He has great possibilities, huge resources and long, very long hands..."

"Like any priest who gets to power," I murmured. "Nothing new under the sun... In Stygia, it was similar. Who knows about the queen's death outside of us?"

"Throne Council, commander of the royal army, General Eresh, chief of his staff and of course the palace's service. In one hour, the Throne Council will issue a statement about the queen's death and regent's taking power. It looks like the interregent will be reign at least three years until Prince Shadarr will reach the age of twenty-one."

"What if the young prince won't live to be twenty-one? Who then becomes the ruler of Zamora? After all, he doesn't have siblings?"

"He has no siblings, he is an only child," Thalia said. "For all gods, what are you... ?!"

"About the coup d'état, Thalia. And that which is creeping."

"Hmmm... Master, step-by-step coup d'état?" Rufus smiled broadly. "I'm afraid that you belive now too much to your imagination!"

I sighed. Rufus might have been good at hacking people and shooting at them with a bow or crossbow, but he was bad politician.

"Well, usually, we associate the coup with rebellions in the army, the speeches of slaves and poorer sections of society. Sometimes it's the rebellion of part of the ruling elite against the second part of these elites. Look at this from this side. Here we have a slow takeover of power by someone who wants this power so much that he didn't hesitate to kill people. First, he took over the throne board, killing your father, General. Now he could send murderers to the queen and be an interregent after her. And in about two years, Prince Shadarr will fall unhappily on his horse or will he have a gun accident... Or a brick from the blue sky will fall on his head."

I looked at Aelius. He was pale and sweat beaded his face.

"It's impossible, Master."

I smiled.

"What happened to your father's body?" I asked.

"It was burnt the day after death," he replied.

"Don't you think about it, General?

He bridled.

"But it was in the summer, during the greatest heat, you could not hold the body of a dead man for so long!"

I looked at him with pity."

"And you're saying that?" I asked him gently like a small child. "Do you have an icehouse?"

He looked at me questioningly.

"Oh my gods..." he whispered, "you're right!"

"Exactly. I'd watch out for yourself, if I were you. Well, I think you know why you're writing reports on inspection of the body and crime scenes?"

He nodded.

"You won't tell me that I'm also threatened with an assault on me?"

"Of course it'is threatening you," I said gently, "if I'm right, then you are the next target on the list of those who are behind the attack on your father and queen. Now let's go search the apartment and royal gardens.

* * *

For the next three hours we searched the rooms of the royal apartments. As we suspected, we did not find anything suspicious. Then I went with Rufus to the rock under which Centurion Geriner's body was found. I had an idea since it was found. But I needed to find material evidence that we had adopted the wrong assumption because I felt that Aelius was wrong. Actually, I was sure of that. Gerinus's body was massacred, battered with rocks, but his face was almost intact. I said almost because there was a small, narrow wound between the eyes. It did not match the wounds inflicted by the sharp edges of the rock, when it fell to the bottom of the precipice, or to the resulting from the impact on the rocky bottom. It did not suit the overall picture of the damage he had. Besides, it was still an open question why the experienced warriors who were there and the queen's courtiers did not react by raising the alarm when the killers appeared in the royal apartments. What's more, they behaved as if the killers were well known to them. This puzzle did not give me peace...

I looked at the rock. Craggy, hanged here and there. It was more than a hundred and fifty feet above the bottom of the abyss. I looked at her exactly where the place from which the centurion fell. About halfway up, I saw a small loop made of rope suspended on a ledge.

"Where was the centurion found?" I asked.

"He was lying here." Aelius pointed out.

"Has anyone searched this place?"

"For what? After all, there is nothing here but stones." Aelius shrugged.

"Hmmm..." I murmured. "And it was necessary."

"What do you mean?"

"Exactly what I said," I replied.

He shrugged.

"We're wasting our time," he said.

"Five more minutes, all right?"

"Well, let it be, Master, but no longer. I've a head ache."

I smiled.

"There's an excellent measure on the hangover," I said looking around on the ground, "just don't drink the day before, and that's all..."

"That's easy for you to say..." he muttered.

Suddenly, something suspicious was in my field of vision. I leaned in and out of the stones I pulled out an object reminiscent of a six-pointed hand-sized star made of heavy metal. It arms were sharp, and one of them was stained brownish. A typical śuriken star. Weapons of ninjas knights - terror of the Assassins. I slid it into my pocket and straightened up. I was sure of my ground.

"We can go." I said.

Aelius clearly came alive. We headed back to the castle.

We went back into the cool interior of the castle corridors.

"General, I have a request," I said.

"Yes?" He replied, raising his eyebrows.

"I'd like to go back to the nether regions for a second and see the centurion's body again."

"For what?" He asked in amazement. "After all..."

"I'd like to see it again," I replied with emphasis, "and at the same time show something to you, General."

He thought about it for a moment.

"Okay," he agreed, "but quickly."

We moved back to the nether regions and after a few minutes we stood at the centurion's body. I looked at his face again and took the śuriken from my pocket.

"Do you know what it is?" I asked.

He shook his head.

"This is a typical śuriken star. Weapon of the ninjas knights," I said. "Did you hear about them?"

"Yes, I heard," he replied, "but what is it?"

"This is a piece of metal in the shape of a star. It is specially polished and profiled to fly steadily to the target, just like that." I said and threw it towards the wall. The star burst into it with a whimper.

"That's how it works," I said, tearing it from the wall, "and now look general," I suggested to him the dirty corner of the star."

"Is that blood?" He asked.

"Yes, it's blood," I confirmed, "and this is his blood," I pointed at the centurion's body.

"Look!" I said and slipped star's arm into the wound. They fit together perfectly. Wound and shoulder of the star.

"Uffff..." Aelius let out a startled gasp. "But what does it mean?"

"Let's get out of here," I suggested, "I'll tell you what it means at dinner and that means three things."

And I went to the exit from the underground.

VI

The dinner consisted of sheep roast with garlic and herb sauce and kasha with some additions. In addition, the cool light Bryth-uan beer, which clearly appealed to Aelius. When we ate, the general looked at me.

"And now tell me, Master, what conclusions you draw from what you found and what you showed me today!"

"Did you find something? Thalia asked timidly.

"Yes," said Aelius, "and I must admit that your man is more and more surprising me!"

"Thank you, General," I answered with a nod. "Can I start?"

"We're waiting!" Aelius answered.

I waited for the servants to take the dishes from which we ate and bring us bowls of water to wash hands and wipe the mouth. When we completed these ablutions, the general slapped me on the back.

"Begin, Master," he said cordially.

"Okay," I said, "but let Thalia keep the minutes.

The general nodded, and Thalia took the stylus. They looked at me expectantly.

I thought for a moment.

"I'll start with the fact that we all thought that the assassination was carried out by a group of assassins who got into the castle by the main entrance and avoided the guards and entered the royal apartments, where the guards standing at the entrance were first killed, and then those people who came to the royal gardens were eliminated in order, and finally the centurion was pushed off a cliff - isn't it?"

The general nodded to indicate that's the truth.

"Then I asked myself a question, namely - how did the killers escape from the castle? And so that nobody has seen them?"

"Maybe they were disguised?" Thalia guessed. "For example, for guards or someone from the castle service?"

"The thought is good," I praised her, "and everything indicates that it was so. But it served them not to ENTER the castle, but to GET OUT of it. Do you understand?"

So, you suggest that..." Thalia said again.

"I'm not suggesting," I said, "but I'm absolutely sure that the killer's commandos entered the royal gardens by the cliffs and then into the apartments."

"How is it?" They looked at me in amazement.

"That the cliff is inaccessible? It's a mistake! During the Assassin's War I saw how Tabbor was being captured, their headquarters on the border with Iranistan. It has been stormed by two thousand Vendhians for a week. Unsuccessfully, finally General Rajiv, who commanded this operation, decided to use a special brigade of mountain archers - the ninjas knights who overcame a sloping rock wall, more than a thousand two hundred feet high, and invaded the mountain stronghold by opening its gates. Rajiv took the Assassins in this way with two fires and almost kill everyone."

"You were there, Master?" Aelius asked.

"Yes, and then I commanded the maniple of the shooters. We have just climbed using special loops of ropes and ropes. Something like this has been used and in this case. The perpetrators went to the cliff. Apparently the centurion heard them and wanted to see what was happening. He leaned over the railing and at that moment one of the killers threw him a *śurikene*. He hit him on the forehead. Gerinus died on the spot, and his inert body buckled through the railing and fell off the cliff."

"And what's next?" Rufus paled distinctly.

"The killers jumped into the gardens and that lured two more guardsmen. They were attacked near the place where their commander was killed and in turn they were killed with blows in the back and throats. The idea was that they would not be able to speak and warn the others. Then the matter was simple. The queen and the women who accompanied her were murdered. Then the guard was lured and murdered in the corridor, and then the last one was killed almost at the entrance to the apartments."

"That seems perfectly credible," whispered the general.

"That's the truth," I replied. "Actually, two-thirds of the truth, that I promised you."

"Where is the remaining one-third?"

I paused for a moment, more for an effect than for a real need. I took a good sip of pomegranate juice, because my throat was dry.

"This one third is like that: the killers were women."

They both looked at me like a revealed deity. In their eyes I saw question marks.

"What?" Aelius asked.

"What???" Thalia accompanied him.

"As you remember, I put one more question at the very beginning of the investigation, namely: why the guards didn't take their weapons? Remember?"

They nodded.

"Exactly. If the killer was a man, then the matter would be clear. But the guardsmen faced not men who were armed to the teeth, but almost naked women!"

And there was silence. I gave them a few minutes to chew and digest this message.

"For Mitra and Ishtar," said Rufus, "it's possible!"

"It's obvious, General," I answered without boasting in my voice.

"But how, for all the demons of Stygia, how did they... do that?" He asked.

"Very simply. They were armed with something like this," I reached into my pocket and pulled out a small switchblade. I pressed the button and a five-inch double-sided blade popped out with a metallic click. "Do you understand now? It can be easily hidden in the palm of your hand. Even a small and narrow woman's hand. One of them approached the victim from the front, and the other stuck a dagger in the back, between the breast vertebrae. You need a steady and strong hand, so I assume that all four women have passed the *ninjas* knights course. But I can't say where."

"Why?"

"Ninjas is an elite formation, guided by a special code. They are cruel and efficient, but they do not kill vulnerable people, old people, women and children. They are used for fighting in the mountains and for secret actions at the back of the enemy. That would be the first case, unless someone trains such killers for their own needs. Besides, we don't know anything about their fighting style. And there are several of them."

"Can woman be the Assassin?" Thalia asked suddenly.

I nodded.

"Yes, but as far as I know, all of them have been caught or killed. Although..." I made a dramatic pause, "it's said that some of them fled by secret passage to the Iranistan side of the border, and from there to Stygia... This information is still unconfirmed. Till this day."

"What does this mean for the world?" Said the general.

"The Third Assassin's War," I replied, "or something like that. Certainly Emperor of Vendhia will be saddened by this."

"Why?" Thalia made a curious face.

"Because he was the Assassins' target..." I answered seriously. "And he almost was killed by them."

I did not finish, because at once somebody rattled on the door and a guard officer entered, who whispered something in the ear to his supervisor.

"Really?" Aelius's face expressed the greatest astonishment and at the same time rage. "Where?"

Whispering again and Aelius, not even hiding his irritation, rose from the table.

"Come with me!" He said in a commanding tone.

"Did something happen?" I asked.

"Another guardsman is dead," he replied in a furious tone, "and this is an officer!"

"Who?" Thalia asked, who knew most of Rufus' men.

"Petreus!" The general growled. Someone found him half an hour ago in the inn at the gate overlooking the Way of the Kings."

VII

We entered the inn where everyday traffic prevailed, only in one of the corners was quiet and peaceful. Two guards in full armed guarded what looked at first glance like a bundle of rags. But when I looked closely, I recognized the human body lying and curled up in a little ball. Petreus lay facing the wall. Beside him lay his short sword in the sheath and the purple coat of a centurion of the guard.

"Who found the body?" Asked the general of the guard.

"Servant Klefaz, general," one of the guardsmen replied.

"Get him here," Aelius commanded and in a moment in front of us stood a small man with Shemits features.

"Speak!" Rufus growled. "What do you know!"

"My Lord, I found him. He was lying like this when I went to this table. And the other one disappeared somewhere."

"Oh, was here the other one?"

"Yes, sir, but he left before I went to the table. They drank together, then the other one went, and when I looked, this officer was not there either. I thought he went without paying the bill and I went to the table, and he was lying there as it is now."

"When did this happen?" I asked.

"An hour ago, maybe a little less," he answered, squinting at Thalia, who showed him the tip of the tongue.

"How did you know he was dead?" I asked.

"I shook him and then I called to the patrol, which almost passed this way and they said that..."

"Oh, sure, I understand." Aelius Rufus looked around and nodded to the patrol commander. "Put him on the table and let nobody get here. We'll see him, Master."

I nodded and Thalia pulleda tablet and a stylus up from her pocket. This woman learned quickly...

Two guardsmen laid Petreus's body on the table. They managed to straighten him and then we saw his face. It was blue, almost black. At the corners of the drawn lips, shreds of foam gathered. I felt a gentle smell of bitter almonds from it.

"Poison," I said.

"Are you sure?" Aelius asked.

"Oh yes and it's about a fulminating action - a one drop can kill a peasant big like prancing, which can be seen in the attached picture."

"What did the other one look like?" I asked Klefaz.

"I don't know, sir," he answered, "I didn't see his face."

"How is it?"

"He was wearing a burnoose and a hood that was slung over his face like Mitra's monk. He was tall, portly. And probably a high family," he added quietly, looking around fearfully.

"How do you know that, you didn't see his face and clothing?" I asked.

"He wore a thick gold ring on his finger with a large ruby eye," he replied.

Well, Shemit - it crossed my mind - that's the most important thing for them... But that was a valuable tip.

"So, Master, are you sure he's poisoned?" General asked.

"If there are no other injuries, I've complete confidence. Besides, this poison kills almost immediately," I replied, "this is the Stone of the Dekerta... By the way..."

I stopped because an absurd idea was born in my head. The Dekerta Stone was used in Stygia and it was made by local priests. It was an extremely lethal mixture of several poisons with instant effect. To kill a man, half-grana of this substance was enough. So it would be another Stygian trace in the matter.

"By the way... what?" Aelius stared intently at my face.

"Tell me, General," I said, "who has an intimate relationship with Stygia? Of all these noble families?"

"With Stygia?" He asked surprised. "As far as I know, half of the city trades with Stygian merchants. We're on the Way of the Kings, so we have several hundred merchants here a month. But why?"

"No, I'm just asking. I'm looking for an anchor point." I replied. This path led nowhere.

* * *

I was lying on a comfortable bed in Thalia's room, who was lying hugged to me with sideways. Her warm presence was soothing, but I could not sleep. I looked at the ceiling, trying to piece together the events of the day. The death of the next centurion gave food for thought. Of course, it could have been a victim of some criminal charges, it could not be proved, but I was sure it was closely related to the attack on the queen.

"You're not sleeping again, my love," I heard her whisper.

I shook my head.

"Do you think about that poisoned centurion?"

"Yhm... That's it," I said in a whisper, just in case, because the rooms of the service were definitely under eavesdropping.

"So what did you come up with?"

"Don't you think about it, my dear," I replied, "just hug and try to fall asleep. Tomorrow we'll have a harsh day."

If I only know what the prophetic words it will be!

"But who could poison him?" She asked.

"Probably the one with who he was and drank wine," I said. "He was drinking Zingarian wine from the vineyards on the eastern slopes of the mountains. It's heavy and sweet, and the local vintners add to it the apricot and peach spirit extract, which gives it almond fragrance. Adding only one grana of Dekerta stone will not change its taste and smell, but it's enough to kill even a man like Petreus. Yes, honey, that's what it's done. And you know what I think about it? I think he was the one who led the four murderers with the exit of service. That is why the palace guards didn't react and four women dressed like cooks or cleaners coming out in the company of an officer aren't unnatural."

"So, honey, the right question is," said Thalia, "for whose commissioned Petreus brought them out of the castle?"

I kissed her on the cheek and she gave me a kiss on the lips.

"You think quickly, my wife." I praised her.

She smiled.

"In the end you're my husband, I wouldn't take just anyone..."

We kissed again. I embraced her and took closer.

"I hope you fall asleep now?" I whispered to her.

She hugged me strong and we lay there in the moonlight. After a while, her breathing leveled up and calmed down. She fell asleep.

And I do not.

I was tired of thinking how to get to Severinus, because I was absolutely sure that he was behind this attack and he was on his way to take the throne of Zamora. And with that thought, I finally fell asleep when the stars began to disappear in the slowly bleaching sky.

Thalia woke me up when the sun was high above the horizon again. I got up and quickly dressed. Then we'd eat something quickly. I had the feeling that during my sleep I found something that was the missing link to solve the final puzzle.

"Tell me, Thalia, has something vanished from the queen's apartment?" I asked her suddenly.

She lifted her beautifully fashioned eyebrows in a grimace of surprise.

"As far as I know, nothing, but we can check it," she said, "do you want to go there now?"

"Can we?"

She smiled with superiority.

"I'm a queen's manor, so I have access there anytime, anywhere, without restrictions. Come!" She said, seeing that I finished eating. She stood up and moved toward the exit and I followed her.

VIII

I was strangely surprised by the thought that it was not about the queen, but about something else. This could have something to do with her plans - someone wanted to prevent her and the possible heir to the throne. Of course, this was another hypothesis, but I had to check it out and that's why we went to the queen's apartments. The castle was undergoing preparations for the funeral ceremony, so no one had time to clean up. At the entrance to the queen's apartment, a surprise awaited us. The door was sealed and closed. Thalia was really surprised.

"Who did it?"

"I think it's on the orders of the Throne Council, Severinus, or Rufus."

We saw the seal, it was the seal of the Throne Council and the personal of Severinus. Fortunately, it was made of hardened wax that did not stick to the wood.

"Ha, ha, we've lucky," I said.

"What we do?" She asked looking around fearfully.

"What we came for," I said.

"But how?..."

"Just like that," I took out my dagger and gently removed the wax seal, then removed a piece of wire from my pocket and bent it in the skeleton key. After a dozen or so seconds of manipulation, the doors opened. Thalia looked at me in amazement.

"But how…"

"What are we waiting for, guard?" I pulled her hand and we went inside.

"What are we looking for?" She asked when she recovered from her first surprise.

"Something what somebody could take away from here. Coils, documents, papyrus, in a word, something that could have been valuable to foreign states or governments and rulers."

"The Queen hasn't had anything like this here, except for the private library, come." Now she pulled my hand into a small room, in which three walls were shelves resembling honeycombs, with the difference that there were scrolls of papyrus and parchment in the cells. Thalia looked around for a moment.

"And what?" I asked.

"I think, there's everything alright," she replied, "but... strange..."

She went to one of the shelves and was looking urgently for something.

"What's strange?" I asked.

"Look here, fourteenth shelf, there was a scroll "Nielburg's Chronicles" and now they are gone."

Now I was amazed.

"Nielburg's Chronicles? You are not mistaken, my love?"

It was a real shock for me.

"No, why?" She turned to me with a fiery face.

I sighed. The "Nielburg's Chronicles" were written over a thousand and a half years ago and constituted a treatise on weapons used by the Atlantic ancestors - the Atlantic, whose civilization preceded the times of the Atlantean Empire. The Brotherhood of the Green Dragon had only one copy in the Library of the Grand Master in Kulalo. A few thousand miles away. And it turned out that there was another scroll of the cursed book, in which there were descriptions and drawings of bizarre constructions. More than one tyrant or madman with sick ambitions on the throne would like to have this book and be able to read it properly. Legends circulated among the populace that it is a book of powerful spells. In fact, it was a book containing technical descriptions of various types of weapons, whose power of destruction turned the Atlantic into abatement and killed all living creatures whose weight was two hundred pounds up. It is thanks to this that all the great animals that were created after the destruction of the titanic reptiles were extinct. After their civilization, there was not even a single stone left standing, and the memory of it only passed from father to son. After the destruction of Atlantis, only the brotherhood and Sages of Shampullah in the Himelian Mountains preserved the knowledge of Atlantis. The survivors of Atlantis hid in the land of Moo.

"My dear, this book is cursed because it contains information about such weapons that are able to lose all life on this planet. And this is our case: Yours and mine. The Brotherhood. That's what the killers were about, whoever they were!"

"What do we tell Rufus?" She asked.

"Truth. We must count on his help and ask him to hunt down the killer's commando before they leave Zamora's borders with the "Chronicles" in their hands. I wonder who knew that the queen had this book?"

"I think everyone," Thalia shrugged, "the queen had it on the outside and in fact, there are some strange drawings... Besides, it is written in the language of Han and that's why she read it and translated mine... Oh, Ishtar!"

"Now you understand why she was killed?"

"Did she know the killers?"

"Exactly," I said. "She may have helped them enter the palace, or... she brought them to the queen. Then they killed her so that there would be no witnesses."

"Chena? Oh, no," Thalia shook her head, "not her, because we spent the whole time together."

"Not necessarily," I said, "she could leave them messages, like me in a dead contact box."

She wondered for a moment.

"You may be right," she answered after thinking, "I haven't always kept an eye on her. And think, two agents in one room... How it can happen!"

"Well, that's our fate," I said, "sometimes you have to sleep with the enemy in one bed."

We went through the library, but apart from Thalia's familiar scrolls with Hyborian lyric poetry and fiction, there was nothing suspicious.

We went through other rooms, but we did not find anything special. Then we slipped out as we came in closing the door with the lock and putting the seal back. We quickly left the royal apartments and after half an hour we found ourselves back in Thalia and Chen's room.

We lay on the bed. Thalia burrowed in me and we were lying like a good old couple.

"What are you going to do? She asked in a whisper.

"Inform the Grand Master," I replied, "this is a priority and in such cases each member of the Brotherhood has unlimited prerogatives, regardless of his rank in his hierarchy and has the authority of the Master. He must recover or destroy a dangerous artifact. Directives are explicit here. We operate here alone, because before the news arrives from Belverus to Kulalo, weeks will pass. Although Vislanian is expanding the heliographic communication network, this episode is still under construction. Messenger from Belverus will be there in a month or two. This rainy season..."

"But we thought that there is nothing dangerous here?"

"That's what we thought after Agaton's death. Until today." I murmured. "The brotherhood has failed to penetrate the royal court and you are the first agent that Master Agaton placed in the capital. Well, we've a nice problem here. I said, clarified to the Crossbowman that the decision to move headquarters from Belverus to Kulalo was premature, but I was voted."

"Who did you clarify for?"

"To the Crossbowman. Lestko is an excellent crossbowman, hence the nickname. Ever since he became a Grand Master, he put down the crossbow and reached for his pen, but he is still one of the best. We are depend on each other, my love. First and foremost."

She closed my mouth with a kiss.

When we finished kissing, a strange thought occurred to me.

"Tell me, what plans had queen?" I asked.

"As I wrote," she answered with astonishment, "she wanted to master all the countries adjacent to Zamora. And she needed something that would help her make this plan."

"A weapons?"

"Maybe, she didn't have this book for nothing, and it was no coincidence that poor Chen got to her court only because of her beautiful eyes. As you can see, she needed someone to translate her "Nielburg's Chronicles" from Kithaian to the Hyborian."

"You lived together here, right?"

"Yes, we do," she replied, "and sometimes we even slept in this marriage bed..." she laughed playfully, "but no, there was nothing that you think about, though I admit that sometimes I had the urge to pet her beautiful dark body. She had nice breasts and you know... Yummy!"

She sighed. I nodded my head with pity in my eyes.

"We were friends only." She said at my disapproval.

I laughed. I have to admit that my imagination gave the view of two young, beautiful female bodies intertwined with each other in a hug and felt a pleasant thrill.

I nodded.

"Where are her things?" I asked.

"Here, do you want to see them?"

"Of course," I said, "I'm still afraid that we've missed something somewhere."

"You won't say that...?"

"I'm not saying anything! I'm just afraid that you were looking the queen, and someone else..."

I did not finish, because Thalia opened Chena's ornate faraway trunk and began to lecture its contents. They were some clothes and stuff, jars with cosmetics and various feminine accessories. Suddenly Thalia was worried and gave me a terrified look.

"Oh, Nertuss," she whispered, terrified, "look here. For the Great Mother!..."

I looked and felt cold, despite the hot day.

IX

There were writing instruments on the bottom of the case: an ink bottle and a few brushes. But that did not scare Thalia. Next to them papyrus lay a carefully rolled up and wrapped in a holster case, marked with number 14.

"This is the "Nielburg's Chronicles"." She whispered, terrified.

I took out the scroll carefully and unfolded it. Among the ideograms of the han script I noticed familiar drawings and diagrams, some tables and graphs. I had a cursed book in my hands.

"We have to destroy it," I whispered, "this is the book from the bottom of Hell.

Suddenly I felt a gentle breeze on my ear and cheek and I heard a gentle shuffle.

Oh, Mother!" Thalia moaned.

"Don't turn around," I heard someone's impersonal voice behind me. This someone spoke in a Hyborian with a strange, hard accent.

I straightened up slowly.

"How many of them are there?" I asked Thalia, who was gray on face in horror. But she did not lose consciousness of her mind and winked twice with both eyes. Four.

"What you have in your hands, give to girl," I heard again.

I handed her the scroll, folded and put in the case, and I actually reached out to her with the scroll, and in the next moment I turned around quickly and blow with it figure behind me. I aimed at the head, but instead of the head there was a black hood. Nevertheless, I felt the scroll hit the opponent in the skull.

He did not expect that, without waiting for a reaction I hit him in the solar plexus, then immediately grabbed him for the black shirt and pushed on the next masked attacker. The push was strong and the attacker was on his sword. The assailant let out a chuckle and slumped to the floor. One less - I thought.

"Thalia, sword!" I shouted. Thalia threw me a katana, which I took out immediately and cut almost blindly, giving back two blows given to me by the next two assailants. The third struggled to take out his sword from the first masked body, which lay still.

One to zero, I thought.

"Take this," I gave the scroll to Thalia, "and hold on to my back."

In the meantime, three attackers moved on us. I managed to snatch out of my belt my dagger, which I took in my left hand. I waited for the attack.

"We don't want bloodshed," I heard the impersonal voice again, "just give us the scroll and we let you live."

I laughed impertinently.

"Ttry to take it from me!" I replied. "Come on!"

They moved at three directions. They tried to reach me with their swords, leading out quick and unexpected cuts, but always a shimmering steel curtain appeared in front of them. They backed away.

"And what's now, you scum?" I said. "Maybe again, huh?"

Now I've looked at them more closely. They were small, masked, in black cloaks. Wild eyes burned in the holes in his face. They moved again, this time they attacked only on one side. They wanted to tire me with the fight with one opponent, to get me later with two of them. It cannot succeed, I thought.

I took two blows and made a getaway. The opponent barely spared the thrust directed at his belt.

Oh, I got you - I thought. With dagger, I stopped another blow aimed at me by the opponent on the left. I supervised the blow and smoothly pushed the thrust to that one who was on the right. Surprised, he did not manage to push this thrust and felt the blade of my sword thrust into his body with a hideous crunch.

Two to zero, I thought. The opponent dropped his sword and began to stain the blood from the wound with his hands.

There were screams at once in the corridor and three Guardsmen with weapons in their hands fell into the room, followed by General Aelius Rufus.

"Take them!!!" He shouted deafeningly, because the voice was according to the height. "But alive!!!"

And then something strange happened. Opponents jumped in the direction of the windows leaving the troupe of his companion to fend for himself. Before we could react in amazement at the sight, the three hooded figures jumped outside the window and disappeared.

We looked at each other and after a second we got to the windows.

Three figures were moving away from the castle towards the south flying on something like colorful, triangular wings. They were already about two hundred steps away.

"Has anyone got a bow or a crossbow?" I asked.

"Shucks..." growled Rufus, "we did not foresee it."

"No one could have foreseen this," I murmured, "even me."

"Devilish tricks, generals," one of the guardsmen said, spitting through his left shoulder, "pfu!"

"Not at all," I said, "ordinary hang-gliders."

"What???"

"Khitaian invention," I replied, "as you can see it quickly applied. Khitaians like flying kites, they always liked it, because it's part of their religion. And they put it into practice..."

"#@#$%$#." Aelius had a complicated curse in his mouth. "But you got one?"

"Yeah, right!" I remembered. "What about him?"

I went over and kicked the corpse to turn on back, then knelt down beside him and with one jerk I tore off the black mask.

"Opppsssss..." One of the guardsmen said suddenly.

"Oh, light..." Rufus muttered.

"Oh, Ishtar!" Thalia exclaimed.

At our feet lay a dead twenty-something girl. Her white skin and light hair contrasted with the blackness of her clothing. The blue eyes were half-closed. I closed them. The body cooled and it was still flexible.

"Æsirka?" Thalia asked stupidly, amazed. "What are they doing here?"

"Mercenary." I murmured. "After the Assassin wars they are full of them here in the Hyborian lands, or even in Khitai. But that's what we was talking about - it's women. And it's trained in Khitaju. They fought in the style of the Wü-i-jin school. Interesting style, only cuts and no pushes. Their swords are not finished too sharply, so they are not suitable for stabbing, just for cutting and chopping enemies. They are sharp as razors."

"But she just died from a thrust."

"She died because she was on the sword of her friend who wanted to strike me, so she was hit with a double force: from the thrust of her sword and her impetus. That's why it came in her so easily. We'll have to look at it more closely."

"To the icehouse with this... carcass," said Rufus with distaste.

The guards took the corpse from the floor and left the room.

We were alone.

"How did you know general that we would need help? Thalia asked.

"I guessed," he replied in a strange tone. "We were at Severinus."

"And what?" I asked a bit surprised. "He told you something?"

"He didn't," Rufus grimaced in disgust, "his service."

"He didn't let you in and you only talked with service?" Thalia asked, astonished.

The general smiled sardonically.

"Service let us in," he said with a wry smile, "he didn't have anything to say anymore. He's been dead for at least two hours..."

X

"What???" We shouted in unison.

"Yes," he confirmed with a nod of his head, "Severinus shared the fate of poor Gerinus. He got the star, this śurikene between the eyes. And what's most interesting, his chambers were thoroughly searched, and the library straightly gutted."

"What about his people?"

"Fortunately, he gave them a day off and he was alone in his palace. When they returned, they found him with the śurikene in his head. Simple conclusion. They killed him and then searched all the rooms. And they didn't find what they were looking for."

"Definitely not," I thought, "because the queen hid it well. In the box of manor..."

"So we are at the starting point, but I'm happy about one thing, my love," I said to Thalia. "Your friend is innocent. What's more, she helped her mistress. And I'll admit, Rufus. that I suspected you."

"Me?" He asked with a bit of bitterness in his voice.

"You," I replied. "You had a motive and occasion."

"And why did you suspect me and don't suspect now?" He asked still with the same bitter note in his voice.

"It's obvious," I said, "you couldn't have killed your beloved woman, that's number one. And secondly: you didn't have time for that. You've just been around your people all the time and no one can confirm that you've been in touch with them." I pointed my thumb at the window. "Because they did it."

He nodded in silence.

"Now both of you tell me what your lady planned during her life and how she planned to do it."

They looked at each other.

"The generals have priority," Thalia said.

"Well," he said after a moment, "I'll start with the fact that the queen was going to create a block of states connected by a defensive alliance. At the beginning, she intended to marry her son with Princess Alaja, the daughter of the King of Turan, and enter with this state in a personal union. Later, she planned to enter into a deal with Khauran and Corinthia to form a federation of four states, to which she later planned to join Brythunia and Nemedia, and continued to Aquilonia and Argos in the West, and Koth and Khoraja in the South. And then Ophir and Zingara. In this way, after a dozen or so years, a community capable of obtaining military hegemony on the continent would arise, and its axis would be the Way of Kings. Besides, it would be a military alliance against the Picts in the west and the Æsir and Hyperboreans in the North, the black kingdoms in the South and the growing empire of Vendhia. But she saw the greatest threat in the east - the waking and growing Khitai. That's where she was looking for the seeds of another war. And she was preparing a defensive alliance capable of opposing it."

"But... it's...." said Thalia.

"I know, but it had a peaceful process. Whoever would not like it would not have to join the federation. In the face of a threat or sooner or later it would happen." Aelius smiled.

"And what's next?" I asked.

"Alaja and the prince are already engaged. Unfortunately, the main architect of the new order and the creator of the Hyborian Community are dead."

"She was murdered by mercenaries from the North in service of..." I hung my voice, "the sultan of Iranistan, who came into agreement with Paikang. It's looking that way. But not only."

"Do you see anything else?" They both asked.

"Stygia. Don't forget that the dead queen Gedrena had similar ambitions and wanted to implement them using weapons. Fortunately, we managed to prevent her and her crazy priests from using it, which would ruin half of the planet. The fortune and her stupidity helped us. Stygia fell out of the game, but as I see it again raises its snake head of Set - a cobra ready to strike."

"Are you sure, Master?" Rufus asked.

"I'll be sure when I look at the corpse of this beauty," I said.

* * *

A warm twilight fell on the city when we left the nether regions. My worst fears have come true. I looked carefully at the body of the dead aggressor. Under the right armpit I found a kind of tattoo in the shape of two runes "S" from the Armanen alphabet and some two stamps, one of which had the shape of a circle and the other a cross. I found something else, which indicated that the progress of the surgical technique was much higher than it seemed to me. Her teeth were amazingly white and equal. It turned out that they were artificial, made of some hard mass, which overlapped the gums like a drawer. Her breasts were surprisingly large and protruding. When I watched them, I found a delicate seam, after the cut I took out strange, semi-transparent cushions from under breasts, which enlarged them. Certainly something like this has not been done in any of the Hyborian lands, let alone the fact that such a procedure that leaves almost no traces on the body would be impossible to carry out at our side. Anywhere on Earth. I was sure of that.

And it was disturbing. Very disturbing.

"You're silent, Master..." Thalia said, when we were alone again in her bed.

"Because I don't have too many reasons to be happy," I replied.

"If you want, I'll give you some reason soon," she said, embracing my neck and hugging me with her whole body, "just say a word... One word, only one..."

I sighed and took her closer to me. We were lying now, hugging with a cheek by the cheek.

"You don't want, my love?" I heard her whisper over ear.

"No, I'm not in the mood," I whispered back. "Too many murders, too much blood shed. And the guilty ones fled."

"Do you think about those... blacks?"

"Yes, about them too. Severinus actually got out of our hands. He entered into conspiracy with the Assassins and sent them to the queen and her companion. He thought he would shoot two hares with one arrow - that he would murder her and at the same time get a great magical book of spells and charms. He failed, because Dobrava was predictable - she ordered Chena to hide it. Well, Chena hid it in her stuff. Severinus did not foresee one thing, namely that there is a secret alliance between the survivors of the Assassins, the Iranian esteem and the emperor of Khitaju. And also the prince of Mer-Arsome regent after Gedrena, the queen of Stygia. The Stygians care the most for rebuilding the state, and like the Khitaians, they are afraid of the power of the Hyborian Federation, whose architect was your mistress. Incidentally, something like this has happened before in Atlantis. That is why the Khitaians also wished to recover the "Nielberg's Chronicles" and the secrets contained in them. So Assassinis murdered Severinus, made a booze in his palace, and they guessed - or Severinus might have told them - that the secret work is in your place. That's why they came running here so fast and wanted to make you a bite-bite, as the Ilbarians say. Then we gave them resistance and actually the thing is over."

"Actually?" She asked. "And what has not been explained yet?"

"The Assassin case," I said, "they were not people."

"Oh no, don't you tell me they were demons?" She laughed.

"Something worse..."

"What?"

"People from the Future," I replied. "And from the worst Hell you can imagine!"

She get serious.

"Is this a joke?" She asked suspiciously. "People can't travel in time."

"Not today, but in twelve or fifteen thousand years, yes."

"How do you know?"

"Do you remember the records of the Crossbowman and Master Haneda who infiltrated Khitai and were in the Crimea Death Cemetery?" It was there that they met with them. What's more, they managed to oust them from there.[17]

"Why from hell?"

"They caused one of the greatest wars in the world of the future. They were defeated, but not completely, and they raise their heads again. They have mastered the possibilities of traveling in Time and intend to steal what we destroy. Their goal is simple - power over the world!"

She sighed.

"Terrible things are happening even in those worlds..." she whispered softly, "that's terrible."

"In addition, we've received information from People of the Future who are fighting with them. And one of them is how you can recognize these bad guys."

"And what?"

"And that, this girl had all these signs. It was they. Followers of the god Hitler."

"Did you say god? There are no gods."

"Yes,but he was a god to them."

"Oh, I understand," she sighed, "and what next?"

If only I knew...

XI

The sky was going dark.

We lay both at the dying fire, listening to the murmur of the stream and the sound of trees. Shadizar remained far behind us. We left him as soon as regent took over - young prince Shadarr, who, as soon as he heard of his mother's death and in hurry came to Shadizar and immediately called himself king without waiting for three years. First of all, he subjugated both generals, and quickly suppressed the Throne Council, which offered symbolic resistance. This has

---

17 This is described in the short story "Fire in the Swamp of the Dead".

prevented riots in both main cities of Zamora, which are frequent in the interregnum period. We had nothing to do there. We both watched as the cursed book burned in the flames of the fire, which cost so many human lives...

"So the mission is over?" Thalia whispered, hugging me.

"Yes," I said. "We're safe now, darling."

We looked at the flickering coals out again."

"Tell me about Atlantis," she said.

"This is history right now." I said. "Which in a few thousand years will be a fairy tale. Although?..."

"Although, what?" She asked.

"Although not. It won't be a fairy tale, but still a living story. Don't forget that what our Brotherhood does changes the reality of our planet all the time. Instead of wasting time and resources for meaningless wars between people, people will fly among the stars looking at them as if they are the lights of distant cities that will have to be visited in the future. It is a fear to think if any part of today's world possesses the knowledge contained in this book," I pointed the fire with a movement of the chin, "and this is terrible knowledge. There was described the most modern generation of weapons of mass destruction, which used the PSI energy field. An energy field that surrounds every living being. If it's deprived of this field, the being dies. It's necessary for it to live and what is most interesting - it's the living beings who produce it. Old age consists in the gradual disappearance of this field and when it disappears, the end comes. Understand?"

She nodded.

"And what's next?" She asked.

"You understand that launching this weapon would be synonymous with the destruction of hundreds of thousands, or even millions of people. And maybe even the annihilation of all living beings all over the Earth... It has once slipped out of control."

"What??? When??? And where???"

"On the Atlantic. 64 million years ago."

"Is the civilization of the Atlantic so old?"

"Yes, very much. Only a few souvenirs left on it in the form of huge statues on Taootoma. And not only because in the Himelian

Mountains, too. There are also small figurines of baked clay and drawings carved on small black stones... They represent the Atlantic and things they could do."

"What happened to them?"

"It's said that the Atlantes have mastered the art of moving in space, and thus flew away where the bright red star Sirius blinks."

"But... it's white and blue!"

"Now yes. But not a million years ago."

She paused.

"How is it known?"

"Our Masters have penetrated deep into the Black Kingdoms. They sailed along the Zarkheba River following the route of Conan the Cymmerian and his beloved Bêlit to the City of the Winged. They wanted to check how much of the truth is in the "Song of Bêlite", and by the way, make a scout..."

"And what?"

"And they got there. And they actually found this city. Of course, there were no Winged People or Demons, but traces of the return of some settlers from Sirius. It turned out, by the way, that Zarkheba is called Niggher - what they read from the inscriptions found there - and that these people were able to fly in the air. Their leaders were Nommo and Ogo. Many times they were flying from Sirius to Earth and back. By the way, it turned out that Sirius is not one, but two stars. One big - two and a half times bigger than our Sun. The other is tiny and white, but its mass is huge and consists of matter called saggala. It float around it for fifty years, and there is also a planet out there."

"Saggala? What is that?"

"It's a matter so much compressed and so hot that one gran of it weight thousand talents, and the heat can kill a man from a hundred feet away."

"Impossible," Thalia smiled perversely, "and what strength is able to do it?"

"The most powerful, yet imperceptible. Omnipresent and at the same time invisible. We see only the effects of its operation, but it is imperceptible to us."

"What is it?"

"Gravity," I replied, "force of gravity."

"I don't understand," she replied, wrinkling her nose.

"You're not only one," I murmured. "And yet it's like that."

"And what's next?"

"Well, they're living on this planet now, circling Sirius, this smaller Sirius, but this planet isn't belong to them. It means it was built by someone..."

"Now you're telling fairy tales," she laughed. "Let's go to sleep."

I covered us with a blanket. We lay staring at the stars. A moment later, exhausted by the slowly passing day, Thalia fell asleep. And I could not fall asleep again and looked at them until they disappeared in the glow of the new day.

11

⁓

ALVFURIANS MASK

I

A warm, gusty foehn wind struck from the Graaskal Mountains. Shutters of the Inn of the Three Trolls, standing on the road from Brythunia to Halogi - the capital of Hyperborea, was pounding. It was just the first spring evening and the shimmering stars flashed in the darkening sky, when a lone rider traveling in two horses appeared from the south. The rider slowly pulled up to the wide open faith and jumped off the horse, releasing his father's armor, who ran out to meet him.

He was not tall and his figure was wrapped in a gray-green warm cape with a deep hood. He looked like a wandering monk-doctor or teacher, but the impression was spoiled by the sight of two simple Zipangian swords that he had strapped to his back so that their hilt protruded from behind his shoulders. The stranger walked slowly to the entrance and stopped, as if searching for someone in the general hall. Hardly anyone noticed him. People on the road tired their way and enjoyed the pleasures of a short break in the journey. Eaten and drunk, played cards and dice. They enjoyed the coming spring, though... In the spring the roads grew thick and the main difficulty was the mud piled up on them.

Hyperborea was slowly opening up to the world, because King Sigvard V allowed the foreigners to enter their inhospitable land ever wider and wider. He quickly learned that it pays off to everyone. Barter and money trade was a much more profitable occupation than looting and killing neighbors, and Sigvard V's subjects quickly understood its principles and quickly grew rich. Within a few years Haloga has more than doubled, and the number of its inhabitants has more than quadrupled. The demand for luxury goods increased and on a daily basis from Brythunia, merchant caravans guarded by strong armed patrols of royal troops glided. Therefore, the appearance of a single traveler interested the innkeeper, who came out to meet a stranger and then the whole on the double and bows led the stranger to the general hall, where feasting different visitors from distant sites. They were mostly Hyborians from Aquilonia, Brythunia, or Hyrkanians, but the bright eye of the newcomer fished out of the colorful crowd of guests also black huge Kushitan and two equally powerful warriors with the appearance of Shemits. Anyway, it was not hard to see - they were provocative and their southern temperament, warmed with wine, sought an outlet.

"Melech! Who you brought here?" The voice of one of the Shemits was heard.

"A significant guest," replied the man called Melech, "and..." he stopped, because the stranger raised his finger warningly."

"What???" The Kushit called, "he threatens you with finger? Well, maybe we'll talk with him, huh?"

"M'vani, please, no arguments," said Melech, "I don't want to have trouble with the king's people here."

The stranger quietly took out his sack and gave Melech several coins. Gold shone in his hand. The eyes of the Amazon woman immediately flashed with greed. An expression of unrestrained greed appeared on M'vani's face. She rose from her seat and nodded to both companions.

"I don't like you," she said, standing in front of the newcomer. "You have two swords and we don't like people like you."

The stranger looked into the drunken Amazon's face.

"I don't want to argue with you," he said in a calm, feminine voice, "so you'd better give up. That's good advice."

M'vani and her companions belonged to this kind of people who treat every kind of courtesy or peace as weakness, and look only for an excuse to start a brawl. Besides, it was the gold he was paying or maybe she was paying, because she intuitively sensed a woman in a stranger, the innkeeper harbored irresistibly...

"But we want it!" M'vani shouted and swung her fist.

The stranger made a quick dodge and the fist slammed into the beam supporting the ceiling.

"*Marr avam lir!*" The Kushit cursed. "You scum!"

"Want to fight?" The stranger asked. "It's better not... You are drunk."

He could not finish, because M'vani shook off her heavy sword from the sheath at her waist and swung it again. Her companions giggled and jumped back into their weapons. All people froze in anticipation of the continuation of accidents. Such windfall - the fight of three Amazons with... - well, with whom? There was a murmur. The viewers felt excitement at the thought of what was going to happen here. Only the visitor stood calmly as if he was not afraid of anyone and anything.

"Do you really want to die?" He asked again in a calm voice.

His hands went to the hood and took it off his head.

There was a muffled sigh, for it turned out that the stranger was a woman. A beautiful woman with noble, regular features, straight white hair, and well-cut eyes with a deep blue on her sunburned face. Now they glowed glumly like the Himelian glaciers in the midday sun. The small but full pink lips now contorted slightly in a contemptuous smile.

"You want to fight me... you white bitch?" M'vana grinded out.

The stranger smiled ironically.

"I'm afraid I'll have to kill you, so let it go, please," she said in her unnaturally calm voice. "Besides, you're drunk and I'm not fighting with drunk ones."

M'vani raised her eyebrows and roared with thunderous laughter.

"You Aesirian bitch!" She cried. "You're extremely cheeky, but I'll teach you mores. You'll be licking my shoes!"

She led out two quick cuts, but the stranger ducked quickly and the blows hit the void.

"For Gorga, Hermino and Kaliano! We'll teach her good manners!" And after a second, swords shimmered in the center of the room.

The stranger stood calmly watching three opponents approach her from three sides.-

"And what now you white bitch, you piss yoursef in fear?" Hermina waved the tip of her sword against the face of a stranger who was still standing without changing her position. "Come on, M'vani!"

The stranger again smiled ironically.

"So far, I was called White Vadera, but if the bitch suits you so much, then..."

M'vani led a cunning thrust into the stranger's belt, while Kaliana tried to push her with the sword on the other side. Hermina raised her sword to the neck of an unknown woman who was so arrogantly and brazenly standing in her way. It could not fit into her head that in the face of death you can be so calm and still waiting for blows...

What the spectators later saw was a spectacular show of Zipangian fencing. White She-wolf twirled around her axis and her hands jerked out two straight blades that bounced both pushes against her. There were two sheaves of sparks, which meant that her weapon was made of solid steel. Hermina's sword did not drop down at all, because Shemit felt the deadly steel of a Zipangian katana penetrate her left breast. The strength left her and sank to the floor, blood pouring profusely. The sword dropped from her fainted hand. She was dying and see her two companions crash on a stranger, giving a battle cry. A second later, a stranger's sword fell evenly at the shoulders of M'vani's head, which fell into an empty beer barrel, and the headless body fell to the floor, straight to the feet of Kaliana in a fountain of blood from cut arteries.

The stranger jumped back only to put one of the swords back into the sheath.

"I can handle you with only one sword," she said calmly to Kaliana. "And when you go to hell, tell your companions that I killed you, Ingrida of Velitrium!"

A murmur of surprise and terror flew through the room. Ingrida was widely known for her prowess and proficiency in the art of wielding swords. The wandering skalds, bards, fishermen and troubadours sang about her skills. Another song has been created about this fight...

"Come on... you... you...!" Kaliana choked on her own words, taking a wide swing.

This blow would have knocked the ox, but Ingrida made a quick dodge and her sword drove with unprecedented precision into the chest of the warrior. It was finish of the fight, because the dead body of the third Amazon fell onto the dirty floor. Purple blood splashed around. Ingrida leaned forward and stripped from the warrior her skirt, which she wiped the sword with.

"Well, that would be enough," she said to the dumbfounded audience, throwing the bloody rag on the fresh corpse. "Does anyone here have any grudges against me?"

The answer was dead silence interrupted only by the sizzle of torches and oil lamps.

"I don't see," Ingrida calmly slipped the second sword into her sheath.

People began to talk again in a low voice and returned to their food and drink.

"Let somebody clean up here," Ingrida said quietly, turning to the attendant, "at their expense," she nodded at the dead Amazons.

"But Lady," said the innkeeper, "what will it be when the news will go to..."

"Don't think about that," said Ingrid. "First of all, they challenged me and there are witnesses for that and secondly I'll go to your king. And I bet a hundred lunas that he won't be happy when he'll know what has happened to me here."

"Do you have witnesses for this, Lady?" The innkeeper asked mockingly. "And where are they? Nobody has seen anything here and nobody will say anything. So?"

"And yet," Ingrida shrugged, "they will be here soon. And they are already here," she said, glancing toward the entrance, which seemed to narrow and diminish, because a powerful man with a height of over six feet and powerful shoulder stood in them. He was dressed in a masking gray-green cape of the Brotherhood, but instead of a sword, he held a stout battle ax in his hands.

"Master Ingrida from Velitrium? Welcome to Haloga!" He cried happily at the threshold, then wrinkled his nose in disapproval as he saw three bloody corpses. "I see you haven't been welcomed here," he added with a low bow, squinting at the innermost owner of the inn. He was known here as a swashbuckler.

Ingrida looked at the newcomer with interest and a bit of amusement. She bowed her head slightly and gave him a seductive look. After all, she was a woman...

"Hello Master Joris from Haloga," she said in a nice voice, slightly bowing her head, "as you can see, I was called a bitch and something unkind, although I'm known as the White Wolf..."

"Well, those girls won't names you like that anymore," said Joris, holding out a hand to her. "Master, I will accompany you to our Commandory. I would not wish a disrespect to you again on this earth..."

"Not yet, Master," she said pleadingly, "I just ordered a supper, so you won't refuse me your company?"

"If a Master from Belverus asks, I won't refuse." Joris bowed to her courtly. "We rarely have such guests here!"

She smiled and said nothing.

They sat at a table on a wide and comfortable bench. After a few moments, the little boy gave them food - veal stuffed with mushrooms and fragrant herbs, browned cakes and light beer. They both brought out the knives and silently got to eat. Joris ate slowly, tasting every bite and taking care not to overtake the woman sitting opposite him. Throwing on food in the presence of a woman has always been considered as crassness. Nevertheless, they quickly satisfied the first hunger.

"Thank you Master, you have great food here, not the scuz that is on the northern slopes of the Himelian Mountains," she said, "and besides, I'm not from Belverus but from Goa. I've been going here for almost three months. I have enough of horse riding."

Joris raised his bushy eyebrows slightly.

"It was announced that you'll come from Belverus, or at least from there came a letter from Lestek the Crossbowman, in which he announced your arrival..."

She smiled delightfully.

"True, but don't forget, Master, that the headquarters of the Brotherhood is now in Kulalo and in Belverus there is only our field facility servicing the solar telegraph and providing independent communication with the Brotherhood Headquarters.

Ingrid wiped her hands in a soft cloth and folded her spring, then slipped it into her pocket. She stood up.

"I'd like to get to Haloga as soon as possible," she said. "I'm used to night driving, so I won't be trouble."

"Not at all, I also like traveling at night, especially warm and spring, under the moon and with such a charming companion at my side..." Joris smiled. "It's a pleasure for me."

"Such a giant, and expresses itself like a skald," Ingrid thought. "So on the road!" She said aloud.

"On the way," the giant clapped his hands at the bollards to bring their horses.

They left the inn. A warm breeze of the spring wind intoxicated them with a wet, fragrant of mugho pine, grass and softened earth, freshness. They got on their horses and, without looking back, melted into the silvery-gray gloom of the moonlit night, aiming for the north.

II

They rode silently next to each other. They were both excited about the night trip. The moon slowly rolled to the western part of the sky and the eastern horizon slightly brightened. After four hours of driving, they stopped for the grazing near the spring beating among a small clump of trees that looked like an island of green among the brown-yellow forest steppe.

"Here we can rest a few hours," said Joris, stopping and getting off his horse.

He came up, reaching out to Ingrid, but she forestalled him and gracefully hopped off her horse.

"Yes, we can, but when we see the first caravan, we move on. I'd like to be in Haloga as soon as possible, "she said. "To tell you the truth, I learned from the Afghulis to sleep in the saddle. Horses need to rest and eat."

She unsaddleed her horses, letting them free, and she lay down on the dry ground wrapped in a thick blanket and put a saddle under her head.

"I advise you to do the same. Master Joris," she said.

He shrugged.

"I don't want to sleep," he said, "I will look after both of us."

He unsaddled his steed and let it go free, then quietly began to kindle a small fire. Meanwhile, Ingrida has fallen asleep and slept with a sleep of the just. Killing three Amazons did not make the slightest impression on her. She lived in a time when a stronger law was in force and only those who were able to defend survived. Or attack. It was just a question of who first drew a weapon and used it.

When she opened her eyes, it was bright and the sun was two cubits above the horizon. For a few moments she lay still watching and listening to the sounds of the forest steppe surrounding her. In the distance, taiga forests were bluing on the silhouettes of mountains. Warm gusts of wind carried the smells of earth and forest. She stretched herself in a catlike gesture and rose silently. Joris sat at the fire, over which a large piece of meat was roasting, spreading a delicious roast.

"Did you hunt something?" She asked sitting down next to him.

"Yes," he smiled, handing her a stick with the portion of roast on it, "eat it, because we will only go to the evening with a break for drinking and feeding horses. But we'll be in Haloga before midnight. Do you have any place to stay?"

Of course, she could stay at the Commodities, where she was entitled to accommodation, but she refused. She preferred to be free to move.

"Yes, I have a younger sister in Haloga. Åsa is the wife of some important dignitary at King Sigvard's court."

"What is her name? Asa?" Ĵoris's eyebrows went up. "I think I know her. She's similar to you, but her hair is yellow..."

"Åsa is the royal sword-bearer's wife," she replied, "and as for hair, she is actually blonde. And her face is similar to me, only she is a little higher."

"Yhm, I agree," said Ĵoris, "they have three children. And her husband's name is Willibald and he is the earl of Leenah County. A long way to north of Haloga, among the ice of the North. On the banks of the Icy Ocean, beyond the mountains of Nordheim."

"That's where the Leenah river is, it's also the name of this ancient city... Cursed City, am I wrong?"

A shade passed through Ĵoris's lovely face. He nodded.

"We studied this city because it's one big underground city. A city complex that was destroyed by some cataclysm. Like an earthquake or something similar. What's the most interesting is that there are four deep craters in the earth within three verst from the four corners of the city. Now covered with snow, filled with ice. It seems that they caused it to be destroyed... Perhaps four Brahmashiras warheads were fired there... Their explosion caused terremoto, which ruined part of the city, and the rest became uninhabitable."

"How many people died there?" Ingrid asked.

"We counted ninety-eight thousand human skeletons in the rooms and tunnels of this city, on its seventy floors. The city was built to a depth of almost two miles, and on its lower floors is as warm as in the Black Kingdoms or in the south of Vendhia... In its darkness grow large, white, black and colorful mushrooms that emit bluish and white-green drizzling light, while in front of them you can even read. They are everywhere, on the ceilings, on the walls and on the floors. This is amazing view in this realm of the dead."

He sighed, as if to some grim memories.

"Interesting!" She said, ending eating. "Will it be possible to visit this place?"

"If you make such a wish?" He answered politely.

She shook her head and wiped her hands on the rag, then stood up.

"No, Master Ĵoris," she said firmly, "this isn't my mission. I'm asking you very much for help in a very sensitive matter, about which only you will know for now, Commander. I mean the Alfvurs Mask."

Ĵoris lifted his long bushy eyebrows slightly.

"We've searched the city of Leenah many times, but unsuccessfully. We haven't found anything that resembles the subject described in the "Nielburg's Chronicle". Anyway, you know that because we sent the report from our search to Belverus when the Brotherhood Headquarters was still there."

"I know that, but in the meantime there have been a few things you don't know about yet, Master."

"What is it?" He asked with undisguised curiosity. "Is there anything new in this case?"

"Of course, Master," she said, packing her stuff and saddling her horse, "when we moved our Headquarters to Kulalo, Master Ewran from Messantia decided to conduct a query of our records and even to compile a list of all the stationery in our possession. At the time of the query, he came across several documents, from which it transpired that fifty-four years ago, Master Agobardus from Galparanu in Taurana carried out an analysis of local legends about the Great Conflict in which the Alvfurians Mask was mentioned. By the way, it turned out that the Alvfurian people inhabited the ice deserts of the North, just on the border between Hyperborea and Asgard. The Cimmerian met with them, who fought not so much with them as with some of their machines. Later, Akira described it in "The Way of Kings" by twisting and embellishing it in his own way..."

"But what is this mask?"

"Just a mask," Ingrida shrugged, "from the descriptions it appears that it was a kind of helmet or crown. It was like a pitcher or rather a calabash[18], which the greater part was a helmet put on the head, and the smaller part in the shape of a sphere roughly bristling with short spikes. The whole thing was made of one greenish crystal or opal.

---

18 Pumpkin type.

"Hmmm... a helmet or a casque is not a mask..." Joris shook his head skeptically, "in that case where did the name come from?"

"Because this helmet has the front part in the shape of a mask covering the whole face. And what's most interesting, there are no holes for eyes. Besides, the legends say that whoever has this mask, or if you prefer a helmet, he can think orders to various monsters and, most interestingly, see and hear what they do."

"And what with this had..."

"...Alvfurians?" Ingrid finished. "They have that they are the last people who used this mask. And it's in the underground city of Leenah!"

They traveled all day with a two-hour grazing when the sun climbed to the southernmost horizon. It was well past midnight when they entered Haloga, which was an open city, and had no defensive walls. There were rumors that the king was going to build such, but so far there was no need. When they knocked on the fortified Gate of Commodities, the clocks began to show midnight. They was tired, so went straight to their rooms. For Ingrid, it was the first quietly slept night after three months of traveling through the huge continent. And for the first time in many days she felt really safe...

In the meantime, Joris could not fall asleep and despite his tiredness, the dream did not come. Ingrid was in front of his eyes and realized that she was a fascinating person he had never met in his thirty-year-old life. And in the morning he was absolutely sure that this acquaintance could change his life...

III

Around noon Ingrid looked around discreetly from side to side, which resulted more from habit and not from a particular need. She went to visit her sister. Åsa lived in a luxurious district of houses built of stone blocks, which gave a sense of solidity and security. For an hour she wandered among the alleys of Alta Haloga - Old Haloga, and after making sure that no one was following her, she turned to Soedra Slopet - a district located on the southern slope of the hill where Haloga was built. It was a routine procedure, which was the way all members of the Brotherhood behaved in unrecognized territory. And that's when she felt a threat. Someone was staring at her greedily.

Ingrid walked along the street mixed with the colorful crowd, stopping at a market stand from time to time and squinting from side to side. She had the feeling that she could feel someone's look on her back - but it was more intuition than experience. When she reached the street leading to Soedra Slopet, she stopped at a market stand with Gunderland materials. She look to the left by the corner of her eye. Nothing suspicious. She bowed her head slightly, as if to look at the art of green brocade and look to the right with her eyes.

He was there. A small man dressed in a gray cloak and with a hood closed to his eyes that sent a disturbing look. If it was not there, Ingrid probably would not have paid attention to him...

"So, indeed!" She thought with satisfaction. "I have a 'shadow'!"

Someone followed her.

Only who and why?

Very few people knew about her mission in Haloga. Crossbowman and Master Alcinoos in Kulalo. And now Joris and no one else. Three - maybe four people including Iris from Ianthe, the wife of Crossbowman. And the Commander from Goa. Five people and no more. All commands and guidelines were encrypted with her individual cipher. Is there any leak somewhere?

She slowly and calmly walked away from the stand and looked around, then slowly and calmly walked along the street. At the third intersection she turned right and then right again and quickly ran to the corner. She looked up at the street and suppressed a whistle at the sight of what she saw. She had already seen two men who were quickly conferring and dividing in two directions. So there were not one, but two 'shadows'... She was absolutely certain now. And again, turning on the streets, squares and alleys, she returned to the Commandory. She went straight to Joris.

"Did you order to follow me?" She asked bluntly, calm and polite tone.

He looked at her with exorbitant amazement.

"No, I didn't," he said, "and you've my word of honor on the nobleman and Commander of the Brotherhood."

"The nobleman's word can cause somebody pain. Two men followed me," she said, "one not tall in a gray sheet with a hood. The second one slightly taller, dressed in a brown coat with black fur. And he had the Hyrkanian cap with ear muffs."

Joris thought for a moment.

"Yes," he murmured, "this description suits every other inhabitant of Haloga... You weren't with your sister?"

"Well, no," she grumbled, "if they were bandits, then of course I won't show them the way to Åsa and her family."

Joris thought again.

"Bandits, you say," he said thoughtfully. "Maybe you're right. Recently, a Black Wolverine band has been operating here. Sophisticated robbers. They robbed a few of the townspeople, and high prizes were awarded for their heads... People say that they are a collection of Hyrkanians outlawed in Hyrkania, to which various rabbles from neighboring countries agreed."

Ingrid shrugged.

"They were professionals and only by chance I managed to track down two intelligence agents. They watched me in parallel, one followed me, the other ahead of us and took me from time to time. There must have been a third one somewhere, maybe it was some woman, but I didn't pay any attention to her. The combination of parallel observation with chess, an old Nemedia school."

"Maybe they were the king's people or rather his minister Sturul, Oyvind's son?" He said. "But then why did they follow you?"

"Maybe because I'm strange here?" Ingrida suggested the thought with a very uncertain voice. "Besides, as you say, they're looking for members of the Black Wolverine band here?"

"Perhaps, but I don't think so," said Joris, "it must have been your Åsa, who told her husband long ago that she was expecting you..."

"She doesn't know anything about me," she murmured. "But did anybody ask you about Brotherhood operations, Master?"

Joris thought for a moment.

"No," he said slowly, "I don't remember talking to anybody except the staff... No, no one outside the Commodities..."

"For sure?"

He nodded.

"For sure. Although…"

"Although, what?" She asked.

"I've remembered it now. A few weeks ago, Count Gurger approached me at the king's banquet."

"And...?"

"Well, he asked me if the Brotherhood is doing some work in the Cursed City. He said he was interested in extracting building materials from Leenah. It didn't surprise me especially, because for a long time there was a thought about getting to building materials from this city. There are huge amounts of marbles, porphyries, granites, sandstones and everything else that could be useful for the development of cities in Hyperborea."

"And what did you say to him, Commander?"

"Nothing that could expose you, Master..." Joris looked at her, "only..."

"Only...?"

"I only said that access to the city is hampered by ice and debris. And that getting there is very difficult and dangerous."

"Is it?"

He laughed.

"Depends for whom. The main entrance is blocked and buckled with boulders and earth as well as ice of a glacier flowing from the surrounding mountains. The Brotherhood has discovered and uses a very narrow, vertical shaft, some emergency exit, or an entrance for installation fitters or something similar, we can only go there on the winding stairs in single file. The shaft is deep at 150 feet and ends with a large chamber from which the tunnel runs connecting it with the sixty-ninth level."

"Not seventy?"

"No, just 69. Level 70 is almost completely polluted. Someone has made sure that the main entrance and the level lying directly under it is completely buried."

"Did you tell that to Gurger?" She asked.

"No. He knew about it, because there is another entrance - a sloping shaft hewn in a soft, tuff rock, probably in ancient times by robbers or gold seekers. It's over three hundred and fifty feet long and reaches 70 levels, to several rooms that were not ruined. From them, the window was pierced to the levels 69 and 68. They were completely emptied of everything that could be removed from there. People don't go farther than level 68. Simply because there are piles of skeletons, and they are afraid of demons..."

"OK," said Ingrida, fully appreciating the situation, "and are there these demons?"

"As much as here," said Ĵoris with a wide smile.

They laughed for a dozen or so seconds. Ĵoris fell silent and listened to her laughter. He was quiet and melodic. Pleasant to the ear. It was difficult for him to get used to the idea that this woman who was able to kill three fighters can laugh so melodious and charming.

"She should be the ornament of the royal court," he thought. "And not going by the mountains and the seas..."

She looked at him.

"I used to be a manor," she said as response for unspoken question, "but it's good for bad skeleton and machinator. I prefer adventure and... solving puzzles from the past. Even if it would cost me my life. Only such a life makes sense."

"Aren't you going to start a family?" He asked, amazed at this unexpected confession.

"Maybe one day, but not yet..." She replied with a grimace of dislike on her pretty face.

"It's a pity!" Said Ĵoris. "You'd be the pride of every home and a star in every court!"

She smiled ironically.

"The pot calling the kettle black," she said ironically, "what about you? You are thirty years old, when you marry, when you will stand over the grave?"

He shrugged.

"I'm not in a hurry, because why should I." He muttered. "I used to have a father, mother, siblings and fiancée. They died at the hands of the Aesirs during one of many wars on the borderland... I got into captivity, but I managed to escape. I was taken over by the Brotherhood and I have already stayed here."

"So we're both with a baggage," said Ingrid thoughtfully.

"Yes," he nodded. "Let's eat something and then we'll think about how to find the damn mask..."

IV

The wind stopped and the weather changed. Dark clouds came over Haloga, from which snowflakes began to fall. So it happens that after a warm wind from the south the weather changed to worse, but it did not last long - two or three days, and again the sun shimmered over Hyperborea.

Using the inclement weather, the White-haired studied the entire documentation of the underground city looking for a place where an artifact could be found. And there's been a few of that, because the city's research lasted almost half a century and that is why the file with documents regarding discoveries in Leenho swelled from year to year, so that it created an impressive thickness of the dossier. She learned, that the 51st and 50th levels were flooded with some liquid that was shining in the dark, but that approaching it was in danger of death. These two levels were the least penetrated. Master Enrinus and his disciple Rabdan had ventured there. They left a description of what they saw there. Description and drawings. Unfortunately - after leaving the underworld, they soon died of a disease of falling hair.[19] Fortunately, they managed to save their observations, which now Ingrida had in front of her eyes. Between level 50 and 51 there was a huge structure that had to be destroyed by some underground shock, because it broke the outer body from which shiny liquid leaked. According to Enrinus, there was breathable air inside, but it was saturated with ozone and some gases that smelled sharply, and the white silver salts turned black. There were many items in the rooms where the vast majority were in excellent condition. Only

---

19 Radiation sickness.

those that were near the 'great cracked cauldron' were destroyed - as Master Enrinus called it. The White-haired guessed that apparently it was a broken energy device, the remains of which radiated lethal energy, as was the case of Vendhia Malbony. Ingrida, at the recommendation of Crossbowman, studied the construction of Malbony, before it was covered with stones, earth and clay. A similar device was found in the City of Ghosts. Master Haneda and his students and apprentices studied them and said they were still working! And what's most interesting, he discovered that he is able to control this device that produced energy in the form of heat and light. She guessed that a similar installation was also in the Cursed City, and it was just as no more dangerous, because it was shattered.After the loss of two members, the Brotherhood found a way to bypass the dangerous area below the 50th level. The next thirty levels were safe, but the lower it got, the hotter it got, and at level 1 the temperature was so high that you could not stay there for too long. However, the calculations made by the Brotherhood indicated that water should start boiling at this level. So the creators and builders of Leenho have found a way to lower the geothermal degree by more than half![20] But that was not the last mystery of the underground complex. At levels from 1 to 30 there was the kingdom of chlorophyll-free plants, and above all the heat- and moisture-damping fungi that most probably constituted some kind of food for the inhabitants of the underground city. The Brotherhood researchers did not find anything else outside of them. A clever system of ducts and pipelines, which even after a few thousand years irrigated these plantations - as Ingrida in her mind called this area - so these levels automatically was out of picture. Perhaps this system cooled the walls and spans of these levels and did not allow the temperature to rise above the end of the biological strength of living beings. The search, therefore, had to be concentrated from the 30th level upwards, of course, except for the prohibited levels 50 and 51, where probably nothing was. But is it for sure?... Unless she does not find anything on the other levels, then

---

20 With a geothermal stage equal to 33 m/1 deg. C on the first level of the city of Leenho, the temperature should be + 98.9°C.

she will also go there. But how? - she did not know it yet. She left this problem for later. The number of 98,000 inhabitants of the city indicated that all levels from the 30th up had to be settled. And she was disturbed by the mystery of their death. All of its predecessors assumed that there was some flyer of poisonous gases from the 51st level, which killed people and the animals accompanying them. Nevertheless, there were dangers of repeating this incident and contamination of levels above and below the 50th and 51st floors. It still was a mystery for her, from where fresh air was taking in, but eventually she came to the conclusion that plants and fungi produce them, and therefore the whole city was one large self-sufficient organism in which people were an important link. And only a link. It was an unexpected discovery which she immediately noted. She had the overwhelming impression that she was facing something that barely brushed her imagination...

Meanwhile, anxious about the course of events, Joris began to suspect that the Amazons who invaded Ingrid did not act on their own instincts, but were sent. And on the same day he pushed his intelligence workers to the Under Three Trolls Inn. In fact, the three Apprentices went there to sniff the situation. One of them, named Soeren, was supposed to pretend to be a student going to the University of Belverus, while the couple Arsia and Lear were to pretend to be traveling song salesmen. The legend was so good that many such people were passing through the taverns on the road leading to Haloga. All three returned after three days and immediately went to the Chamber of the Commander. Joris took them immediately.

"Report," he ordered dryly.

The apprentices looked at each other.

"Arsia, start," said the Commander, "you were a song salesman with Lear, and what?"

Arsia smiled slyly.

"Yes, Commander," she confirmed, "we went to this hostel and there we started playing our roles. We went quite well and even made some gold lunas for our songs about gods and heroes. And then, with a glass of wine, we talked to the servants about white-haired woman who had defeat the three Amazons."

"And what's next?" Joris was impatient. "What did you find out?"

"Well, Commander, these three warriors appeared in this inn almost four weeks ago. At first they behaved calmly, as if they were waiting for someone, but as time passed, it was getting worse. They had huge amounts of gold, so no one would get in their way, and they gutted and drank unconscious... They said they were going to Haloga and... they were not moving from the inn...

"To the day when Master Ingrida arrived."

"Yes, Commander, to the dy of her arrival. After their death, a whole pouch full of gold was found. Someone did not grudge them money for a riotous life. It was almost a hundred and fifty gold lunas, not counting pearls, stones and other valuables. Their weapons were also worth the fortune. It could have been war trophy, but they spend a lot of money. During the day they slept, at night they would drink and party with men, that they liked. But always only one of them - the other two watched downstairs... To the day of arrival of White She-wolf."

The Commander pondered for a moment.

"OK," he said, "thank you for the good job. And what do you say, Soeren?"

Soeren stood up and smoothed his long golden hair.

"Commander," he said, "I was an itinerant student and I managed to sneak into the favors of the beautiful Anfis, Hyrkanian, who is employed there. She served them all this time.

"Anfis is your lover?" Joris asked bluntly.

"Yes, Commander, I've already reported it to my Master." Soeren said it calmly, but with a slight blush on his young, handsome face. "We are going to get married, but not yet.

"Sure, I understand," said Joris, "but did you find anything out from her?"

"Yes," said Soeren, "every week a man came to them. Man. Not tall, dressed in gray, unobtrusive robes... And what's most interesting, he was there that evening, when this incident occurred. Anfis described this to me minutely because everyone was waiting for the result of this fight. When it was over and you, Commander, you entered the inn, that someone sneaked out of the general room and disappeared."

The Commander raised his eyebrows slightly, not allowing any additional expressions of emotion.

"Are you sure about it, Soeren?" He asked in a voice that made hard notes.

"Anfis is absolutely sure of that," Soeren said it with undisturbed calm, "she has not deceived me yet."

Ĵoris thought about it. The news that he was near someone who was the client of the attack on Ingrida or his messenger gave him absolute certainty that the events of that evening were not accidental, and that - worst of all - someone blurted out the secret of the White She-wolf's mission. He vowed for himself. He did not talk to anyone about it. Apart from him in Commandory, no one knew the date of her arrival or who was to come. All information was triple encrypted with his personal cipher, which only Crossbowman and he had access to. And yet, unknown someone knew who was going on and most likely for what. It was a mathematical certainty. Not good, he thought. - Completely wrong. Someone tries to get into the possession of the same as the Brotherhood, and in such cases the goal has sanctified the means..."

"Commander?" Arsia spoke in a questioning tone.

He forgot their presence. He waved his hand.

"Are you still here? Thank you, you can leave. Good job." He said in a casual praise, because he was already thinking about something else.

And it was not a happy thought. It was obvious that someone had betrayed and that the traitor was outside the Commandory...

V

He sat deep in bleak thoughts. He had no idea what to do and who to trust. One thing was certain - again the Brotherhood faced a confrontation with someone who wanted to reach for power over the world and did not have any scruples. The Brotherhood was public and its branches were accessible to everyone, but it was guided by its own laws, and the most stringent of them concerned the recruitment. Others - nevertheless rigorous - protected its secrets. And these secrets were most often mad with insane greed and greed for rulers, and above all priests of various religions - most often gods of darkness and Hell. So far, the Brotherhood has managed to find and neutralize most dangerous artifacts after the atomic wars of gods-as-tigronauts from Atlantis, Mu, Lanka and other mythical lands. But now there was again someone who wanted to obtain an ultimatum weapon with the help of which he could gain real power over the Hyborian world.

Legends about the Alvfurians Mask said that it was a device that allowed to direct machines, that without energy were only piles of dead scrap iron, but the legends also brought different, equally amazing information about the possibility of influencing human minds and enslaving them at a distance. And that sounded very disturbing. It was impossible to allow the Mask to be in the hands of a madman. He was a little reassured by the knowledge that the Mask must have had its source of power, without which it was useless, but he did not have that certainty. He was not sure. And that was why it was necessary to resume the search in the underground city of Frigida, which was penetrated by him and Master Ariette and Students... He was absolutely sure that at no level there was something that would almost resemble a mask or helmet. He simply knew, because for many long days, they cataloged all the artifacts found there, which were not too many. Actually, they were only on levels above 65, because they were preserved by coldness and ice. Even corpses of people and animals. However, below the temperature grew and everything that was made in non-durable materials was destroyed by moisture, heat and ubiquitous, glowing mold.

The candle in the candlestick fired the last flame and went out. He looked for a new one and lit up after a few moments. It got bright. He sat down again in the chair and closed his eyes.

And the last cases related to the arrival of the White She-wolf. Intuition told him that solving this puzzle would not be easy and simple. The only point of reference was Count Gurger. It was a peculiarly naughty figure - a happy companion, a drinker, a reveler and a high roller. A typical brick. It is not known why the king kept him at the court, and not in Gurgerlandia, where he should stay. It was the only clue and it had to be checked. He decided to watch Gurger in the morning, through his trusted people in the court and members of the Brotherhood.

Gurger from Gurgerlandia. He did not fit this story. A small, almost dwarf with ugly, monkey ears and runny Shemian eyes. He resembled a mountain troll or kobold, which are full of northern legends. In court circles, it was said in a whisper that he was the hero of several scandals, but it was strange that this was the end. Nobody proved anything to him and it made him gain direct access to Sigvard V. Perhaps that's what made him a man with two faces - thought Joris. - And maybe even more than two. Like Sviatovid-Triglav in the Kingdoms of Borderlands...

A silent squeak of the door interrupted his meditations. Ingrida entered his room. She stepped noiselessly to him. He pointed to her seat without lifting his head.

"Please, sit down," he said kindly. "What do you come with?"

White-haired took advantage of the invitation, and Joris only now looked at her with amazement. Because there was something to be surprised about! She, who wore a gray-green robe of the Brotherhood with Master's silver-green brooch, was now dressed in a loose, semi-translucent white and turquoise dress that emphasized the slenderness of her legs discovered to her round knees. Green and white pleasantly contrasted with the warm color of her body. She did not have any jewelry except some thin Vendhian bracelets on her wrists and a thin chain on her ankle. Her delicate, small feet usually hidden in riding boots were now shod with exquisite eastern slippers. She was beautiful.

She smiled at the sight of his enchantment, enjoying the impression she had made on him.

"What's the ceremony?" He asked to say something and break the stage fright.

She sensed it immediately.

"After all I'm a woman," she said lightly, "and sometimes I allow myself a bit of luxury and coquetry..."

Joris felt confused again. There was something incredible about this woman, which forced people to obey and ordered to be scared of her. On the other hand, it attracted him, which he discovered with amazement when they got to know each other better. What he saw now was a clear signal intended only for him.

He cooled out instantly. Ingrida liked him very much, but he dared not dream about it, because she and he... To go with her through life. He has not gone so far in his dreams. But he felt that she is the one, the only one...

"What would you like to talk about, Master?" He asked politely. She got serious.

"About my mission." She said. "The truth is, I have to ask you for help."

"As a member of the Brotherhood, you have it..."

"...assured, I know that," she interrupted, "but I need someone to come with me to Frigida, the Cursed City. I know it's over two hundred miles through the rocky-ice wastes, but I've to go there. I'll tell you why. Well, I'm going to penetrate levels 50 and 51. I need someone who risks life and, at best, health."

Joris had already completely recovered from the stupor which was evoked in him by the sight of the changed Ingrida.

"That's a sure death!" He exclaimed.

She nodded calmly.

"I know that," she said, "but I'll be absolutely sure, and you, Commander, when someone enters and searches the 50th and 51th levels."

"The relations of our brothers are clear. Staying at these levels is a sure, terrible and long death. I won't let you do it," he said calmly. "Not for your death."

White-haired got up and came to him. She put her hands on his shoulders and looked into her eyes.

"I'll go there because I've to do it. I'm a Master and I've the right to risk only my life. It's just that someone has to go there to get the job done. I need someone to take the materials from me and bring them to the Commodities, if I can still write, and if not, he will repeat what I tell him."

"I won't let you alone there," he said firmly, "and if you must go there, then we'll go. You and me. And we'll do it together. And I don't care that we'll die."

She looked at him and something unexpectedly flashed in her sapphire eyes...

She took a deep breath in her lungs.

"Was... was that your... confession?" She asked quietly.

"Yes," he replied. "Since I saw you for the first time, I haven't experienced peace. And since you've put it this way, you don't leave me a choice. I'm going with you."

"You can't," she said, "you're a Commander, and you can't leave the Commodities just because..."

"...you know I can," he replied, "but I won't allow you to die alone. Don't you understand that we've just confessed love? And if you are sticking your's neck, what should I do? I couldn't live without you..."

Their hands met over the table and they never came back to this topic again that night.

VI

The next day, Ĵoris gave his intelligencers orders to follow Count Gurger, wherever he moved. Besides, after discussing the problem with Ingrida, they decided to wait for the "shadows" that followed her. For this purpose, she again tried to visit her sister, but on the route of her walk, the intelligencers of Ĵoris were deployed, who were tasked to pick out her "tails" from the crowd.

The weather of appointed day was nasty, which favored the intentions of Commander and Ingrida. Therefore, it was assumed that on such a day most people would be sitting in taverns, beer-houses and inns, and the "shadows" would be quickly tracked and eliminated. It was also hoped that they would be captured alive and then interrogated. The Brotherhood did not use cruel methods - delinquents got used to drugs that broke the will of a man better than clubs and cudgels. That is why the Brotherhood agents were so successful in extruding from people interesting information... Of course, when someone could not drink the serum of truth, traditional methods were used, such were the times...

Ingrida left the Commodities and began to wander around the streets of Old Haloga. Behind her came a couple of intelligence workers - Kay and Arlene, who pretended to be in love, hugging and hugging each other about a hundred and fifty paces from White-haired. Meanwhile, the second team of Brothers began to set up on the route leading to Soedra Slopet. Everything was going well and nothing interesting was happening. Ingrida entered a route surrounded by brothers - Ĵoris decided on a chess variant of external observation, because it enabled continuous observation of both Ingrid and the potential target, which were foreign "tails". In fact, after a few minutes the reconnoiterers saw a "shadow" sneaking behind White-haired. When the "shadow" equaled one of the alleys, two scouts dragged him in and overpowered him, and then tied him.

At the signal of the director of the action, Ĵoris, he was quickly thrown into a litter and taken away from the street. Meanwhile, Apprentice Karup watching the route noticed the second "shadow" as he left the block and followed Ingrida. Together with his partner Astrida, they approached him, but the "shadow" realized that he was being watched and dived in the nearest alley. They both rushed after him, and Astrida whistled in an agreed way, letting them know that they were pursuing. The "shadow" ran two blocks and stopped at once. Karup was faster and almost reached the figure who stood motionless in the middle of the road, when the figure made a sudden movement as if raising something to his mouth and Karup felt something stuck in his left cheek. At the same time, he heard a muffled "ptfuuu...". He felt dark in front of his eyes and sudden powerlessness cut his legs. He lost consciousness before he fell to the ground...

Astrida panting fell to a friend. She gave a cry and fell into his inert body. Karup lived, but he was unconscious, breathing poorly, and there was a miniature arrow in his cheek. The girl looked up, who stopped on the black figure standing ten paces from her. In her hand was a foot-long tube, from which she probably blew the arrow. At once the figure removed the hood with a calm, almost majestic movement, and Astrida's astonished eyes showed the beautiful face of a young woman. Her eyes were gray, merciless eyes, but the weirdest were the hair - black with gray strands falling on her shoulders. The apprentice was pole-axed for a moment, because she expected everything, but not that.

"You killed him," she said in an icy voice, reaching for the dagger, "I won't give you away, whoever you may be."

"I do not think so," she heard her pleasant, calm voice, "in a few minutes he would regain consciousness. Why are you chasing me?"

"Why did you follow our friend?" Astrida answered with the question.

The stranger's eyebrows went slightly up.

"Friend?" She asked, surprised.

"A friend, as a matter of fact," Astrida growled, "so?"

The stranger looked at her with irony.

"Listen to me," she said firmly, "I don't know who you are, but I object to that tone. First of all. Secondly, Ingrid White-haired is my friend who I want to protect against her enemies. She once saved my life and now I pay her debt. And third..."

"...so we're playing in the same team," Astrida finished calmly, "I'm Astrida from the Brotherhood of the Green Dragon, and this is Karup. Who are you?"

The woman hid her weapon and helped her raise and seat Karup, who was slowly coming back to consciousness.

"They call me Gray Wolf, and my name is Doriana. We know each other from the Assassin's Wars. We fought together in Vendhia. I don't belong to the Brotherhood, but... Let's say I sympathize with you. Oh, somewhere here is the Red She-wolf - Baella."

"It's the one we caught?" Asked Astrida.

"How was she dressed?" Doriana replied.

"In a gray-brown fur coat and a furry, Hyrkanian hat," said Astirida, remembering the "shadow" her colleagues had disposed of.

"It's not her," Doriana shook her head negatively, "she's coming here anyway."

Indeed. The red-haired woman was approaching them quickly. Karup slowly stood up and supported himself on the arm of Astirida.

"What about her?" Doriana asked.

"She came to her sister without problems. She had a tail, but I see that your friends took care of it. Who are you? She turned to them."

Astrida introduced herself and Karup.

"So what are you going to do?" Karup asked.

"If your master is under your protection, that's fine. We'll spend some time here and return to the trails..." Baella smiled predatory. "Once we were three and we were power. Three She-wolfs from the Himalian Mountains... old history."

"Yes, old," Doriana sighed, "we'll escort you to the Commandory and meet your master Ingrida... Well, well, who would think. Master of the Green Dragon Brotherhood!"

And both women laughed.

On the same day, all three of the She-wolfs met after a long separation - their memories were endless. In the meantime, Joris set about processing the prisoner who was brought in a litter to the Commander's dungeon. It was a young, maybe sixteen-year-old boy, who was tied to a pole in a special chamber resembling a torture chamber. Recalling with the mood, because the Brotherhood did not use physical violence and there was nothing in it that would involve torture. After a few hours the prisoner was given food and drink. He was admixed with a mixture of agents that weakened the will and broke the barrier of resistance to hypnosis.

"Well, let's wait another hour," said Joris to the White She-wolf, watching the prisoner through the secret eye in the wall of the interrogation room.

After an hour, they started the interrogation, during which they found out only that some stranger instructed him to track Ingrida, for which he got a hundred silver Grzywna in cash. He is to meet with him tomorrow at about six in the afternoon at the Under Swords in Ostra Gade in the wealthier Haloga district.

It was a good news. Ingrida dismissed both friends, claiming that she would be safe and that she would soon return to Goa. Doriana and Baella did not believe in it anyway, but they promised to guard her sister, Åsa, which was very handy to her, because it gave her complete freedom of movement. She could now deal with the proper purpose of her mission.

VII

There was no meet with a man who ordered observation of White-haired. It happened, but he slipped from her hands because he was found dead. Someone killed him with a firm and heartless hand. The stranger had died from blows with a knife or dagger in the heart and kidney. Each of these blows must have been lethal.

"Someone did damn good work here," said Ingrida, watching the body of the slain. "This seems to be the work of the Assassins. It's their blows and their hand. I've seen something like this in Vendhia," she added in a quieter voice.

"That was to be expected," snarled Joris. "By the way, where did your old comrades find out about your mission?"

Ingrid's eyes darkened. She was furious. He too.

"Not about the mission, but about leaving. And completely by accident. It is simply Emperor of Vendhia who convenes all those capable of carrying weapons, because he is preparing another expedition against the brigands of jetes and Assassins on the northern slope of the Himelian Mountains, in Ghulistan, and above all on the southern edge of the Wahuan desert, because he wants to have safe trade routes to Turan and Khitaju and Zipango . They looked for me and found my track in Goa. Someone in the Commandory told them I went north and they followed me.

"Well, now I understand that someone could have been saying too much and it interested somebody..." Joris murmured. "...who got interested in the purpose of your journey and you are known with certain reputation..."

He made a sad face, but she hadn't been misled by it.

"OK," she replied conciliatoryly, "because this was the first thing that came out. And so far we have a draw: one to one."

"Well, rather zero to four," Joris chuckled, "at least in the corpses. But there is no evil, which would not work for good. We know that someone wants to find this same as you - the Alvfurians Mask!"

White-haired also laughed.

"I don't share your optimism. In any case, I'm sure of only one, "she said with certainty," and the fact that Assassins is behind all this.

These three Amazons were for sure. This is evident from the style of the fight and their behavior. They were drunk and it was the reason of their failure, if they were sober, my scattered body would be on the floor. This one," she nodded to the corpse, "was also killed by Assassin. He or she. This time it was a precise job. Faultless. Someone is trying to close the door that we're trying to open. And they are successful for now."

"So what do you propose?" He asked a little helplessly. "From what you said, we're dealing with Assassins."

"Doing our job." the White She-wolf shrugged. "And I think that we won't wait long for the next guest or guests."

Getting the language in the inn did not give a satisfactory result - nobody saw anything. The man was killed in an imperceptible way, and only one of the servant girls, seventeen-year-old youth remembered that a woman sat down for a moment. She had the appearance of an ordinary harlot, so she did not pay any attention to herself - there were many such wickets providing paid erotic services in the district and they paid no attention.

"But she drew your attention," said the Commander, "what exactly?"

The girl thought for a moment.

"She was only dressed and painted like a whore," she said thoughtfully, "but she moved differently than they did."

"Differently, I mean how?"

"It's hard to say, sir. Her movements were like... a warrior..." A cerebration was painted on her pretty face. "Just like that. She moved, like you, lady."

She looked at Ingrida.

"Yes, exactly," she added more confidently. "Skillfully and springy, and at the same time somehow... dancy...?"

"Can you tell me what she looked like?" Joris asked and drew out a sketchbook and coal from the folds of his cloak.

The girl gave a description of a mysterious woman which Joris moved on thick paper with quick but precise movements. After a quarter of an hour, he had a picture of the memory of the alleged murderess.

"Did she look like this?" He asked.

The girl nodded, staring at the drawing with a certain admiration.

"You are a great artist," she said in reverence.

"Thank you," said Joris, "is this her?"

"Yes, sir, it's her."

White-haired exchanged glances with Joris and bowed her head slightly as if in a gesture of confirmation.

"Are you sure?" Ingrida assured.

"Yes, lady," she replied.

"What do they call you?" White She-wolf asked.

"Ylva, my lady," the girl replied. "I come from Haloga."

"So, listen to me, Ylva," she said gently but firmly, accentuating every word, "you must disappear from here and out of the city for a few days. Go to your parents, get stuck in your home. And don't get your nose out for at least a month."

"For Thorus!" She whispered terrified and involuntarily knelt in front of the White She-wolf. "Lady, is there something threatening me?"

"Yes, Ylva" Joris scooped her up from her knees, "you're in danger from the hands of those who killed this man. Only you've seen a murderer, or rather a murderess. Pack and run. And the sooner the better for you..."

Ylva jumped up and ran out of the room where the body was laid.

"You didn't need to scare her so much," said Joris. "Now she'll run away and the murderer will guess that she is a witness of crime and kill her at the first opportunity."

White-haired shrugged.

"They must have already guessed," she said, "but the sooner she disappears, the later they will get her. I hope we'll be faster."

Joris sighed heavily.

"I hope so..." He muttered.

* * *

A week passed, during which nothing serious happened. White-haired was preparing for a trip to the Cursed City. She was surprised to learn that it was only 40 miles north-east of Haloga, which meant about two days' drive. Joris led her out of mistake - because it was about 40 Hyperborean miles, which meant 250 Hyborian miles and not two days, but at least two weeks of traveling through the difficult ice wastes and mountains of Nordheim... So she had to go there with all the supplies and equipment to survive in such difficult conditions. Despite the fact there was almost spring in southern Hyperborea, in the northern slope of Nordheim, there was still winter. The only consolation was that since the Brotherhood was not able to go out there implicitly, no one else could not, and therefore the situation was under control.

Joris came up with a way to get out of Haloga so as not to draw anyone's attention to the expedition. The city was abandoned in small groups - 2-3 people with a small amount of equipment and always at night, to not pay anyone's attention. At the end of the week, a six-person expedition was already halfway to Frigida. Ingrida was supposed to join them by following the tracks that had left their sleigh on the snowy slope. Of course, these were not only traces, but also secret signs known only to members of the Brotherhood.

But before she left she had an event that turned out to be fateful... She was about to go out into the Commandory's yard, where a sleigh was waiting for her when the door opened and an Joris stood by her. He was dressed in fur boots and a jacket, ready to go.

"I'm going with you," he announced without preliminaries.

She looked at him in amazement.

"But we agreed..." She began, but he did not let her finish.

"I'm going with you no matter what. If we will die, then both of us." And in response to his astonished gaze he added. "Besides, I can't imagine that I could sit here calmly knowing that you are in danger!"

She did not speak, but her face was blushed. She has never heard anything so wonderful, a soothing balm on her heart.

"Joris, thank you, but I don't want to expose you to certain death. I don't require this from you..."

"No more words!" Joris grabbed her in his arms and gave her a hot kiss. "We are going together and if we have to die, then we die together."

And she felt that her knees got a little weak because her happiness. Without a word of objection, she sat on a sleigh and he took a seat next to her. After a while they went together to face the adventure...

VIII

After two weeks of hardship of journey, they reached the place where there was a descent to the Cursed City of Frigida, also called Leenho. White-haired was surprised because from the descriptions she developed a view that turned out to be completely wrong in the face of hard reality...

She imagined that this city would manifest itself with a dark spot on the smooth surface of snow or eternal ice, meanwhile wandering through a maze of cracked ice toros with only lightly buried with fresh snow. Frigida was perfectly masked and the traveler who passed over it had no idea that there was a bustling human anthill below the layer of ice and ground.

"There was something," she thought, "but now there is no one here alive..."

They rode along the huge ice blocks that had become detached from the gigantic glacier and slid into the valley to form an amazing labyrinth, and after traveling a few, the brother-guide stopped the sleigh in front of a huge pile of stones that had traces of machining with a human hand.

"It's here, Commander," he said, extending his hand.

They stopped the sleigh and began to unpack them.

"You have supplies here for a week," said one of the brothers, "and then...?"

"I hope it won't be necessary," replied Joris.

He did not want to say that after the 50th and 51st level penetration, they would not be alive anymore...

He issued a series of commands and the brothers quickly camped. They were to remain at the top, and Ingrid and Joris prepared to go underground. He wanted to wait until dawn, but after a short consultation they decided to go down as soon as possible. The brothers pulled the heavy hatch in a joint effort and a cloud of steam erupted from the inside, which began to cover everything with frost. It looked a bit like a geyser.

"We're going down," said White-haired, "the sooner the better."

Joris looked at the setting sun.

"Will I see it again?" He asked himself in his mind.

They looked into each other's eyes, then put their backpacks on their backs and, following the spiral staircase, plunged deeper into the Cursed City of Leenho...

* * *

They went through the first three upper levels without problems. Signs and arrows drawn by the underground researchers pointed to a road that was cleared and safe. The levels no. 70, 69 and 68 were almost completely covered with rubble. It was obvious that there must have been a powerful earthquake here, but the shaking had to be horizontal because mainly the partition walls were destroyed. And what's most interesting - the ceilings were damaged to a minimal degree.

"Do you think it was the result of these four explosions that it writes about in the documents of your Commandory?" She asked, lighting the ruined walls.

"Probably," he replied, "Master Enrinus made the model of this city with any similarity, and then detonated explosives of various power, so that he managed to determine the power of device that could have caused such destruction. And do you know what happened?"

"What?"

"The fact that the 50th and 51st level couldn't be destroyed even with charges of many times more power. Even 100 times bigger! Therefore, the cause of the failure of the energy producer, if it was such a producer, had to be different."

"Hmmm..." She muttered. "You're right. If I was going to destroy this city, you know what I would do?"

"What?"

"I'd launch a series of low-power missiles in the city center, one after the other. I think five would be enough to destroy them to the first level."

"So you think...?"

"I'm sure that these four explosions were not intended to destroy the city, and that the energy products could have been destroyed due to a technical failure, not hostile action."

"Why you are so confidet?" He asked, astonished.

She smiled in the darkness with only the brightness of their torches and the greenish-blue shining of the walls.

"Because it's logical. Nobody tried to destroy this city, and I'm afraid that nobody, or almost nobody, knew about its existence, until it was discovered by gold and valuable searchers, who then spread the legend about Alvfurians. Then the Brotherhood became interested in it."

"Oh, you're right."

After four hours of descent, they were at the 52nd level.

"Well, we're almost at the goal. What we do?" Joris asked.

"I suggest rest," she said without conviction.

"A great thought," said Joris and laid two sleeping bags on the floor. They both had enough of going down to the heart of the Cursed City. Their legs ached.

"By the way, it is interestingly made here," said Ingrid, "it should be very warm and hot, and it's just... warm. We're almost a mile underground.[21] In the caves I visited, at this depth, we walked almost naked and sweated terribly. We drank a few quarts of slightly salted water, because the heat was unbearable... Only that let us survive there.

"It must have been interesting," Joris murmured.

She looked at him and after a moment they both laughed.

"You mean our sweating?" She asked mockingly.

"Mmmm... and more! How much were you undressed?"

She smiled again. All guys are the same - she thought.

---

21 At this depth, with an average geothermal level, the temperature should be + 49°C.

"Absolutely," she replied, "it simply couldn't stand there in the clothes. Even in your underwear."

"And why did you go there?" He asked in astonishment.

She got serious.

"In those caves there were some metal remains..." she thought for a moment, "...objects. We don't even know what it was, because they had crumbled to rusty ash in their hands. Some were already calcited..."

"Where was it?"

"In the complex of caves in one of the ranges of the Himelian Mountains, on the border with Meru, about one hundred and twenty miles south of Sumero Tso. An amazing land. You can see the action of human hand and time in it. There you can really learn a lot about passing..."

The cheerful mood faded and Ingrida lay down in her sleeping bag. Tired of walking down the stairs and ramps won and after a few minutes she fell asleep. She dreamed that she was wandering the levels of Frigida. In the uncertain light of the walls she sees stacks of some pieces of wood and spherical objects. She leans over one of them and sees to her horror that it is a human skull. At once in her eye sockets, red fires ignite, and the skeleton to which it belonged begins to rise. She jumped from him terrified to the highest limits only to see the next skeletons rising from the place of their eternal rest. In the red glare of their eyes, they run away running along the labyrinths of corridors and rooms. And they follow her. With the last of her strength, she throws herself into the only corridor leading down and runs up the stairs towards the armored doors, on which she can see the clear numbers 51. She opens them not without difficulty and sees the blue liquid of deadly liquid spilled on the floor. She does not think long and falls into the glowing space. It is surrounded by objects, but she is frantically searching for something that falls into her field of vision at once. It's a big opal helmet. She runs up to it, hearing behind the sound of splashing and chopping mixed up with the clatter of bones hitting the floor. She turns and sees a group of skeletons glowing red with empty eye sockets slowly approaching her. Nightmarish characters celebrate her around and surround her from all sides. Bony fingers stretch out to tear off her clothes and cling to her naked, vulnerable body in an icy, bony, deadly cold embrace... She gives a shout and with all her strength puts a opal helmet over her head...

Someone tugged her shoulder hard.

"Ingrida! Wake up!" Joris exclaims full of anxiety. "What's up with you?"

He breathes a sigh of relief. She is panting and she is sweating, her heart beats fiercely.

"Nothing has happened," she murmurs, "it's just a nightmare."

"Yes? What did you dream about?" He asked with sudden interest.

She told him about it. He listened carefully, then quietly burned the fire and lit the torch.

"I don't believe in dreams. Speaking of sleeping, we probably slept for eight hours." He said calmly. "There's a day now on the top. So what - are we going?"

Ingrida has already recovered her's wits.

"That's why we came here," she said, "now we're going to do something to eat and...", she thought for a moment, "...and on the road!"

She did not tell him that it would be the last meal in their lives and he understood it anyway.

IX

And so that is what they did. It was not so much about food but about calming down before the death journey to the lower floor of the City. They had no doubt that they would share the fate of Master Enrinus and his student. They had hoped that they would find what they were looking for, and it encouraged them that their lives were not in vain. But the case looked hopeless, because they knew that they would not get out of it alive. Master Erinus lived two or three days and his student died even faster. They managed to convey a report about these floors, thanks to which Ingrida could immediately eliminate some places and narrow down the search.

After a few minutes, they stood in front of the armored door. They were identical as in a dream. The White-haired shuddered involuntarily looking around, but around them the silence of the underworld reigned.

She drew air into her lungs like before jumping into the water. She was afraid not so much of death as the fact that she would not find a cursed artifact and her death would be futile. She glanced at Joris. He was pale. He was also nervous.

"Are we going?" He asked.

She nodded, swallowed and reached into the door handle. She turned it and pushed it. They opened slightly and they both entered the stuffy darkness. The door closed itself silently. Light shone under the ceiling. They were in a floodgate. Compressed air sizzled.

"Floodgate," said Ingrida, "the last safe place. You can still leave from here."

He looked at her, then simply took her in his arms.

"No," he replied.

And he kissed her on the lips. Slowly, sensually. She clung to him with her whole body. I did not even love him... - she thought with regret.

"I'm going with you," he said. "I couldn't live without you."

And White-haired felt her warmth on her heart, and that fear and doubt leave her. Joris also picked up the pieces. Now he reached into the handle of the armored hatch and opened it. This hatch also opened silently.

They crossed the high threshold of a gas-tight door and entered the shiny blue space of level 51.

"Where are we going?" He asked.

"For now straight, then left and third street to the right. We've three hours, then we will start to feel the effects of radiation." She said firmly. "So let's start!"

They moved ahead. It smelled of ozone and something like sea salt, but in a much higher concentration. Puddles of luminescent, radioactive water did not occupy the entire floor space, so they avoided them as much as possible. But they knew that the radio-active steam and gases coming out of the water from the broken installations also penetrated into their organisms. It only postponed the moment of death, but it did not go away. They quickly crossed the road and stood on the threshold of the large hall. Its surface was covered with various boxes or dark metal cassettes. They quickly browsed their contents - unfortunately, they were all empty or filled with objects that did not look like a mask or a helmet.

"There is nothing here," she said with disappointment in her voice.

"Yhm..." murmured Joris, "and where now?"

"Two blocks away is a similar room, and behind it the energy production hall," she said in a certain voice, "if it was a producer at all..."

She broke off with a sudden thought.

They ran again. Time was shrinking to them and the result was zero. They felt the first pains and the skin became red with radiation. In addition, White-haired felt nausea and light dizziness.

They searched the next rooms. There were no mask.

"We go to the main hall," she ordered, "it must be here, I'm sure of that!"

"I envy you with this certainty," said Joris.

"That dream was not accidental," she said, "and I believe it was a clue!"

"So remember the way and go!"

She looked at him.

"I'm just trying," she replied calmly with an effort on her face. "We're back to the floodgate!"

And she went back and he followed her. They felt worse and worse. The third hour of searching was approaching. A point of no return - Joris thought.

He did not regret life. It was only a pity that when he will die he would leave Ingrida, whom he fell in love at first sight. That he would never see her again and hear her voice. That he will not share his life and family happiness with her. He knew that gamma quanta penetrating him would kill his body's cells at any moment and neutrons would pierce the skin's shell and penetrate into his body, ravaging them inexorably and systematically. But in spite of everything, he hoped he would find this damned mask and destroy it before someone could use it against people and the world.

He felt worse and worse, life was leaving him faster and faster. Despite the effort of the will, he moved more and more slowly. The senses dulled, the pains intensified. They moved again from the floodgate, and Ingrida slowly moved toward the corridor, other than the one from which they came. He looked at her and frightened. Her face was pale, covered with drops of sweat, but it did not frighten him. Her eyes were wide open and glassy. They stared at the bluish dark with unseeing eyes. After a while, he understood - Ingrida put in a hypnotic trance that would help her find her way. He followed her for some time, then he stumbled on some threshold and fell to the floor. He said with horror that he did not have the strength to get up. White-haired went on automatically. He saw her figure moving away in the perspective of the corridor. And then he was overwhelmed by weakness and the darkness of death, which came to him with a slow, merciless step...

Meanwhile, Ingrida walked insensitive to the powerful radiation surrounding her. Her will focused on just one thing - remembering her dream and finding a helmet that was an Alvfurians Mask. She was walking more and more slowly, but she was walking. Half an hour later, she found herself in the room she had seen in her sleep. Then she woke up from a trance. A terrible pain almost knocked her off her legs. She took a few steps and saw the Mask in a bluish drizzle.

Exactly the same as seen in a dream.

Only that it was behind a thick, transparent sheet. It might have been on the other side of the Moon as well...

For a moment she was overcome with despair. So all efforts, terrible nuclear death, that's all for nothing! She consoled herself that if she can not get to it, nobody can. A miserable comfort, but always. The strength left her and she sat down opposite it. If only I could lift this surface... - she thought.

"Just open, you damn pane!" She exclaimed in thought.

And then something impossible happened.

She swayed for a moment, because the pane rose silently and the helmet shone with opal glow.

She shivered with joy and fear. Out of joy, because what she was looking for was within her reach. Out of fear, because she understood that she only launched something by the power of her thoughts and that something is still active and may prevent her from destroying the Alvfurians Mask.

She reached up for the mask and pulled it out of her socket. Then, thinking little, she put it on her head. It fits perfectly and after a while she felt gentle pricks in the scalp. She did not know that the Mask had inserted the electrodes into her nerve nodes connecting to the brain.

"I'm here for your orders," she heard a voice coming from everywhere and out of nowhere.

"Who's here!" She exclaimed. "who's here!?"

There was a moment of chilling silence. Ingrida understood. Whatever it was did not react to the voice, only to the articulated thought. The discovery mobilized her to the next effort. The body would not listen to her, but her will and thought remained.

"Who you are?" She thought with all the effort of the will she still had.

X

And she heard answer.

"Here's the system... I'm waiting for your instructions..."

"What system?" She asked in thought.

"The one you call the Alvfurians Mask," the answer came.

"But you used a word I don't understand..." she replied.

"Because it isn't exist in your language," replied the mask, "I'm waiting for your orders."

She felt a twitch of hope.

"What can you do for me and my companion? Can you cure us?" She asked this question, because at the moment only this problem was the most important for her.

"Command accepted," she heard in response. "I start the treatment process. I need to move you to another place, the local alpha, beta and gamma and neutron levels are too high."

After a while, a cloud of fine particles materialized in the middle of the room, which fell to Ingrid. After a moment she felt her body lose weight and float into the air. It lasted a few minutes and then she fell into the blackness of sleep.

She woke up in a room whose walls shone with an even, white, shadowy glow. On her head she still had a opal helmet, the front part of which was transparent, so she could see without any obstacles. She sat down, feeling new forces pour into her body with each breath.

"Death was with me and Mask saved me." She thought. And then her heart squeezed with terror.

"Joris!" She exclaimed. "Joris, where are you!!!"

"Don't shout," she heard behind her, "I'm here."

She turned her head. Joris lay on the next table. His face was pale, but the colors were slowly returning to his cheeks.

"We're live," she said with a squeezed throat, "you're here!"

"I am, my dear," he confirmed. "I see you succeeded!"

She breathed a sigh of relief and told him what she had lived through. He listened to her without interrupting.

"So Mask has saved our lives," he concluded as he finished, "so it isn't a weapon."

"It isn't," she nodded. "This is a universal tool and a doctor in case of..."

"We were very close to the other bank." He muttered slowly getting up. "Now we'll have to get out of here."

"How are you?" White-haired asked. "Because I'm pretty good. And I'm terribly hungry!"

Joris listened to his body for a moment.

"Me too," he said with astonishment, "but we've to get out of here somehow..."

She nodded.

"Where should we move this... system?"

To the camp on the ground," he said anxiously, "I feel something bad is happening there."

Ingrida concentrated and expressed her wish. Rainbow dust swirled around them and after a moment the cold air struck them.

The dust disappeared somewhere and they stood knee-deep in the snow about fifteen steps from the camp...

Joris first wanted to tell her that she had directed them so far away from the fire, but he immediately understood why she did so. In front of them were about twenty people who stared at the fire of the camp and six unsuspecting young people.

Joris looked at them closely - they were people of different blood and from different lands. But one of them was connected - hatred and cruelty written on their faces. And lust for murder.

"They're Assassins," White-haired whispered.

"A lot of them," he replied, "about twenty. Ours may not be able to make it."

"We will jump there and warn them," she said.

"We can't make it..." he whispered.

"We can, we can," she murmured, grabbing his hand, "watch out!"

The rainbow dust moved them to the center of the camp, and at the same moment they heard the assassin's battle cry, which fell on them unimpressed by what they had seen a few seconds ago. They stopped a few paces from them. Their leader appeared in front of them.

"Listen to me you white bitch and you Hyrkanian bull!" He shout. "You will give us what we're looking for and you'll be free!"

Yeah, right," said Ingrida, "how did you find us?"

"The tracks, you stupid woman," replied the leader, spitting contemptuously. "And what did you think you would hornswoggle Mollak? We follow you in your footsteps from Fort Ghori, you white bitch! And finally I got you!"

"And what will happen if we won't give it back?" Joris asked. "What are you going to do to us, you goat hooli from the slurry of Haloga?"

"We'll take it!" Replied the Assassins' leader. "You give it voluntarily or not?"

"No!" Ingrida replied haughtily and laughed impertinently. She had returned completely to the old form, and the screech of steel sounded like the most wonderful song in her ears. "Come and take it! I hope I can kill you and spay you like your little brother."

She met Mollak during the Assassins War. Together with his brother Wollak they were famous for their cruelty. It was not until the end of the war that the pursuit group of White She-wolf managed to hunt down Wollak in his mountain hideout and liquidate along with several dozen Assassins. Mollak managed to sneak out and escape, but he has sworn revenge ever since. Now he drew the scimitar and pointed to them.

"Take this bitch, and I'll take care of this bull! Let's get going!!! We'll play with her and then with her sister and friends in Haloga!"

And he laughed at the horrible, weird laughter from which the Apprentices felt cold on the bones. The White-haired breathed a sigh of relief, because it meant that Åsa and her companions were safe at the moment. Assassins did not manage to get them.

The thugs moved on them.

The White She-wolf grinded a blade of shallow steel from behind her back and cut the nearest one, which bounced off the curve with a Hyrkanian sword and, in turn, led a snaky thrust to the torso. Ingrida made a jump and turn, from which she moved her foot kick to the opponent's jaw. She hits. With some satisfaction she heard the crack of breaking bones. Assassin groaned to the ground and moaned. Two others crashed at her, but they did not make it, because the axor of Joris, who stood in front of her, had been dealt with them, separating her from the Assassins.

"Kill them!" He shouted in his stentor voice and waving a bloody ax and a small round shield. "Use the Mask!"

Ingrida jumped back. She concentrated and thought a wish. Nothing happened. She understood at once - the system or whatever it was that worked so as not to harm people. She understood in flight that it was necessary to formulate an order so as to kick away the assailants.

"Take them to the top of that mountain," she thought, staring at the looming peak of some giant mountain in the distance.

"Accepted." She heard in response.

She hoped that the system would listen to her and that it did. A huge rainbow cloud crashed into attackers and surrounded them tightly, then rose to thirty feet up and took the shape of a rotating disk. Joris and his men watched as the disk grew in altitude and speed toward the distant peak. Having reached it, it melted in the air and disappeared... From this distance they could not see what had happened to the attackers. But they least cared about them now - they had some other, pressing things to deal with.

Ingrid at once became weak and fell to her knees. The mask must have been some kind of transducer and amplifier of her brain energy, because its use exhausted her strength. Joris picked her up and laid her on the sleigh, removing the helmet from her head. She took a deep breath and was very pale.

"I'm weak," she whispered.

"We run away from here," said Joris, "but now! Collapse the camp."

The youth quickly recovered from the sensation of the effect of the opal helmet on Ingrida's head. They tucked up the tents and loaded them on the sleigh. They extinguished the campfire and buried mainly in the snow. After a while, nothing indicated the traces of their stay in this place... They harnessed the horses and stood by the sleigh.

"We're ready." They reported.

"We're going from here. Mission accomplished." He said somewhat quieter.

The sun was slowly hiding behind the mountains. Meanwhile, on the glacier, the Seventeen Assassins cursed and threatening them helplessly tried to go down a great ice tongue, but after a few hours they all died in ice crevices and under break down snow-ice bridges. A few was sweep by the avalanches of powerful seracs, shaken by their screams. The scourge of the northern Vendhia fell into a narrow chimney and was covered with an avalanche of ice hunk. His body was found in the valley after two centuries. The wolves have torn it...

After two days, the team returned to the Haloga commandory.

XI

"Do you know, my dear, what it all reminds me?" Ingrida asked in a sweet voice of her husband, when after the wedding ceremony and finally feast, they was alone, lounging in the pool with hot water.

"What's up, my sun?" He answered with the question.

White-haired sat down opposite him and looked into his eyes.

"Shemit Legends about their god. Almighty, the only one. Think, now we're almost omnipotent. We have the Mask and..."

"Are you going to desert?" He asked with astonishment.

"No, but think how much good you can do with it!" She just said. "I think its destruction would be a mistake."

"And keeping it, even more," he said firmly, "we don't know what it actually is."

Triumph flashed in Ingrida's eyes.

"Besides me," she said with a sly smile, "I know what it is."

Joris sat up straight at once. He was intrigued to the highest degree because he knew that his wife knew something about it what he did not have the slightest idea. And he did not get wrong.

White-haired came over and sat on his thighs, he felt the feel of her body and felt lust. But he took control quickly, waiting for her words.

"Tell me what you know," he said.

"I'll tell you, but not now..." she teased him.

He put his arms around her and hugged her. They kissed passionately in the clouds of steam.

"That's enough," he whispered, "because I'm going to rap you."

She giggled and bit him in the ear.

"Let's get out of here, now," he said, "because I'll die at heart attack."

He stood up and left the water. Ingrida also came out of the pool and wrapped herself in a wide towel. They went out to the room and lay down at a table with wedding bouquets of roses. They lay huddled against each other, inhaling their sweet scent.

"Now say what do you know," said Joris.

She teased him for a moment longer, finally graciously yielded.

"First of all," she said, "the mask is simply indestructible. Someone has tried for it. This is a kind of brain bioenergier amplifier that uses the life energy of whoever uses it - do you understand?"

"That's why I was so tired when we kicked away those... thugs on the glacier. This, however, required a lot of energy..."

He nodded.

"Secondly: The Mask is used to control some complicated mechanisms composed of many dust-like elements, which if necessary and the degree of complexity of the task merge into larger aggregates. This we have seen in action, it is this rainbow cloud."

"Sure, what's next?" He asked, puzzled.

"Thirdly, it's not a weapon. I mean, it can't be used directly against a human, unlike the talisman that Gedrena had and which was neutralized by Halidor and Sonja..."

"Wait a minute," Joris shook his head, "and what does have one to the other?"

"It has that both can only be handle by a woman!" She cried with triumph in her voice. "Do you understand? Mollak thought that if he got it in his hands, he would become the master of the world, not a chance!"

They lay silent for a moment.

"You know that Mollak did not act alone, only on someone's behalf?"

"I think I know who," she replied. "Prince Menkaur. He was the one who mingled with the Assassins and hefted them with gold from Kamroon Island! Our guys tracked them down when they gave them at least 50 gold talents - now we know what it was all about. By the way, it is completely sick. I wonder how much gold Mollak got for getting this Mask?"

"He is a rather primitive type and I think he content himself with a mere piss," murmured Joris.

"But there is another objection in this matter," White-haired said, cuddling up to him.

"What?" Joris was surprised. "I think everything is clear."

"Do you remember what I said about the Mask's properties?" She asked. "I remind you that only a woman can use it. Like the Talisman."

"Do not finish, I understand," said Joris, "you think that Menkaure has a woman who..."

"Exactly," she said. "And she is the most dangerous of all this company. You have to tell the operation commanders on the northern slope of the Himelian Mountains, because they are catching the Assassins so far, but really dangerous people will escape them."

"So, what now?"

"You have to go to Belverus and give a warning about it to Goa and Kulalo, but first of all to Goa. The Crossbowman's daughter has her influence at the court, so she'll go easily with it."

"It will take a long time," said Joris.

"Don't forget, dear, that you have me, and I have a mask," she said, "thanks to this we'll shorten the path to two days."

"And your friends?"

"They have already gone, just after the wedding feast."

Joris's eyes flashed for a moment.

"You can't do it," he said with concern, "that transfer will consume a lot of your life energy."

"Yes," she replied, "but this process is completely reversible, because the energy can be replenished and thus half a day of flight, a day of rest and the second half of the flight. The day after tomorrow we can be in Goa... Will you agree, Commander?"

"Well... I don't know..." he said hesitantly.

"Come on, agree! Please!" Ingrida put her arms around his neck and kissed him on the lips, then gently licked and pinched the skin on his neck and torso with her teeth...

Now he was teasing her, and finally he stripped off her towel and took her in his arms. They both fell to a wide bed. White-haired sat on his hips and absorbed him, and after a few minutes a cry of pleasure came out of her throat. Joris drew her to him and now he was on top and she firmly pressed her underbelly to his lower abdomen. Her eyes went dark and after a moment they both fell into the red mist of pleasure...

After a quarter of an hour, they moved away from each other, panting heavily.

"Madman." Ingrida gasped, looking from under half-closed eyelids at him.

"Madwoman." Joris grunted, panting heavily. "Savage."

And they both laugh of themselves. They hugged each other, this time only to enjoy their closeness. Silence was brake by her.

"Joris, will you let me go to Goa?" She asked quietly and humbly.

"No," he replied firmly.

"Why?" She asked miserably.

"Because if you want to go anywhere, only with me," he said in the same tone, "do you understand?"

She kissed him strong and hot.

"My dear, of course," she whispered, "I didn't expect anything else."

And they hugged each other again.

And two days later, they flew to Vendhia to meet another adventure.

THE END